To Move the World

An Historical Odyssey By

Brent Monahan

TO MOVE THE WORLD

An Historical Odyssey

BRENT MONAHAN

Copyright 2005 by Brent Monahan

ISBN: 1-59507-114-8

ArcheBooks Publishing Incorporated
www.archebooks.com

9101 W. Sahara Ave.
Suite 105-112
Las Vegas, NV 89117

Hardcover First Edition: 2005

ArcheBooks Publishing

CRITICAL PRAISE FOR BRENT MONAHAN

For *Book of the Common Dread*

"A real page turner. If chills and thrills are to your taste, then Brent Monahan provides a feast."

Robert Bloch
Author of *Psycho*

"Monahan breathes new life into the vampire theme... The novel is clever, thrilling, and, above all, entertaining."

Library Journal

"An old-fashioned page-turner of the best sort. Easily the best addition to the vampire genre since Anne Rice's *Interview with the Vampire*."

Indianapolis Star

"The sort of well that Umberto Eco tapped in *The Name of the Rose*... Brent Monahan delivers much more than gore."

Atlanta Journal & Constitution

"The modern vampire classic."

Locus Magazine

DEDICATION

For Jim Wiley
And his
Agriogianis heritage

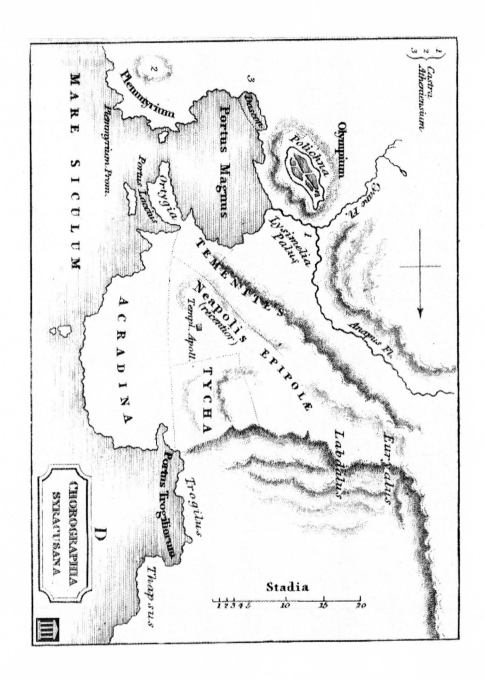

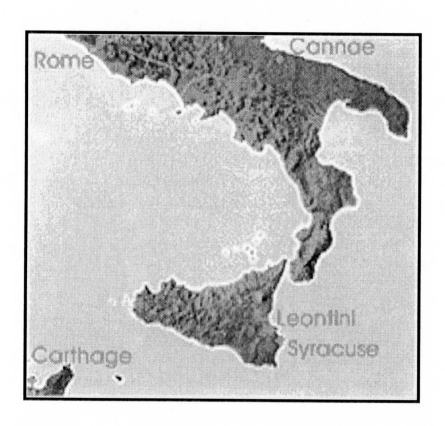

CAST OF CHARACTERS

Adranodorus – Husband of daughter of King Hieron

Archimedes – One of ancient Western civilization's greatest mathematical minds. Unlike his contemporaries, he designed practical applications of his theories. Great-uncle of Leonides

Amara – Wife of soldier and wrestler Apollonius

Anaximander(Petrus) – Son of Leonides

Apollonius – Best friend of Leonides

Apollos – Father of Leonidas

Archidamus – Contemporary of King Hieron of Syracuse. General of the Syracusan army until Hieron's death

Athena – Daughter of Leonides

Aurora – Daughter of consul and great Roman soldier Marcus Claudius Marcellus.

Azar – Slave of family of Thalia

Calandra – Wife of Eustace, mother of Thalia

Carthalo – High-ranking officer in Hannibal's army

Cleomenes – Wealthy quarry and rope-making businessman of Syracuse

Crito – Servant of Archimedes

Diocles – Agent of Timon

Dion – Eldest of Apollos' sons, brother of Leonides

Dionysius – Tyrant of Syracuse who built much of its fortifications

Epikydes – General for Syracuse under regime favoring Carthage

Eustace – Father of Thalia

Gelon – Son of Hieron, father of Harmonia and Hieronymos

Hamilcar Barca – Father of Hannibal

Hannibal – Carthaginian general who invaded Italy

Harmonia – Daughter of Gelon, granddaughter of Hieron

Heraclia – Daughter of King Hieron

Hieron – General of Syracuse, later self-declared king and benevolent despot

Hieronymos – Grandson of Hieron

Hippokrates – General for Syracuse under regime favoring Carthage

Ioannis – Agent of Timon

Irene – Servant of Archimedes

Leonides - Son of Apollos, great-nephew of Archimedes, soldier of Syracuse

Marcus Claudius Marcellus – Four-time Roman consul and celebrated general for the Republic of Rome

Marcellus – *see* Marcus Claudius Marcellus

Melampus – Member of Silent Storm

Menander – Member of Silent Storm

Myreon – Middle son of Apollos, brother of Leonides

Nereis – Daughter of King Pyrrhus, wife of Gelon

Phidias – Father of Archimedes and Apollos

Philistis – Daughter of Leptines, wife of Hieron

Protesilous – Member of Silent Storm

Ptolemy – Ruling family of Egypt from time of Alexander the Great through the Roman Republic

Severinus – *see* Sixtus Severinus Callusius

Sixtus Severinus Callusius – Tribune of Rome

Thalia – Beloved of Leonides

Timon – Chief minister of King Hieron

Themistos – Husband of Harmonia

Xenophanes – Member of Silent Storm

Zoippos – Husband of Heraclia, daughter of Hieron

CHAPTER I

Delivering a king's message can be dangerous. Delivering the message to an irascible genius has its own set of challenges.

Dhows glided downstream on the Nile past the rail of my barge, their sails appearing like beaten gold leaf as they filtered the fierce morning light. The Egyptian sun pressed against my sweat-slick skin like a hot iron. I had left Alexandria two mornings before, after paying homage to Alexander the Great at his golden tomb. My great-uncle had abandoned Alexandria's awe-inspiring library, I learned, four weeks earlier. I was told that he had left to "work on the fields of Memphis." Despite having reached his seventieth year, my great-uncle was ever busy with work. Generally, Archimedes occupied his time pondering pure abstractions. Yet among the great Greek mathematicians of our time and of ages past, he was unparalleled in his penchant for applying knowledge.

I am Leonides, of the same lineage that produced Archimedes. My family is Siracusan. My father named me for the king who commanded the Spartians at Thermopylae against the overwhelming forces of Xerxes the Persian. I stem, however, from Korinthian and not Spartian roots. He

1

selected the Spartian name because Leonides fought with unsurpassed courage on behalf of all the Greek states. My father is as unique as Archimedes in his own way; he holds an unprovincial outlook on the world, and he instilled his unprejudiced attitudes in me. Among the vast majority of old guard Siracusans, despite the fact that their Korinthian ancestors founded this city more than 500 years ago and their blood has intermingled many times, anyone who cannot trace his bloodline back to Korinthos is deemed inferior. Such narrow-mindedness is apparently a sad trait among all races.

Siracusa was the greatest city on Sicilia. The primitive tribes who scratched out their existence on this island before we arrived are but a dark memory. Over the centuries, and at various times, the Greeks established colonies on the island's southeastern quarter—the Carthaginians on the western half, and the Romans on the northeast quarter. All of these settlements were created with the intent of control. Sicilia is set squarely in the middle of the Mediterranean Sea, like the hub of a watery wheel. Any race desiring to spread its influence throughout the region must dominate here. Therefore, heritage periodically proved not a matter of pride but of dread.

The other reason my father named me Leonides was because my destiny since birth was fated for warfare. I was the third son. I would inherit nothing of the family business. My father's thought was that in a period of turmoil I could rise dramatically in society as a professional soldier. It was also his attempt to give his family an advantage during times of the sword. My father had never known war. He knew enough of history to doubt that such a state could continue through my lifetime.

Whether I became a successful warrior because of natural talents or because I had no other choice, I do not know. What I know is that I grew to stand the width of a hand taller than any other man in my family, with a proportionately stronger build and more powerful thrusting arm. I tell you candidly, but with humility, that I can carry without tiring greater burdens than virtually any other man I know. The Unseen Creator also gifted me with the eyesight of a bird of prey.

Siracusa had been a peaceful city for decades before my birth. The man who commanded our troops was quite old and knew only outmoded techniques of warfare. When I reached my eighteenth birthday, my father made a great sacrifice on my behalf and sent me to Korinthos for a year to study military science. According to the sealed letters sent home with me, I acquitted myself well. When I was twenty-two, the city hosted five days of athletic contests that emulated the Olympiads of our native Greek homeland. I won the victor's crown of wild olives for the most honored event, the pentathlon.

In spite of warfare that touched our city across the centuries, Siracusans were not known for starting conflicts or for hiring ourselves out for those of others. We prospered by farming, craftsmanship, and trading. So it was that in my own land, during a protracted peace, my martial training and my scroll of recommendation were not held with any particular reverence. Periodically in one or another of our agoras someone would stand upon the public platform and wonder aloud why we needed even a skeleton army of 440 soldiers stationed inside the city. Did not every freeman at eighteen receive his spear and shield in expectation that he would defend Siracusa to the death? Why had the old practice of creating soldiers purely in times of need from the landed and wealthy citizenry been abandoned, they asked of a crowd of taxpayers ready to listen.

Citizens of Siracusa who did not recognize me—which naturally was the vast majority—sometimes looked upon my uniform with open displeasure, perhaps thinking I was a mercenary brought in from some other country. There was neither adventure nor respect in Siracusa. Consequently, when I was summoned by Hieron, the ruler of our city, to drag home my great-uncle from Egypt, I went with only one secret regret in my heart.

When I learned of my great-uncle's unscheduled trip to the city of Memphis, I importuned the captain of a military barge bound for the headwaters of the White Nile for a ride. He was happy to oblige the soldier of a close trading partner country. He knew the Greek that was spoken in Egypt, and we managed a pleasant conversation for several hours, as I watched the strange trees and plants dotting the banks glide by, listening to the gentle splash of oars entering the water. The only elements that dampened my spirits were the great river's gnats and flies, which were as pestiferous as the mosquitoes that rose like an evening fog out of Siracusa's Great Harbor marshes in the warm seasons.

After debarking on the second day of my river trip, I required the better part of the afternoon to locate my great-uncle. I must admit that I divided my attention between searching for him and gawking at the amazing ancient structures such as the White Walls palace and the Temple of Ptah. Even after visiting Korinthos and Athenai, I had always thought of Siracusa as an enormous city. However, I was told and then saw with my own eyes that Memphis contained twenty times as many people as my place of birth. Fortunately for me, I learned early on that Archimedes confined himself to the river bank at the southern extreme of the city.

I recognized him from a distance, from his wealth of yellow-white hair, from skin much lighter than that of the Egyptian fellahs who surrounded him, and from the full-length chiton he wore, despite the heat. Around him, the uniformly thin natives worked in simple loincloths. He stood with his arms folded in patent satisfaction before a long wooden tube whose bottom end rested in the river and whose top end rose over the earthen dike. One of the fellahs turned a crank on the top end with maniacal energy. Between his legs cascaded the waters of the Nile. Archimedes' old eyes at last focused on me—and knew instantly why I had come. His brows knit with displeasure for several moments. Then he stretched out his vein-covered hand.

"Strategos!" he called out, using the sarcastically inappropriate nickname he had bestowed on me two years before, "come and see what I have invented!"

"A water mover," I replied, content to delay for the moment the weighty reason for my presence.

"Where is your vision? It is a land changer." He turned his back to the great river. "Look out to the horizon!"

I gazed across a valley of maturing grain. Summer was hard upon the land. The vibrant green of new life had been all but bleached from the waving shafts. Beyond them, the color of barren earth was that of death.

"Do you know what a river is called that flows through a desert and that irrigates a narrow strip of land on either side?" Archimedes asked me.

"It is an exotic river," I replied.

"Correct. Before they invented hieroglyphics, these people developed dikes and sluices, to increase their arable land substantially. Their population grew; their power and wealth grew. They dominated this part of the world when other peoples still scavenged to survive. However, in rainy years the river overflowed the dikes and turned the fields to swamps. In dry years, the river level dropped too far to extract its water. The Nile was always greater than the pharaohs. But now, with my invention, they may truly defy Nature. They can lift water up the banks whenever they choose, into vast irrigation ditches. What is more, they can pump out areas that become too flooded. When a thousand of my inventions are built, that desert on the horizon will also bloom."

"But what value is it if an army comes to steal all their grain?" I asked, thinking as a soldier and seeing no sign of military might around Memphis.

Archimedes was not daunted. "I have no power over that. But what if the enemy's navy is swamped in a great storm? The Egyptian navy can pump out the water as quickly as it enters."

I was no match for his mind. I asked, "How does it work?"

"Inside the cylinder is a central shaft. Around this rises an incline plane. One only needs to be careful that the bottom end remains under the surface of the water."

In Siracusa when I was a child, Archimedes had shown me how I might place a hollow reed into water, press my thumb over the top opening, and be able to lift the liquid up inside the tube. But this was clearly an entirely different principle.

"Why does the water rise up the shaft?" I asked. "Why does not the water fall naturally to lower levels and the air above not push it back down?"

Almost from the moment my great-uncle began to explain, he lost me. His language was one of mathematics and physics, far beyond my ability to understand. Nevertheless, I nodded my head soberly until he had finished. Archimedes had a positive opinion of my intelligence, and I would do nothing to change that. This was not out of personal vanity but rather fear of loss. The old genius had no patience for those with average

5

or low intellect. My father assured me that decades of arguments and entreaties by my family for him to treat less gifted men with respect had fallen on deaf ears.

"I thought you had come to Egypt to learn, not to teach," I commented.

The old man shrugged. "I was told about the parched fields and journeyed here to face a challenge. Think of how many more may be fed from this simple invention!" He glanced at the sword dangling from my side. "Let me reverse your earlier scenario: Perhaps I have preserved this country from needing to invade a neighbor because of famine."

"Perhaps," I conceded.

"The more one learns, the greater the ability to make valuable applications. Hieron promised that I might stay in Egypt for a year. Alexandria is a lodestone that attracts great minds from many nations. I have learned much." Archimedes clapped his hands together, wiping off dried dirt. "But you appear after six months to coax me home."

"I will not coax you, Uncle. I have a direct order for you in my pouch," I told him. "Hieron's seal is pressed into the wax. The message is 'Return to Siracusa immediately. Your services are required.'"

His cracked lips pursed. "What services does he speak of?"

"I know not," I replied, although I sheltered a guess. "You may stay here three more days." I held up three fingers to amplify my words. "A fleet of our galleys departs from Alexandria six days hence. Tidy your affairs."

"Back to the flat world," he said, in an equally flat voice.

"What does that mean?" I asked.

"In Siracusa the world is flat."

"It is flat everywhere," I replied.

"Not so," he insisted, smiling at my having taken his bait. "Long ago, when I read Eratosthenes of Cyrene's proof that the world is a sphere, I was sure his calculations and observations were correct. By coming here, I have learned that the Egyptians also developed their own proof some time ago. Their scientists created two huge sand hourglasses that emptied at precisely the same moment. Then they transported one of the timepieces up the Nile some 4,000 stadia."

6

Archimedes sidled down the embankment to the muddy river edge, beckoning me to follow. He bent with a rheumatic groan and picked up a thick length of dead reed. In the smooth mud, he rapidly drew with the tip of the stick representations of the sun, parallel rays issuing from it, and a curving world.

"On a day of perfectly clear weather, they placed poles of equal length into the ground at the two places. When the glasses emptied, each team measured the length of the shadow cast on the ground. The shadows were of different lengths! This could not be so with a flat world. But see you not in my drawing how a curved Egypt precisely accounts for the discrepancy? They were not only able to prove from the differing lengths of the shadows that the world curves, but they also estimated its circumference. Their calculation differs a bit from that of Eratosthenes, but either figure would keep you awake tonight if I told you how large it is. Suffice to say that Alexander should not have wept for lack of world to conquer."

Impressed as I was with my uncle's theorems and applications, I knew from my own life's experiences that the world was flat. Numbers, letters, and other symbols, no matter how elegantly they were arranged, could not alter the evidence of my own eyes. I began to sputter out a dispute that the sun's rays might not arrive parallel everywhere when Archimedes raised his hand to stop me.

"If I provide a third proof—one that you will have to accept without understanding even a single equation—will you linger several weeks and tell Hieron you could not find me?"

"What kind of proof?"

"That's my secret. We shall need to return to Alexandria for me to show you."

In the end, I told him that I might be convinced to pretend I had not found him, since his scheme at least required him to come back with me as far as Alexandria.

Four days later, Archimedes directed me to the top of Alexandria's wondrous lighthouse, which is as tall as seventy-five men standing upon each other's shoulders. From my lofty perch on a particularly clear afternoon, I was able to see incredibly far out across the Mediterranean.

Straining my eyes, I watched a minuscule mast emerge out of the water on the horizon. Presently, the entire bireme rose as if out of the waves. Minutes later, another vessel reversed the process as it sailed toward Crete. Only if the very waters of the ocean curved with the earth was there an explanation for what my own eyes beheld. As he had promised, without a single equation Archimedes had changed my world from a flat one to a round one. I had no idea how much more profoundly he would change my world in the years to come. Nevertheless, obeying my direct order from our king I dragged him onto a ship bound for Siracusa.

CHAPTER II

Exciting as it was to view the pyramids of El Giza, the ancient pal-
aces and temples that flanked the eternal Nile, I was elated to see
my home island rise into view out of the vast Mediterranean. Our
mariners were well experienced, and we moved toward Siracusa almost
directly, out of nothing but dark, rolling waters. I put myself at the bobbing bow as soon as the call was sounded.

As we drew close to land, the plateau of Epipolai emerged below the
hazy blue mountain ranges, defining the northern limit of the city. The
wind blew westerly, necessitating the sailors to bend thirty and six oars
against the waves. As we struggled nearer, the whitewashed walls of
Achradina and Neapolis became visible beneath Epipolai's cliffs, and I
could just discern the indentation of the Little Harbor that defined the
southernmost point of the Achradina district. The waters took on a
brighter blue hue as we came out of the deep, and I, an inveterate lands-
man, breathed a sigh of relief. A little closer brought into view the fortress
and the Temple of Artemis atop the out-thrusting district of Ortygia.

The fleet, consisting of both cargo and warships, rowed resolutely toward the Great Harbor that lay south of and behind the Ortygian peninsula. On the opposite side of the mouth of the harbor at the southern extreme of Siracusa lay the rise of land called the Plemmyrion, with its line of protective walls and its own fortress.

My home looked prosperous and secure from the water, and I remember smiling with pride. Siracusa was a splendid city, holding virtually every comfort, entertainment, and vice that the civilized world had to offer. Its weather was generally mild, its skies and waters unsurpassed hues of blue. Visitors from around the Mediterranean kept the city vibrant and modern. Most importantly, it was the city where the gods had chosen to place the most beautiful young woman in the world.

We reached Naso Point, where the rough ocean swells were tamed by shallow waters. When at last we had passed through the harbor mouth and I could make out the stretches of saltwater marshes that formed the western end of the largest harbor on Sicilia, I quit the bow and saw to the disembarking of both myself and my great-uncle.

My first duty upon returning to Siracusa was to accompany Archimedes to his home and see that all was in order. His long-time servants, Crito and Irene, had kept the place in good order. I expected no less; it was their home as well. Having been informed of the arrival of the fleet while it still lay beyond the harbor, they had seen to the gathering of flowers and the purchase of extra foodstuffs. Little truly was needed to accommodate Archimedes; his demands were few and simple.

My great-uncle had never married. Any woman clever enough to have merited his respect would never have endured his nature. On most days, he barely registered that the servants existed. He ate because they placed food before him. He slept when he could think no more, whether it was at midnight or noon. He would have worn the same clothing until they were rags were fresh changes not laid out for him. All that truly mattered to him was the world of the mind.

I will say to his credit, however, that he was a clean man. He enjoyed almost every day visiting the public baths that adjoined the main city gymnasium. It was there also that he made his greatest effort to imitate normal men, listening to conversations, asking questions of the matters of the day, and sometimes even contributing to mundane discussions. Every

Siracusan man knew who he was and treated him with the honor and deference he deserved, and although he never commented on it, I am sure he enjoyed the daily evidence of his import. He was, after the poet Theocritus, the most famous creative Siracusan native of our century. But Theocritus had left the city when they were both young men, choosing Egypt and the island of Chios over his birthplace. Theocritus was now dead. Archimedes had not shared the pedestal for many decades.

Archimedes' dwelling lay in the district of Achradina just west of the agora. It was an unprepossessing home for such an exalted dweller, a mere four rooms with a traditional courtyard and garden in the center. The largest of the rooms served as a workshop. He had a bedroom no larger than that of Crito and Irene. The last room served every other need and purpose.

The center of the courtyard was dominated by a pit of fine sand, with a consistency somewhat like clay. Archimedes demanded little of Crito, but in two of the pit's four corners, he expected to find earthen jars perpetually filled with water. The jars were pierced below the mouths with small holes, so that the water could be sprinkled upon the sand just enough to keep it moist. At the rate that Archimedes calculated, papyrus was simply too expensive to be consumed. A stick drawing in sand substituted for charcoal or ink on papyrus or the wax slates and styluses given to schoolchildren. Several times in my youth I watched silently from the safe shadows beyond the doorway as he worked across the pit until it was covered with geometric shapes and calculations. Sometimes, he would pause and transfer a few figures to papyrus before drawing a fine rake across the sand. Other times, he would destroy everything in a frenzy and saturate the sand with violent aspersing, all the while muttering to himself.

After warmly clasping the servant couple, who were almost as old as he, my great-uncle hurried out to the courtyard. Several thoughts had come to him as we crossed the Mediterranean, and he was compelled to prove them out in the sand with no further delay. I followed him into the sunlight.

"Do not linger too long here, Uncle," I admonished. "You were given leave to visit Egypt by Hieron. It was he who underwrote your journey and who maintains this house and its servants for you. Once he learns of your return, he will expect your appearance at his court immediately."

"By and by."

"Before nightfall," I said for his own good. To command his attention I grabbed his long stick so that he could no longer draw.

Archimedes yanked the stick from me with irritation. "Yes, yes! By nightfall."

Experience had taught me that there was good chance of him not leaving the house on his own. "In fact," I decided, "I will deliver myself to my father and mother, change my clothes, and take food. Then I will return. We shall visit Hieron together. I am also expected to report."

"And I will be expected to perform like a trained baboon."

In truth, very little was demanded of my great-uncle by the city's king. Hieron the Second was in my estimation not a bad man considering he had made himself dictator. He had ruled for almost sixty years, like the benevolent despot described by Plato. I am sure he would have been deposed in all that time had he not known how to please the people. Never once was his hundred-man personal guard called up to protect him. In our long history, Siracusa has experienced despots, conquerors, limited democracies and oligarchies. Each one apparently sufficed for its time, since the city has survived for more than 500 years. A free spirit like Archimedes, however, would have bridled at the requests of any regime. I left him bent over his sand, stick in his right hand, his left hand combing absent-mindedly through his beard, muttering as always.

Δ

I had not told my great-uncle the absolute truth of my afternoon itinerary. I did not walk directly to my parents' home. As my father often said, "The greatest general is named Love. He conquers all." From the moment of leaving Siracusa, despite my excited anticipation of visiting Egypt, my heart looked ever backward. Each day closer on the return my spirit was that much lighter, imaging that I was regaining a control which in fact I did not have at all.

My first visit was to the stall of one of the most frequented jewelers in Siracusa. From one of my bags, I produced for selling three items of jewelry that had been fashioned more than a thousand years earlier. My main focus in Egypt was fetching Archimedes home, but my secondary goal was to turn half a year's salary into a small fortune. This was only possible by first finding and then negotiating with tomb robbers who worked the Valley of the Kings. I was not proud of supporting such ghouls, but in my position as a soldier in a peacetime city, I could think of no other stratagem to advance my wealth. I told myself over and over that robbing princesses who had led privileged lives on this earth and who probably had no need for its gold and precious jewels in death was justified in making happy two lovers whose lives were just beginning.

For my less-than-noble efforts, I managed to triple my initial outlay. I was now a man with respectable funds. After transferring some of the coins to a new and small pouch, I hastened to the home of the maiden Thalia. She was the third surviving daughter of Eustace the wine merchant. The largest cargo galley in the fleet that bore me home was filled with amphorae holding prized Peloponnesian wines that would replenish his shops.

Thalia was the youngest daughter of Eustace and Calandra, and was the apple of her father's eye. She was fifteen, clearly of marrying age, but he rejected parting with her. Her mother doted on Thalia as well. If she had been born to a poor family, her parents could have used the accepted argument that she would have to be the daughter who remained unmarried, to care at home for them in their old age. Theirs was, however, one of the richest families in Siracusa. Four servants tended Eustace's house, and another nine slaves labored on behalf of his shops. Moreover, their other daughters lived in the same district, almost within shouting distance. Most importantly, Thalia possessed a sheer force of will more powerful than the rest of her family combined, and she was determined to be married.

In my eyes, Thalia was Aphrodite reborn. Beauty, grace, brains, and breeding combined in her in such abundance that one wondered how many poor young women the gods had cheated to gift her so profligately. I prayed daily that she would stay inside her house weaving, lest the entire male population of Siracusa be at her feet. Fortunately, my love for her was requited.

Of course, love has nothing to do with marriage. Daughters, being little better than property, have their husbands chosen for them by their fathers and mothers. As a poor soldier seeking to win Thalia, I might as well have determined to duplicate the labors of Heracles. But love is blind to reason, and so I plotted and schemed, feeling content that Thalia had not been promised to another, so that I might soon rise to a position where Eustace would change his mind about keeping his youngest at home and desire me for a son-in-law.

I struggled from not entirely an impossible situation. My father and Eustace were known to each other and subscribed to more or less the same politics. I was noted throughout the city as the victor of the pentathlon. My brothers were married and could not have competed for Thalia's hand even if they loved her. I had counseled Thalia not to pester her father to consider her marriage until I had advanced myself. She had agreed. I was the great-nephew of the most famous man in Siracusa, and we were both related to the king. Human upheavals had begun in Sicilia, upheavals that no doubt would involve military might. In a single battle, I might cover myself with glory and have the offers of a dozen fathers. This might set Eustace thinking in the same vein. Hope sang my song softly but insistently in the distant trees.

Thalia's house lay in Ortygia, the district of the government and the rich. When my ancestors first arrived in Sicilia, Ortygia was an island shaped roughly like a pregnant woman in profile looking out to sea. It had obviously been part of the mainland several thousand years earlier, but the action of waves had carved a channel wide enough so that few could have thrown a stone across to it. Nevertheless, it was not such a gulf that it long defied the creation of a wide causeway with breakwater moles on both the Great and Little Harbor sides.

Now as a peninsula, Ortygia was nonetheless a formidable bastion against attack. Its cliffs rose the height of two standing men above the waterline at high tide, and they were solid rock. Atop this stood high, thick walls. During his ancient reign, Dionysius pushed out the island's inhabitants and made the entire place his citadel. When the city became more democratic after his death, parts of this complex were torn down, and the rich again built houses, favoring the greater security of the fortified peninsula. It was, in a phrase, the most exclusive district of Siracusa.

The home of Eustace lay not far from the causeway. Many houses of Epipolai, Achradina, Tyche, and Neapolis were one room wide, with but one more room behind. The street frontage of this residence stretched sixteen paces. It had a small front courtyard with a portico. Beyond this, I learned from Thalia, lay eight rooms encircling a far grander courtyard. The home, in fact, ran the full depth of the block on which it stood.

I rang the bells fixed on the entrance alcove centered in the tall outer wall. Presently their boy slave opened the heavy door, recognized me, and allowed me into the courtyard. I had a small coin ready in my hand, and I pressed it into his as a bribe for silence, instructing him to find Azar and to tell her only that I had returned.

While I waited, I gazed on the herm that is so common a fixture at the entrance to Greek homes, the stone pillar featuring the head of a man and a phallus. Eustace wished to coax the god Hermes to protect his home and to bring it fecundity, but he would not marry off Thalia. The sound of lyre music drifted across the courtyard, indicating that my love was at home. She was the only one of the household who currently played the instrument. I prudently backed through the door into the street, peeking in from time to time.

Azar appeared, moving swiftly despite her age and arthritis. She was Thalia's governess and had, in fact, been the chaperone to all three of Eustace's daughters. According to the woman, she had been taken from her tribe when she was six. Considering the virago's personality, I was convinced that her tribe had abandoned her. She had a tongue like a butcher's knife. She could only recall that her homeland was southeast of the Caspian Sea, for she brought little more with her than her name. She had been owned by two families before Eustace bought her from a sea captain, the second of these families residing in Korinthos. She had been purchased when the eldest of Eustace's daughters was born, and must have been fifty by the time I first met her. Whether or not Thalia was married, her value to the family was swiftly diminishing. They might elect to keep her out of kindness or from a sense of obligation for her many years of service. Just as many families in similar situations, how-ever, sold such slaves if they could get a good price or tossed them out if not and never asked how they would survive. Azar was, therefore, ex-tremely anxious about her immediate future. I did what I could to capitalize on the fact.

Azar carried on her head a large water jar. She turned after she slipped into her sandals.

"I'm going for water," she announced to the house. No one replied.

I gathered up my belongings and raced ahead of the old woman. On Ortygia, there is only one place to fill water jars. The fountain of Are-thusa lies near the western verge of the island. In spite of the fact that salt water surrounds the spring on virtually every side, the water bubbling up from it is fresh, cold, and extremely pure. Clearly, a fissure from deep in the earth exits through the island, and the water seeps down from the mountainous countryside that lies only a few stadia west of the city. Across the length and width of the spring, in distinct clumps, grow stands of papyrus which are periodically harvested. Waterfowl land there and were also harvested for Hieron's dinner table.

On the landward side of the spring, a depression had been dug and a small structure raised above it. Inside, a parapet wall created a basin, so that jars might be filled without bending. Water cascaded out of the back wall through a pair of bronze boars' heads. Since the women were obliged to fetch water every day, the island's agora market had been lo-cated just beyond the fountain. Down one adjacent street, owing to the amount of water their craft consumed, lay the shops and furnaces of the metalworkers. The air resounded with the beating of hammers.

I preceded Azar into the water house. Luckily, no one else fetched water at that moment.

"Her mother was with her," Azar explained, setting down her jar. "Tomorrow morning, however, Thalia and I come to buy warp weights in this market. She now has her own loom."

"I will be here," I assured. I set on the lip of the parapet wall the new skin pouch that contained a tenth of the money I had earned from selling the ancient Egyptian jewelry. Azar snatched up the purse and dropped it down the neck of her chiton between her breasts.

"If you count what I have given you already in past months," I said softly to her, "you may live comfortably for a year."

"You mean if I am dismissed. And what happens to me after that year?"

"With your help, Thalia and I will be married, and you will have a home for the rest of your life."

The care lines around Azar's' eyes did not soften. I assumed that she mistrusted me.

"I give you my word as a soldier," I added.

"What use is a soldier's word? Swear instead by Artemis," she insisted.

"I swear."

Azar released her pent up breath with relief.

Two women entered the water house with jars. We moved away from the basin.

"How is she?" I asked.

"More beautiful than ever. By far the most beautiful young woman on this island. And healthy. She will bear many fine sons."

"Is her love for me unchanged?"

"She loves you still. But beware! You now have a rival: Cleomenes, who owns the quarries."

Cleomenes also lived on Ortygia. He was the only son of a family who had monopolized a good portion of the quarrying business in Siracusa for 200 years, ever since we defeated a force of Athenian invaders. Those not massacred were imprisoned and worked to death in the same quarries. When he was twenty-four, Cleomenes' mother had died of a blood disease. The following year, his father was crushed supervising the reclamation of a large wall. At the relatively young age of twenty-six, Cleomenes found himself in charge of no fewer than 100 quarry workers and another three-dozen or so women who assembled cord and rope in the humid caves created by the quarrying. He was, in short, a very rich man.

Perhaps because Siracusa was such a large city, I could claim to know no more than 200 citizens by name and perhaps another 200 by face. I knew of Cleomenes because my family was also rather prosperous.

17

As in every other city, the rich associate with the rich. Truthfully, the quarry owner was better known to my brothers, who operated the family businesses. They were the ones who passed along at dinner news of his rise to fortune, along with the ebbs and neaps of the fortunes of other families.

Cleomenes was four years older than I and also never married. I had to admit that he was not repulsive to look upon. He seemed ever of a good humor and was well spoken of. In short, he was someone to respect and fear as a rival for Thalia's attention. The greatest factor against him was that his family (and, therefore, all who worked for them) had traditionally opposed Hieron and his regime. This included an attitude that Siracusa should align itself with Carthage and resist Roma. I found it difficult imagining Eustace blessing a union between one of his children and the child of such a disloyal family.

"His attention is good in a way," Azar hastened to add. "Because he is the first suitor to broach the notion of Thalia leaving them, he risks the ill feelings of both Eustace and Calandra."

"But if they should relent," I countered, "he would be first in line."

"Thalia is making sure her parents know her indifference to him," Azar assured.

"Only indifference?" I said.

"You are a man; you would not understand," she told me, pressing the small pouch through the wool of her dress to feel her coins. "Your beloved does what she can. I tell you about Cleomenes not to upset you, but rather to spur your efforts on your own behalf if you would not lose her."

We parted moments later, after I splashed a quantity of water upon my face to soothe its burning.

Δ

When we entered the forecourt of Hieron's audience chamber, I was prepared to leave Archimedes alone and return when separately summoned. Instead, Timon, the ruler's chief minister indicated that we should enter together. I did not know the chief minister well, but his smile was too broad and his eyes too pinched at the corners for my taste. These features proved nothing unwholesome about him, but I had heard that he was firmly in the control of Roma.

On the previous appearance I had made at Hieron's court, more than half a dozen people had surrounded him, from his ministers and scribes to his astrologer and his woman who fanned him with ostrich feathers, to his son Gelon, who ruled the city with him. This time, however, the chamber was empty, and Hieron did not wear his crown. Nor did he bear in his right hand the scepter of power. All that indicated his kingship was the robe he wore over his toga, dyed with the royal Tyrian purple derived from Murex shellfish. Timon drew the large bronze-sheathed doors shut behind him as he departed, sealing us in.

"Greetings, Cousin!" Hieron cried out to Archimedes.

I suddenly realized that the king had never felt the need to mention his kinship to me. He rose with effort from his throne and descended the three steps to meet my great-uncle on the main floor. If Archimedes was old, Hieron was ancient. He had only weeks before attaining the age of eighty-nine. Archimedes' hair was the color of flax; Hieron's was sparse and silver. A vast webbing of wrinkles crisscrossed his face. Despite his age, he fought decrepitude valiantly, struggling to hold himself erect like the warrior he had once been.

"Did you learn much in Egypt?" he asked.

"Not as much as if I had been allowed to stay another six months," my great-uncle answered boldly.

"Yes, I am sure. And what of the political scrolls you carried?"

"That third of Alexander's empire is stable. Peace reigns. The Ptolemies are secure. Our trade agreements remain in place."

"Good to hear." Hieron gestured to two camp chairs off to the side of the space. "Bring a chair up to the throne for your great-uncle!" he directed me.

"What is this urgent service you require of me?" Archimedes asked, with an irritated edge in his voice.

"Patience, my celebrated mathematician! First, regale me with news of your adventures and your discoveries!"

I sat as well, but did not move the other seat from the shadows. Archimedes began reluctantly and with palpable resentment. He glanced in my direction. I spread my arms and swept out the shape of a huge sphere. He nodded and began to speak about the world being round like the moon. With each sentence, he grew more animated. He simply could not maintain his anger over being recalled to Siracusa in the face of his enthusiasm. Within a few minutes, he was spouting formulae and using terms I am sure Hieron had never heard, smart as the ruler was. But, as I did when Archimedes babbled about his sciences, the king nodded slowly and affected an easy smile.

The old genius rattled on for at least ten minutes, with hardly a moment taken to draw breath. When a distant trumpet signal sounded, however, indicating the sighting of some vessel or fleet approaching the harbor, Archimedes paused. Hieron used the moment to best advantage.

"What do you think it is?" he asked. "A battle fleet from Carthage?"

"Has Carthage rebuilt its fleet?" Archimedes asked.

"It has. I entertained two of her ambassadors in this very hall not three months ago. They spoke softly and smiled a great deal, but they held the word of their new fleet over my head like an axe."

"And why would they possibly want to use it against Siracusa?" My great-uncle raised his eyebrows in an ingenuous gesture that attempted to belie his provocative question.

"Because, as you well know, no matter whether the world is flat or round, Siracusa lies in the middle of it. Considering the conflicts raging across the strait, how could the Carthaginians not fix their attention upon us?"

"Ask the war questions of your strategos here," Archimedes said, making me cringe from his mockery. "As you yourself say, I am a mathematician."

"Which gives you control over physics," Hieron countered. "Which applies to everything that stands or moves upon the earth, does it not?"

"Certainly."

"Which, therefore, must embrace the defense of our city. This is why I sent Leonides to Egypt to fetch you home."

Archimedes shook his head gravely. "A disservice to both you and me. You have high walls and a standing army already assembled."

20

"What I have ready," Hieron huffed, "is not one-tenth of an army."

"Then you certainly have citizens willing to fight. We are no different from any other Greeks. Our pride and our sense of honor compel us to trample each other in our haste to volunteer. Moreover, our city is ringed by Dionysius' defenses, which have stood nearly 200 years. The cliffs of Epipolai to the north would discourage any prudent general. The swamps to the south have defeated at least one of our ancient enemies with their diseases. What more do you require?"

"Believe me that more is indeed required. How much, I do not know," Hieron replied. "And that is precisely the problem. I do know that the art of warfare has advanced since Dionysius built our walls. If you recall the histories, he established a scientific warfare laboratory. This is how the belly bow that shoots bolts so far was invented. Think of how successful a laboratory at your command would be! Leonides can help you. He has learned the modern ways of battle and siege."

"The Greek methods only," I hastened to interject.

Hieron raised his thin forefinger to punctuate my qualification. "Precisely! Not that of the Romans or the Carthaginians. We need techniques better than theirs. Together, you two can spot weaknesses. You can anticipate enemy stratagems and build against them. I feel with a certainty that this city will be drawn into war within months."

Archimedes struggled up from his chair. "I am a scientist. What you ask for are architects and engineers. Perhaps I could have gathered information in Egypt, if you had entrusted me with news of this crisis and let me stay another three or four months, but..." He shrugged. "I shall think on this. Please excuse me. I am exhausted by a long sea voyage. I need my rest."

Hieron's jaws tightened with swallowed annoyance. He flicked his boney hand out and pointed his forefinger. "Think hard, cousin! You will return here when you are rested!"

Archimedes was compelled to knock upon the chamber doors to have them opened. When he had passed through and the doors were closed again, Hieron indicated that I should occupy the seat Archimedes had held.

To Move the World

Δ

Before I set another word of my tale to this scroll, it is of utmost import to my reader to understand something of the great forces at work which compelled King Hieron to recall Archimedes from Egypt. Without a broad context, I fear all the rest that I shall relate to you as gathered by my own eyes and ears, fearsome as it may be, will not provide sufficient impact.

About the time of the founding of our city, several Greek states other than Korinthos had established colonies all around the Aegean Sea and up to the shores of the Black Sea, across the lower third of the Italian peninsula, on Sicilia, Corsica, and Sardinia, in parts of Gaul and Hispania, and even on the Egyptian region of the Mediterranean in Cyrene and Naucratis. This was virtually a necessity because of the growing Greek population. The poor soil of the mountainous homeland demanded it, and it allowed them to trade pottery, metalwork, cloth, and olive oil for much-needed grains and lumber.

The seafarers of Phoenicia, meantime, had spread their race across the entire northern shore of Africa, to the western edge of the Egyptian provinces. They had ranged beyond the Pillars of Heracles, ventured into Hispania, and had begun their own empire, with the city of Carthage and its magnificent harbor at its center. From their point of view, the entire western half of the Mediterranean was theirs.

Added to this mix is a race of people—some said Greeks fleeing the Persians—who moved into the central valleys of Italia at almost the same time as our Korinthian ancestors occupied Sicilia. They called themselves the Latini because they lived on the Latium, which in their language means the Broad Plain. Eventually, when they realized the strategic value of its location, they consolidated a few settlements at a vital Tiber River ford into what had become the thriving city of Roma, named after one particular tribe among them. The rest of the civilized world began calling those in that region Romans, using the word with respect. Of all the peoples who occupied parts of their great peninsula, this aggressive race dominated. The regions they did not directly control had mostly joined in a confederacy with them. This was generally out of fear of being conquered outright. Consummate imitators of other races' successful experiments, these Romans also began creating colonies beyond their peninsula—on Sicilia, Sardinia, Corsica, and westward into Hispania. By the time I was born, there was no question that overlapping racial ambitions must result in rivers of blood.

I have already said that despite its location and power, across 500 years Siracusa has rarely extended its spheres of influence in a military manner. Thus, it is supremely ironic that she and her ruler, Hieron, should have taken actions that began such destructive and protracted conflicts across the whole of the western world.

The city of Messana commands the straits between Sicilia and Italia, where the turbulent waters inspired the legend of Scylla and Charybdis in ancient times. A tribe of brutal mercenaries called the Mamertini had invaded Messana some forty-seven years earlier and taken it over. Since Messana was a Greek settlement, Hieron felt compelled to come to the aid of its citizens. However, because our city has little tradition of warfare it was having no success at its siege. Hieron sent ambassadors to both Roma and Carthage, to see if either might consider a mutual protection alliance with Siracusa, the other Greek cities of Sicilia, and the Greek settlements of southern Italia. The Carthaginians responded rapidly with a powerful army that had all but swept the Mamertini out just as the Romans arrived. The Romans exercised Hieron's invitation and also attacked. When the admiral of the Carthaginian force accepted a parley with the Roman general to discuss the taking of the city, the Romans captured him and held him for ransom.

According to Hieron, although he preferred the help of the Romans, their general's action was so ignoble that he was compelled to side with the Carthaginians against them. Having the advantage of a shorter supply route, the Romans triumphed. The next year, to punish Hieron they marched into Sicilia and down the coast. Before they were able to reach Siracusa, Hieron sued for peace. For forty-five years, Hieron and Siracusa were confederates of Roma, but not without a smoldering resentment among most of the Siracusan people. The city was expected to supply monetary tribute and food supplies to this warlike tribe. For all this time, Roma and Carthage have been warring back and forth, on Corsica and Sicilia, in Hispania and Africa, exhausting their resources and the flower of their youth.

The remarkable adaptability of the Roman mind had led me to believe that they would eventually win the titanic conflict. When their wars with Carthage began they had no navy, and Carthage controlled the western Mediterranean. However, in the thirteenth year of Hieron's reign, the Romans captured a Carthaginian warship that had been driven to shore in a storm. Within two months, they had studied the ship and built an astonishing 120 copies. While they amassed their fleet, they trained their would-be seamen and their warriors on land models and introduced large boarding planks so that their soldiers might compensate for the skills of the Carthaginian sailors. Within ten years, the Romans had mastered seafaring and dominated the western Mediterranean. In Siracusa, the majority of us believed that this advantage would end the back-and-forth fighting in Sicilia, and would result once and for all in Roma's triumph in the year they decided to invade Africa.

We were mistaken. Out of Carthage emerged a highly competent general named Hamilcar Barca. Hamilcar refocused Carthage's sights on Hispania. In a ten-year period, he swept across that land, bringing to his side wealth, provisions, and auxiliary troops. When he died, his campaigning was continued by his son-in-law Hasdrubal and by his son Hannibal.

Hieron's court was kept constantly apprised of the Carthaginians' schemes by Roman ambassadors. Last year, finally having enough of their old enemy's successes, Roma decided to send one army to Hispania and another to Africa by way of Sicilia. This did not come to pass. The reason was the surprise invasion of Italia from over the Alps by Hannibal. His very boldness shook Roma to its foundations. As Hannibal moved south, several of those clans surrounding the Romans, who feared and envied them for so long, threw in with the enemy from Africa.

Thus, in the waning summer days of Hieron's fifty-third year of reign, Siracusa found itself squarely at the fulcrum point between warring giants. For months, Roma had been petitioning Hieron to raise an army of auxiliaries. As the Italian countryside was laid waste and thousands of Latini farmers were drawn from their land for soldiering, greater amounts of food than that dictated by the peace treaty needed to be imported from our region for the Roman armies. If we refused their demands, they might well send a few legions to our city to sack it and remove by force our wealth and food stores. As if this threat was not enough, one month before I left to fetch Archimedes back from Egypt we received word of a rebuilt Carthaginian war fleet. The most reasonable strategy we could imagine was that Carthage would capitalize on Roma's distraction by retaking Sicilia. Naturally, Siracusa and its king had every right to be worried.

Δ

All this roiled in my mind as I watched Archimedes disappear through the doors of Hieron's court.

"I ought to take his home from him for his insolence," Hieron said. "Or at least have him scourged." I knew from the tone of his voice that he would do neither. In all his years as ruler, it was said that Hieron never once had any citizen killed or even exiled for opposing his will. His respect for Archimedes was much too high to impose punishment.

"He is correct that he has no skills as a builder of defense works," I pointed out to the king.

"If he wished to absorb such knowledge, he could do so in a matter of weeks," Hieron answered.

"I believe a great deal of his disinterest is because he is philosophically opposed to war," I said.

Hieron began to pace. "Philosophically, so am I! Why do you think I have continued to pay the Romans tribute, to allow their war galleys to harbor here? It would be wonderful if I could believe that they would fight our battles for us and never think to occupy us as well. Isn't Archimedes just as opposed to having his throat slit by invaders? Isn't he opposed to the destruction of his own city? Shall we send him to Carthage and Roma to reason out a peace throughout the Mediterranean? Does he believe that will succeed?"

I had risen when Hieron first addressed me. I bowed before delivering my next words. "Do you know the story of the donkey in the stream,

25

your Highness?"

"No."

"A shepherd comes to a stream where a farmer is cursing. It seems the farmer's donkey has stopped in the middle of the water and will not move. 'I have tried to offer it food; I have yanked on it; I have pushed it; and now I am cursing at it, but it will not move,' the farmer told the shepherd. 'Have you tried to reason with it?' the shepherd asked. 'You try to reason with it!' invited the farmer. The shepherd picked up a stout branch from the edge of the stream. He walked up to the donkey and struck it hard between the eyes. The donkey was so stunned that he allowed himself to be led from the stream with no more resistance. 'I thought you were going to reason with it' said the farmer to the shepherd. 'I will,' replied the shepherd. 'But first I had to get its attention.'"

After the king had finished laughing, I said, "My great-uncle is just as stubborn as a donkey when he sets his mind against something. I believe that, little by little we must get Archimedes' attention to the gravity of this matter and lead his mind in this direction."

"How?" Hieron asked. "This is not a donkey we are talking about."

I paused for a moment to choose precisely the words I needed. "By a series of challenges, wherein he demonstrates his genius in applying theorems to various practical purposes. And by exposing him to the defensive needs of the city," I answered. "You must supply the first, your Highness. I will work on the second."

The king relaxed back onto his throne. "Fair enough."

"This will not be an easy task," I warned.

"Decidedly so."

"If I succeed in my challenge, may I look forward to advancement?" I dared.

"If you don't succeed, you may not have to worry about advancement. Whether you are a foot soldier or a general, you will either die or be enslaved if Siracusa falls. I cannot rely on either our cousin or on the continued benevolent protection of the Roman armies. I have too long allowed our people to grow fat and wealthy ignoring the need for their own military might in this harsh world."

Hieron leaned far forward. "Tomorrow, the citizens of Siracusa will learn of a general levy. All freemen from the ages of eighteen to thirty-two will be required to report for basic military training. The tradesmen first, then the farmers according to their harvests. One year from today, I want Siracusa to be able to field at least 5,000 infantrymen whenever the trumpets may sound. How much you are able to convince Archimedes to become involved with the defense of Siracusa will determine how high you rise." He waggled his fingers. "Do not dally. With your young legs you can catch him before he reaches his home!"

Δ

The home of my parents lay in Neapolis. Because I had received my orders to fetch Archimedes back to Siracusa directly from Timon, King Hieron's chief minister, and not from my commander, I dared to delay a night in the city before reporting to the fortress of Euryalus. My mother greeted me with great hugs and copious tears, as if I had been to the end of the world. My father was less demonstrative, but I could tell that he was glad to see me safe. He immediately sent one of the slaves out to alert my brothers.

Apollos is my father's name. His father was the brother of Phidias, who was a businessman by day and an astronomer by night. Phidias was Archimedes' father. Apollos' business was that of paint, whitewash, and stucco. Nowhere else in Sicilia was sold such a vibrant red or such a durable blue as from my father's shop. My elder brother, Dion, had learned the craft of grinding and mixing the pigments, freeing my father to concentrate on the selling, importing, and exporting duties. My second brother, older than I by a year, was Myreon. From a craftsman who used my father's pigments he had apprenticed to learn the art of mural painting. Dozens of rooms throughout Siracusa were livened by his depictions of favorite scenes from Sicilia and from the homeland of Greece, as well as fanciful recreations of the exploits of gods and heroes. Of course, only my father's pigments were used.

Myreon and Dion were summoned by my father. Once they were inside the place of our births, my father announced that the four of us would not dine there that night, but rather celebrate my return with a professional symposion at the house of Exadne. She was of the hetairai, the women who entertained men in the evening. Although I had been to such houses in Korinthos and Alexandria, I found Exadne a particularly highly cultured and educated woman and her house one of unique beauty. My brother Myreon validated my admiration of the wall murals depicting women athletes, scenes at the same time exotic and erotic. The floor of the dining chamber was of the finest tessera, the mosaic formally patterned around the edges, but representing the Mediterranean in a central circle that teemed with octopuses, mollusks, eels, and fish.

In acknowledgement of my too-many days bobbing upon the Mediterranean, my father ordered not the fruits of the sea, but rather emptied his purse for several brace of quail. With them we ate bread, onions and cabbage, and a porridge of lentils cooked in a delightful sauce. For dessert we nibbled on figs, grapes, and honey cakes. I occupied the same couch as my father, while Dion and Myreon shared another. Across the chamber reclined a man whose name I have forgotten who was a ship's outfitter, along with his son and two of his friends.

When the meal was ended I was chosen as the symposiarch, to determine what proportion of water should be added to the wine. I decided that the night called for dizzying delight, and my decision was approved by all. After our drinking cups were drained and we had debated and riddled ourselves to near-exhaustion, the other group retired from the ornate dining room to private, inner chambers, leaving myself and my family alone in the andron. I used the opportunity to share with my brothers in subdued tones the news that they would soon be expected to serve military duty. Dion, to his credit, greeted the news with the fervor expected of a man and a Siracusan. Myreon looked as though he could already feel a spear going through him.

"I will serve, of course, but I despair of ever having any aptitude for war," he admitted. "Are there not outsiders we can hire who have experience as soldiers?"

My father shook his head gravely. "There are always men who are willing to accept pay for fighting, but few of them can be depended upon. They take the salary for years and do nothing but parade around by day and cause trouble by night. Then, when the enemy is within sight, they manage to disappear. The only ones who will fight fiercely for our city are those who love it and live in it."

"There are other reasons not to hire mercenaries," I said, looking at my father. "Did not Siracusa once suffer from their kind?"

Apollos turned the crater upside down, signifying the end of drinking. "Indeed. This was when Hieron first took rule. They were violent and injurious to the citizens and even threatened mutiny. This is an excellent example of Hieron's mind, and why he has survived for so long as king. This was at a time when the Campanians had seized Messana. He had at his disposal a force equally composed of citizen soldiers and mercenaries, and he chose a site near the river Cyamosorus to do battle. He arrayed his cavalry on the right, his home force on the left flank under his command, and the mercenaries in the middle. He made it known that the plan of attack was to engage with Siracusa's mercenaries first and then surround the enemy with a double flanking envelopment. The trumpets and horns never sounded the crucial call; the Campanians were allowed to overwhelm and annihilate the mercenaries. Hieron withdrew his loyal troops to Siracusa. Thereafter, Hieron himself chose those who would serve the city with spear and shield."

Apollos seemed content to conclude the story there. I had heard this and more from my commander at the fortress. I asked him if I might finish the tale. He nodded.

"The same Campanians who had crushed Hieron's mercenaries foolishly concluded that these were the best Siracusa had to offer. Therefore, they marched south and began fearlessly raiding our confederate towns and villages. Hieron recruited more citizens, armed them, and put them through a stringent period of training. When they were ready, he led them out of our gates and engaged the Campanians near the river Longanus on the plain of Mylae. The enemy attacked with virtually no battle plan and was decisively beaten. Their leaders were captured and executed. From that day forward Hieron was called king."

"We will fill our army with citizens, Myreon," my father said. "And you will serve with honor." In the silence that ensued, he laid down his coins and led us out of the house of Exadne.

As we walked through the winding streets toward my boyhood

home, my father said to me, "While you were away, Philana's sister reached her fourteenth year. How long has it been since you have seen Xantippe?"

My father spoke of the sister of Dion's wife. Women of Siracusan households which could afford slaves rarely left the house, and if they did, they wore veils or hoods over their faces in the streets and at the market. I admitted that I had not looked upon her in more than a year.

My father said, "She is a woman now. She has long since placed her toys in the Temple of Artemis. Her father and I believe that she may be a good match for you. She is as smart as a woman should be, healthy, and of good spirit. Shall we arrange for you to meet with her?"

"I own no home, Father," I reasoned, seeing Thalia in my mind's eye. "Professional soldiers rarely can afford to marry before the age of thirty."

"But you could at least look on her and speak with her," he persisted. "You know I did not impose my will implacably on either Dion or Myreon. If you decide that she pleases you, I am sure she can wait until she is sixteen for the formal marriage. And then she can live with us until you have advanced yourself and secured a house."

I feared even the first step toward the trap. If I met with Xantippe and rejected her, I would create discord between Dion and his wife and in-laws. If I acted even mildly interested in her, my father would negotiate the dowry the next day. In Siracusa as in other Greek cities, the engagement is the formal and binding contract and the marriage only the outward tying up of ends.

"Not now," I evaded. "With this building of the army reserves, I will be much too busy to think of a wife."

"Or is there another reason?" Myreon formed the fingers of his right hand into the letter of the alphabet that implied I was a homosexual.

An instant later, my father's palm swept hard against the side of Myreon's head.

"Why do I deserve that?" my brother asked, laboring to conceal a wicked grin. "In his work he associates with only men."

"And in your work," my father countered, "you associate only with walls. Does that make you as thick as one?"

30

Dion burst into laughter and pushed Myreon hard against the side of a house. "Be careful little brother!" he warned him. "You will be among those same men soon enough!"

Δ

For those who wonder if Cupid's arrow can pierce the heart cleanly in one draw of the bow, the answer is yes. Both Thalia and I would eagerly have attested to the same. We first laid eyes upon each other at the great amphitheater that takes advantage of the hill that slopes sharply up from Neapolis into the Epipolai district. The occasion had been a city-wide celebration of the successful gathering of summer crops, and it coincided with the third full moon following the summer solstice. Tents had been pitched in the city's open lots for the farmers who came in from as far as 200 stadia distant. An animal fair was conducted; the temples teemed with citizens offering sacrifices; the theaters provided imported entertainment; a scaled-down version of the Olympiad was conducted on the competition fields and in the gymnasia.

As I have stated, I acquitted myself as the best in the grueling pentathlon, scoring the most combined points for running the length of one stadion, broad jumping, wrestling, and throwing the discus and javelin. The afternoon following my victory, a troupe of players from the island of Naxos performed an Aristophanes' comedy called *The Birds*. I can remember neither the plot nor the witticisms of the play. I have forgotten what must have been splendid sets behind the players. I do not recall the look of the actors' persona masks or how well the young men portrayed the parts of the women. All I committed to memory that afternoon was every contour and nuance of Thalia's face.

The amphitheater of Siracusa is justly famous not only for its size and construction, but also for its clever placement. Plays, song festivals, and orations are begun halfway between when the sun has reached its daily zenith and when it disappears over the mountains to the west. For the vast majority of the audience, therefore, it lies behind their shoulders, sparing their eyes from its glare. As the entertainment wears on, the air grows gradually cooler and the light grows easier on the eyes. Naturally, since the rows of seats curve in concentric semi-circles, those on the far left and right receive light to their profiles. As the hero of the day, I was invited to sit in the front row amongst the members of our royal family, on those special marble seats with backs. Upon my head was affixed the crown of wild olive leaves, lest anyone wonder who I was.

Not five minutes after taking my seat, I noticed the family of Eustace moving along the orchestra to the left flank of the first row. With him entered his son, his two older daughters and their husbands, his wife, and one other woman, who was slender and quite graceful. Of course, in public the women of all but the most common families cover their faces either with veils in the warm weather or hoods when it is cold. Since, however, it is considered that at the theater all eyes are fixed on the stage and that the only parts of a woman a stranger may see are the back of her head and her shoulders, they are allowed there to lower their veils. Thus it was that I beheld the fifteen-year-old Thalia when she exposed her face. I viewed her in half profile, and what I gazed upon in my opinion was the embodiment of perfection. I knew that I acted rudely, and I averted my stare after several seconds. Yet time and time again, my eyes stole back to her. Perhaps it was on the fifth or sixth occasion that our eyes met.

It was as if an invisible thunderbolt passed between us. Even at the distance across the orchestra circle I saw her eyes studying my face, taking in the crown of olive leaves with patent admiration. I wished then that women would have been allowed to view the men competing, so that her approval could have been all the more amplified. Our eyes locked. She did not look away, as maidens are taught to do, but boldly returned my rapt stare. A smile stole across her face. For the next two hours, we played a silent game of flirtation. She laughed wonderfully, and she knew it. Whenever something uproarious occurred on the stage and the audience reacted, her cheeks elevated and her lips drew back from her perfect teeth. The next moment, she would cast her eyes in my direction. When she departed the theater, my heart left with her.

The next day, I found my way to her parents' house and lay stealthy siege across from its gate. When Azar left that morning to fetch water, I followed her and offered my first bribe.

"Thalia's parents do not wish her to marry," she had told me bluntly. "And if she ever does, it will not be to a lowly soldier."

I protested that if such were the case, she risked nothing in acting as a go-between. Clearly, I would soon be told as much by Thalia and sent on my way. I pressed another coin into the old woman's hand. It was thus arranged that since the Festival of the Harvest was still in progress, Thalia might go to the Temple of Apollo in Neapolis to offer prayers.

For three days straight, accompanied by her governess, Thalia prayed. Each day I was also inside the temple. In thirty stolen minutes all told, we confirmed that our love was mutual and that our future together was all but ordained by the heavens.

Only five times in all did I speak with her before I was compelled to depart for Egypt to drag Archimedes home. One occasion was a massive fete at Hieron's palace for the wealthiest and most privileged families of Siracusa, a periodic ploy of the king's to take the political temperature of the influential men and confirm that they were sufficiently content to continue supporting his regime. The patriarchs were taken into the palace walls for advising and to build consent, but their families remained in the great courtyard among the sword dancers and musicians, picking food from the tables and viewing monumental statuary and clever displays fashioned from flowers and plants, all of it lit by a hundred torches. Thalia and I had plotted to arrange that our families would arrive at virtually the same time, so that reintroductions were made all around. Without arousing suspicion, I was able to flatter both her father and mother, and they were able to put my face with the name of the victor of the pentathlon event two months earlier. Although she was veiled, I was able to spend another ten minutes or so alongside my beloved, pretending that we were engaged in the idlest of chats.

One other time I saw the keeper of my heart alone in that first year, and this was in the Ortygian agora. Ordinarily, well-born women did not go to the marketplace. The fathers did the daily shopping with one or two slaves in tow. If the mothers needed items for food preparation, housekeeping, or weaving, they generally sent out their servants. From time to time, however, on such occasions as choosing the raw materials for fashioning dresses or draperies, the women ventured forth. Using just such an excuse, Thalia was allowed to leave the house.

Behind the clothmakers' stalls, on a street that radiated out from the agora, lay a deep and narrow alley with two doors that were barred from the inside. Within this alley I waited, and, with Azar guarding its mouth, into it Thalia eventually stole. My being was already aflame with the expectation that I would gaze upon her up close up with no veil and no distractions.

I was somewhat confused when she appeared wearing a full robe over her chiton. The himation is meant for cool nights and cold days, but this was a warm late-summer morning. As she took her final steps toward me, she unfastened the garment's belt and let it drop. Then she drew the robe over her head, and I saw the reason she had worn it. Underneath, the material of her dress was all but invisible. It was made of that magical fabric imported from the mysterious Far East that the Chiosans fashion into what they call a coa vestis. I could see through its gossamer fineness the shape of Thalia's breasts, the rosy color of her nipples, and the dark triangle between her thighs. She stood before me as still as a caryatid column, and yet she might just as well have been writhing like a Babylonian harlot for the lust she produced in me.

"It is my mother's," Thalia said, grinning at my astonished reaction.

"You should not have taken such a terrible risk," I answered, despite the indescribable joy she gave me.

"I know. But I cannot give you myself, so this is the most I can do for now." Thalia's breaths became shallow and rapid as she registered the extent of my excitement. "Touch me," she said in a whisper.

I took her arms and guided her around to the alley's back wall, so that my bulk would protect her from any chance glimpse by a passerby. Then I slowly explored her form, passing my hands with gentle reverence over her breasts, down her flanks, and across her stomach, over her hips, to feel the taut curves of her buttocks.

Thalia gave forth a low moan. Then she laughed lightly. "My little brother has given me a new nickname: Callipygia."

She did indeed have shapely and beautiful buttocks. Much as I reveled in the look of her beauty and in holding her, so much more did I fear some sudden disaster of a tradesman coming through one of the barred doors. I hurriedly scooped up her belt and robe and beseeched her to put them back on. When she had, I took her again in my arms and thanked her over and over for her offering, in between raining kisses upon her sweet, full lips. If I had been in her thrall the ten months before, I was then her abject slave. I reminded her that I was related to the king, reasoned that the military leaders of the city were rapidly aging and would soon retire, and pledged that I would rise to such a level that her father would be eager to have me as a son-in-law. In all of this, Thalia encouraged me, all the while running her delicate fingers up and down the muscles of my arms. I informed her of my duty to travel to Egypt and swore to take good care of myself. She, in turn, swore to be inconsolable until my return. By the time she pulled away and raced down the alley, my entire body was aflame.

So it was, the day after my return to Siracusa from Egypt, that I found myself in the same dead-end alley, awaiting my beloved. I had dressed in my full soldier's regalia, the better to impress her, careening back and forth between the narrow walls as I impatiently paced.

At last, two shadows darkened the entrance to the alley. Again, Azar took up her guard. Again, Thalia raced to me, drawing down her veil as she came. Then her lips were upon mine and her hands upon my cheeks.

"I prayed daily to Poseidon to keep you safe," she exclaimed.

"Then he, too, must love you," I said. "The crossings were both without event."

"I have missed you so!"

"Only the greatest poet could tell how I have missed you," I echoed.

Thalia stepped back a pace. "All the way from Egypt!"

"In truth."

"And what have you brought me?" she asked.

My heart sank. I struggled for words. "I would have brought you the very pyramids if I could have."

"How romantic! But what did you bring?"

"Thalia, my darling," I said, "you know well that I could bring you nothing. If I gave you a vial of precious perfume, your father would immediately smell it and ask who gave it to you. If I brought you sheets of fine cotton for your bed, your mother would learn of me in a trice."

Thalia's eyes remained bright and undaunted. "Of course. I know that you cannot give me gifts until you are able to announce your intentions toward me. But that doesn't mean you aren't laying them aside. I know the depths of your love. You could not possibly have traveled all the way to Egypt without getting me something. Tell me what!"

I could not master my sigh. "Earrings," I heard myself say.

"I adore jewelry!" she enthused, as if I could not see the necklace of coins from twenty foreign lands upon her chest or the ornate gold pins that created the sleeves of her chiton. "Tell me about them!"

"They are of the finest beaten gold, cleverly hinged, with malachite and lapis lazuli stones. And they belonged to a queen."

"Which queen?"

"Do you know of many ancient Egyptian queens?"

"No. But why should that matter?"

"The wife of Thutmose," I lied, grasping for one of the kingly names I had heard on my travels. "It was stolen from her treasure chamber, and I obtained it at great cost and personal risk."

Thalia went up on tiptoe and crushed my lips with a kiss of pure passion.

"Bring them for me to see the next time we meet," she said. Her face grew serious and even a bit hard. "Yesterday, when Azar told me of your return, I heard a jingling from under her chiton. Later, I went through her belongings and found a purse filled with the images of Hieron, Gelon, and Arethusa. The purse looked like it belonged to a soldier."

"It's an Egyptian purse," I replied.

"You have been buying Azar's favor and assistance."

"Naturally. Why else would she help me?"

"Don't," Thalia said, emphatically. "You have given her half enough coins to buy her freedom."

"Have your parents spoken of selling her?"

"Selling? Who would have her? Do not give her even one more coin!" Thalia ordered.

"As you wish," I said.

"She is my slave, not yours. You do not have to be kind to her anymore, in fact."

"It costs me nothing to be kind."

"She is a perverse creature, fond of telling others what to do and think. Kindness only makes her more sharp-tongued and independent." Thalia reaffixed her smile and changed the subject, giving me news of her home.

The noises of the market reminded us all the while of the danger of our meeting. After not nearly enough moments, she pulled from my embrace and backed down the alley.

"I shall wear those earrings on my wedding day," she said.

And then she was gone.

Δ

Not ten minutes after leaving Thalia, I stood before the jeweler to whom I had sold the Egyptian treasures. I will not share his name to spare his family shame. I knew when I sold to him that he was a character of questionable reputation, at least when it came to business. So it was with a certainty of trouble that I put myself in front of him so soon again.

"I need to buy back one-third of what I sold you yesterday," I told him, staring at the very earrings I had described to Thalia.

"You do?" he said. "That is most strange. Which do you speak of?" When I pointed to the earrings, he said, "Oh, misfortune! They are already spoken for. I am merely holding them until the buyer can gather the money. An advance has already been put down upon them."

I had expected precisely such an argument. "I will pay you twenty-five per cent more than you paid me for them."

He laughed. "But I have said that they are already as good as sold, and the buyer is willing to pay twice what I gave you."

I matched his lie with one of my own. "I expect to travel again to Egypt within the year," I said, "and I will bring you five times the treasures I secured the first time. I will only do this if you sell back the earrings. Otherwise, I go to your competitor. For the earrings, you will make twenty-five per cent profit in less than one day."

The old haggler studied my face for the truth and weighed future promises against present profits. "For fifty per cent," he said, "I will risk the anger of a valued customer as a favor to you."

I listened to a growing buzz of chatter in the stalls around us. Old men were embracing young ones. Matriarchs who never deigned to visit the marketplace were searching out their sons. Then I looked past the crafty bargainer's shoulder to several young men who were forging links into golden chains.

"Are any of those lads yours?" I asked.

He pointed to the one seated closest to him. "He is."

"How old?"

"Just eighteen."

I turned dramatically to listen to the crowd and verify my surmise over the tumult. When I turned back, I said, "Do you know what causes the excitement around you?"

"No. I am too busy dealing with you, young soldier."

"A levy has just been announced for reserve soldiers."

"Are we at war?" he asked, his eyes wide with fear.

"Not yet. The city is merely improving its ability to defend itself. Your son will be called within a few weeks." The father calculated furiously behind his crafty eyes.

"It is likely that he will train under me," I said. "What is his name?"

"Patroclos. He is called Patroclos."

"A noble fighting name, indeed. But Homer tells us that his namesake fell in battle. I might serve as his Achilles, to protect him," I pointed out. "I will have those ear bobs back for twenty-five per cent more than you paid me, or your son will find himself training without a friend."

Moments later the earrings were mine again. Of all the hundreds of laws the observant Jews follow, they have ten great commandments. These ten were supposedly directly given to their prophet Moses by their One God of All. One of these is "Thou Shalt Not Steal." I had not stolen the jewelry myself, but in purchasing it from the tomb robbers I had certainly encouraged their next crime. To repossess the earrings, I was reduced to lies and threats, the fact of the jeweler's gouging reputation notwithstanding. In all my life, I had never before stooped to such depths, never before so compromised my scruples. But I had also never before had the chance to win Thalia.

CHAPTER III

The 440 professional soldiers who served inside Siracusa were not the parasites many of its citizens imagined, even in times of peace. Throughout the night, patrols of two or three moved through the dark streets of the various districts, insuring peace and safety. The city gates required guarding. Walls needed to be patrolled. Outposts had to be manned at both the Little and Great Harbors, to watch against sudden invasion from the sea, and also to ensure that runaway slaves did not slip onto the vessels. Slaves needed to know they could not rise up against the city. We also augmented Hieron's one-hundred-man personal guard when he and members of his family moved among the citizenry at festivals. For this we wore no uniforms and were lightly armed, so that Hieron might give the appearance of having the confidence in his subjects to wander unguarded. Nevertheless, it was important work.

Another 440 soldiers served outside of the city walls. These cost the citizens of Siracusa nothing. They were paid by a tithe on the earnings of the seven towns, fifty hamlets, and 100 or so estates surrounding Siracusa. This was justly demanded by Hieron, because all these places depended on Siracusa as their window to the world. The percentage of their earnings paid for the guarding of the harbor, to help build cargo ships and war galleys, for the maintaining of the roads that connected them to the city, and for protection from the roving brigands who preyed upon the road traffic. These places were subservient, not as Roman colonies were, but rather as true confederates. Many of them were so pleased by Siracusa's protection that they trained no soldiers of their own, compelling ours to pursue their occasional thieves and murderers.

If every man who counted himself a soldier was totaled, Siracusa yet did not have 1,000 men serving on the day Archimedes and I returned from Egypt. For a city of our size, this was a statement perhaps unique throughout the Mediterranean. We could no longer afford such complaisance.

As soon as the edict to build the army reserves went out, the obligations of the veterans increased. Some switched to the crafts of fashioning weapons and armor, consulting with the metalworkers of all the districts to create equipment as modern as that of our potential foes. More than the normal number looked after the many quartermaster needs of a vastly increased army: tents, shovels, cooking gear, enormous stores of grain and dried meat, fish, and fruits. The commissary was increased. The most senior veterans took on the task of drilling the raw recruits into one smoothly functioning juggernaut.

There were those of us assigned the onerous task of combing the city for men who had not voluntarily reported to the agoras on the day of the levy. Fortunately, they were few. A man who evaded service was a man without honor, which was regarded as one step above a murderer. The truth was that many who were not called wished to serve. Any man who paid no taxes was not eligible for call, and most of this group were deeply embarrassed to be of the right age and not able to wear a uniform. This searching, for the first month, was my task. If I could not find the cowards in their homes or places of business, the taverns and houses of ill repute proved excellent hunting grounds.

Soon enough, we had enrolled the roughly 5,000 men Hieron wanted. We could not train them in a single body, but rather mustered

768 at a time. The last large army that Siracusa had formed had been roughly copied from those of the great Macedonians, King Philip and his son Alexander.

The bulk of those colossal fighting forces were speira, or squared masses of men that, linked together like chain, formed irresistible phalanxes. These speira were sixteen men deep and sixteen men wide, and the initial shock weapon was a spear long enough to reach through row after row of men, meant to impale an approaching army as the thorns of a dense bramble bush will stop the rush of the strongest man. The second weapon was the shield, which was quite heavy and nearly as long as a man. The objective was to use the shields not only for protection but also to bowl over the front lines of the enemy, so that those behind could hack them to pieces on the ground. Once the opposing lines met the depth of each mattered, since man after man behind the first one pushed forward, adding his weight to the mass in driving the enemy's force backward into confusion. Truth be known, it was brave work, but not challenging.

Simple mathematics proves that each Macedonian speira was comprised of 256 men. Our main unit was called instead a syntagma, or gathering, and had only 192 men. Our battlefront was sixteen men wide but only twelve men deep. The reasoning of my superiors was that we would be fighting defensively and in closed quarters. If any of our walls were breached, a line twelve spears deep would be enough to repel a force coming through a narrow opening. In fact, with 122 stadia of walls and two harbors to defend night and day during a siege, it would likely be impossible to gather a full syntagma together during a momentary crisis.

The main point of the massing was for precision drilling and to hammer home the concept that every man's individuality had to be sacrificed for the common cause. The smallest working unit consisted of six men. A marching line of twenty-four men collapsed into four side-by-side ranks of six upon the initial cry of the commander, followed by a trumpet signal. I will not trouble you with all of the minutia of creating battle order, but suffice it to say whether they marched in a single or double column, each man knew precisely beside whom he belonged, and in quick time the disciplined cohort could face an enemy with a solid mass of spears and shields.

Getting to such a point, however, was not easy. The raw recruits would begin to step off as soon as the order was given, without waiting for the trumpet signal. They were allowed to get themselves into trouble, colliding with each other and dropping their shields, to show them just how ignorant they were. The habitual failures were given marching duties with full armor and assigned extra wall guard.

The army had no power over—and little connection to—the palace guard. This assured the king the loyalty of enough men to guard his person if the general of the army chose to overthrow him. Only seven long-time veterans commanded our initial 880. The oldest, Archidamus, served as strategos and had been an under officer when Hieron led the field. Reporting directly to our general were Urian and Lysander, valiant and highly disciplined men. They headed the cavalry, which consisted of 100 of the surplus beyond the 768 in the ranks.

The commander of each syntagma division was named the syntagmatarch. He stood at the far right corner of the front rank, with an officer in charge of the left half of the unit, named a taxiarch. Our first division was headed by a man named Hippokrates; his brother Epikydes commanded the second. The third division's leader was Archelous, and Paulus commanded the fourth. My aspiration was to become a syntagmatarch as quickly as possible. With the army expanding so rapidly, my special training in Korinthos and my triumph in the pentathlon gave me high hopes despite my youth.

As long as Archimedes divided my attention, I knew that I could not maintain the presence required to earn merit in Archidamus' eyes. While the general was aware of the Promethean task I had been given by our king, he was hardly sympathetic to the time it took from my other duties. Therefore, I redoubled my effort to convert the old curmudgeon as quickly as possible.

In spite of his annoyance at me for not allowing him to stay in Egypt, my great-uncle and I became significantly closer during our sea voyage than we had previously been. When I came to him and invited him to walk with me "for exercise" he did not question ulterior motives but laid down his drawing stick and accompanied me. He did not even complain when we climbed out of Neapolis through the higher district of Epipolai.

I took him outside the city walls among the groves of olive trees that had been planted only ten years before and which would not begin to yield a harvest for another six years.

Of his own accord, Archimedes said, "If you want to improve the defenses, you must remove these trees."

"It is true," I granted. I said no more, hoping he would continue. He walked over to a patch of sandy soil and looked down.

"I shouldn't expend even a moment on this. War is evil," he pronounced.

"Men die," I granted, "but it is necessary to advance a race."

"By 'advance', you mean to spread into other parts of the world."

"It is why we are here in Sicilia. The mountainous lands of Greece would not support the growing population. Many would have starved as numbers increased."

Archimedes began walking again. "Then let those who cannot fight for their share of food starve. It is a way to eliminate the weak from the race."

"You only offer this hypothetically. Surely you do not mean it."

"Do I not?"

I could not read his face. "But it is cruel."

"Then the cruelest manner of winnowing excess population is war," he stated. "It eliminates the fit men on both sides, those who should live to pass on their vigor and intelligence."

I felt as if I had stumbled into one of Plato's dialogues. "War has existed since before history, and, I am sure, will go on long after we are dead."

"Because killing is easy," Archimedes said. "Alternatives are difficult. Telling people that they may not have as many children as they want is difficult."

"Your wisdom is rare, Uncle," I said, and then to shift the discussion: "If you had but one of your discoveries to be remembered for all time, what would it be?"

"The ratio of the volume of a sphere to a cylinder in which it perfectly fits is two to three. Moreover, the surface of that same sphere is two-thirds the surface of this circumscribed cylinder, including its bases."

Thinking of his water screw and his platform that used counter-weights to lift men straight up the side of a wall, I could not contain my amusement at this apparently inapplicable discovery.

"Yes, laugh," he said, not taking offense. "But it is the mathematics that I developed to be able to prove this fact that makes it so important. And is not the fact of exactly two to three wonderful? Does it not speak of the elegance of creation? If fate is kind, you will be allowed to outlive me. Do me a favor: Above my resting place, have those who love me set a sphere beside a cylinder in marble and, beneath it, my name and the formula. I shall write it down on paper for you."

"It shall be done," I said, as a little shiver went through me contemplating the great man being no more.

Archimedes stopped and stared at the Hexapyli gate to the Epipolai district. "I know little about architecture," he said to me, "but any fool can tell that such a gate is an invitation for a battering ram."

The door, massive and reinforced with metal as it was, stood parallel to the wall, barely inset.

"And how should it be improved?" I asked, careful not to ask him directly how he would improve it.

Archimedes pointed to the ground. "Do me a favor and pick up that stick." When I had handed it to him, he smoothed out a space of dirt with his sandal and began to draw. He drew lines representing the thick walls on either side of the gate, but he left a space in between. Directly in front of the entrance and parallel with the existing wall, at double the width of the roadway, he placed another wall which stood alone but which extended beyond the width of the space beyond. He redrew the roadway to go around this outer wall on both sides. He then created a duplicate of the new wall on the opposite side of the main walls. Between the new inside wall and the old defensive wall he indicated two portals. These, however, were at right angles to where the old door had been.

"This front wall I have imagined is very thick but quite low, so that soldiers stationed on the parapets can shoot over it at any enemy that approaches. It is nonetheless high enough to prevent a battering ram from being wheeled over it. Not at least until the wall is removed. By building a simple wall, you could kill many of your enemies or else dissuade them from attacking that point. Even if they succeed in removing this outer wall, when they bring the ram forward, they will not face a wooden gate but a doubly thick set-back wall. These gates at right angles cannot possibly be assailed by a ram; the space between them is too small to angle in a ram of effective size and to turn it. Moreover, if the enemy tries to build fires against the doors to burn them down, they can be attacked from above on three sides."

"Incredible!" I marveled. "It is marvelous in its simplicity. This is exactly what Hieron wants of you."

"I doubt that I have more to contribute," the old man said. "I see a wall, and I think 'build it higher and thicker.' There is no genius to that. I am ignorant of warfare and modes of defense."

"I can show you what I know."

"It would be much quicker and simpler for you to tell construction engineers. I believe that even Hieron is beginning to concede as much. He has stopped pestering me about the walls and has asked me to solve another problem. A much more difficult problem, I should say."

"And what is that?"

"He has recently had a new crown made. A wreath really. Not for his own head but rather to set upon the head of that statue of Zeus beside the palace altar. It mimics the intertwined olive branches of the champion, with a host of delicate leaves set at various angles. In other words, it is a very complex shape. Because the wreath has already been consecrated by the high priest, I am forbidden to alter it in any way with tests. Consequently, it defies the task of calculating its volume."

"And why would he want that done?"

"He believes the jeweler who fashioned the crown has cheated him out of a quantity of gold. He suspects that the man mixed silver in with most of the gold and kept a few ounces of the more precious metal for himself."

"Can he not weigh the crown to determine if the man cheated him?"

"No. The weight is precisely that of the amount of gold supplied."

"What of the color of pure gold against that of the crown?"

"I have experimented with that. A small amount of silver may be mixed to the gold without changing its color."

I asked the jeweler's name. I was not surprised to learn that the man who sought to gouge me and the one believed to have cheated Hieron were one and the same. I shared with Archimedes that I knew from experience that the man was not above such thievery.

"Then I shall have to give the matter more serious thought," Archimedes decided. He rubbed out his drawing with his sandal and consulted the angle of the sun. "I have walked as far as I will today. Let us return."

Δ

One week later to the day, Archimedes had his answer. I had fulfilled my morning duty of mustering a new cohort of men for training and was headed toward the bathhouse that my great-uncle frequented. I was still perhaps a hundred paces from it when Archimedes rounded the corner at high speed, talking aloud to himself. To my amazement and that of the other men in the street, he wore nothing more than a towel around his flabby middle. His feet were bare. His hair dripped water.

"What is wrong, Uncle?" I cried out.

"Nothing, nothing. Everything is excellent! I have found it!"

"Found what?" I asked, but he had already dashed past me.

I debated following him home, but elected to cleanse myself first and then visit his house. I was certain I would find him there drawing in his sand pit, bringing to life whatever new formula had sprung to his mind while he was relaxing in the warm water.

When I entered the bathhouse, the place was abuzz with Archimedes' antics.

"You are his great nephew, are you not?" one of the men asked me.

"I am indeed."

"Did he pass you in the street?"

"Wearing nothing but a towel."

"Exactly."

"What happened?" I inquired of the group of men.

"I was in the bath right beside him," a very hirsute man volunteered. "He likes to talk with me, because mathematics is a hobby of mine. For my part I wither when he approaches, for his mind is so in advance of mine. For example, today he was prattling about cattle of the Sun grazing upon the fields of the Trinacian Isle and being divided into four herds of different colors. He was making my mind ache."

I knew well the feeling.

"He was so engaged in sharing the problem with me that he kept emptying jars of hot water into the bath until it had risen almost to the level of the floor. I could see that he would get water everywhere when he lowered himself, but he is Archimedes, and who am I to correct him?"

"Go on," I said, tiring of the man's digressions.

"Well, then he did lower himself, and the water did run out all over the floor. He stopped his lecture on the cattle in mid-sentence and just stared for the longest time in silence at the puddles of water. Then he raised himself partway out of the bath. After a time he reclined again, saying nothing."

"And all of a sudden, he leapt out!" another man supplied, stealing the storyteller's thunder and earning for himself a withering look. The interloper had fixed his gaze on me and was oblivious. "He leapt out," he repeated, "as if the water were scalding. And he shouted 'Eureka! Twice he shouted it, in truth."

"I heard him say the same thing," I shared. "'I have found it.'"

"What did he find?" another asked.

"Perhaps someone dropped an article of jewelry in the water," another surmised.

"Don't be an idiot!" the hairy man scolded. "Archimedes cares nothing for gold or silver."

With those words, I forgot my bath and left the building, moving with long strides to my great-uncle's house. There, I found him seated at one of his work tables rather than in the sunny courtyard. He had taken quill to papyrus and busied himself in drawing what looked to be a basin with a lever and two masses suspended above it. I waited quietly until he at last noticed me.

"What is it that you have found, Uncle?" I asked.

"The answer to the problem of Hieron's wreath!" he proclaimed. "At least I believe I have it. I will have to conduct an experiment to be sure, naturally."

"Naturally. And what is this answer?"

"That a body immersed in a fluid is buoyed up by a force equal to the weight of the displaced fluid. Does that not make perfect sense?"

I supposed as much.

"Think of a galley or argosy," he said to me. "Why does it float when a stone will not? Because, by its shape, the volume of water it displaces is greater than its weight."

I began to understand what he meant. He pointed to his drawing.

"I will secure from Hieron an amount of gold precisely equal to that given to the goldsmith. This I will attach to the end of a pivoting lever that shall act as my scale. To the opposite end of the lever I will attach the wreath. Then I will immerse them both into a tank of water. If the scale remains in balance, then the wreath was made of pure gold. If it tilts toward the mass of gold, then the wreath has a greater volume because its density is less. Silver is lighter than gold, you see?"

Three days later, the jeweler was thrown into prison. His son was mustered immediately into the army; his wife was compelled to live with her sister and brother-in-law when the jeweler's house was confiscated. The contents of his shop and his equipment were auctioned off and the money used toward buying iron for spears. Months later, I came across the wretched man in chains within the bowels of Euryalus, fashioning spearheads.

Δ

During the hectic months of building the army and my task of shepherding Archimedes, I remained in a near-frenzied state over my lack of communication with Thalia. I saw her about six weeks after returning from Egypt, to show her the earrings. Other than that, I was reduced to sending her messages that a public scribe wrote onto papyrus. As always, my go-between was Azar. Too much danger existed in my delivering notes to Eustace's home. I needed a go-between who would neither care unduly of the mutual love between me and Thalia nor be inclined to gossip about it. The person arose in the form of my best friend's new bride.

48

Strategos Archidamus encouraged the men of his army to engage in physical contests and provided time for such pursuits. Among those who wrestled, I met a man named Apollonius, who was six years my senior. He also stood taller than the other men of our force and proved to be an outstanding wrestler. As I grew to know him, I found that his ambitions were no less than mine. He was also frustrated by the static nature of our command and the lack of opportunities for advancement.

As soon as the army began to grow, however, Apollonius was promoted to the rank of taxiarch. This freed him at last to marry the young woman to whom he had been engaged for two years. Her name was Amara, and she was a lovely and kind creature, who always thought of the needs of others before her own.

Apollo, as he was known to his friends, bestowed on me the great honor of serving as his best man. The banquet was held at the home of Amara's parents, where the pledges the lovers first made at their betrothal were repeated and dowry and guest presents were set out for all to admire. The marriage gods were invoked. Earlier in the day, sacrifices had been made. Some of the animals were given back for the feast. Wine flowed freely. The one who drank the most was the groom. Both the bride and groom smelled sweetly from the ritual baths they had taken in perfumed sacred waters.

Siracusan marriages are particularly enjoyable because for this festive occasion men and women mix freely together in one place. The women are dressed to the limit of their wealth and rouged, painted, and powdered to the limit of their art. I suffered exquisitely that afternoon and evening, wanting Thalia by my side.

When the feast was ended, a procession was formed to carry the couple to their home. Owing to the fact that Apollo had only begun to earn more salary, his father gave his son the second floor of their dwelling to begin their life together. The two families lived but three blocks from each other, which was not nearly enough distance for the revelry the throng intended. What was more, a chariot had been rented, as was the custom, to transport the bride and groom to their home. Amara sat in the middle. As best man, I should have stood to Amara's left while Apollo handled the rig at her right. My comrade, however, was far too drunk, and so I took the honor of driving. Directly behind us came Amara's mother and girlfriends, bearing torches. The remainder of the party followed along, singing and playing on whatever instruments they had brought. Apollo directed me to take many wrong turns, precisely to prolong the ride.

Apollo's mother and father waited at their house, his mother holding a torch high in the night to light the bride over the threshold. They offered sweetmeats to us all, and Apollo's father recited a speech of welcome to the bride. Then the couple climbed the steps together, fleeing from the hooting and crude jokes alluding to their marriage bed.

The following day, as was also the custom, Apollo's father offered a meal for only the men of the wedding party. I took the honored place on Apollo's couch directly behind him. Again, the groom drank too much. Apollo was not an inveterate drunk, but once he began drinking during a celebration he could not stop. This was his one failing. During a lull in the festivities, his lowered inhibitions caused him to question my melancholy attitude the previous day. Finally, I shared with another man the secret of my love. I shared as well the many impediments in the way of not merely a future union, but even in finding a means by which to communicate.

"Worry no more," Apollo said. "My home and Amara will serve as your go-between. Have Thalia's servant visit as frequently as she may dare. Amara will hold the tokens that Thalia sends you and vice versa."

Apollo's generous offer did much to ease my constant fears that I would lose Thalia. Each note that she sent to me renewed my hope, no matter how mundane her messages. Always, she assured me that her love was eternal.

Without Thalia's messages I might have thrown myself off a cliff in a fit of despair, for I had heard quite by chance that my unknowing rival, Cleomenes, was becoming richer by the day. Owing to the needs of rebuilding and improving the many defensive walls, he had to double the number of workmen in his quarries. Moreover, the demand for rope, which his women workers produced, had also radically increased. By the time the city was prepared for invasion, I expected he would find himself as rich as the legendary Croesus.

His good fortune notwithstanding, Cleomenes was younger than thirty-three and therefore was expected to serve his military training and to make himself instantly ready when the trumpets of war were sounded. To his credit, he was not one who evaded duty, but rather, like the vast majority of men, hurried to enroll. His cohort for training was not summoned until the onset of winter. I had been watching the rolls carefully for his name to appear. Although he had never put in a day of military service, he showed at the camp wearing finer gear than the veterans owned. Moreover, behind him walked a male servant who was perhaps thirty-five, carrying a breastplate, greaves, helmet, short sword in sheath, and shield. All but the sword and shield were ornate and fashioned of solid, shining bronze that showed no sign of use.

Cleomenes was certainly not the only one to bring a manservant with him for the training period. He and the others of the wealthier districts had been informed that they would have to pay for their servant's lodging and food, and this did nothing to deter them. The more common citizens watched such blunt parades with dispassion; the practice had been going on since Spartia first fielded an army. The quartermaster corps also had no complaint, as Cleomenes relieved them of supplying his equipment.

Bringing full battle regalia for the initial period of training, however, was an ignorant mistake. Only helmets, shields, and spears were issued for the first month. The common man got his payback watching the rich man next to him struggle up a cliff and jog down a long, dusty roadway wearing twice the weight. As the months wore on, I wondered why the rich young men who had trained earlier did not pass the word along to like friends who trained later. I assume that the answer lies in the old adage "misery loves company."

Even though my father knew his father, Cleomenes had no idea who I was, despite my unusual name. It was spoken in his presence several times without his showing the slightest sign of recognition. I bided my time for several weeks, until I learned that he had been assigned guard duty on the wall close by the harbor. I was determined to speak to him at last, in my capacity as master of the watch.

If an inexperienced sentry on night duty is found asleep at his post the first time, he is put in front of his cohort, humiliated, and then made to serve the same duty for a week. If a man is found asleep at his post a second time, he is marched out to an open field, striped of his weapons, and beaten to death by his comrades. Any man, raw recruit or veteran, who is found to have deserted his post when the master of watch comes around is hunted down and similarly beaten to death. His head is also displayed for a time on a pike as a lesson to all. Such punishment is not excessive. The fate of an entire army or city depends on the alertness of its sentries.

That midnight was filled with clouds, with not even a veiled moon to light it. A part of me hoped to find Cleomenes sleeping. However, he was not only at his post, but he also detected me from a good distance and called out for the password. To test him, I answered with the wrong response. He hesitated for only a moment and then blew on his horn. Within a minute, five other soldiers were at our side on the wall. I identified myself and ordered the other guards to disperse and turn back any others who might respond. I congratulated Cleomenes for his proper execution of his duty and collected his slate with the wax password scribed into it. His chest rose with pride.

I lingered for a time to speak with the man. I would like to say that I heartily disliked him, but he seemed in general a decent fellow. I encouraged him to speak about his civilian life, and he was only too happy to respond. He readily answered all my questions, as I probed my unwitting rival for weaknesses I might exploit in denigrating him in the eyes of Thalia and her parents. Realizing that he would hold nothing back, I inquired if he had a wife.

"I would be engaged tomorrow if I had my way, but the girl's parents believe she is still too young to wed."

"Who is she?" I asked.

"I'm sure you wouldn't know her," he said, foolishly assuming that no professional soldier without high rank came from a successful family.

"And she is beautiful?" I asked.

"Exceedingly. But just as importantly, her father owns city wine shops. Rare and exotic wines are my passion, and I am certain that, over the years, marriage to his daughter will save me a fortune." He laughed at his own wit. "Moreover, she has only one brother. He is younger and seems frail. He may not live to adulthood. In that case, the three wine shops would be divided among the three sisters."

After ten minutes of conversation, I judged that Cleomenes was shrewd in watching out for himself, but he was not especially smart. Predictably, however, his opinion of his intellect and sense of humor were exceedingly high and offered freely. "I" was his favorite pronoun. Never once did he ask about my family, my marital status, or even my career as a soldier. When we both began shivering for lack of moving in the cold night air, I left him and continued my review of the sentries.

Once I had finished with the second watch, there was nothing for me to do until I patrolled the third watch around two o'clock. The more I thought about Cleomenes, the more morose I became. I found myself moving toward that narrow street in Achradina bounded on one side by the hovels of the poor and the other by the sea wall. Only a blind man would not have known what the principle trade of this street was, as every other house had a balcony extending over the street. In the early hours of the night, the courtesans would hang over the railings in various states of undress, coaxing the men inside like Odysseus' sirens.

I was not picky. I turned into the first house of rapture. If I had considered myself unlucky for the past month, the Fates smiled on me that evening, delivering me into the hands of a tender and understanding young woman who was content to substitute for my beloved. Her cries of joy at least seemed real, and she professed again and again that the woman who would eventually have me would be indeed blessed. Her name was Iris, like the goddess of the rainbow. I saw her only one more time, but like the rainbow of the legend, she gave me hope to march on through the months ahead.

Ironically, this lowly prostitute to whom the gods had apparently been so cruel professed to petition them all the time. She encouraged me to visit every temple and shrine I could, to offer prayers and sacrifices to any god who might hear me concerning Thalia.

I must admit that since my early youth, I had doubts that the gods were anything like men and women in immortal form. We wish them to be so out of our own vanity, but in truth the wisdom of men compared with whatever has the power and knowledge to fashion the world and the heavens must be akin to that of ants regarding men. Is it not hubris for any man to profess to know what the gods look like, much less tales of their intimate existences?

I wondered if the Jews with their One God of All or the Zoroastrians with but one god of good and one of evil are more accurate than we with our pantheon of deities. I wondered if the One, the Two, or the Many really cared what we did, desired our rituals and sacrifices to them, or ever listened to our pleas.

Nevertheless, in my desperation to possess Thalia, after coming to know Iris, I prayed often and with fervor. I struggled to believe, because if I lost my faith there would be no one but myself to help win her.

CHAPTER IV

Four months passed since the citizens first levied arrived in the city's main fortress, signaling the start of the fifth cycle and the fifth month of training. We were approaching the cold, dark days of winter, and my spirits were also dark and cold, both from not having seen Thalia and from lack of promotion. The snytagmas and taxiarchs for the fifth cohort had been selected, and I was not even chosen to be a taxiarch. My close friend Apollo reminded me that fully 400 of our original army had seniority over me. I countered that I not only had the benefit of special military training in Greece, but that I was also the champion of the last pentathlon. He saw the logic of my arguments and suggested I take the matter boldly to the strategos.

Archidamus smiled when I sputtered out my frustrations in his field tent.

"If it is a matter of my age," I argued, having prepared my speech by reciting it fifty times in the midst of an orchard, "I would welcome taking 196 striplings to train. The veterans complain the most about those who are only eighteen or nineteen. I would offer no such complaint."

"It is not a matter of your age," Archidamus said. "It is two other matters. The first is a direct command from Hieron. When I nominated you for promotion he ordered that you not be overly burdened while you concentrate on the task he has personally given you."

My head swam with ambivalent feelings. I simultaneously rejoiced that the strategos had been considering me after all and despaired that I would ever bring my stubborn great-uncle around to working on Siracusa's defense and rid myself of the ongoing assignment.

"The second matter I have also spoken to the king about," Archidamus went on. "I am unhappy not using you to your full potential. Probably this would not be realized as a taxiarch even if you were granted your request. Hieron and I agree that you are meant to head a specialized group of warriors. You are aware that the census revealed enough citizens between the ages of eighteen and thirty-two who qualify to form twenty-two syntagmas."

"Not including our original number," I stated, overeagerly.

Archidamus gave me a fatherly nod. "When those cohorts are filled, there are yet ninety-four qualified citizens left over. They shall be trained as rigorously and in the same disciplines as all the others, but my thought is to keep them in reserve. We have no idea when our army may be called to serve. Perhaps never, although this I doubt. However, one truth is certain: In the coming months, among our 5,000 and more, some of this number will die of accidents. Some will die of disease. Others will emigrate or desert the city. Seventy of this surplus will supply these contingencies." He paused.

"And the other twenty-four?" I asked.

"They will also replace men. Special men taken out of existing units. You have helped with the training of all four initial cohorts."

I confirmed that I had.

"Have you noted a few who perform difficult tasks such as climbing and stabbing with a minimum of noise and motion?"

"I can think of perhaps twelve who stand out in my mind."

"And, I am sure, you will be able to select another twelve from among your veteran brethren." Archidamus leaned forward on his camp chair. "You know that this army we are building is not meant to conquer but to defend. Naturally, they will be drilled in field operations. But once they have the rudiments of soldiering, we will concentrate on the defense of the walls and how to regain territory if any of the districts are occupied. At the same time, I must plan how to break a siege, Leonides. Was this covered in your training in Greece?"

"An important element is being providential. That is, laying in a great surplus of food and securing water supplies if sufficiently warned," I recited from my Korinthian training.

The strategos shook his head. "I seek strictly the purely military concerns."

I said, "A good plan is to hold an army outside your walls and to attack the enemy from behind while he is engaged in siege activities. Or else enlist an ally to do this."

"Yes, the best of plans," the general agreed. "But we lack the resources to create two armies. Further, we cannot depend on allies. The Greek colonies on Italia asked King Pyrrhus to help them so many years ago. He won battle after battle, but could not win the war due to the size of the Roman armies. There will be no help from our Greek brothers. Moreover, whether it is Carthage or Roma who attacks us, inviting the other to defend us also invites being occupied from that time on."

"Are you thinking about demoralizing the enemy?" I asked.

"I am. If they see our walls high and thick and thousands of well-armed and able men atop them, that will weaken their resolve. Can you offer a second element?"

I thought for a moment, in light of the hints he had given me. "They will also be demoralized if we can break their blockade from time to time and bring in fresh food and other necessities."

Archidamus reached out and tapped my chest. "Precisely. The Romans are famous for bicircumvallation, but our city is too large for that to succeed. The Athenians tried it under the leadership of Nicias, and look how we crushed them."

I knew what the general meant. When an army laid siege to a city, it was necessary to keep the people from slipping in and out. Consequently, when feasible they built another wall behind their force and laid out

57

guard posts not more than a stadion apart.

"Since we have 100 stadia of outer walls, and an enemy cannot watch all of them at every moment," said Archidamus, "here is what I propose: Before either a Roman or a Carthaginian army approaches, by land, by sea, or both, we devise a plan that sets dates and places for breaking the siege. This will be both by land and sea, but your concern will only be the land. For example, if Hieron's astrologers calculate that two years from now there will be no moon on the seventh night of that year's seventh month, we will plan that night to bring in supplies by the Epipolai gate. This information will be kept by only a few of the most trusted citizens of our city and its confederate towns and villages.

"On such nights, the territory around the particular gate will have to be cleared of enemy patrols and to make sure the enemy does not lie in wait. Diversionary attacks will need to be created elsewhere. Such a troop of men by their very nature need not exceed more than two dozen. These warriors must be remorseless killers. They will need to be strong, swift, and silent. Above all, they must be able to climb up and down ropes as easily as monkeys climb trees."

I had often fretted that the defensive nature of our army severely restricted opportunities to shine in warfare. Pushing ladders off walls with pikes or pouring boiling oil onto a siege machine from a parapet covered no warrior in glory. There was no brilliant strategy to it. The suggestion of the general, however, promised glory, adventure, and the opportunity to extemporize in military fashion.

"I accept this challenge!" I affirmed, standing in my excitement.

The strategos gestured for me to sit again. "Good, good. Since this will be perilous work, you as commander will receive the salary of a syntagmatarch," he said. "Do not begin spending tomorrow; this will come to you only after a siege has begun. For now, there will be a small increase in the amounts of salt, grain, and coin you receive. Naturally, you may not recruit from among the other officers, and you may not draft anyone. Each member must volunteer, as you have."

What I deemed most important was that I had not been forbidden from talking to various men and using vivid images. I had often been told that I am persuasive when speaking from the heart, and I meant to use this to full advantage. My mind buzzed with possible candidates.

"King Hieron is quite enthusiastic about this concept," said Archidamus. "In fact, he has suggested a name. You have heard of the crack battalions of famous past armies—the Immortals, the Sacred Band, the Companions?"

"Of course."

"He suggests that since you and your men will not be seen or heard but only felt, that you be called the Silent Storm."

I was not to understand until weeks later the wisdom of bestowing an imaginative name upon the group for the purpose of recruiting. Such wisdom, I suppose, comes with the age and position both Archimadus and Hieron had attained.

Naturally, the romance of heading this bold venture demanded that I get the news to Thalia immediately. At my first opportunity, I visited the house of Apollo and delivered into Amara's hands a tightly wrapped scroll tied with a bit of red cloth and generously sealed in three places with wax. Thalia had instructed me months earlier to handle messages in this manner, and her missives to me were delivered in the same condition.

With this letter, I also reported Cleomenes' crass words about wanting to marry Thalia for access to good wines and with the hope that her younger brother would die. I felt that at last I was gaining the upper hand over my unwitting rival.

Δ

Rather than rush into my new assignment, I approached it with the same kind of scientific dispassion as that demonstrated by my great-uncle. I did not hurry to surround myself with old friends. In fact, I ended up choosing only seven veterans for the group. I understood that, after all, the military training they had had up to this time had very little to do with the sort of stealth, speed, and surprise in which my band required to excel. For all but the high officers and the cavalry, soldiering was a simple task. It required the knowledge of how to march and form up for battle, how to drive forward into the belly of the enemy ranks with your spear, and when the numbers thinned and your spear was left in an opponent's middle, how to employ your shield and sword until you won or lost. This and the courage not to break rank were the basic demands for the great mass of any army.

The finest armies moved slowly in battle, weighted down by heavy helmets, armor, and shields and with all but those in the front and back rows and the far flanks hemmed in on all sides by dense ranks and files of fellow soldiers. They seemed to me like a collection of giant, disciplined beetles, with soft cores of flesh and organs under formidable shells. Shells, however, are the undoing of many beetles once they are turned on their backs. Similarly, if swift movement is required of heavily armored men, they cannot run fast or far. Moreover, if one is able to get behind the armored soldier, a thrust in the side among the armor straps or across the muscles of the calf or behind the knee will kill or cripple him. For such fighting, armor is only a hindrance.

I developed a litany of mottos. One was: "Surprise is better than armor." Another was: "What cannot be seen cannot be struck." My observations and mottos became the guiding precepts for my group. We wore no greaves over our shins and only stiffened linen breastplates over our chests. Our helmets were made of thick leather rather than bronze, to absorb rather than give off sound. Even our shields were specially made, of smaller size and padded around the rim with leather. We carried not the traditional phalanx thrusting spears that are three or four times as long as a man but light throwing spears with a greater proportion of iron. We wore the traditional short sword in a sheath on our belt, but we also carried a hatchet or a knife. The hatchet we taught ourselves to throw at a target of wood from three times a man's length. We trained with the knives to creep up on sentries and silently slit their throats. Even our uniform and shields were especially fashioned in blacks, browns, and muted grays, the better to blend into the night.

Of the seven veterans I chose, not one was older than twenty-five. From among the new recruits who volunteered neither were any over that age. Only three in all had wives, and none yet had children; I needed each man to be fearless, with little more than glory and rewards to live for.

Every man of the eventual cohort that formed the Silent Storm was exceedingly brave and noble, and I respected and trusted them all. Although I tried never to show it, I must admit that I had my favorites. These were Protesilous, Melampus, Menander, and Xenophanes.

Protesilous was a veteran and was known to complain about the lack of opportunities to slake a bloodthirsty nature. He hunted wild boar with a spear, which was as perilous a sport as any man can find. His talent with a sword was unmatched among his peers.

Melampus had become an orphan at ten and had lived by cunning and wit around the docks, gradually working his way up to respectability. He could make himself as a shadow, even in broad daylight and could get past locked and guarded places with disquieting ease. The Spartians, who underfed their boy trainees and so encouraged them to steal food, would have been particularly proud of Melampus. I never asked him about the particulars of his larcenous talents, and he never volunteered information. For one who could become so silent, he possessed a beautiful singing voice, which we encouraged him to use at night when we were encamped on maneuvers in the fields.

Menander lived for physical activity. His body was sculpted like that of the statues of the war god Ares. He was also a third son, but his father had been a nobleman. Menander's father was killed by a certain cowardly back-stabber named Himerius. Menander publicly gave him three days to live. The murderer surrounded himself with hired guards, but Menander found a way over rooftops into his home, gouged out his eyes, broke his back, and threw him out a window into the street.

Xenophanes was another of our veterans. He possessed no special skills or storied history, but he completed any task handed him in quick order, and he showed more common sense than any other man I had ever met. Thus, he was readily accepted by the group when I eventually chose him as my second in command.

We trained through the winter and into spring, until we had honed our needed skills to razor sharpness. I was in fact so dedicated to this task that I sometimes forgot to feed the fire of my obsession with Thalia. Looking back, I realize how valuable this distraction was in masking my loneliness. The day-to-day association with my fellow soldiers and my periodic visits to the homes of my family did not fulfill the needs I had for that unique class of intimate companionship. Those like Archimedes, who can be content purely in a world of abstractions, are rare. The good among us need to give affection every bit as much as we wish to receive it. I could conceive of no vessel other than Thalia to satisfy this compulsion.

Because of the building up of the Silent Storm, I also visited Archimedes less often than I should have. Out of desperation, I finally broke down and confessed to my great-uncle during one of these visits that Hieron had set me the task of cajoling or tricking him into working on the defenses of the city. Archimedes was not surprised. He told me that for my sake he would have acquiesced, but he candidly could think of little more than making the walls higher and thicker, clearing away the land before the walls, and changing the shape of the gates.

Despite the falseness I had played with him, he continued to walk with me on occasion when the weather wafted pleasant. Once he did pause before a certain stretch of land as we approached one of the city gates. He studied the terrain for some time.

"I am looking at this now as an enemy would," he said. "I am very pleased that the ground is so smooth here. I can run my men right up to the walls or roll siege machines forward with no trouble. Might not a trench some little distance out from the walls not confound me? Better still, a series of three trenches, with the last one fortified and a low wall in front of it for our army? The first two trenches would be attached to rivulets held back by gates that may be knocked out, so that when the enemy draws near they will fill with water or mud. Or if that is not possible in the dry season, they might be filled with sharpened stakes or dead, dry bramble bushes. Are there many archers in your army?"

I told him that there were not.

"Foolish," he said. "I would place the farthest trench at precisely the limit of your archers' range, so that they barely need to aim."

After I had transmitted them, the simple observations of the great mathematician occupied a considerable portion of our populace for many weeks. Hundreds of soldiers and civilians alike dug trenches, collected wood for bows and arrows, studied existing bows in order to learn how to duplicate them, and trained in a completely new skill. Hieron was so pleased by these improvements that he relieved me of my assignment of hounding my great-uncle. The canny old ruler, however, had not abandoned his part of the same task.

In the middle of the spring, a great fleet of grain ships arrived safely from Egypt. The cargo in the holds of these galleys replaced the extra supplies we had been compelled to ferry to the Roman armies. However, the truth was that the delivery more than answered this need. Four buildings near the harbor had been converted to grain warehouses, and these were almost filled with the excess. Plans against siege other than enlarging the army and improving the walls were being implemented.

Hieron was mightily pleased by Egypt's response to his request and to the fair price that the reigning Ptolemy had asked. As partial thanks for the Egyptian ruler's friendship, Hieron caused to be created as a gift the largest galley that had ever been built in Siracusa. The ship was so large that it was designed not with the usual single mast but rather three. It was built in traditional fashion on the edge of the harbor, upon wooden ways and with the stern toward the land. When the time came to push the vessel off its ways and into the water, however, it was found to be too massive to move.

Immediately, Hieron summoned Archimedes to his palace. The king had listened throughout the winter and early spring to his cousin's numerous perorations on the extreme efficiency of compound blocks and tackles. To bait Archimedes, the king pretended not to believe him and in fact openly mocked him before his court as a genius gone mad from his own notoriety. Rising to the bait, Archimedes had thrown down upon the marble floor the staff he had begun using to support himself.

"Mad am I? I say—would that there was another earth above our own or a way to ascend to the moon. For if I but had a place to stand upon, I could move the world!"

"The world?" Hieron repeated in a mocking tone. "I have a single galley that cannot be moved right now in the harbor. I will buy you a new pair of sandals if you can launch it."

"Give me two days," Archimedes shot back. "Two days to prepare, and I will move your ship."

To Move the World

In fact, the preparations took three days. They also employed no fewer than sixty shipyard workers. Four enormous pilings were sunk into the muck, two at the distance of a man out from the vessel's bow and two more near the ship's midsection. Then seemingly every block and pulley in the harbor was gathered, along with stadia lengths of nautical rope.

Another myriad of workers had been charged with building two reviewing stands on either side of the dock. The first held the royal family and its sycophants. The wife of Hieron's son Gelon, who was named Neiris, sat beside her daughter Harmonia and her son Hieronymos. Neiris was the daughter of the notorious King Pyrrhus of Epirus, he who won battle after battle against the Romans but at such great cost to his army that he eventually lost the war. Hieron's daughters Heraclia and Damarata sat with their husbands Zoippos and Adranodoros. These four were known to be extremely ambitious and were not liked nearly as much as the king or his son.

The second reviewing stand held members of those families who had recently contributed the largest funds for the strengthening of the army and the laying in of stores. Among them sat Eustace and, beside him, my Thalia. She nodded her head slightly when my eyes found her among the others. I was sure the fact that I stood next to Archimedes was not lost to her. I saw her once lean toward her father, speak a few words into his ear, and point in my direction.

When the time came for the demonstration, two sets of ropes were tied to the dock pilings. The use of ropes to warp ships from docks and ways is an ancient practice. The complex system of blocks and pulleys Archimedes had devised constituted the difference. As impressive as the riggings were, however, I could not imagine such a monstrous ship being moved by fewer than a hundred rope pullers.

The dock itself began to groan and shift with the weight of the shipyard workers. The king was compelled to order half of them back a distance.

"If you insist that I do this alone," Archimedes said in his loudest voice to the king, "I will do so. However, it will take a good deal of time, for I will need to walk back and forth, constantly tying off ropes and then untying them. Would you grant me, oh King, that since you and I are both of advanced age and have long since seen the flower of our youth wilt, that we together might equal one average shipwright?"

"A king should never admit failings, particularly of age," Hieron called out, playing to the crowd. "But if I handle one of these ropes, I promise to use only half my strength."

At this the witnesses burst into laughter, followed by applause. Gelon assisted his father by holding onto the rope and ensuring that it did not slip back. No one with eyes would have claimed that this provided much additional assistance. Gelon had passed into his sixth decade a few years before, and rumors circulated that his health was in decline. Anyone who had observed him in the months prior to this demonstration believed the rumors.

Archimedes spoke several sentences of instruction to the king, in a voice too low to be overheard even from where I stood. Each man then took hold of his rope and began to pull.

The amount of cordage that passed through the maze of pulleys was quite staggering. Many coils lay upon the dock before the groans of wood moving against wood was heard. Nevertheless, slowly but inexorably, the vessel could be detected crawling forward. When the proof that Archimedes had won the wager was undeniable, Hieron nodded to one of the dock foremen, and a hundred men rushed to the galley to complete the launch. As the ship's bow cut into the harbor's water, a roar went up from the crowd.

The king embraced his cousin. "Is there nothing you cannot accomplish?" he asked.

"Nothing, as long as it involves winning new sandals," Archimedes replied.

Hieron leaned in to Archimedes' ear and whispered a few words. Once my great-uncle had received the full complement of congratulations and the throng was dispersing, he moved to me and said, "We have both been summoned to another private audience with our king. Why do I feel that my actions here today have cost me more than I have won?"

Δ

To Move the World

"I apologize to you, Cousin," Hieron began, once Archimedes and I were sealed with him inside his audience chamber. "It had only occurred to me to get you to think about the construction of the city walls and harbors. To me, engines and machines are instruments used to gain entry to a city and not to defend it. A week ago, the notion came to me that such contrivances could also be designed for defensive purposes. The only reason such things have not been devised is for lack of a genius to put his mind to the issue. Any man who can move a huge galley single-handedly can certainly make Siracusa impregnable."

"Once again, Cousin," Archimedes replied, lightly mocking the king by using the same familiarity, "I must say that I can be of minor use, since I know virtually nothing of the art of siege or of the engines now in use, either by the Romans or the Carthaginians."

"Do you love the city of your birth?" Hieron asked.

"Certainly I do," avowed Archimedes.

"You have no qualms about serving it?"

"I always have, in every regard."

"And your hesitancy has nothing to do with pride or obstinacy?"

Archimedes sighed. "Have you not baited me enough this week?"

"Then the only consideration that remains is how much you are willing to sacrifice to help insure that it will not be destroyed."

"Speak more!" Archimedes invited.

Hieron pointed to the mathematician. "For your age, you seem hail enough. I understand that you are able to walk ten or twelve stadia with Leonides on an afternoon."

"I can do that and more when I use a staff."

"Good. I remember fondly how I felt at seventy. I thought then that I was exceedingly frail and the husk of my former self. But I have continued another nineteen years. The aches and pains I had then seem nothing now. I now know they did me no long-term harm." Hieron glanced toward me. "I am proposing that you travel for two or three months in Italia with your great-nephew. You will travel incognito, as his servant."

Before Archimedes could object, Hieron held up his hand. "Let me tell you how serious our troubles have become. The Romans have sent spies throughout our city. They claim to be administrators, bargaining the price of various provisions. But the same so-called administrators have visited virtually every drinking establishment in the city and have been buying drinks for all men at a rate no low-level functionaries could afford. Questions they ask of our more intemperate citizens focus on our defense. They say they have observed the improvements of our walls, note the increase of men in military uniform, and question why we are laying in such large stores of grain."

"Is this something for the Silent Storm to handle?" I asked.

Hieron shook his head. "They are not to be harmed within our city walls. If the Romans question our attitude toward them now, so much more will they mistrust us if their agents disappear. No, it is much better to bring answers directly to the Roman consuls and to feign complete allegiance to their cause against Carthage.

"Leonides, when the spring harvest is ready two months hence, you will accompany the tribute fleet. You will volunteer information that your king greatly fears the new Carthaginian fleet. You will truthfully say that I have been threatened by their ministers. This truth will help the Romans swallow the lie that we have heard rumors of new legions being formed by the Carthaginians precisely to capture southern Sicilia. You will say that we have bestirred our entire city, so not to be caught undefended when the Carthaginians suddenly appear at our doorstep. As our resident expert in defense, your king has sent you to its ally against Carthage to view any Roman attempts at city sieges and to interview their engineers for instruction on defending ourselves. Thus, we will learn our stronger enemy's greatest tricks from that enemy himself."

"I hope spies were not among those who viewed my demonstration yesterday," Archimedes worried. "Otherwise I will be recognized. This ruse will be exposed, and Leonides and I will both be put to death."

"Only highly trusted citizens and their families watched you yesterday," Hieron assured. "You hold an enviable position, Cousin," he said. "Your name is famous throughout the Mediterranean, but your face is not."

"I keep waiting for a coin to be minted with my likeness," Archimedes quipped, "but it never happens."

"I am glad of it," returned Hieron. "You have said that you dislike the Romans."

"That is true. When one says that they are a bellicose people, one has said practically all that distinguishes them." Archimedes turned to me. "I am old enough to remember forty years ago clearly, the year after our city capitulated to them and began sending tribute."

Hieron nodded, as if he knew the story Archimedes was about to tell.

"Both the Roman consuls returned with their legions later that year and advanced on Agrigento," my uncle began. Agrigento was south of us, at the southern tip of Sicilia.

"The Carthaginians had overrun the town. The Romans laid siege. Carthage attempted to raise the siege from the outside, but suffered losses and ill fate. The city fell. This was almost a purely Greek town, Leonides," my great-uncle said. "I had dear friends in Agrigento. They did not invite the Carthaginians in. Nonetheless, it was sacked by the Romans, and its people were sold into slavery in Italia. This is their way. They export war like others export grain or cloth. I fear that their race wishes to emulate Alexander and to control the entire world."

"Then protect us from them," Hieron urged.

"I must admit, it would put my new sandals to good use." Archimedes turned to me. "What say you, Strategos? Can you and I do this thing together?"

"Most assuredly, oh Puller of Ropes," I countered.

Hieron's laughter sealed the agreement.

CHAPTER V

As one who truly fears the sea, I was not happy when I learned that the fleet carrying myself, Archimedes, and our city's semi-annual tribute was bound for Trinitapoli. Neither I nor Archimedes had ever heard of this forsaken place. The town was all the way around the bottom of the peninsula of Italia, well into the Adriatic Sea. I had thought that the fleet would make its usual trek up to Neapoli or Ostia and unload there. It seemed that the main force of the Roman army, however, was encamped near their eastern coast, close by the forces of Hannibal. Due to Hannibal's raiding and foraging, the Republic's army was in dire need of provision.

Since Siracusa did not export war, we possessed a limited number of warships. Our fleet for this journey was protected by only six triremes and four biremes. We stayed close to shorelines so that we could beach as soon as we sighted what looked like hostile galleys. We were slowed by a patch of bad weather and slowed further by dropping off trading goods with our sister towns and cities of Locai, Patelia, and Tarentum. Despite former efforts, Roma had not at this time subjugated the Greek colonies on the lower end of the Italian peninsula. It was necessary to keep the crew and the slaves well away from the inhabitants of these places, because if they learned our final destination our cargo would have been confiscated or burned. It was a thin beam indeed upon which Hieron attempted to balance.

As we approached the beaches south of Trinitapoli and ran up our flags, we became aware of a detachment of cavalry that appeared and disappeared on the cliffs for perhaps fifty stadia. These were Romans who were sent out to watch for us and who set signal fires where we were to land. A portion of a legion waited to guide and guard us to the Roman encampments. I had expected even a larger force, but I was assured that Hannibal's soldiers were not near.

The tribune sent to escort us was Sixtus Severinus Callusius. In the Roman manner, he had three names to my one, signifying that his family was Callusius and that he was the sixth one to possess the name Severinus. He was a large man, even a bit larger than I. I judged him to be about forty years of age. His nose had been badly broken in the past, and I learned later that in his youth he had engaged in the brutal type of boxing that uses metal weights wrapped in cloth over the knuckles. He presented the image of being a soldier's soldier. Severinus took his duty very seriously and showed no indication of having a sense of humor. In fact, when we first met him he was wearing a scowl.

"I was told that you would bring a force of 400 auxiliaries," he said in excellent Greek. I had picked up some Latin in Siracusa, and I had been practicing it diligently since learning of my mission, but my proficiency still left much to be desired. I was glad that the prolonged greatness of the Greek states and Alexander's conquering army had made Greek the common language of the world.

"Your emissaries petitioned for that number," I replied, handing him the scroll with Hieron's signet seal and bearing my credentials. "However, we regretfully must decline. We face a different Carthaginian threat on our front and can spare no men. Until a few months ago, we had fewer than 2,000 soldiers to defend our city." I would not tell him the real number, even though I knew that spies had undoubtedly brought his Senate very accurate figures.

My news caused the tribune's eyebrows to elevate.

"What is more," I reminded him, "we are not a subject of your republic."

"You are allied by treaty with Roma," Severinus said, forcefully.

I did not want to antagonize him any further, so I held my tongue. Archimedes came up beside me. I knew this would be the old genius's first test, and I was extremely anxious to have him assure me that he would pass it.

"This is Alonzo," I lied, in way of introduction. "He is my manservant."

Archimedes smiled blandly, bowed, and said nothing. I had made him promise over and over that he would speak only with me and that he would put forth every effort to seem slow instead of brilliant.

Severinus barely acknowledged my companion, which pleased me. He concentrated on our beached ships, counting them. In this he seemed satisfied. For my part, I noted that his detail included about 600 infantry soldiers and almost 100 cavalry. I also noted that they had arrived with an optimistically large number of wagons and pack donkeys.

"Your provisions are sorely needed," Severinus shared. "Our army burned as much of the crops as possible around Hannibal all last summer and fall. Of course, this affected us as well. He escaped from our forces in the Falernian lowlands, crossed the mountains to the east, and attacked the town of Gerunium. The town had great stores of corn. His barbarians killed all its inhabitants and filled their houses with his booty and provisions. He most recently besieged a little village called Cannae which held an army supply granary. Killed everyone there also. The monster."

Δ

As a soldier of Siracusa, I was fascinated by the doings of both the Carthaginian and the Roman armies. I and my comrades importuned every stranger passing through Siracusa for news of their movements and tactics. I will not set down here all that I heard of Hannibal's stunning surprise appearance through the Alps into the top end of Italia, how he rallied foes of Roma to his side, eluded some armies and annihilated oth-

71

ers, bringing the fight to his enemy's homeland. His strategy was based on a belief that most of the tribes of the peninsula hated existence under the Roman yoke and would come to his aid when he showed them that he and his force could indeed beat their oppressors.

During the twelve months prior to my arrival with our tribute convoy, Hannibal had moved boldly and inexorably toward the southern third of the Italian peninsula. This was the region least controlled by the Romans and whence the Carthaginians could best hope to wrest away provisions and support troops. Near a place called Trasimeni, he struck at one Roman legion while it waited to unite with another, moving his army into position at night under a nearly full moon. By hiding units of his pikemen and cavalry in hillside defiles, he was able to assault the Romans through a fog from two sides at once. A vast lake lay on the third side, and into this water thousands of Roman soldiers retreated, to drown or to be slaughtered at leisure. According to Hieron, the Romans had won so many battles against less formidable foes in the preceding decades that they never learned to properly send out scouts. They paid dearly this day, losing their consul Flaminius and suffering the slaughter of half of a 30,000 man army. The other half, allies, were released by Hannibal without ransom. He proclaimed that his war was only with the Romans, cannily hoping his clemency would encourage more confederate towns and regions to defect.

We were informed in Siracusa from several sources that the unaccustomed disaster near Trasimeni shook Roma to its foundations. The Romans had not suffered such a defeat since the days of Regulus. While they were trying to absorb this injury, insult was added. Each year, Roman citizens elected two consuls to rule and particularly to lead the armies. Flaminius' partner was Germinus, who commanded the other army. He had sent 4,000 cavalry ahead of his infantry to bolster Flaminius' force. Unlike the Roman, Hannibal had his scouts dispersed across the country. They let him know of this detachment. Again through ambush, he was able to kill most of this contingent as well.

While the Romans quaked at the double disasters, Hannibal moved south past their city. As I have already stated, his clear strategy was to recruit massive forces from the southern part of the peninsula. Some towns and cities had only recently been forcibly annexed to the confederacy; others anticipated such a fate. Once the general had gathered a clear advantage of numbers, most assumed he would return to lay siege and then destroy Roma.

Incredibly, after suffering such great losses Roma was able to raise from its own citizens and from allies a 14th, 15th, 16th, and 17th legion. When I heard this news, my mind grew dizzy. Our city could perhaps raise 10,000 combatants in time of great need; this people, after having already fielded thirteen legions, could recruit, train, and outfit another 20,000 infantry and 3,000 cavalry! When I heard this, I became convinced that Hannibal, as brilliant a general as he is, has little chance of ultimate victory.

We heard that Hannibal had ravaged the eastern coast of Italia, moving south with the summer, then cutting directly west and striping the Falernian Plain and its cities of everything of value. Just when the Romans thought they had boxed him in, he sent a huge herd of captured oxen at one entrenched enemy force during the predawn hours. Tied to their horns were bundled of sticks which were set on fire. When the sentries spied what they supposed were torches, they sounded the alarm. The army roused itself and rushed forward to fight, only to meet a stampede of crazed oxen. While they dealt with the confusion, Hannibal rushed his army past them. He crossed the Apennine Mountains just as winter set in, attacking Gerunium for its large stores of corn, and erecting a camp fortified with trench and palisade.

In reaction to the impetuous pursuits of Hannibal by Flaminius and Geminus, Roma decided to place total power for six months in the hands of a cautious nobleman named Quintus Fabius Maximus. The man had served well during the first war with Carthage and had been credited with a victory over a Gallic people named the Ligurians. Fabius chose as his master of cavalry Marcus Minucius Rufus, who had formerly served as a consul. As we sailed from Siracusa, we learned that Fabius and Minucius were each leading new legions south toward Hannibal's forces.

Δ

Thinking back on Archimedes' description of the Romans slaughtering the entire Greek town of Agrigento, I was annoyed at the tribune Severinus calling Hannibal a monster. Instead of rebuking him, I said, "I assume you have been told that Alonzo and I will accompany our tribute to your camp."

"I have not," Severinus replied.

I pointed to the scroll. "The command from my king is contained there. It is essential that we learn your needs in terms of trained soldiers, in both numbers and tactical skills. We also must learn your ways of siege and defense against siege if we are to hold another fresh Carthaginian army at bay to help you."

These words struck home with the tribune. He nodded his understanding and indicated which wagon we should visit in order to receive wine and food.

With so much help, the ships were unloaded in less than two hours. As we left the beach, our ships were already moving out into the sea. Even though I am fearful of deep water, I looked back at them with longing. I turned and peered into the rolling countryside with misgiving.

"Are you absolutely certain that Hannibal's forces are not foraging in this area?" I asked.

"Rest assured," returned the tribune. "The combined weight of eight legions lies between us and Hannibal."

"Fabius' time as dictator has lapsed," I noted. "Was his position renewed?"

"No," Severinus supplied. "We have two new consuls: Gaius Terentius Varro and Lucius Aemilius Paulus."

"Are they in the field?"

"They are. Roma functions with Marcus Claudius Marcellus and Lucius Posthumius Albinus as its praetors. We have recovered well from our recent defeats."

I was unwilling to believe his words were objective, and I determined to form my own opinion when I saw the newly assembled army. With so many foreign names being hurled at me, I barely noted that of Marcus Claudius Marcellus. If anyone had told me at the time the major role this man would play in defining my future, I would not have believed him.

CHAPTER VI

annae was not nearly so far from the coast as Severinus had led me to believe. I had prepared myself to camp overnight in the open, and I wished to see how temporary defenses were erected by a Roman force, but this did not happen. Instead, sheep, goats, wagons, pack donkeys, and men all moved together at a constant speed, heading almost directly south through the afternoon and into the early evening.

I was provided a horse and rode beside Severinus, who relaxed his guard against me somewhat as we rode and gradually expanded upon his replies to my many questions. As I have reported, he willingly divulged that a full eight Roman legions were now encamped in the valley of the Aufidus River. Moreover, these were not the pared down legions of 4,500, but rather ones numbering around 5,000 men. To this mass were added 1,600 Roman cavalry, formed of the most elite citizens of Roma itself. Their allies contributed a little more than 13,000 infantry and 4,800 horsemen. The highest intelligence estimate of the enemy's number was

40,000 Carthaginians and allies, with some 8,000 horsemen.

"Their general is bold and clever," Severinus admitted, "but there is no finer soldier in the world than the Roman soldier. We have hounded him for the better part of a year, refusing to give battle on his terms. At last he is out in the open, with no mountain crevasses to hide his forces. If he confronts us man to man, we will crush his army. If he attempts to retreat, we will chew at his rear until we devour him piece by piece. He must do something soon. We are halfway through the summer, and he has not moved in months. Those cities to the south whom he petitioned for aid are holding back and waiting for this one great battle, to see whose boots to lick."

As we rode, Severinus bragged about the Roman innovation in line warfare. The phalanx of Alexander's day, he declared, was obsolete. Just as was done in the great Macedonian general's day, the Romans set out harassing troops in front of the main body of men. These are called velites and are the lowest level of allies. Too poor to afford armor, they compensate with speed. They approach the assembling enemy force and pelt it with light javelins and stones hurled from slings. This they keep up until their weapons are exhausted or until they are pursued. They then fall back quickly.

Falling back, however, is not the problem it had been for the equivalent of velites used in front of phalanxes. Those fighters needed to retreat to the sides as well as backward, to clear the solid and deep line of the main force. A massed phalanx might stretch out like a mythical snake for four stadia. Not so with the Romans. Their lines are more fluid. The word Archimedes used was permeable. Severinus gave me the name the Romans themselves used for the strategy, which was the "quincunx" formation. He explained that this could most clearly be imagined as the sort of board used for various games, on which dark and light squares alternate. The dark squares represent the array of the Roman army moments before battle is initiated.

The front maniples of the mass are collectively called the hastati. It is made up of the youngest and most impetuous warriors, with each legion having 1,200 to 1,500. Behind these come a formation of like size and make-up called the principes. These are the men in the prime of life, with more experience. A third formation, called the trairii, advances behind the principes. It is composed of only half as many men, but these survivors of years of Roman empire-building are the least likely to falter.

The maniple units of each line were compounded into squares sixteen men wide by sixteen men deep. However long this total mass stretched, it marched with open field between the units, precisely the same sizes as the human squares occupied. Once the front formation came within range of the enemy, the back eight rows swung around to the left on command and closed in with the front, forming one solid mass.

According to Severinus, the most effective innovation of the legions is the carrying of two spears. These are not the sort of mammoth thrusting lances used by our Greek phalanxes, but rather, hurling spears. A heavy spear is fastened behind the legionnaire's long shield. In his right hand, he carries a lighter spear, which can be hurled a greater distance. These light spears have heads made of softer iron which stick in the enemies' shields and cannot be easily dislodged. This compels the antagonists to abandon their shields. Moments later, the hastati warriors unhook their heavy spears and hurl them as well. The ranks behind them rest on their right knees, with their shields and spears tilted upward to ward off missiles.

Those in the enemy advance lines not killed outright face the onrush and crush of the long Roman shields, followed by the blades of their cut-and-thrust short sword, adopted from an Hispanic design and called the gladius. If the enemy holds against the hastati and exhausts them, horns are blown. In good order, the remaining front-line Roman soldiers retreat, creating holes for the advance of the principes. These men come through sixteen wide and deep and expand to the right, allowing the hastati to retreat and rest. Only if both these front lines are deemed in danger of collapse are the triarii sent in as a shock force. The rotation of exhausted and fresh forces make sense to me. Anyone who has tried to hold up a shield for half an hour while delivering blow after blow with a sword knows precisely what I mean.

The least dependable of the allies are held back as accensi, or reserves. More allied infantry are used on either flank, as well as the cavalry, to ensure that the main force is not enveloped. However, in the mind of Severinus, the center of the field always determined the outcome of battle.

As Severinus was so confident in this attitude, I therefore assumed two things: This strategy had worked over and over in past decades, and that from the top ranks down, all Roman soldiers were expected to accept this as incontrovertible. And yet Hannibal had won again and again and never lost. I was overtaken at that moment by the thought that Severinus perfectly represented the Roman mind. I could not fathom why he had not questioned the system's miserable failure at Trasmeni. So firm was his belief in the Roman method that when I worried aloud about this and about Hannibal's superiority in horsemen, he laughed.

"We can be tricked only so many times. That was indeed clever, but he made use of mountains and a lake. You will see no such concealing terrain here," he proclaimed with confidence. "And as for his horsemen, no cavalry on the earth can penetrate the Roman ranks on an open plain!"

When I had agreed to Hieron's plan of traveling to Italia to learn about their manner of conducting war, I had no idea Archimedes and I would be immediately exposed to action, much less the greatest battle yet waged on that peninsula. Even as we traveled down the valley with its low-lying hills on either side and spotted the first Roman encampment, my mind labored to construct what I might say to convince one of their consuls to send me and my great-uncle out of harm's way in quick order.

"This is our minor camp," Severinus informed. "We had both camps on this side of the river, but Hannibal moved his camp in response. Our larger camp lies beyond. There!"

I already gazed in awe at the size of the closer encampment, until the tribune pointed. Then I focused on what I had assumed was the city of Cannae. It stretched more than five stadia across the valley. I should have expected as much, as the size of the combined Roman legions and their allies exceeded the population of my city.

"You'll be able to see the position of Hannibal's camp within the hour," Severinus reported. "Once the sunlight fails, there will be a hundred fires and another hundred torches showing over there."

"Beyond the crest of the hill?" I asked, anxiously.

"No. Ahead of it. A fast runner could cover the space between our ramparts and theirs in about six minutes."

Archimedes regarded the horizon with a baleful expression.

"We continue to the farther camp," Severinus said with a grim smile, as if he wished to increase our anxiety.

I have no fear of battle other than that I might die in disgrace. In fact, after all my training, a part of me was anxious to engage a foe in mortal combat and prove that my skills went beyond winning olive branch wreaths. This war, however, was supposed to affect me and what I held dear only indirectly. Moreover, I was extremely concerned that Archimedes, the pride and perhaps the ultimate protector of our city, was being exposed to such danger. Nevertheless, there was nothing to be done but to prevail upon one consul or the other to have us escorted to Roma as soon as possible.

In the dying daylight I studied the construction of the Roman fortresses that had been thrown up in the middle of the open valley. Severinus noted my interest.

"The proper method of encamping is to send ahead one tribune and a survey team, to mark out the camp," he supplied. "This, of course, depends on the size of the army. If possible, elevated ground is chosen. If the ground is determined to be too sloped, lower ground is chosen. The surveyors carry a number of spears with flags tied to the tops. One man uses a tool called a groma for sighting, and the others drive the spears into the ground at his direction.

"A white flag is placed where the consul's tent will be," the tribune continued. "The open space around it is called the praetorium. This is traditional, from when the leaders were called praetors and not consuls. A red flag is placed on the side best suited for foraging and securing water. This is the side for the legions. All is done in strict order. It never varies except for its scale. You will see the result soon enough."

"And how do you protect yourselves while you build the fort?" I asked.

"The baggage trains are placed behind the line that will become the rampart. The velites, the cavalry, and half the infantry stand in formation between the builders and the enemy. Then, the rest of the army digs the ditch as quickly as possible and heaps up the rampart just behind it. If there are two legions, the front and rear of the camp are created at the same time. The allies construct the sides. As each length of ditch and rampart are completed, the various maniples are marched inside. The velites enter next, the cavalry last."

As we drew near to the entrance facing away from Hannibal's army, I noted the confusion of sharpened stakes that lined the outer rampart walls. They were formed of small tree trunks that branched in many directions and had been planted so that they overlapped and would cause maximum damage to an enemy force that had to disentangle them quickly to get past.

"Each soldier carries two stakes with his gear, so that we do not have to waste time making them afresh," Severinus explained. "Every possible element has been considered so that the entire camp can be created in a matter of hours."

"We enter by the porta decumana," Severinus said, as we went around a high pile of earth in order to get into the camp. The design was much like that which Archimedes had drawn for me outside the Tyche gate in Siracusa. I traded knowing glances with him as we passed it.

The tribune said, "Since the design never varies, every soldier knows precisely where he belongs."

Moments later, I understood just what he meant. Beyond the ten soldiers who guarded the portal a distance of open earth stretched to either side. Farther back stood rows of tents, lines of wagons, and make-shift pens for the animals, all in perfect regimentation. Our caravan moved down a path that ran straight as a spear. It was, I would later learn, called the Via Praetoria. On either side were bivouacked the cavalry units. Behind them were the triarii, then the principes, then the hastati, and finally the allies. One third of the way into the square camp, we came to a road at right angles, called the Via Quintana. Another third of the way, a road at right angles led to the right and left portals. This was the Via Principalis. Beyond this lay the tents of the consuls, the prefects, and the tribunes. Here also stood the storage areas of the camp and the assembly forum. Around this were arrayed the support units and other auxiliaries.

Archimedes brought his donkey up close to mine and leaned over.

80

"You see manifested in this the order of the Roman mind. There is nothing here that is highly innovative, but they are very practical and very disciplined. Such a mind is greatly to be feared."

I nodded. Anything that so impressed such a genius warranted my full attention. Around us stood a complete city which had been erected in a matter of hours. Looking on its orderliness and sheer size, it was not very difficult to understand how Severinus exuded confidence. And yet Hannibal's string of victories tortured my thoughts. I therefore pressed our tribune for an immediate audience with one of the consuls, to formalize our contribution to their effort, to present Hieron's scroll, and to petition for immediate conduct to Roma.

Although Severinus held the status of tribune, he commanded no centurions or troops but was instead a liaison with all the groups supporting the camp who were not soldiers. Even if he served on the line, he did not merit the ear of either consul. I needed first to get to a prefect and plead my case. The prefect would approach a consul on my behalf. After more than an hour, I was led into the tent of a self-important man named Petillius, who did not speak Greek, and who barely allowed Severinus to begin translating my words before he had an answer.

"The primary reason for your presence here," he told me via the tribune, "was to deliver your tribute. This other request of your king must wait. Do you not understand that we must focus all our attention on the battle at hand? Do you not understand that we have no men to spare to conduct you to Roma?"

Before I could formulate a response, he added, "I do not intend to belittle your need or your offer of Siracusa acting as a bulwark against another Carthaginian force. Nevertheless, nothing can be done now. The enemy's army lies between us and Roma. Further, his cavalry ranges far and wide on forage. Even if a troop of our cavalry conducted you straight west, you might be detected and killed." He offered an insincere smile and set Hieron's petition to the side of his camp table. "No, the safest thing for you to do is to stay here with us until we crush them. There is no safer place in the whole of Italia." Then he looked down at a map on his camp table, waiting for me to disappear.

Severinus seemed somewhat embarrassed by my treatment. He

clapped me on the shoulder and shook it. "Petillius is correct about your safety," he assured. "We have an overwhelming superiority of numbers. Hannibal was insane to begin this war on our ground. What he does not understand is that our last census revealed 770,000 men of age to bear arms within the sphere of our protection. We have only one-seventh of our citizens and allies serving."

At these words, I conjured up the image of an ocean leviathan swallowing every fish in its path. I could not see how they would not some day be camped outside Siracusa's gates.

Δ

When I located Archimedes, he was ambling back from the western rampart.

"By patience and diligence," he said, "I found several men who speak Greek. They express confidence in the outcome of this battle, but I can tell that beneath their swagger they are frightened of an army that has ranged up and down what they consider their peninsula for so long."

"Should we find our own way to Roma?" I asked him.

"We no longer even have our scroll from Hieron," he answered. "I think we are trapped here for the time being. We must pray that our Roman enemy triumphs over our Carthaginian one, at least in this battle." He raised his forefinger. "But coming here has not been entirely futile. I have determined that there is nothing to learn about siege with this army. Hannibal was unable to transport his machines over the Alps, so that he has not been able to lay siege to any city. Instead, he attacks towns and villages, habitations with low walls and poor defense works that are easily overrun. Since he never gets into a major city, the Romans have not needed to employ their siege instruments to dislodge him. Hannibal would not allow himself to be so bottled up at any rate."

"How then are we to learn about siege?" I asked.

"Do you think the old veterans in this army have not had such experience? As long as we have been allowed into their camp, they see no reason why they should question my interest. And those on the ramparts are allied velites, lacking the suspicion of their Roman masters. I have received a veritable treatise on the battering ram from one veteran. And I have learned another thing: One reason they can raise such large armies is because their government allows them to levy between the ages of eighteen and forty-six. That is twice as many years as our enrollment. They can be required to serve as many as sixteen total years in that time. The only reason this is possible is because this race operates an enormous slave system. The slaves, naturally, are obtained from their many conquests. Conquest yields slaves; to conquer ever more lands requires many years of fighting for their citizens; fighting requires slaves to do their work at home. The cycle cannot be broken without a collapse of their way of life. I intend to learn how they keep such a large servant population in line, how they discourage revolt. Even putting aside the deplorable ethics of slavery, it seems to me a dangerous system."

I thought about Irene and Crito, the slaves who had been given to Archimedes by Hieron. I am sure, however, that Archimedes never thought of them as such. I know he never treated them as anything but equals who provided for his comforts in exchange for a home and the necessities of life. I, too, felt an intense interest in seeing how the Roman slave was treated and kept in his place.

I led Archimedes to the tent that we had been assigned, where we shared space with several independent blacksmiths. I reminded him not to show his intelligence with such musings. He thanked me and affected a convincingly blank expression. I must say that when he put his mind to it, he could act quite effectively as if he had no mind at all.

Δ

I awoke before first light, having suffered a dream-troubled sleep. I took myself outside and walked through the morning mist. As the first rays of dawn swept into the valley, I saw that I was not the only restless one. Soldiers sat outside their tents with spears in hand, carefully honing their points with files. Others polished the bronze of their helmets. Most had black feathers or horsehair knots rising out of the helmet crests. I thought of how cats bristle their fur when attacked, to look larger and more fierce, and I was sure that this and not beauty was the primary reason for such tall decorations. Teams were at work baking and preparing the first meal.

The tribunes reported to the tent of the consul who would command the army that day. On this day, it was the turn of Gaius Tarentius Varro. Sacrifices were offered to the gods and omens read by augurs hired by the army. A particularly bad omen, I was informed, might confine the army to the camp for a week.

The days were still long some six weeks after the summer solstice. Light streamed across the camp as the trumpets sounded reveille. The city came to life, like an ant nest disturbed. I marveled at the ordered chaos from my place on the top of a rampart. Men fell into ranks and files and were counted. Groups marched to and from meals. Animals were fed. The main avenues were swept and sprinkled with water to minimize dust.

As I ate, I became aware of a faint rumbling to the northwest, like distant thunder. Others, too, looked up. The first meal was forgotten or hurried as men streamed to the ramparts.

The army of Hannibal was on the move. Its main force had exited their north gate and was parading to the place where the plain widened, on the north side of the river. Regiment after regiment marched out, led by an unruly pack of skirmishers. On either flank came troop after troop of horsemen.

I assumed that Hannibal walked or rode at the head of his enormous army, but I could not spy him. I was mightily impressed by the army's size and orderliness. However when it wheeled as one entity to face the encampment in which I stood, I felt a shiver go through me. The discipline of changing direction and forming more than 40,000 men smoothly on the oblique was almost unthinkable, and yet it was being done before my eyes. Each time horns and trumpets sounded in unison, a definite action could be observed. In between the signals, only the tromping of thousands of sandals and hooves could be heard.

Then the terrifying creature that was Hannibal's army halted.

A deep roar went up from more than 40,000 throats, rolling across the plain in great waves of sound. This was soon augmented by a cacophony of spears beating against shields. The Carthaginians taunted the

Romans, daring them to emerge from the protection of their walls.

A veteran ally soldier who hailed from a Greek city, and who had befriended me, turned and consulted the area around the consul's tent.

"No scarlet cloak on a spear," he said to me. "Hardly a surprise that we decline. Where Hannibal stands now, he could escape north with little trouble. We also know he has more cavalry than we do. On the north side of the river, he has too much room for them to maneuver. The consul will wait until he offers on the south side."

The thunderous baiting continued for over an hour. When the sun had climbed well into the sky the great army quit the field, showing the same discipline with which it had appeared. My loquacious acquaintance took me by the shoulder and guided me down the back of the rampart.

"The show is over for today. Hannibal won't let his men stand in armor all morning, exhausting themselves in the sun. He needs them fresh for the real battle tomorrow."

I thought hard that day about the discipline of Hannibal's army. I had been assured that it paled in comparison to that of the Romans, but I could hardly imagine it being improved upon. I was not at all as sure as those around me that victory was guaranteed.

The idle day and the evening that followed allowed Archimedes to interview half a dozen more veterans about the nature of Roman siege and siege machines. He learned of the usual prefabricated boat bridges that went with the army, the battering rams, the catapults. He received detailed descriptions of the mantlets, the hides, and the wooden beams generally carried to erect wooden towers. But none of this equipment had been brought with the army that Roma had sent rushing south, riding on a great tide of intense anger and lust for revenge.

When Archimedes returned to my side, I wondered aloud if perhaps we should abandon the fortress and head south toward the Greek cities that dotted Italia's southernmost shores.

"I also observed this morning's display, and I am unnerved," Archimedes confided. "We will not be allowed to leave at this hour. However, I have heard that a certain group of civilians will move themselves south to the fortress of Cannae at first light. I would like to be among them."

CHAPTER VII

A large part of the civilian group to which Archimedes had alluded on the previous night turned out to be a caravan of camp-following prostitutes and their protectors. I was not surprised to see them hurry from danger, but I was astonished to find Severinus leading their retreat. As he came alongside my horse, he took pains to explain that he rode to Cannae not to guard us, but rather to establish a signal post. The little town stood on the highest outcropping of rock among the valley's southern hills, within sight of all three encampments. From there, the tribune would be able to look down upon any formations on the south side of the river and, by using flags, warn his commanders of surprise maneuvers attempted by the Carthaginians on the Roman left.

Severinus rode between a pair of able-looking cavalrymen. Strapped to their horses were several spears, to which had been attached cloths of different colors. The three formed the vanguard of a motley convoy of wagons and a small herd of goats.

Archimedes rode on a donkey well behind the parade, apparently not bothered by the dust being kicked up. When I dropped back to encourage him to move faster, he gestured me close to him.

"I have figured it out," he said. "Severinus is far too solicitous of these women and their keepers. He is getting on in years and must provide for his future. He is quite happy, I think, in serving as the tribune liaison to the non-combatants. On our way into the camp, you must have noted the caravans circled up in the distance."

I assured him that I had.

"One caravan holds the peddlers who will pay the soldiers for the spoils of war they collect, whichever side wins. The other is made up of slave dealers, from Delos or some other place. They also do not care who wins, so long as they can purchase captives to sell. I have been led to understand that prostitutes and their owners are more of the parasites found in these same make-shift camps. Do you not find it curious that these women were allowed to operate inside the Roman camp, especially before an expected battle?"

"But I am certain the soldiers are not allowed beyond the ramparts," I hazarded.

"Severinus is well paid to allow their presence," judged the old calculator. "Imagine how much salary young soldiers are willing to lay out to lie in the arms of a woman on the night before they may die. Plenty of profit to go around each dawn. I imagine the bribes ascend through the tribune directly to the consuls. Your tribune is protecting his second source of income by taking them out of the camp."

"I do not care about his profit," I said to my great-uncle. "What bothers me is his complaisance and that of nearly every other officer concerning who leads them. Would you allow a butcher to cut your hair?"

"Certainly not."

"Or to build the house over your head?"

"No, indeed!"

"But is not commanding an army an even more important charge? Should their consuls not be professional soldiers instead of merely politicians who got their positions because of wealth?"

"Do not seek an argument from me," Archimedes said. "A general may also be a butcher, but one who slaughters men must have a different set of skills than one who slaughters dumb animals."

"They fight a man who has practiced warfare his entire life. Has he not shown them that his knowledge and tactics are superior to theirs?"

"The Romans are cock-sure. They depend on sheer size and a particular penchant for organization," said my old mentor. "We shall see today whether or not this is sufficient."

I looked at the group ahead of us. I focused on two scribes whose satchels were weighted down with letters to parents, sweethearts, and wives. One wagon held the equipment of a pair of blacksmiths. Another wagon belonged to a custom armorer. A third was driven by the servant of a physician who had catered to the nobles in the camp. A fourth bore the pair of augurs whom the consuls used to predict the outcome of the battle. Fully five wagons were used by the prostitutes, the man who owned them, the two giants who protected them and who looked like retired military men, and the four creatures who were either eunuchs or caprices of the gods.

We had forded the river with little difficulty and rumbled over denuded fields to a highway which ran by the citadel of Cannae. The town stood just above that highway, accessed by a road that wound halfway around the hillock before entering the main gate on the southeast side. Evidence of Hannibal's assault on the town earlier in the year was abundant. The hillock covered not more than five acres. Upon its crest were approximately two-dozen dwellings, built on either side of a single, straight street. At the end of this street, where the hillock plunged precipitously, stood a small fortress. This largest among the structures had also served as the town's granary. The backs of every house had been constructed with no portals or windows, and between them rose high walls, so that all the structures together had once formed a respectable barrier to assault. Obviously, however, the town had not been made to resist an army of 40,000.

As we entered, we saw that Cannae's gate had been destroyed, even to the small towers that flanked it. In several places the walls between buildings had likewise been pulled down. Just outside the town we had spotted dozens of freshly-dug graves. It was a sad place, devoid of humanity and mutely attesting to the horrors of war.

Severinus led the little caravan into the deserted town's street. As soon as the animals were penned, the entire contingent climbed onto roofs for a view of the expected battle. Several of the women carried shades to protect their skin from the sun, early in the day as it was. I felt ill at ease staring at so many woman with their faces bared to the world, their profession notwithstanding.

The spectacle in the valley was already underway. The larger Roman army had left the camp we had also occupied and was crossing the river at two fords.

"Paulus leads today," Severinus informed. He and I crowded into the lookout tower of the fortress, with the tribune's adjutants on either side. Each assistant carried three spears with signaling scarves. "He will bring the fight to Hannibal. He is not as wary as the butcher's son."

The tribune spoke of Consul Varro, whose father controlled a large portion of the meat market for Roma. Severinus' words were spoken with clear disdain. I took this opportunity to resume the discourse I had with Archimedes only minutes earlier.

"I understand Consul Varro does not have much soldiering experience," I remarked.

"Neither does Paulus," Severinus revealed. "But what does that matter? They exist merely to give the command. The army and its officers know what to do. At least Paulus is not afraid to send us into battle."

The man's hubris jolted me. I wanted to bark at him, "Do you not understand that you face a man with a soldier's brain and that he may not do what you wish him to do? Who will give new orders if your enemy's tactics require you to adjust?" Instead, I asked, "Have Varro and Paulus at least served together on the field?"

"No."

I was immensely glad to be out of the encampment and at least somewhat on our way out of danger.

We watched the legionaries stream from the second camp, which lay just northeast of Cannae on the plain. I waited with barely-contained excitement to view how eight legions would form into one fighting machine.

"We measured the width of the plain between the river and the foothills," Severinus told me. "It is a little more than ten of your stadia. We are able to build the hastati and principe thirty ranks deep and still extend across the entire valley with our allies and cavalry on the flanks. Nothing Hannibal puts in our way will be able to resist such massing."

I watched in wonder as his words became fact. A solid line of men soon extended from river to hillside, with about 6,000 velites positioned out in front.

"You see our cavalry on the right?" the tribune asked. "That will steady the more exposed side. The cavalry closest to us are our allies." He grinned. "And now I will tell you a secret. Nearly 10,000 men have been held inside the main camp. The triarii and an equal number of allied infantry. Shortly after the battle begins, they will hasten to Hannibal's camp and overrun it. He will lose all his tents and provisions even if some of his force escapes the battle. There will be no last stand behind his ramparts that will kill thousands of our men over a period of days. Excellent strategy, don't you agree?"

"But the trairii are your guarantee against disaster," I worried.

"They are not needed on the line. One Roman equals two Carthaginians, and we outnumber them by 10,000 without the triarii," he boasted.

Finally, the Roman line came to a halt. It extended across the valley on the oblique, from northwest to southeast, as if there were too many of them to crowd in at right angles to the river and hills. More probably, this maneuver was in expectation of the right flank being hit hardest.

"Finally!" Severinus exalted, pointing. "The enemy accepts civilized battle instead of running and playing tricks."

I found the words 'civilized' and 'battle' incongruous, but I refrained from comment. From the west, this time on the south side of the river, marched that same colossal enemy force I had witnessed the previous day outside our camp.

"I can't make out their standards or colors," Severinus complained.

As I have already stated, my eyesight is extremely keen. I reported to him those standards and colors I could make out.

"His center is Hispanic and Celtic infantry," Severinus translated. "The Celts are most expendable to him, so he places them dead center. The cavalry on his right are Numidians and Carthaginians. The nobles of his city are the ones wearing the red cloaks. The Numidians wear white tunics and sit upon leopard skins. I admire their style. Good horsemen. And they carry shields covered with elephant hide."

"Your horsemen carry no shields," I noted. "How can the Numidians?"

"They have taught themselves how to ride and direct their horses without using reins. They must develop very strong thighs."

I was dismayed at the fact that Severinus' attention to the enemy cavalrymen fixed on their outfits and style rather than the distinct advantage he had revealed in their fighting with shields. In my mind, that was equal to putting another thousand horsemen in the field.

"That leaves Hannibal's left to his Hispanic and Celtic cavalries," Severinus went on. He made a purring noise in his throat. "Therefore, all those now in the front ranks must be Africans. So much the better. If we kill Hannibal's countrymen first, the others will break."

"Behind his skirmish line," I observed, "his main force is forming a bow. See how the companies on each end hold back. What do you make of that?"

"He believes he can drive a wedge into our middle and break our army in two," the tribune decided. "Regulus and Geminus will hold him. They command the center. Varro heads the west wing, and Paulus leads the right."

"But no single man coordinates the entire Roman effort," I confirmed.

"No. It is too big for one man to control."

My thought was that it was too big for one man not to have control. "Have Regulus and Geminus at least fought together?"

"I do not believe so. Do you note how we have arranged it so that Hannibal's troops fight with the sun in their eyes?"

In this Severinus was correct. However, within another hour this advantage would disappear. Hannibal's troops, on the other hand, had their own advantages. Because they stood on the inland side of the plain, the land sloped down toward their opponents. This made their advance easier or that of the Romans more difficult. Moreover, as this was the height of summer, the hot Sirocco winds that crossed the Mediterranean from the Sahara Desert would blow into the legionnaires' faces throughout the day. Not even an advantage of nearly one-third more men on the Roman side made me feel safe.

As Severinus said his last words, the slingers and pikemen of both sides had ventured within striking distance of each other. From our distant venue we could hear only the faintest noise. Individual shouts were impossible to discern. Coming to us as one mass, it sounded like the plaintive moaning of a night wind. Neither could we see the conflicts among individuals but rather only registered mass movements. I knew, however, that light spears were flying from both sides and that balls of lead capable of piercing a shield were being flung by the hundreds. Even the onset of battle was a fearsome event.

The armies drew ever nearer.

The African pikemen fell back with astonishing speed and discipline, reforming behind the two wings of cavalry. Seeing this, the tribune growled with vexation beside me. The dust of the horses masked the precise formations that Hannibal's crack troops were creating. Already, his unusual convex crescent center and the swift reforming of the African pikemen proved to me that Hannibal had developed a complex plan. In opposition, the Romans continued forward in one great line, looking from where I stood little different from Alexander's storied phalanxes.

"Our triarii will dash for their camp soon." Severinus leaned intently over the little fortress' parapet, as if his effort could improve his view.

We watched in silence for several minutes. Then I pointed to the far end of the plain, near the river. "They bring more cavalry," I reported. "Hundreds more. They seek to break your right."

"Gods!" Severinus exclaimed. "Where did they get them all? How could they have concealed so many from us?"

I thought of the Roman disinterest in scouting and in the Carthaginians' penchant for it and realized that an extra thousand unaccounted-for horseman might have constantly been crisscrossing the countryside gathering information.

In the heat of the battle I temporarily became a Roman, wishing their side the win. As Severinus did, I fixed my attention on the first action of the battle, which was the reinforced cavalry charge on the Roman right.

"They hold! You see? They hold!" Severinus protested.

I saw a different scene. The charge had certainly been blunted, but little by little the right wing gave way. On the Roman left, the Numidian horsemen skirmished and harassed the lines constantly. It was clear that they were trying to draw the Roman left wing forward and thin them out so they could slip past, but it held together tenaciously.

Trumpet calls resounded across the plain, and the velites retired via the Roman center. The legionaries meantime beat their light spears against their shields to indicate their impatience to begin the slaughter. The remnants of Hannibal's light forward troops withdrew as well.

At last I beheld the working of the quincunx formation. Once the velites had passed behind the main line, maniple after maniple of legionaries raced forward in precise order, filling in the gaps. The trumpets and horns sounded again, and the Roman center charged.

Long days must have been spent drilling the Roman infantry on precisely when to throw their light javelins. Almost as a single body, they paused momentarily at a given distance and let fly such a torrent of missiles that the space between the forces grew dark. Hardly had they released their first spears when they started forward again, drawing out their heavy spears as they advanced. The Celts and Hispanics had barely lowered their shields to pull out the first flight of spears when the second began to rain down upon them. I spotted little wavers in the Carthaginian lines as particular areas buckled from the shock of the missiles. Moments later, more men filled in the line atop the fallen.

I have never heard such a terrible din as when thousands of shields collided at top speed with thousands more. The weight of the Roman masses became immediately evident. Their enemy seemed to be compressed backward. Then the force of the attack was absorbed, and the slow, deadly business or pushing and hacking began in earnest.

Behind the hastati, the principe companies waited patiently for their turns, resting on their right knees. They beat their shields in encouragement. Behind them were only the survivors among their velites.

"We begin to win already," Severinus judged after another quarter hour. What had been a convex crescent of enemy fighters facing the Roman middle was now a straight line.

"A fire," I noted. From the northwest hill behind the Carthaginian forces rose a column of smoke. "Is it a signal, I wonder?"

"Just as possibly cavalry raiders setting fire to stores," one of Severinus' cavalry guards speculated.

I looked for some discernable shift among Hannibal's main troops, but minute after minute I could detect nothing beyond the inexorable push of the Roman center into the core of its enemy. Then something within caused me to turn my attention from the plain and gaze at the hillocks and vales to our southwest. Within their concealing rills, slowed by the unevenness of the terrain, moved at least 500 more cavalrymen. Both wings of the Roman army were barely holding their own. Clearly, this force added enough power to crush the Roman left wing.

"Look!" I called out. "Signal your velites to move to the left!"

"I cannot do that," Severinus revealed. "The flags only signal the nature of the danger; they cannot recommend an action."

At that moment, screams from the women and eunuchs on the rooftops below us caused us to look directly south. A troop of about twenty enemy cavalrymen galloped toward the entrance to Cannae.

Without thinking, I grabbed the three signal spears propped against the wall unused. I dashed down the stairs to Cannae's street and raced toward the ruined gate. Behind me came Severinus and his second adjutant.

"Block the street with those wagons!" I commanded the blacksmiths and armorer as I rushed to the ruins on the right side of the gate.

The cavalrymen ascended to Cannae in two groups, the first comprised of six men. When they were almost to the open gate, I stepped out of hiding and thrust the first of my spears. It struck my target squarely in the chest, knocking him cleanly off his mount. As I reached down for the second spear, I saw out of the corner of my eye another rider bending low to attack me with his sword. I ducked under his swing, taking a glancing blow to my helmet. He continued into the town. I stood and hurled the second spear. This effort was not as true and drove into that rider's horse just below the mane. The horse cried out and tumbled over sideways, crushing its rider beneath its great weight. A fourth enemy slipped from his horse when it reared wildly in reaction.

Severinus had brought with him another of the spears, and he raced out with it raised to attack the last of the initial horsemen. From his mad dash to the gate his unstrapped helmet had turned askew on his head, so that the hinged chin piece blocked the periphery of his view from the fifth rider. This Numidian charged at him from the flank with a long lance. I had just enough time to pluck my sword from its sheath and to hack across the legs of his horse. The beast crumbled, throwing its rider over its head and onto Severinus. The lance flew uselessly away as the man thrust out his hands to cushion his fall. He sailed directly into the tribune, driving them both to the ground.

By this time, one of the riders whom I had caused to spill had risen to his feet and ran toward the pinned tribune, sword drawn. I stepped into his path. Neither of us held a shield. Our duel devolved purely to attack and parry. I did not toy with him to test the range of his skills but quickly used my best feint and drove my blade deeply into his neck. As I had been taught, I followed through by stepping into him rather than reflexively backing from his counterstroke. His hacking motion landed with no effect against my chain mail. I wrestled the sword out of his hand while his lifeblood pulsed hotly onto me.

In Korinthos I was instructed that all too frequently the skills of any one soldier have nothing to do with his survival in a pitched battle. So it was for me. As I struggled out of the grip of the dying warrior, the second group of enemy cavalrymen reached the gates. I, Severinus, and one of his adjutants had ventured beyond the walls to blunt the charge. Without my seeing it happen, the adjutant had been struck and killed. Severinus lay on the ground, choking the life from the man who had been thrown onto him. Both of us should have died. Eternal honor to Publius, the man who owned the prostitutes, and to his massive guards for stepping boldly in the path of the second enemy unit and holding them at bay until we could retreat. As it was, one of the prostitute guards was killed and the other wounded.

I released my dying enemy, and Severinus struggled to his feet as Publius yelled for us to retreat. He and his wounded companion used spear and shield to cover us as they pretended to throw at the enemy horsemen even as they backed away.

To Move the World

While Severinus and I scrambled over the wreck of one of the towers, four more of the riders charged past us into Cannae. After they passed through, two wagons were pushed across the entrance, blocking the way to the rest. I was not happy over the prospect of facing enemies on both sides, but I soon found that those at my back were more than engaged by the blacksmiths and armorer brandishing spears from behind the wagons and the many women and womanlike creatures on the rooftops flinging down loose stones and debris. Even the two scribes and the physician ventured out from hiding every few moments to hurl objects. From many directions missiles rained upon the five cavalrymen. Owing to the confusion of the wagons and the many milling animals of our caravan, they found precious little room in which to maneuver. As soon as those cavalrymen outside the walls heard the volume of shouting and viewed the plight of their companions, they quit the hillock.

By careful maneuvering and with the use of my last spear, I was able to kill one man who refused to abandon his horse. Two others managed to escape over rooftops and thence down the hill. The last two attackers were surrounded. We deprived them of their dignity by allowing the women and eunuchs to stone them to death. When they lay still, the feminine creatures descended on them like the Harpies of legend, kicking their lifeless bodies. Not satisfied with two kills, the troupe flew toward the gate with rocks in hand and hair trailing wildly behind them to see if there were any others to finish off.

Archimedes appeared from hiding. As we listened to the outraged shrieks of the women, he shook his head. "War could be worse," he speculated. "If women fought it, no one would be allowed to live."

Δ

In reflection, I believe that an enemy lookout spotted me and the three Roman soldiers on Cannae's fortress tower, and enough horsemen were dispatched to eliminate us. The size of our contingent, civilians notwithstanding, caught them unaware. If the purpose of the small detachment that stormed the town was indeed to prevent us from signaling about the stealthy approach of 500 more of their kind, then clearly they succeeded. Either that or our signal was seen but it was already too late to adjust the battle line. Certainly, there were no 10,000 trairii and allied reinforcements on the field of battle to face the new foe.

By the time we attended to the wounded and wearily remounted the fortress turret, we saw that Hannibal had gained the upper hand. Both Roman wings were in collapse. The Roman center had succeeded in driving the enemy's center back into the reverse of their initial formation. Now, the bow in their line surrounded the Roman line and threatened to encircle it. I saw that Hannibal had purposely allowed his forces to give ground and not resist the great mass of the Roman army. Despite the theoretical protection of a river on the right flank and hills on their left flank, the Romans had allowed themselves to be enveloped on two sides.

Within what seemed only minutes, the cavalrymen and Hannibal's crack pikemen had wheeled to attack both Roman flanks. We watched in mute horror as the proud Roman army became so hemmed in that its soldiers could barely wield their weapons. I knew that the Africans were spearing them almost at will. I saw no sign of the legion in Hannibal's fort coming to their comrades' aid. I knew that, at best, the Romans had suffered another defeat; at worst, they would be annihilated, and the way to Roma lay open.

Severinus faced me and kneeled. "It is our tradition to call the man who saves you Father. My life is forever in your debt."

"'Forever' may be a meaningless term unless we press south," I told him, offering my hand to help him up. He grasped my arm just below the elbow, in the Roman manner, and then moved swiftly away to command our retreat.

CHAPTER VIII

I will not delay in setting down the outcome of the battle of Cannae. Some of what I set down here was not known by the Romans until many days later. The consul Paulus was struck by a stone from an enemy slinger only minutes into the conflict and mortally wounded. The consensus estimate of the advantage of Celtic and Hispanic horsemen over the Roman cavalry on the right was three to one. Despite this, the Romans and their foot support were only slowly pushed back. The left at first held. It could not, however, advance alongside the mass of the Roman center when those tens of thousands moved forward. Similarly, a gaping hole was left between wing and center on the right. At the first opportunity, Hasdrubal, Hannibal's brother-in-law, exploited the gap on the river side with a reinforcement of cavalry and from that point harassed the center's right flank and eventually attacked the army's rear.

Considering the battle's final outcome, little doubt remained that Hannibal had cleverly planned the slow retreat of his center. Apparently, the Romans came within a quarter stadion of overwhelming the enemy infantry and sending it into flight, but Hannibal himself directed from the rear and was able to encourage his men to hold until the line had formed a semi-circle around the Roman center. Once this occurred, the thousands of African pikemen he had reserved for the wings turned inward. With the Carthaginian cavalry harassing the Roman rear, the envelopment was complete. The trairii and their allies who had been left behind in the fort never emerged to counterattack. Ironically, they who were supposed to prevent Hannibal from defending his camp ended doing the same thing inside their own on the following day.

Paulus died. Geminus and Regulus died commanding the center. In all, eighty of Roma's senators lay on the field when the battle ended. Most of the equites, those men able to afford a horse and heavy armor, died. Much later, I would learn that of the 300 seats allowed in the Roman Senate, 177 vacancies had been created by this single battle. Of thirty-three tribunes, twenty-nine were lost, as were almost all of the praetorian rank. Petillius would not be delivering King Hieron's scroll to either consul. I prayed that someone inside the camp had the presence of mind to burn it, along with all other strategic documents.

Many of these intelligences I collected from among a bit more than 10,000 survivors who slowly gathered in the town of Canusium, a day's march southwest of Cannae. Unintentionally, our little caravan provided the vanguard of this retreat. A more defeated and dejected stream of men I have never seen. Later, I learned that approximately 3,800 other fighters for the Roman side escaped east and north. About 10,000 of the surrounded central mass surrendered. 7,000 of these were Roman citizens.

Hannibal sent ten of the higher-ranking prisoners back to Roma, along with a high-ranking officer of his called Carthalo to act as an ambassador. Carthalo's primary charge was to negotiate for ransom. He was also instructed to tender an offer to negotiate for peace if the opportunity seemed to arise. The Carthaginian was not allowed to pass through the gates of Roma but was halted at the Albion Hills by a lector. He was made to wait there for several days while the ten prisoners reported to the Senate and while the issue of ransom was discussed.

The notion of peace negotiations was rejected out of hand. Better every Roman should perish, the Senate vowed, than that a foreign power be able to claim it had won a war on Italian soil.

Hannibal's ransom offer was, I thought, fair. He asked 500 denarii for each horseman, 300 for each foot soldier, and 100 for each slave. The Senate refused to pay the ransom. Many among the body would have allowed families to pay for their men's release, since the loss of such a large part of the Roman armies was crippling. However, one of the older nobles argued eloquently that cowardice could not be rewarded by redemption. So, the allies were released as was Hannibal's custom, and the 7,000 Romans were sold to the slave dealers and shipped to Greece.

Upon learning of the Senate's decision, one of the ten officers who had pledged to return to Hannibal's camp bolted from Roma. He was hunted down and delivered back into captivity, so that the city's honor might not be blemished by his unwillingness to serve the rest of his life as a slave. The day that I learned the news of the Romans refusing to ransom their own citizens I lost my last illusion of these people treating Siracusa with anything less than the harshest brutality if my city ever closed its gates on them. My choice of ally swung silently to Carthage.

The estimate of Severinus was that 36,000 Romans and allied soldiers were lost in a single day. This equaled nearly the full size of Hannibal's army. Carthalo was pleased to deliver to the Senate news that their side had lost only 5,710 men. In a little more than a year, Hannibal and his forces had managed to kill about 75,000 men on their enemy's home soil. In spite of Severinus' boast that this so-called republic's census had revealed 770,000 able men, I thought it impossible for Roma to recover from such rapid attrition. I expected that those most recently acquired confederates and those tribes brutally brought under Roman control would defect. I also expected that neutral tribes and the cities and towns of the southern extreme of the peninsula would now cast their lot in with Hannibal, to rid themselves of this warlike, acquisitive people from the Latium plain. I dared to hope that with so much happening in Italia, Siracusa would be left alone for many years.

Δ

Once the headlong race to escape Hannibal's army had slowed and the Roman army survivors were sure they were not being pursued, they dropped by the sides of the road like winter leaves. Only the heaving of their chests proved that they were not dead. Having won our little skirmish in the town of Cannae and survived, my reaction was the opposite. I was, in truth, elated. I had triumphed in my first combat. I had been granted by the gods the rare privilege as a soldier to view a great battle from a vantage that was highly instructional. I had witnessed the initial naïve confidence of an army and what defeat does to morale. I had learned vicariously the wages of underestimating a foe. I now fully understood the critical need for gathering reliable intelligence. In short, I had absorbed much more than the crafts of siege and siege defense to take back with me to Siracusa.

Consul Varro appeared in Canusium on the next morning, leading the last remnant of stragglers. From where I had observed the beginning of the battle, it had seemed to me that Gaius Terentius Varro had acquitted himself best among the four top officers, holding the left until Hannibal's surprise 500 horsemen swept down on his flank. Evidently, from the behavior of the soldiers who surrounded him on the retreat, their opinion was the same: The butcher's son had proven as valiant and competent a soldier as anyone else on the field. I did not mark this as a heartening observation.

Δ

By virtue of his rank, Severinus was one of the highest surviving officers. He therefore possessed power, and some of that power benefited Archimedes and me. He kept us close by him and never failed to tell the story of how I was the first to notice the flanking cavalry charge and the one who had saved his life. For a Greek and one not on the true field of battle, I swiftly became known as one of the few heroes of the day. This loosened many men's tongues to my inquiries. My loyalty to the Roman cause was never again questioned. When I asked about siege defense, veterans who spoke Greek vied with each other to explain the minutest details of the craft. As much as possible, I kept Archimedes by my side, so that he would not have to benefit from the knowledge second-hand.

Protecting my genius great-uncle from exposure was a constant trial. He held his tongue only with the greatest effort. For example, when the last of the survivors dribbled into Canusium, Severinus and several other officers set themselves down to calculate the rations needed for the next three months. As apparently none of the top quartermaster officers had survived, the tribunes labored against their ignorance.

"It's not that difficult," Archimedes broke in with exasperation after about fifteen minutes of their wrangling.

"What does the slave say?" one of the tribunes asked.

Severinus translated. The group stared at my great-uncle. Some of them looked with anger, some with disbelief, and some with amusement. I shot Archimedes my own look, which the Romans undoubtedly took to be punitive. He knew that he had temporarily forgotten his role as simpleton.

"So, old man, what is your estimate of the wheat and barley that we need for the next three months?" Severinus invited.

Archimedes snatched up a little stick from the ground. As I had seen him do so many times in the reckoning box of his courtyard, he scribbled figures. These, however, were nonsense. "Three times three times three times three," he replied with a broad smile.

Severinus again translated to the group. While the men roared with laughter, I commanded 'Alonzo' to look after his donkey and my string of captured horses.

As soon as I could get away, I visited with the old genius and received from him the correct calculations, which Archimedes had made in his head. These I brought back to the group a few hours later. They proved identical to the figures that they had taken the entire morning and a full committee to assemble. My reputation rose another notch.

Δ

The town fathers of Canusium did not want any part of the Roman army. They expected the full force of Hannibal's army to arrive at any moment. They greatly resented being pressed into labor to strengthen their town's defenses. Moreover, if the Carthaginians never arrived or if the walls held, their store of provisions was barely enough to feed their residents for the winter much less 10,000 fighting men. Varro allowed them to complain, because he and they both knew that the army could not and would not leave unless relief arrived.

Archimedes and I elected to linger with the army, despite the danger. Probably nowhere else on the peninsula could we receive such a first-hand education in strengthening a town against attack. We watched existing walls thicken. We saw new walls go up in front of the old ones, as a first line of defense. We noted how the stones were laid and cemented, where openings were placed to allow missiles to be directed down on an enemy from relative safety, and how those openings could be created without locally weakening the wall.

In surprisingly few days, couriers delivered word from Roma regarding the citizenry's reaction to the stunning defeat. The bad news was kept from the general army, but Severinus had to share it with someone. I seemed the safest vessel.

Roma expected at any moment that Hannibal would be storming their walls. The city gates were sealed, to prevent wholesale flight. The former temporary dictator Quintus Fabius Maximus took charge in the panic, purposely withholding the casualty lists. All feasting and entertainments were suspended. One patrician who was spotted leaning out of a balcony drunk and wearing a banquet wreath was clapped in chains and deposited in prison.

There was not a street in the city without mothers, sisters, and wives weeping openly for their dead men, in spite of an earnest attempt to keep all married women indoors. More than a dozen women had committed suicide upon hearing the news. Many cleansed temple walls and floors with their tears and their unbound hair. Those who had lost husbands spat on those whose husbands had not volunteered.

Scapegoats were sought. Varro's name was vilified, despite his honorable command during the battle. He was burned in effigy. He had been the one, they all remembered, who had whipped up the Senate to send the eight legions south, saying that to tolerate Hannibal on their soil even one more day was to make the world question their strength.

"The Fabian senators," Varro had been reported saying, "tell us that their policy of hounding Hannibal rather than attacking him directly is preserving the Republic. But in preserving us, they keep us from conquering the man." The politician was also singled out for encouraging the members of the Senate to join him in enlisting, so that almost two-thirds of their numbers were now dead.

Two of the Vestal virgins were accused of having had sexual relations with men and enraging the gods. One immediately committed suicide. The other was buried alive at the Collina Gate, the portal where the city had expected their army to return in triumph. The revered Sibylline Books were consulted by the augurs. They revealed that more human sacrifice was required. A Celtic couple and a Greek couple were singled out and buried alive in the cattle market. I was glad Archimedes and I had not hurried to the city.

Not long after we had absorbed this barbarous news, another set of couriers arrived in Canusium. The Roman Senate had elected Marcus Claudius Marcellus to take command of the remains of the eight legions. At the time, he had been serving in command of the entire Roman fleet, most of which was harbored in Ostia. I knew that I had heard his name before, but I could not remember where.

"I had told you about him shortly after we first met," Severinus reminded me. "You asked if we still had a dictator."

It suddenly came to me. "He is one of two praetors who ran Roma while the consuls were at war."

Severinus gave me a patronizing smile. "Neither the consuls nor the praetors run Roma. That is done by the elected Senate and by hundreds of appointed city officials."

I understood. Those elected to lead this race of men were invariably away managing their armies and navies. As Archimedes had once said with disdain, the main product of the Romans was war. I thought that the more correct answer was "expansion," but my answer was rarely possible without incorporating his. Severinus emphasized that personages were elected in his country, as if to chide me for living in one ruled by a dictator. I did not feel at all chastened. Our dictator was benevolent, and by diplomacy skillfully kept our men from perishing in war. Considering the Roman system was supposedly a republic, its citizens seemed to have little say in how their men spent the best years of their lives, if they lived at all. To me, their government seemed no better than the old Spartian state. If their citizens did in fact choose such a way of life, I both pitied and feared them.

Δ

Each day brought more news of Marcellus' exploits. As soon as he was appointed supreme leader of the main army, he dispatched 1,500 marines from his fleet to Roma to help strengthen its defenses. The next day, he ordered the second legion of marines to Teanum Didicunum to secure the Via Latini as a first line of defense against Hannibal marching on their capital city. The third day, we learned that he traveled by forced march with a small force to link up with the remaining soldiers from Cannae, who cowered behind Canusium's walls. On hearing this, Varro started back to Roma to offer his sword and his bare neck. Contrary to the conjecture of several tribunes around us, when Varro arrived home he was not singled out as the cause of the massacre. Rather, the Senate went out to the city walls as a body and welcomed him home.

By the time Marcellus arrived, I expected to look upon a competent leader. I was not disappointed.

By a caprice of Fate, it so happened that Severinus had served under Marcellus in years past. He had prepared me to meet a man who was the complete soldier and a devoted family man. I was told that he was fifty-two years old, yet even though he had lost the hair on the top of his head he did not look much older than Severinus, whom I knew to be forty. He was a man of average height, but I could tell even with his armor on that he owned an enviable physique. He carried himself like a champion. In this I was not surprised, since Severinus had entertained me several nights earlier with the tale of how Marcellus had accepted the challenge of a Gallic chieftain named Viridomartus to combat before the start of a battle. This happened only six years earlier, when Marcellus was past his prime and would not have been considered a coward for declining. Such challenges from northern barbarians were common. Less often were they accepted. Only three times were they won. Marcellus killed the Celt in quick order and for this was awarded spolia optima, the spoils of honor, which were the arms taken from an enemy chief.

I was not introduced to the man until several hours after Severinus first met with him. When I entered his tent, he stood and offered his arm.

"This is the warrior I have heard so much about," he greeted in Greek, through a good smile. "Would that we had had a thousand of your mettle at Cannae."

I did my best to maintain my humility.

"You killed four of our enemy in as many minutes?" he asked.

I nodded.

"And he is the pentathlon champion of Siracusa as well," Severinus bragged on my behalf. I knew then that Archimedes had been talking again.

"I am sorry that the scroll from my king has been lost," I told Marcellus. "It asked that, as an ally, I be instructed in the latest innovations in defense against siege."

I told him about the emissaries from Carthage to Hieron's court, of their veiled threats of a new fleet, and their pressure to change our city's allegiance.

"Indeed this fleet exists," Marcellus shared. "Five days after the Cannae battle, a fleet was spotted beyond the harbor of Siracusa. They lingered awhile, as if looking for our fleet possibly harbored there. Then they sailed on. Where they went, no one yet knows."

"I saw the scroll Leonides speaks of," Severinus affirmed, "but it has indeed been lost."

Marcellus waved his hand. "No need to verify this man's word," he said. "I can see that he is as truthful as he is valiant."

The praetor asked for my rank. I gave him the reply that Hieron had commanded.

"You have no equivalent to my title," I answered. "I report only to my king and my strategos, who is like your consuls in the field."

"Then you and I are roughly of the same rank," Marcellus said.

I blushed at the older and more-experienced man's words. "That cannot be true, sir. We are but a city. You lead the fate of a country."

He put his arm on my shoulder. "Be that as it may, you are most impressive for your age. We shall spend time together as soon as I feel I have control over this mess."

As I was escorted from the tent, I heard him say, "Well, we are bound to improve next year, my fellow Romans. Imagine how badly you would have been defeated if Hannibal still had both his eyes!"

Of all his attributes, the fact that this warrior could find humor—even amid such despair—impressed me the most. It was said of Hannibal that he possessed a fine sense of humor. Perhaps, I mused, Roma had at last found the Carthaginian general's equal.

CHAPTER IX

Archimedes and I lingered with the remnants of the once-great Roman peninsular army until it had been determined for certain that Hannibal was not pressing north to Roma. As we had suspected, he occupied himself fully on gathering allies. Triumphant as he had been in the previous twelve months, he still had suffered considerable losses. I am sure thoughts of the equally victorious but ultimately defeated King Pyrrhus filled his mind. He needed reinforcements badly, and he and his agents ranged from Apulia, through Samnium, and across Calabria collecting them.

Marcellus gave us the best of possible escorts to Roma. Severinus rode by my side, with almost fifty other mounted nobles. Our way, marvelous to say, was well scouted. Marcellus had insured an open highway back to the capital city.

This leg of our journey required four days in all. I must admit that my excitement grew each day we rode closer. I cannot convey my disappointment in viewing this hub of the Roman Republic, either from outside its walls or inside. Having visited Alexandria, Korinthos, and Athenai and living in Siracusa, I expected that the would-be rulers of all of Italia and more would have built something as least as grand as these great cities. The only thing impressive about it were its seven hills. Even these are not of the majestic height that many travelers describe. I am sure that not one stands more than a sixth of a stadion above the ground of the forum.

On first viewing, Roma strikes one as a violent collision of villages. It has grown up with no rhyme or reason. I am aware that the oldest cities are the most unplanned, but in light of the absolute order of the Roman encampments, I was mightily disappointed by the narrow, constantly twisting streets with awnings and balconies making already-dim passageways even darker. Because Roma lies among many hills, the smoke from its thousands of hearths and furnaces collects in the valleys and gives the air a depressing pall.

Siracusa has its share of two-story dwellings. In Roma, I found many apartment buildings of three stories and even a few of four. This further contributes to its cramped feel. Further, most structures are poorly-constructed masses of timber and mud brick. Many displayed cracks that hinted they would not stand for more than a few decades. Their red brick compounds the dark aspect of the city. The more expensive structures such as the temples are formed from the local rock, which is called tufa. It is generally yellow-gray but sometimes dark-gray in color. It can be damaged by simply digging a knife into it. The roofs of the city are almost uniformly made of wood, with terra cotta tiles covering them. I would not care to be in most of the districts if a fire started. I was assured this calamity happens with frequency.

The best building material I saw was Roman concrete. It is quite strong and allows large open areas to be created in public buildings, with barrel-vaulted ceilings above. Generally stucco is applied over it, but this is not of the quality that my father's shop offers. Nor are the colors of the buildings which are painted as vibrant. Particularly disappointing was the Temple of Jupiter Optimus Maximus.

The Servian Wall that encircles Roma was built long ago. It encloses a space far smaller than that of Siracusa. Consequently, the city has run out of room, and expansion goes upward. An underground aqueduct which brings pure water from a distance of about sixty stadia makes possible such overcrowding.

In fairness, I cannot say that all of Roma is ugly. The forum is comparable to that of our agoras in Siracusa. Moreover, the Palatine Hill is lovely. It is dotted with the townhouses of the wealthy. The Clivus Victoriae in particular, a road near the crest of this hill, offers an impressive view down into the forum.

On the Capitoline stands the city's fortress and the Temples of Juno Moneta and Jupiter. Other smaller temples such as those of Castor and Pollux, Janus, Saturn, and Vesta are scattered throughout the city. Naturally, the shops and government buildings are arrayed around the forum. When I looked for a great library such as that of Alexandria, I was disappointed yet again. These are not a people who engross themselves in reading, debating, and learning. Disappointing also are the theaters and the baths. They have no amphitheater such as the one we have built. They also do not delight in dance and theater as we do. I had heard for many years about the Roman penchant for entertainments that honor warfare. I was particularly disappointed that the mock combats among as many as twenty-two gladiators had been suspended due to the extended period of mourning. Likewise, all chariot races had been postponed indefinitely.

Down near the Tiber River and its bridges lie the markets for animals and perishables such as the Forum Boarium for cattle and the Forum Holitorium for vegetables. Between this and the swampy land, the smell is terrible. Also, not far from here the Cloaca Maxima, the great sewer of the city, empties.

Fortunately for the look of the city, the higher parts of most of the hills have not been developed. I am sure this is due to the cost of building on uneven ground. Between the Esquiline and Palatine Hills lies a cemetery, but the other cemeteries lie just outside the city close by the various gates. As with Cannae, two that Archimedes and I walked through held a chillingly large number of freshly-dug graves. I pictured the image of Hannibal's forces attacking this city through the cemeteries and dying there atop these new graves. I sincerely wondered if the gods would be disappointed if all races, like the Romans did with their mock combats, suspended military conflicts. I wondered also if perhaps we exist merely for their sport.

Δ

Because of the life-debt that Severinus insisted he owed me, I had no choice but to stay at his house. In truth, I was very grateful for his hospitality. The structure stood at the bottom of the Palatine. It was neither one of the cramped apartment dwellings of the plebeians nor the spacious city domus of the most privileged patrician, but a home about twice the size of that of my parents, befitting a successful businessman, soldier, and politician. It boasted a central atrium with an impluvium in which decorative fish swam. The requisite triclinium occupied one of the home's back corners for dining. Added to the bedrooms, storage rooms, and the quarters for the slaves was a study, which Severinus called a tablinum. Of this room he seemed most proud. It held chairs with backs and two tables fashioned from bronze. The oil lamps were particularly beautiful. While I admired the space, I thought of Archimedes' critical, but probably correct, comments concerning the tribune's lifestyle being improved by contributions from the owner of the camp prostitutes. He also owned and reaped the benefits of two estates in lands that the Romans had occupied in recent decades.

Severinus received a tearful, touching reception upon his return to his family. He had three children, a son and twin daughters, who were exceedingly well behaved. His wife was a pleasant woman named Cornelia, who did not act unnerved at the unexpected prospect of keeping two Greeks under her roof. Neither she nor her children, unfortunately, spoke Greek, which made communication stilted and perpetually embarrassing. Although her husband was forty, she could not have been older than thirty, and her daughters were nine and son seven. Like the Siracusan soldier, the average Roman soldier could not afford to marry young.

While Cornelia had a servant show Archimedes to his quarters among the slaves, Severinus teased his children. As soon as he dismissed them, Cornelia lost her smile.

"Do you remember before you left that the priests said they observed the statues of the war gods sweating blood?"

"Yes, of course," Severinus replied.

"They swore that this meant the gods urged full war. Now they are saying that they misread the sign. I think someone should kill these particular priests and banish the rest forever. Useless parasites!"

"Is this a suggestion you wish me personally to act upon?" Severinus asked.

"No, husband. I wish you to submit a petition to the Senate."

"Offer our coin and sacrifices to other temples," the tribune countered.

"I have. Those women whose men still lived were told of the defeat first," his wife revealed, taking his hand. "I thought I would die until they arrived at our door."

I knew that I was intruding on moments the couple wished to spend alone. When I suggested that I should go to my assigned room and unpack, they would have none of it. They labored then to include me in their discussion.

"The food rationing has been most vexing," Cornelia reported. "The meat, fish, and vegetables still are in short supply."

"I and my servant should stay at an inn," I said.

The couple blanched at my suggestion, and I feared I had greatly offended them.

"The inns are for scoundrels and thieves," Severinus declared. "We will have no such thing. In fact, you will benefit my family with increased ration when I make known your presence to the proper officials."

"The rationing of grains has lessened since the food gift of your king arrived," Cornelia managed to communicate to me.

This was the first I had heard of such a gift. Hieron had not made this intent known to either myself or Archimedes. His decision to throw Siracusa's loyalty completely behind Roma was no doubt made before the debacle of Cannae. Yet, it could not have been made but a few days after our departure from the city, else we would have sailed on this more direct route with far greater safety. Hieron had sent to Roma under Roman escort fifty more ships loaded with grain, only days after dispatching

Archimedes and me with the required tribute shipment. Cornelia let us know that he had also sent a statue of Victory, fashioned from almost twice my weight in gold. Ordinarily, gifts were uniquely fashioned for other monarchs or states. I knew this statue well. It had been made before my birth and was perhaps the most costly votive piece in our city. Something highly disturbing had compelled our ruler to include it on very short notice. I looked forward with expectation to learning what political pressures had sparked such precipitous actions.

"The Senate is voting whether or not they should accept this statue," Cornelia said. She looked at me with question in her eyes after she spoke to her husband, as if I could explain its arrival. I was somewhat unnerved by her stare.

Severinus translated his wife's words.

"Why would they not accept such a valuable gift?" I asked.

"Usually gifts are refused from anywhere other than cities with full citizen status," he answered. "We do not want to be considered a dominating people who demand such gifts. Nor do we want any other race to believe we need such contributions."

Each day, from incidents such as this, I came to know Roman pride a little better. This emotion had contributed mightily to their defeats at the hands of Hannibal. I wondered if it might work as well to the favor of Siracusa.

"If the Senate decides in favor of the statue," Cornelia continued slowly, while keeping her eyes on me, "there will be a formal acceptance and dedication. It arrived with only a secondary ambassador. Perhaps you will be chosen as the representative of your city."

Neither husband nor wife knew how unimportant I was in the great scheme of Siracusan affairs. I declined to disabuse them and just nodded.

"I will see that we have enough food," Severinus told his wife. He soon after took me out to see sections of Roma which I had not observed on our entry tour. Archimedes came with us. One could sense the pervading mood of mourning. The women were still largely absent from view. Only old men and children seemed to walk the streets. Vendors did not shout out lustily for attention. Bargaining was half-hearted. The drinking shops were all but empty.

To Move the World

The main purpose of our journey was gathering information on siege and siege defense. As we shopped, I reminded Severinus of this. He took us directly to the Via Sacra, which held the fabricating shops of several dozen weapons and warfare contractors. A few of the owners Severinus knew personally. He made an introduction and then made clear that I was to be treated with great respect and given answers to all my questions. I noted carefully the locations of the factories of the tribune's friends.

Δ

Even divorced of the period of general mourning, the Roman sense of propriety forbade more than three guests in a home on non-festival days, and not more than five for festivals. This first evening in Roma, Severinus told me that they had invited one other person. This was to be a woman named Aurora. She was the daughter of Marcus Claudius Marcellus. I had been told by the great praetor's own mouth that of five children born to him he had one son, also named Marcus, and one daughter surviving.

"Marcus instructed me before we left Canusium to see that you meet his daughter," Severinus told me. "As you have no doubt suspected, he has a great respect of the Greeks. Of their culture, their learning, their literature and philosophy."

"He said as much to me," I revealed. "He also said that he greatly regrets that his military duties have prevented him from becoming more skillful with our language and writing."

The tribune nodded. "But his daughter has had the time. Marcus has instilled in her his love of all things Greek. The son is considerably older and serves in a legion in the north. Aurora minds her father's household."

"Where is his wife?"

"Dead, blessed be her soul."

"Then I shall be most happy to dine with the daughter of the great Marcellus," I said, picturing a creature perhaps fourteen years old.

114

Δ

To maintain our ruse, the otherwise-renowned Archimedes could not dine with us. He made do with the slaves of the house, two of whom spoke Greek. I could not even linger with him that night or see that his needs were adequately cared for.

I was presented a toga to wear. I wrapped it around myself and fastened it together as best I could. To be inside a house again after so many weeks of the rough life constituted a major luxury. It set me in a temperate mood even before the first cup of wine was poured.

Aurora arrived with but a single male escort, whom she commanded to return to her house the moment she stood inside Severinus' atrium.

"We can feed your servant," Cornelia told her.

"Thank you, but he does not eat among slaves."

Clearly, Aurora was not a frequent enough visitor to the tribune's home for this information to be known. Unperturbed, Cornelia smiled and turned to me. "Here is our honored guest."

While I was introduced and praised, I studied the child of Marcus Claudius Marcellus. She was no girl-woman but one full-grown. Her figure was mature. I later learned that she was all of twenty-one. In height she was like a younger person, for she stood a head shorter than I. Her eyes were highly animated. Their sharp intelligence commanded attention. But her face overall was not one to rivet a man. There was too much of her father in her, and I thought that such a stern demeanor could never inspire adoration. If she had ever demonstrated traces of girlish giddiness, they had long since vanished. Since she was not married, I made the snap surmises that either she was too plain to get herself a husband or, more likely, since she was high-born and the daughter of a great man, ordered to stay at home and serve her father. I thought of Thalia and of her possessive father, Eustace, and my heart ached to return to Siracusa.

Aurora's voice was low-pitched. She spoke softly, but she also spoke slowly and clearly, so that I missed not a word of what she said. The other reason I missed not a word was that she spoke perfect Greek. It was, in fact, rather archaic and formal, learned as much from studying texts as from conversing. My Greek was, naturally, of the Sicilian dialect, but she seemed to have no trouble dealing with it.

Aurora used the Claudian cognomen, indicating that she stemmed from one of the most noble and ancient families of Roma. She was not called Marcellus, because this appellation that indicated a warlike nature had been bestowed solely upon her father, for his many successful years as a soldier.

Respecting her father as much as I did, I was most anxious to make a good impression on the daughter. I asked her many questions about her city. She was content to answer me in terse sentences. I did not, however, feel that she disliked me. On the contrary, she smiled often and averted her eyes.

When we were led into the triclinium to eat, Severinus suggested that we speak Latin so that I might practice for my upcoming interrogations of the makers of military materials. Being extremely polite hosts, he and Cornelia spoke slowly and used simple words whenever they could. Aurora would supply a Greek translation each time I became confused. Otherwise, she seemed mostly content to listen.

We dined that evening on hare and sausages, with chickpeas and lettuce as side dishes. For desert, Severinus had found pine nuts and apples in the market. The fare was not in any way a feast, but I enjoyed it nonetheless.

The meal ended all too soon, and Aurora said that her escort would arrive within a few minutes to bring her back home. I asked how far that was. She said it sat but the length of three streets up the hill. Looking into the open sky above the atrium, I saw that night had fallen with a particular darkness. I refused to allow her to return home with only one man by her side. I swiftly doffed my borrowed toga for the other article I had been given, which was called a synthesis. It was a more abbreviated costume that allowed me much more freedom of movement. Around it I buckled my sword.

When I returned to the atrium, the male servant had arrived. Severinus, Cornelia, and the servant all regarded my reappearance with raised eyebrows, but Aurora slipped her hand into the crook of my arm and asked me to take her home.

The moment we were beyond Severinus' threshold, Aurora asked, "Do you think it is proper that women should think about philosophy?"

"I know no reason why they shouldn't," I replied. "After all, they live in the same world as do men."

She nodded sharply. "Just so. And as you might imagine, I am not welcomed among those few Roman men who have seriously studied Greek philosophy. As far as women go, I have yet to meet one who has read sources directly."

I suddenly felt out of my depth. I have to this point in my narrative scrupulously avoided the fact that at this time in my life I could barely write more than my signature. My reading beyond street and shop signs and military slates was slow and labored. When I sent letters to Thalia, I always relied on the services of a scribe. Yet I considered there to be no more important building in the world than the library of Alexandria. I had an enormous respect for those who read and wrote with ease, and I would gladly have become part of their number, but I was a third son. Such advanced education was not to be wasted on me. My father's investment in my betterment had gone toward shipping me to and from Korinthos and in having me educated in the ways of war.

Because I lived as a military man no stigma existed among my associates and friends concerning my poor abilities to read and write. Most were no more literate than I. However, every time I stood in Archimedes' presence, I felt that I would momentarily be caught out and forever banished from his irascible sight. Now, once again, with this Roman daughter of a man I greatly respected, I felt the curtain being inexorably drawn back on my ignorance.

"As a military man, my depth of knowledge about philosophers is rather restricted," I truthfully told her.

"I understand. I'm not talking about the arcane ones such as Anaxagoras or Empedocles. Surely you've examined the work of Xenophanes of Colophon. Why do you think his assertion that God is one and omnipresent was not adopted?"

I lengthened my stride somewhat to reach her home all the sooner. The old male servant, however, could not be hurried and compelled me to slow again. I had hoped that she would ask questions about Socrates,

Plato, or Aristotle, knowledge of whose thoughts every citizen had drilled into him whether by family or the bit of formal tutelage any child from a modestly successful background receives. Even if she had asked about Epicurus or Zeno, the father of Stoicism, I might have been able to parrot one of the opinions I had heard at dinner or in the baths. However, the only Xenophanes I knew of was the man who served as my second in command for the Silent Storm. I had a sinking feeling that the Xenophanes Aurora asked about was truly ancient. No one I knew spoke of him.

"Why has the Jews' one god not prevailed in their part of the world?" I evaded, calling upon something I had heard while traveling up the Nile.

"Because no one wants a god who cannot protect his own people," Aurora replied.

"It is a matter of believability," I said, stating my own conviction. "How can one god possibly watch over the rivers, the oceans, the sun, the winds, the people, the weather, the harvests?"

Aurora squeezed my arm. "Yes! You are right! It is precisely because the more primitive man imprints his own limitations on the supernatural. It is, after all, vanity that kills the notion of one great deity."

I swallowed her unintended swipe at my intellect and launched an offensive, to prevent her from posing an even more thorny philosophical question. I inquired about the homes we walked by and who lived in them. She freely replied. Soon enough, we stood at her portal.

"I have enjoyed meeting you," Aurora said through a smile conveyed not merely by her lips but by her entire face, which was highly animated if not beautiful. "Will you linger long in Roma?"

"I do not know."

"At least a week?" she asked.

I shriveled inside my clothing. "Yes, at least that long."

"Then I hope I will see you again." She pivoted to enter her home, and then turned back. "A bit of advice: the synthesis you wear is meant only for use inside the home."

I felt myself blush to my roots. "Why did everyone allow me to walk outside like this?"

"I assume Severinus and Cornelia did so because they did not wish to embarrass you in front of me. I said nothing because I enjoyed looking at your arms and legs. Good night, Leonides."

Having said her piece, Aurora vanished inside a domus that even from the street looked more elegant and spacious than that of the tribune. One striking difference was the home's forecourt, which featured a burbling fountain in the center and lush plantings on either side.

The servant bowed his head respectfully before closing and locking the iron gate. I lingered for a minute, leaning against the outer wall. Thalia's house had a forecourt. I closed my eyes and could envision its details. I recalled the phallic herm. I pictured our private moments in the alley off the Ortygian agora. I heard her voice inside my head and the playing of her lute. I dredged up the image of her first smile at me.

With a sigh, I turned toward the house of Severinus.

Δ

For three days, Archimedes and I flattered and cajoled the craftsmen of Roma's warfare shops. In a certain way, I was further disappointed to hear that there had been no startling breakthroughs in siege techniques in recent years. In another way, I was greatly relieved. At the same time every standard machine, including the ancient battering ram, had received improvements. That instrument now featured a practical, thick metal point instead of a blunt, decorative ram's head. Instead of being carried by many men, the ram was quickly rolled up on four wheels. The wheels were chocked, and the ram was immediately swung into action from a framework above. Not surprisingly, this was called a horse. The horse had evolved to be covered with a wooden roof and damp hides or seaweed. This "shell" was called the tortoise. It protected the ram and its engineers from dropped stones and that long-employed mixture of boiling oil and other nasty ingredients invented by my Greek ancestors.

From the defenders' prospective, the ram was now countered by lowering padding from the parapets. Hoists were installed at gates and other weak points, to attempt to grab this more effective ram and haul it up.

To the old attack method of slowly building up an earthen incline to the level of the top of a city wall had been added the laying down of logs in crisscross patterns on either side, to lessen the amount of earth needed. The recommended counters to this tactic were to heighten the wall in that area, to build a second wall behind the targeted section, or to tunnel under the wall from the inside and remove dirt so that the pile collapsed when a mass of soldiers used it for an assault.

We learned that a new strategy had been added to that of sapping, by which was meant tunneling under a city wall and collapsing it. Because the civilized world had learned the value of carrying waste away rather than letting it rot inside cities and attract plagues, any city of size and import now had a sewer system. The Cloaca Maxima of Roma had existed for 300 years. Such giant drains had proven the Achilles heel of several besieged cities. The remedy was to install strong iron bars across the sewer just inside the wall and to inspect the place every few hours. If enemy engineers worked to remove the bars, oil could be floated on the water and then set on fire. The smoke killed them if the fire failed to.

Siege towers on wheels had begun to sport iron-clad sides and hurling instruments on the penthouses. These weapons had advanced the most and fascinated Archimedes. They were fashioned of wood and iron and most often featured compound bows and ratchets. The secret of their throwing power lay in sinews that could be greatly stretched. By demonstration, we saw that such machines could be made to hurl a stone half as heavy as a man half a stadion!

Sharing words is one matter; drawing pictures is another. Inside the shops, we were careful only to speak with the weapons designers and builders and set nothing down. However, as soon as we had returned to Severinus' home we set the various inventions to papyrus. Between the old genius and me, we were able to reproduce designs and proportions of the machines with great accuracy. We felt that our perilous journey to Italia had at last been made worthwhile, and we agreed that to stay another few days could improve our knowledge enough to merit the risk.

Δ

On the morning of our third day in Roma, as we walked toward the Via Sacra to importune the weapons makers, Archimedes and I saw a most disturbing display. A young mother dragged a child not older than three years along the street against its will. It made a great protest. Suddenly, the woman came to a stop, grabbed the child by both shoulders, shook him enough to jolt him into momentary silence, and then in a low but pointedly warning voice said, "Be quiet! Hannibal is at the gate! Do you want him to hear you?"

At this the child's eyes widened with terror. He immediately ceased his crying. I wondered if the woman had invented the threat herself or had heard of its effectiveness from another young matron. Looking at the boy, I had no doubt that Hannibal would soon join the ranks of ghosts, centaurs, and harpies who were employed to cow children.

"Ignorant sow!" Archimedes pronounced after we had passed the scene.

"Perhaps the mothers of Carthage will one day say 'Marcellus is at the gate'," I speculated.

"And they will be just as ignorant. But you would not hear such nonsense in Siracusa. Our women are wiser," Archimedes decided. "I understand Roman women are allowed many more liberties beyond not wearing veils in public. They speak before being spoken to. They contradict their husbands in public."

"They do speak frankly," I said, thinking of Aurora's admission that she enjoyed looking at my physique.

"They speak openly about sex," my great-uncle continued.

"But they are also bred to regard their virtue above all else," I reported, repeating the words of Severinus.

Archimedes snorted. "If you call the sentence of death for adultery a form of breeding, I agree. Do you not think the Roman man would be equally as virtuous if he could be put to death for infidelity?"

Archimedes' desire to debate combined with the subject of women caused me to confide in him. "You know that I dined the other night with the daughter of Marcellus."

"Yes. What is she like?"

"Nothing to look upon. Pleasant enough of disposition. But too curious."

"Curious? About what?"

"Greek philosophers."

"Truly? I wish I could have dined with you."

"I wish you could have as well," I truthfully replied. "Yesterday, she sent an invitation asking me to dine with her at the home of Marcellus tonight. I declined, using business as an excuse."

"Business is not conducted in the evening."

"It was all I could think of. I cannot twice offend the daughter of the great Marcellus," I said. "What shall I do if she sends another invitation?"

"Go."

"But she will want me to discuss philosophers. Xenophanes, for one."

"Xenophanes was no philosopher!" Archimedes said with annoyance. "He was a religious leader and poet. Perhaps she meant Xenocrates, the pupil of Plato."

"Tell me of both," I said. "And then tell me what you know about Anaxagoras and Empedocles."

Archimedes stopped walking. "Does this woman attract you?"

"No, no," I said with emphasis. "I simply do not want to repel her with ignorance. She has a silly illusion that all Greeks are learned, and I do not want to disappoint her."

"All Greeks are learned," Archimedes replied. "All except our soldiers. As we walk to and from each shop, I will instruct you. I am pleased to have you show some intellectual curiosity, if only to impress a Roman woman."

Δ

Aurora's second invitation awaited me that afternoon upon my return to the house of Severinus. Armed with my new knowledge, I sent one of Severinus' slaves to accept. When I arrived that evening, I hoped against hope that I would dine among other guests or relatives.

Aurora alone greeted me.

She wore a dress that the Romans called a palla. It was wrapped much like a toga, but it was gathered under her breasts by a golden band.

The dress itself was shot through with threads of gold, so that it caught the light from the lamps and caused a pleasing, glittering effect.

The first time I met Aurora, she had worn her hair tied back in a bun and fixed with a pin. This evening her hair was fashioned into ringlets in front of her ears and woven behind. A serpent of gold wound itself up her left forearm. Altogether, the changes made her look less severe and more feminine. For my part, I had decided to bow to the Roman style while I was in Roma and have my beard shaved. I drew the line, however, when the barber suggested that he could get rid of the last stubble and keep my beard from growing back for several days if I would let him scrape my face with a pumice stone.

Aurora had been sitting in her father's garden when I arrived at the gate. She did not call for a servant, but let me inside herself. I had brought a bundle of freshly-cut flowers, which I handed to her.

Her mouth curled into a wry smile. "Should I accept these? We are told to 'Beware of Greeks bearing gifts.'"

"That only warns Troizens about gifts of enormous wooden horses," I rejoined. "And that was a long time ago. We have since become much more civilized and trustworthy."

Aurora filled a wide earthen jar with water from the fountain as I spoke and proceeded to arrange the flowers skillfully in the jar. "You have become the most civilized people in the world, in fact. Considering that the Greeks were inside the horse, I always thought the saying should have been 'Beware of gifts bearing Greeks.'"

My laughter caused her to laugh as well. She led me back to her bench. We sat and talked for a long time, accompanied by the soothing murmur of the water fountain. I told her I had finally remembered some facts about various philosophers and doled them out. However, I also warned her that what I shared was the extent of my knowledge. She seemed pleased, as she should have been. I repeated the precious remembrances and opinions of one of the greatest geniuses of the world.

We were summoned to dinner by the same male servant who had come to the house of Severinus to fetch Aurora. Owing to Marcellus' rank among the citizenry and the size of his city domus, I was surprised not to see more slaves scurrying about. Inside the home also waited one woman, who spoke to Aurora with no trace of deference.

I was led along a large peristylum to the dining room. Mosaics decorated the courtyard walls. Aurora explained that they depicted bird's eye views of various cities of the Republic. Inside the triclinium, I marveled at great murals that put the work of my brother to shame. Four huge landscapes completely filled the walls up to the ceilings. The harmony of their composition immediately struck me. Each wall featured a scene captured in a different season. Across from puffy summer clouds raged leaden winter ones. Opposite a dry creek bed and colored leaves, a vigorous spring stream tumbled through verdant foliage. Half hidden within each mural were animals, but they were not easy to find, as if they naturally hid from human viewers.

I told Aurora that my brother was a professional painter. "Most of his efforts depict either the deeds of famous men or of the gods."

"The gods are fictions of idle priest minds," Aurora declared. "And the fewer humans in the world, the better off it would be."

By this time I was not caught off guard by the woman's radical attitudes. "Did your father allow you to dictate the seasonal theme to the artist?" I asked.

"He allowed me to paint whatever I wished. I am the artist."

My head reared back at this news. I recovered as quickly as I could. "I have never heard of a private person painting murals."

"Much less a woman."

"Frankly, yes. But I also frankly tell you that your artistry exceeds that of my brother and the masters who taught him."

"I am flattered." Aurora arranged herself on one of the couches and indicated for me to sit across from her.

The first course had already been set at the table. No one else reclined in the dining room. Only the one woman servant moved in and out, setting and removing the dishes, pouring wine, providing water and towels for our fingers. We dined on crab pounded and peppered and served in a golden broth, on fowl stuffed with leaves and grapes, and on sprouts seasoned with coriander, onion, cumin, pepper, raisin wine and a dash of olive oil. For desert, we ate delicious honey cakes that put those the Siracusan women made to shame. I should say I feasted; Aurora ate lightly.

The meal was one of the best I had ever consumed.

"Do you mean to tell me that only one woman cooked all that?" I asked when we had finished.

Aurora smiled. "No. Haki helped. I did most of the cooking."

I again struggled against my surprise. "You cook wonderfully."

She cocked one eyebrow. "Thank you. You have a question?"

"Does Marcellus keep only two slaves for this huge house?"

"I have four who help me. Two live in another part of the city. None is a slave. I despise slavery." Aurora sat up with her back to the wall. "You are a circumspect man in your speech, which is a laudable attribute. However, I could read between your words the other evening how you feel about our Senate's decision to allow our men to be sold into slavery. Is this because they are fellow soldiers or because you, too, despise the selling of humans as property?"

"I would never allow myself to be made a slave," I vowed, avoiding her question. "Therefore, I can hardly imagine anyone else being happy in such a condition. However, I will not say that I would go so far as to speak out against it."

"Why not?" my hostess asked.

"Because slavery is practiced by most of the world. If I were about to be conquered, I would fight until they were forced to kill me. However, many would rather survive under any condition. Certainly, after an enemy is conquered you cannot simply allow him to continue to live on his land."

"Why not?" she asked again.

"Because he would rise up later. Moreover, he would rise up with vengeance."

"Take his weapons from him. Station armed garrisons in his land, and pay for those garrisons with a tax. Tax him well for losing."

"Both difficult," I replied, uncomfortable with the subject and wanting to put an end to it.

Aurora shook her head slowly. "It makes me sad to hear a Greek man say these things. Your ancestors invented the concept of individual freedom. By what justification or mental equivocation can they keep slaves?"

125

"Precisely because of what I have said." I thought back to arguments I had heard defending slavery. "If this were not a just solution, Socrates, Plato, and Aristotle would have argued against it, would they not?"

Aurora's lips pursed. I thought I had finally silenced her. Then she said, "I must admit that Socrates' silence on this subject, given that he was willing to die rather than suffer banishment for his opinions, confuses me. Plato unfortunately did not speak out either. However, he once said that 'a slave is an embarrassing possession.' Aristotle I believe was afraid to speak out. But he knew it was wrong. He wrote, 'There are people who consider owning slaves as violating natural laws because the distinction between a slave and a free person is wholly conventional and has no place in nature, so that it rests on mere force and is devoid of justice.'"

"These are direct quotations?" I asked, considerably impressed.

Aurora nodded. "I did not receive these second-hand, but read them myself from Greek scrolls. You who know about so many other philosophers should not be content merely to draw on Socrates and his legacy for opinions. What about Euripides, who said, 'Slavery is that thing of evil, by its nature evil. Forcing submission from a man to what no man should yield to.' Your Stoics consider it the greatest wrong committed by one man against another."

I drew in a fortifying breath. "To bring this full circle, you say you supervise the servants in this household, and none of them is a slave."

"Precisely. I strive to live by my conscience and the natural laws of justice."

"Does your father keep slaves?"

"He does. They work the estates he owns. However, he allows his daughter to act upon her convictions, which is a rare quality for a Roman man. Do you keep slaves?"

I was glad to say that I did not. I told her that I had but one servant, and he was old and slow of wit. I admitted that my parents owned some slaves, but I also told her that my father paid them enough that they could buy their freedom within seven or eight years. I made a point of telling her that two former slaves had elected to stay on in our employ after purchasing their freedom.

I did not feel that Aurora left me at her front gate with as much enthusiasm as she greeted me. This did not make me happy. At the same time it did not upset me. I had labored to please her in order to indirectly please her father. If she spoke to him about my less-than-revolutionary attitudes toward slavery, I was sure that he would take my side.

When she closed the gate after me, Marcellus' daughter did not speak of another invitation.

CHAPTER X

S ix weeks to the day after Archimedes and I departed Siracusa, all my personal Fates converged on Roma to play sport with me. The morning passed with no extraordinary occurrence. We began it by walking slowly, as if meandering, past both the inner and outer sides of Roma's defensive walls, noting how they had originally been built and how modifications were being made. When we could view no more without attracting attention we headed down to the Tiber, to interview boatmen who had come up from Ostia, to see if they knew when the next convoy would sail for Sicilia or at least Neapoli. According to two of their number, the next fleet sailing south would occur four days hence.

We then visited some sites of Roma that I had not yet viewed. I was particularly interested in seeing the spoils that Marcellus had dedicated to Jupiter Feretrius following his single combat victory over the Gallic chieftain. That highly polished helmet and shield were not the only articles of battle hanging on the temple walls. Despite myself being a soldier, I marveled at the irony of men fervently petitioning peace and prosperity from the gods by offering items of discord and death to encourage favor.

128

While we stood inside the temple, a rite of sacrifice was in progress. Rows of onlookers surrounded the priests. As the pungent smoke curled toward the hole in the temple roof, the high priest called heavenward in a booming voice.

"God of Death and War, bring infernal terrors to the city of Carthage. Visit plague upon its army, its people, and its generals. Let the earth open and swallow them. Let them be consumed in fire."

I watched the crowd nodding their assent fiercely. Roma was a city aflame with the human passion for revenge.

Δ

It was not until early afternoon in the food markets down by the Tiber that events and people began to converge to direct my life. As in Greek cities, the daily shopping is generally done in Roma by the man of the house. Since there was no patriarch at Marcellus' house and as Aurora was so independent, she happened to come to the stalls of the Macellum market soon after we did. Archimedes' attention was fixed on the purchase of a bronze measuring instrument that lay among all manner of disparate paraphernalia, and I observed his technique as any good apprentice watches his master.

"That is the finest example of its type in the world," the seller proclaimed in passable Greek when Archimedes picked it up. "200 denarii is entirely fair."

"Show me how it works," Archimedes challenged.

The man struggled with the instrument.

"As I thought," my great-uncle crowed. "If you have no idea how to work it, how can you know its value? 100 denarii."

The man threw up his hands in a gesture fit for an amphitheater. "100? The thing came from Korinthos! I paid 130 myself!"

"Then you were robbed because of your ignorance. 110."

The man took the instrument out of Archimedes' hand. "Impossible. You think I do not know workmanship when I see it? And I have never seen another of its kind, which means it is rare. Not for one denarius less than 150."

"I will make due with the one I already own. I paid 100 denarii for mine," Archimedes said to me in a clearly audible whisper. He reached for my arm to turn me around. "Come!"

"You say I was robbed in purchasing this?" the shop owner complained to our backs. "Would you compound my sorrow by having me robbed twice over the same item? 135, and that's my final offer."

"130, and at least you will have lost nothing for your foolishness," Archimedes answered.

The owner held out his hand. "Deal!"

Archimedes opened his purse and counted out the agreed-upon denarii. As he took the instrument into his possession, a low-pitched voice sounded from behind us.

"Nicely done," praised the familiar feminine voice.

Both the old man and I whirled around. I had a sick feeling that Aurora had been watching the bargaining for some time.

"Good day, Mistress Aurora," I said, erecting a bluff face.

"Good day. Is this your traveling companion then?" she asked.

I could not lie for fear of being exposed by some other trick of bad fortune. "Yes, he is. Alonzo, please meet the daughter of Marcus Claudius Marcellus."

Archimedes knew better than to lapse into a sudden seizure of stupidity. He bowed gracefully. "I am charmed."

"I understand that you are a freeman," Aurora said to my great-uncle.

"That is correct," he answered.

"And did you earn your freedom with such hard bargaining?" she asked.

"As a matter of fact, he did," I said.

I watched Aurora's unveiled lips curling down. She addressed me. "Curious, then, that your servant has a reputation for being slow of mind. Did you not say so to me yourself?"

"Sometimes when we travel, I have a reputation for being deaf instead," Archimedes replied for me. "All travelers are at a disadvantage in foreign lands. Master Leonides has evolved these ruses for me so that he may learn more than is offered his own eyes and ears."

Once again, Aurora looked at me. "Very clever of you. But why are you purchasing the instrument of a mathematician?"

"It will be a gift to my great-uncle. He is Archimedes."

Now Aurora's assessing eyes shifted to my old companion, even as she continued to speak to me. "Truly? How wonderful for you! You are too modest in keeping such a relation a secret. Apparently, you surround yourself with brilliant men."

Archimedes, annoying me greatly, could not resist bowing at the compliment.

I said, "My father taught me always to associate with those more clever than I, even if they are servants. Would you like Alonzo to bargain for you?"

"No. I manage well enough, thank you."

"Master, we should be going," said "Alonzo," coming up to rescue me. "You will be late for that appointment if we tarry."

"Quite so," I agreed and excused us. We walked away at a stroll. Neither of us dared to look back in case Marcellus' observant daughter still watched.

"Who will she speak to about this?" Archimedes worried.

"She is all but a recluse," I assured him. "But we must devise a reason for a quick departure. I do not want to wait four days for that convoy."

"It would be a pity to have gained so much knowledge for Siracusa, only to die in Roma," Archimedes said, as he held his hand palm up. "You should have presented a bigger offering at the temple; it has begun to rain."

Δ

The news could not have been worse when we returned to the house of Severinus. Generally the wealthy Romans support a host of clients and hangers on, and Severinus was no exception. Since his return to the city, he had spent at least an hour every morning listening to their complaints, schemes, and petitions. This day, he had been so mercilessly assailed that he had put off one interview until the afternoon. So it was that he was escorting out a harried-looking man whom he addressed as Cotilus as we entered his home.

"I have the most interesting information to share!" the tribune exclaimed, as soon as he returned to the atrium, where I sat waiting. "Marcus Claudius has returned to Roma!"

I felt the crucifixion nails pounding into my hands.

"He barely left!" I exclaimed. "What could compel such a swift return?"

"Do you know of Nola?"

"It is a town of middling size."

"But of strategic value. Not one to lose," Severinus said. "A number of its inhabitants are militating for a popular uprising to push out our presence and to turn the town over to Hannibal. This would be one disaster too many."

"I take it this is not a Roman town."

"No. We have had allegiances with the southern Campanians for so long, no need was felt to establish colonies there. Now we pay the price."

"Why does Marcellus not take the town?"

"You know better than you did a month ago that siege is difficult and protracted. Marcellus cannot move against Nola without the express order of the dictator. He returns to Roma for that purpose."

Again, owing to the dire crisis, another dictator had been appointed for six months. This one was named Marcus Junius Pera.

Severinus added, "The Roman people expect Pera to supervise personally such an operation if it proves necessary. One reason they have elected him is that he is a cautious man. They are still smarting from following Varro's strategy of engagement. Marcellus needs to address the Senate and impress upon them the desperate situation, so that they will shove Pera out of our gates. He is too clever and prudent to make decisions on his own that might ruin him."

I thought then how I lived in terrible times. While Severinus spoke, I watched the runoff of the rain from the roof dropping into catch basins elevated on either side of the central pool. Looking up through the exposed space in the center of the house, I could see dark and angry clouds racing across the heavens.

"Rain is good in the late summer," Severinus remarked. "At any rate, Marcellus has been given leave to address the Senate tomorrow. He expects to linger in Roma no more than two days. He does me the honor of dining with us tonight."

I looked forward to reuniting with the great soldier. Among other things I had learned while in the capital city was that Marcus Claudius Marcellus had twice served as its consul. The last was six years earlier, directly after his stunning victory over the Gauls. His modesty had prevented him from making any reference to this great honor when I first met him. What I did not look forward to was the prospect of seeing his daughter at his side and my presence possibly inspiring her to tell the story of my brilliant manservant who bargained so well for a mathematical tool on the behalf of Archimedes. I asked if Aurora would accompany her father.

"Certainly. I could not very well invite the father on his first night home without inviting the daughter. I hope this pleases you."

"I like her well enough," I replied, being polite.

As I contemplated this impending calamity, the Fates introduced another player onto the stage of my personal tragedy. We heard a rapping on the front door. Severinus' male servant answered.

A small, elderly gentleman with a pronounced pot belly entered the atrium.

"Augustus Terentius!" Severinus exclaimed, rising with arms open. I stood as well.

"It is good to see you, my friend," the old fellow declared as he allowed himself to be warmly embraced. "Especially after thinking of all the friends gone through the Collina gate who will never return."

"Yes, terrible indeed," said the tribune. He introduced me with his usual enthusiasm.

"Then I have indeed come to the right place," said Terentius. "A high-level ambassador has just arrived from Siracusa, and he seeks out a man and his servant. The man he seeks stands before me."

"Do you know this ambassador's name?" I inquired.

"Timon."

"A man about sixty years of age with a hooked nose and deep wrinkles about his eyes?" I qualified.

Terentius nodded. "And a bridge between his front teeth."

I nodded. This was not a mere ambassador but Hieron's chief minister. Only the most dire circumstances could have drawn Timon to Roma. This, swift upon the heels of the gifts of fifty shiploads of grain and a golden statue. I felt perspiration break out on my forehead, and there was nothing I could do to stop it.

"Several men volunteered to search you out," Terentius told me. "Whoever succeeds is to bring you to the Senaculum."

Δ

I fetched Archimedes, and we followed the old Roman with haste to the center of the city. We found Timon pacing inside the small public building. As soon as we were alone, he gestured for us to follow him. We walked with him into the rain.

"The walls may have ears," he warned. "I am glad at least to see you both safe. Have you learned what you came here to learn?"

We assured him that we had.

Timon pinched the bridge of his nose, as if to forestall a headache. "That at least is good news. Gelon has died."

I could not say that I was surprised in any way. At the ceremony where Archimedes and the king moved the huge galley, Hieron's son looked as if the shades of Hades were fastening themselves to his heels.

"He had been bleeding for some time," Timon expanded. "It was not a good death, but he bore it bravely. The real tragedy is that Hieron himself does poorly. Naturally, the death of Gelon was a great shock to him. But the man is also approaching ninety. Would that his body were half as hale as his mind. If he lives another year, the populace of Siracusa will be fortunate indeed. In the meantime, he has set out explicit instructions on the course of actions we are to take to protect our city. That is why I am here."

I gave him a nod of understanding, prompting him to go on.

"I understand that tomorrow the Senate holds session," Timon said.

I confirmed this.

"As soon as day breaks, I will begin my campaign to see that our statue of Victory is accepted by the Roman people. There must be no question whatsoever as to the mutual admiration of the people of Roma and Siracusa."

Timon had always been known as Siracusa's foremost promoter of subservience to the Republic. The first thought that went through my head upon hearing his words was that the man was exploiting the death of Gelon and Hieron's infirmity for his own purposes. I was not completely dissuaded from this opinion even after hearing his next words.

Timon said, "Four days after Hannibal's victory at Cannae, a galley arrived with the news. I must tell you that it produced a change in the attitude of our people like that of a sudden sea wind. Fully half of the city believes that the Carthaginians will win this war."

"Has the shift been loud enough for Roman spies to hear?" Archimedes asked.

"More than loud enough."

"This was the reason for the extra grain and the gift of Victory," Archimedes concluded.

"Yes. We had to reassure the Romans that at least those who control the city remain loyal."

"After what we personally witnessed, I may be counted among those who doubt the Romans will win," I admitted. I briefly outlined my reasons.

"And your thoughts, Archimedes?" Timon asked.

"I do not believe that victory is guaranteed for either side, but we have no long-standing peace treaty with Carthage. We do with Roma, and this is no secret to the Carthaginians. It makes most sense to stay as we are until compelled to change," my great-uncle said.

"Exactly so!" Timon said to him with enthusiasm. "I would have you back home as soon as possible to spread your thoughts. Everything possible must be done to quell the rise of anti-Roman sentiment.

Timon pointed to the rain-soaked plaza. "On this front, every effort must be made as well. I am not convinced that the statue will be accepted. In order to ingratiate us further, I have brought with me ten young men. All are unmarried. All are of better families of Siracusa

which are unquestionably loyal to Hieron and in favor of our city continuing as a Roman ally." Timon named the young men. I knew of half.
Menander from the Silent Storm was among them.

"I have done this speculatively," said Timon, "but my idea is to offer
these young men as husbands to the wives of men sold into slavery. This
will at least save these women from poverty and remove them from
Roma, so that they will no longer serve as reminders of defeat. I know
that the Romans disapprove of their citizens marrying non-citizens, but
these women have inherited their husbands' disgrace. I trust this will en-
dear us to the Senate."

"This will prove a difficult adjustment to both our young men and the
Roman women," I judged.

"It will. It is not a sacrifice lightly made," said Timon. "But it is the
will of their fathers, and thus it cannot be refused." He cleared his throat
and lowered his eyes. "I bring news to you specifically, Leonides."

"My family is well?" I worried.

"Yes. They are fine. This is news of another family. Thalia, the
daughter of Eustace, is now engaged to Cleomenes."

My heart felt as if it had been ripped from my chest. I struggled to
find voice, but for a moment could not draw a breath.

"When did this happen?" I asked.

"Two weeks ago. Cleomenes was one of the most vocal proponents
for changing our allegiance to Carthage."

I watched Archimedes step back from me, as if allowing room for my
patent agony.

"What does that have to do with Thalia?" I asked, too stunned by the
moment to reason it out myself.

"Eustace is loyal to Hieron. He does whatever the king asks. Thalia
was offered as a prize to silence Cleomenes and secure his loyalty."

Finally, my brain began to function again. "Why do you tell me
this?" I said, more a demand than a question.

"We learned about the mutual pledge of love between you and the
daughter."

"And do you not wish to maintain my loyalty?" I nearly shouted.

"You are a soldier of Siracusa. Your loyalty is assumed."

"And I am a nothing in comparison to Cleomenes' power. He can dictate his opinion to his hundreds of workers."

"True enough," Timon granted. "You had no chance with Eustace's favorite child."

"How did you learn of our love?"

"That is a state secret. Do you understand why I have chosen this moment to deliver such bad news myself, rather than letting you wait until you return home and learn it yourself?"

Now anger poured out beside my sorrow. Insult was being added to injury. "I also am to marry a Roman woman."

"That is correct. I thought you should know about the daughter of Eustace, to make this acceptance easier. Your father has offered you as husband for the good of the city. I have the scroll with his sign among my possessions. There is also a scroll from Hieron petitioning your cooperation with this necessary action."

I had no more chance of gainsaying my father than Thalia had had with hers. I lowered my head in resignation. Anger and sorrow, however, continued to flow like molten lava, turning hope to ash.

"You will begin to live again when you forget the daughter of Eustace," Timon counseled with a gentle voice, as if he had read my mind. "In truth, you both conjured an impossible dream." He patted my shoulder with affected sympathy. "Better to let it die now. Fix your goals elsewhere. There are positive aspects in this turn of events. In recognition of your sacrifice, Hieron has decreed that your temporary rank is to be made permanent, along with the salary. This is also awarded for willingly exposing yourself to the dangers of this journey. Remember that you can divorce the woman chosen for you at a suitable time. What do the Romans call their document of marital dissolution?"

"A letter of repudiation," I said.

"Just so. Any excuse will do: She is a shrew; she has grown ugly; certainly if she is childless. That, of course, is up to you."

"But if this is a woman with children?" I said. "What would become of a Roman woman in a Greek city with no support?"

Timon shrugged. "What would become of her now in Roma? If her parents or in-laws choose not to help her, she and her children will go on the dole. If times grow worse, they will starve. She should be grateful to escape to Siracusa and to have a fine man like you protecting her."

Before I could torture myself and Timon with more questions, Archimedes stepped back into view.

"Much as I empathize, talk will not better this situation. Can we not get out of this rain?" he said. "One more matter must be broached here: Leonides and I are in danger of being exposed at any minute." In terse fashion, he spoke of the bargaining in the market and Aurora's chance witnessing.

Timon's cheeks puffed out in exasperation. "This, too, shall have to be dealt with. Fortunately, I have agents in the city. She must be silenced as quickly as possible."

I looked at Archimedes with great agitation.

The old man shrugged. "You wanted me to help defend our city? I agree with Timon. It is not merely our lives weighed against hers. The fate of Siracusa may lie in the balance."

Δ

The bed I was given to use at the house of Severinus had taut rope webbing and fine mattress stuffing. Nevertheless, when I lay down to nap before dinner I could find no rest. The dilemma of how to save me and Archimedes without harming Aurora might have confounded even King Solomon. In order to forestall action and to prevent some ill-timed plot, I had informed Timon that Aurora's father was now at home and that any attempt at murder in his domus would result either in his death or the deaths of the agents. The chief minister absorbed this intelligence without comment and did not deign to share his thinking with me. I further informed him that both Marcellus and Aurora would dine with Severinus, Cornelia, and me that evening. My deferentially-delivered suggestion was that Timon wait to give the order for death until Marcellus was occupied addressing the Senate. I knew that this consummate politician's nod in response might only mean that he understood what I advised, not that he would choose to act upon it.

Sleep also contended with my miserable thoughts about Thalia. I wondered how she had received the news of an undesired union with Cleomenes. Images of her in the quarry master's arms swam into my head unbidden. Between thinking of her fate and that of Aurora, my head throbbed.

Never had I felt so impotent.

Δ

Toward dusk, the great warrior and former consul arrived with Aurora on his arm. Unlike his daughter's previous arrival with only an aged servant, Marcellus was escorted by two armed men who looked like they could have bested a battalion. When they assured themselves that the house was secure, they posted themselves outside the front gate for the remainder of the evening.

"You have impressed my daughter," Marcellus confided shortly after arriving. "This is no mean feat."

"I am similarly impressed by her," I truthfully answered, assiduously avoiding Aurora's eyes. "Her skills at cooking and painting alone make her an unforgettable woman. Add to that her ability to read and her knowledge of poetry, literature, and philosophy, and she is unique among her gender."

"Yes, remarkable accomplishments for a woman," Marcellus said, without letting go of his daughter's arm. "But let us speak about a truly important subject. You have heard from Severinus of my difficulties in the south?"

I told him I had.

"In the wake of Cannae, some southern confederates have defected. Others will follow. I fear that we will lose by next spring twenty per cent of the territory we use to recruit soldiers. Some members of the Senate are about to propose that we free virtually all the prisoners and allow them to fight for their freedom. This would provide us with enough men to fill two legions."

"How many people do you estimate are held in Siracusa's prisons, Leonides?" Aurora broke in.

"About 400," I answered.

"You see?" she said to her father. "They hold 400, and we hold more than enough for two legions! Either our laws are too harsh or our system fails its people, or both. But what can we expect from a people who keep a flock of sacred chickens in their capital to predict the future?"

Marcellus held up his forefinger in warning to his daughter. "What do you think of this idea?" he asked me.

"I suppose I would at least give them the choice."

"Why do that?" said Aurora. "They are meant to die, just rough stones to grind away some of Hannibal's army. And think of all the bread we will save when they are dead!" She knew that her second interruption had crossed the line, and she moved away from her father as quickly as she could and sat by herself at the edge of the atrium pool.

"I have been too indulgent with her," Marcellus apologized. "Her mother died when she was eight. I was always away. When I returned home I could not find the heart to speak crossly to her. She needs beating."

I held my tongue.

Marcellus looked briefly at his child, shook his head, and then turned back to me. "Other senators suggest that we make a similar offer to some of the more fit slaves. An offer of freedom if they defeat Hannibal. Do you think this is a dangerous precedent?"

I told the commander that if I were a consul and could gather an overwhelming force against Hannibal, I would employ it as swiftly as I could, before his army had time to recover fully from Cannae and before he had time to recruit more allies.

"I personally am unsure," Marcellus confided. "I am glad to leave this in the hands of the Senate. Now that Hannibal has shown he is not yet ready to attack Roma, I am to be given the 20th and 21st legions from the city. This is good news. My work here is to see that Marcus Junius Pera is sent into the field. My hands are tied without him in the south making quick decisions."

A few hours earlier, I had beseeched Archimedes not to show his face during the dinner party. The last thing we needed was to remind Aurora about his gifted bargaining skills and what he bargained for. Mercifully, he seemed to have eclipsed himself.

Severinus joined us. The discussion moved to the need to keep vital towns open to guard lines of communication and supply.

Marcellus said, "While this is being done, I personally intend to lead the cavalry to hound Hannibal's rear guard and his supply trains at every turn. I will not let him rest. The word is that he fears my name. I intend to use my reputation to prevent him from breathing."

"So long as you are not rash," Severinus counseled. "This man is a maker of traps. You must not be drawn into one. You are far too important to lose."

"Yes, yes," the old commander said, which was his way of silencing the tribune's chides.

Severinus was called away by his wife.

"Do you know why Aurora remains in my house?" Marcellus asked as soon as we were again alone.

"I suppose she is a great treasure, and you wish to have someone you can trust managing your home while you are gone," I ventured.

"Not at all. She is a Claudius. This should make her a treasure under any circumstances. But no Roman of aristocratic blood will have such an opinionated, outspoken woman." He snapped his fingers at his daughter and crooked his finger to bring her to our side.

"Have you bored Leonides with your low opinion of Roman men?"

"I leave that to you, Father. You know my opinions better than I," she responded.

"In that you are correct, since I have had to endure them over and over and over. There are certain foolish people, Leonides, who believe that any other race, any other place, and any other time are superior to their own."

"I am not of that class," Aurora bristled, although the sound of her protest was weak.

"Or is it only anything that is Greek is superior to anything Roman?" Marcellus goaded.

"We are a people consumed by property and possessions," she said to both her father and me. "Our greatest arts are practicality and pragmatism. The Greeks had and have their priorities straight. They play as much as they work. They laugh as much as they cry. They exercise their minds as much as their bodies."

"My daughter sings this song to anyone who will listen. She tells everyone about the sayings carved into the pediments of the sacred temple at Delphi: Do Nothing Too Much and Know Thyself. And yet she lectures far too much. She also forgets herself. She forgets that she is a Roman woman and seeks to be Greek. She does not weave as every woman should, but rather spends her time reading Greek treatises and essays. Reading, reading, reading."

"You bring me the scrolls," Aurora said softly.

"Because it is the only way I can get you to smile."

"If I love the Greek mind and way of life better than ours, it is your doing," she accused.

Marcellus nodded several times. "So it is. I have passed on my love of Greek virtues to you. But I have never forgotten that I am a Roman. I have not forgotten that we, too, are a great people." He looked at me. "You are a level-headed man, Leonides. What shall I do with this woman?"

"Give her to me," I said.

Marcellus laughed. "Is this spoken truly?"

Aurora blinked in astonishment. I averted my eyes from her.

"Yes, truly," I said. "I would have her."

Marcellus pivoted and called out loud for his long-time tribune friend. Severinus appeared through the triclinium doorway.

"What is wrong?" he asked.

"Now here is a startlingly turn of events. Did you not feel the world move a moment ago?" asked Marcellus. "What do you think of me giving Aurora to Leonides to be wed?"

Without the slightest hesitation, Severinus said, "An excellent notion, if he will take her. She will not have any Roman man, and no Roman man will have her."

Aurora's eyes pooled with tears. She turned to flee the group.

"I have not dismissed you," Marcellus said.

Aurora stopped in mid-stride, with her chin raised and jaw set.

"Not being her father, perhaps you will have the courage to beat her," Marcellus told me. "I will even give you a choice: You may opt for the more formal marriage. With this, I will provide a generous dowry. Or, if you fear you can control her no better than I, you may opt for usus."

Aurora drew in her breath sharply at her father's words. Her eyelids batted swiftly. I knew before another sentence had been spoken that he had insulted her.

"With usus, you need only take her into your house and to your bed," Marcellus explained. "If you allow her to spend at least three nights within the year outside of your house, either you or she may reclaim your freedom."

I was dumbfounded that the noble father of this intelligent and highly sensitive woman would suggest that I take his daughter as did the most lowly plebians, in common law marriage.

"I formally accept engagement," I told Marcellus.

"Bravely said!" Severinus exclaimed. "And for your courage, I shall add to Marcellus' dowry with a purse of coins. But do not think I do this because I owe you my life, Father."

Marcellus offered me his hand, and I took it.

"My good host," Marcellus said to the tribune, "send your swiftest slave to fetch an aedile before our young Greek comes to his senses. Sempronius lives but four or five doors down. He will do to formalize the engagement. We shall make this night truly memorable."

By this time, tears streamed down Aurora's cheeks.

"Why do you cry, daughter?" Marcellus asked. "Does this not realize your fondest wish, to have a worthy Greek husband and to live in a Greek city?"

"I cry because I shall miss you, Father."

At this, Marcellus gathered his daughter into his arms. I saw that his eyes, too, brimmed with tears. As quickly as they appeared, he blinked them away.

In spite of my unremitting misery, one tiny part of me was happy with this decision. In both Greek and Roman society, the engagement and not the marriage ceremony was the legally binding part of the agreement. The marriage had to do with receiving blessings from the gods for peace, prosperity, and progeny. It provided an opportunity for family and friends to share the joy—if there was any. But those who were poor did not even celebrate. Engagement was enough. Once the woman's father gave her to her husband, she was his property. As such, she could not testify against him or in any way incriminate him.

I took Aurora's hand in mine and drew her aside. "You understand that you can say nothing about me, my doings, my possessions or servants from this point forward, even if you are asked by a high judge?"

I was surprised that she showed no confusion by what should have seemed a strange question.

"I understand perfectly," she said.

While we waited for the aedile, who had both governmental and religious authority, I found the opportunity to slip into the back of the house and find Archimedes. I told him of the astonishing events which had just passed. He received the news with no comment. I further directed him to leave the house the moment the hosts and guests retired to the dining chamber, to find Timon and break the news. At least, I reflected, the sport of the Fates had allowed Aurora to live, had spared Archimedes and me from exposure, and had kept Siracusa safe from Roman attack.

CHAPTER XI

I ronically, I became more impressed with Roma after I left it. As our group boated down the Tiber to Ostia, I noted that both sides of the river were dotted with prosperous towns and villages. Moreover, while Siracusa's two harbors had more space, the harbor of Ostia serviced twice as many vessels, hailing from dozens of ports. The vitality of the port city was unmistakable. Its lighthouse was the second biggest one I had seen, after that of Alexandria. Evidence of military activity could be viewed on roads, wharfs, docks, and ships.

I left Roma in the company of Archimedes and my new wife. With us went Timon, who was as anxious to return to Siracusa as I. He had by his side two guards, who may very well have been the agents he would have sent to murder Aurora. One of our secondary ministers was left behind with the ten young sons of Siracusan citizens, to negotiate their engagements to women who would now have the horror of losing their husbands compounded by moving to a foreign city where few spoke Latin.

To Move the World

The golden statue of Victory had been accepted by the Roman Senate, which greatly satisfied and relieved Timon. The mutual love of the two great cities was proclaimed and set down in document. Special trade agreements were approved. Mutual protection was reassured by both sides, although Timon declined to put his signet to wax regarding this last business.

On board with us went two large trunks carrying Aurora's clothing, jewelry, toilet and health articles, and cooking equipment. A large wooden closet went as well, along with two chairs with backs, a pair of high bronze oil lamps, a table, and her bed. There came as well a large linen satchel with a shoulder strap which she insisted on carrying herself. In this lay sixteen scrolls. Each was protected by a wooden cylinder. Their combined weight caused the little woman to list to one side when she walked. She transferred the bundle often from shoulder to shoulder but refused to turn it over to anyone else's care.

Seven of her scrolls had been purchased at great price by her father. These were all works of Greek poets and philosophers. The other nine she had created by having her father borrow texts on his reputation, then laboriously copying every one of their words herself. These as well were written in my tongue, although not all the authors were themselves Greek. Two were histories. One was a treatise on medicine. Two were philosophical works. The remainder were plays. These facts I learned before and during the voyage, not because I cared to know, but rather because Aurora was intent on me knowing.

I carried my military equipment onboard and left old Archimedes, who was compelled to maintain his false persona a bit longer, to see after my clothing and the rest of my kit. I also carried a large box made of beautifully inlaid wood which had a daunting lock. The box held the combined dowries of Marcellus and Severinus. If I remained married to Aurora for three years, I would not need to return the sums to either man.

The fleet we departed with was enormous. It was bound for Neapoli with trade, with provisions for the peninsular army and with the two legions freed up from defending Roma. No fewer than sixty triremes and quinqueremes protected our seaward side. Amazingly, the same port had

146

only a few weeks earlier sent out more fighting galleys, to join with others from their base in Sicilia. Together, this armada of 120 warships was to commence a random patrol of Sardinia, Corsica, and the coast of Africa.

The new Carthaginian fleet of 70 ships had scored a recent triumph in overtaking a small convoy ferrying Roman envoys to Hispania. It had also beached on the west coast of Italia well above Ostia and raided as far inland as Pisa. Hannibal's escapades were not the only Carthaginian offenses. Two leviathans ranged upon the waves, and a gigantic sea battle seemed inevitable when one finally found the other. The only element that could forestall such action other than the Fates was the season. The Mediterranean is ever an uncontrollable highway, but generally in the late spring to early fall it is clement. Once the days become shorter than the nights, it grows restless and hungry. Then entire fleets can be swallowed in a single hour, no matter their size.

Owing to the rising sentiment in Siracusa against Roma, Timon had elected to leave our home city not via the royal galley, but rather onboard a simple trading vessel. It was this same Siracusan ship we took for our homeward voyage. The curve of its front and back ends brought them considerably higher above the waterline than its middle. The rear also held four tiny compartments. One of these went to Aurora and me; another to Timon; the third to Timon's guards and "Alonzo." If these guards recognized my great-uncle as one of the living treasures of their city, they were well enough trained to say nothing.

At the opposite end of the ship lay compartments in which Aurora's belongings had been stored. Since the vessel had delivered its cargo of grain and olive oil, it rode high in the water. Little else occupied the main hold beside ballast stones and six donkeys. These beasts were no different than those found across the length and breadth of Sicilia. Their presence seemed strange to me, but I refrained from posing the question.

The leg of the voyage from Ostia to Neapoli took but one day. We saw many fishing boats near the shoreline, but nothing out in the deep. The weather was clear. I had thought that the time would pass uneventfully. However, at one point Timon and his guards stood on the starboard side while Archimedes, Aurora, and I stood on the other. It

147

was at this moment that Aurora, who had been as silent and contemplative as I during the previous three days, chose to speak.

"The pretense must end sooner or later," she said. "Can I not begin to call Alonzo Archimedes now, or must I wait?"

Archimedes laughed deeply, keeping his eyes fixed on the shoreline.

"When did you know?" I asked.

She fixed her eyes on mine. "Would you believe me if I said that it was in the market?"

"No," I admitted. "I believe when I commanded your silence directly after we became engaged."

"You are wrong," she said flatly. The slightest hint of a smile curled one side of her lips.

"Am I? Then if you knew that one of us had entered Roma under false identity, why would you not tell the authorities?"

"For what purpose should I speak? To have you exposed and unbalance the delicate alliance between our cities?" She turned to Archimedes. "You are one of the greatest minds of our time, sir. I wish you to judge if the logic of my words prove that I could know your identity and still not speak of it."

"I am delighted to serve," said Archimedes. He stepped around so that Aurora could address us both at once.

"Assume I tell the truth about guessing your identity in the marketplace. What goes through my mind then? I say to myself: Here are two men, clearly Greek and clearly from Siracusa. One is a military man. The other is a genius in disguise, known to employ science for practical purpose. What could they want in Roma that Roma might not willingly give them? Could it be secrets of warfare? Could it be defensive weaknesses of Roma? And why would they want such secrets? To attack my city? To consider that Siracusa, which has such a long history of peacefulness, would send a force to attack Roma is lunacy. Are they then agents for the Carthaginians? I do not think so. Perhaps the soldier might be, if he was so ordered. But not the great Archimedes. He would only work on behalf of his own city. Leonides freely admits to Severinus and others that he wishes to learn the latest art of siege and siege defense. However, he always moves about with his servant at his arm. You both spend your days on the Via Sacra. If you do not wish to attack Roma, then you wish to defend Siracusa. I ask myself if I wish you to succeed in your plot. What do I say?"

"You clearly allow it," I answered.

"And why?" Aurora continued.

Archimedes said, "Because you do not like war. You do not like the ways of your people."

"Exactly! And because, while I have never seen it, I suspect that Siracusa is a wonderful city. It does not wage war on other races or even across its own island. It embodies all the strengths of Greek culture without the weakness of the old Greek warring states. I say to myself: Such a city should be allowed to defend itself. I am most pleased, therefore, not to tell anyone about the presence of Archimedes."

"Thank you," said my old companion. "I judge that you indeed knew me in the market." He took Aurora's hand and kissed it. She broke into a beaming smile.

In the space of three breaths I thought first of Thalia, then of the unavoidable commands of my king and father to wed, then of the many women without husbands in Roma I might have had a choice of wedding, ones younger, taller, more beautiful, less contentious and opinionated than the one standing in front of me.

As if she knew how angry I was at both her and the situation I had been placed in, Aurora confessed, "I held my tongue for you as much as for Archimedes, Leonides. Even if I thought you would give information to the Carthaginians, I would not have betrayed you."

I thought then of how she had betrayed me by not admitting all this before I asked her father for her hand. "You were a traitor to your city and your own father."

"My thoughts and actions have made me a traitor a thousand times over," she affirmed. "Roma is overjoyed to be rid of me."

And now I was tethered to her.

"And if I think or do things you do not agree with, will the vows of marriage prevent you from betraying me?" I asked.

I prepared myself for any of half a dozen reactions. One might have been a bold admission that she would indeed work against my will. Another might have been just as bold a repudiation. A third might have been more deep reasoning to reassure me. Instead, Aurora said, "When you know my heart as well as you believe you know my head, you will never again think that." Immediately she took herself away, to stand on the ship's starboard side.

"You are thinking that the woman tricked you into marrying her," Archimedes said. "And you are resenting her for it, are you not?"

"Why shouldn't I?" I fumed.

"Because she presents a cornucopia of good traits. I do not know this Siracusan woman you loved, but I would be astonished if she is more of a woman than Aurora."

"She is twice the woman," I affirmed. Since he gave me the opportunity, I rattled off Thalia's many strengths, including beauty, intelligence, and musical ability.

"Then you really must introduce me," Archimedes said. "If I were your age, I would have used my wit to have gotten this one away from you. I looked in vain my entire life for one such as this."

"Why? Because she owns scrolls and argues about philosophy and drama?"

"Precisely."

"She is a man in a woman's body."

"What is wrong with that? Do you particularly like the normal woman's mind? And it is not such an unpleasing body after all."

"Not when compared with Thalia," I said. "You only know her surface."

"That alone is fascinating," he rejoined, not put off at all by my bitter reply. "With many women, they are no more than they appear. This one has depth of character. You, my great-nephew, will have the privilege of getting to delve beneath that surface." He raised and lowered his hoary eyebrows several times, as I have seen older men do when watching prostitutes. "Will she be an easy woman to know? No. An easy woman to handle? No. An easy woman to please?"

"No!" I supplied. "And that is the worst of her. She will be too much work."

"Things of value are only gained by much work. Such work, believe me, is never too much. If you worry so much about her spirit, then take her to your bed three times a day and do what a man of your age and vigor does best. That will boil some of the spice out of her." Having said his piece, the old man also left me.

I stood alone.

As I looked at the hills and vales of the Italian coastline, I told myself I should have felt happier. The woman I had been shackled to was held in high regard by the man I regarded highest. And yet I could not rejoice. I had no desire "to delve beneath the surface" of Aurora.

I wanted Thalia.

Δ

Our contingent stayed in Neapoli at the pleasure of the Roman Republic. A recently vacated villa provided us elegant accommodations. Aurora and I were given a room with a window that looked out on a lovely garden. Even when night fell and I drew the shutters, the sounds of water, wind, and an owl drifted into our chamber.

I had allowed Aurora to stay with her father for the four nights following our engagement, owing to the fact that she might never see him again. I understood that they dined every evening with friends so that Aurora might say her farewells. During the days, she put her affairs in order. I did not see her until we met again at the Tiber wharf.

In Neapoli, I told her that sea voyages always drained me of energy. We lay down in the same bed, but I turned my back on her. She did not protest. I knew that she would not cry. I also knew that I would soon enough perform my husbandly duty. She was, after all, my wife, and I, being a man, required a vessel for my passions. But the passions of my body were nothing compared with the passions of my mind, and I still mourned for the death of the dream Thalia and I had created. I still ached to possess her. A part of me did not want to violate our vows by coupling with my bride.

Δ

The next morning, Timon rose late. I had been awake since dawn. I knew that it would not be a good day to travel; the sky was washed with red. Timon, however, was furious at having overslept. He would hear of no other plan but to get to our ship and have the anchor weighed the moment his feet touched the deck.

Timon had been told that a Roman supply fleet was due to sail across to Messana, Panoramus, and thence to Lilybaeum. This would at least give us an armed escort to our island. The admiral would also arrange for us to be escorted overland by a century of men as far as the border between the Roman colonies and the Greek region of Sicilia. But Timon would have none of this either, since this fleet would not sail for another six days. He elected rather to command our ship to follow the coast of Italia into the territories of Roman allies, then Roman enemies, and finally Greek colonies. As a ship of Siracusa, the only worry we would have with this plan was the sudden appearance of pirate galleys.

We sailed out of the harbor of Neapoli at mid-morning. Within two hours, the clouds darkened and the waves crested sufficiently even for Timon to choose the shore over further risk. We turned into the Sarnus River and beached. Here stood the town of Pompeii, which had been established as a Greek colony from almost the same time as Siracusa. It had recently been directly absorbed by Roma and was beginning to take on Roman influences, but on the whole it looked extremely familiar to me. For one thing, it was not the jumble and confusion of streets that Roma and Ostia had been, but was rather laid out in rectilinear fashion, as were all the Greek colonies. For another, it possessed all the requisites of a Greek town in familiar architecture: four temples, two baths, bakeries, wine shops, a forum, and a palaestra for sporting events. The entire town, with its ineffectual-looking tufa and limestone outer walls, could not take more than half an hour to walk around. I was told by the man who volunteered to guide us for two denarii that it had a populace of only about 12,000. And yet it had an amphitheater for spectacles and two small theaters for dramas. It also abounded with brothels.

Pompeii was a resort town. Its baths had caladaria, or heated waters, no doubt owing to the dormant volcano Vesuvio that dominated the landscape. Several dozen Roman nobles and plutocrats had established villas in the town, which gave it the necessary cachet to attract others. The relaxed nature of the resort was especially evident in its statuary, its murals, and its mosaics.

Everywhere, the images of Priapus and phalluses were celebrated. The shape of a penis and testicles could be seen even on the paving stones. Our guide knew many servants and slaves, so that we were allowed to peek into some of the brothels and some of the homes with particularly graphic renderings. We viewed paintings of the three nude graces, of Priapus weighing his genitalia, and of men and women or men and men coupling in no fewer than twenty positions.

The guide had asked me with merry eyes if my new wife would be offended by such displays. I responded that she was a woman who sought edification from every possible place, and that both she and I might only benefit from the tour.

Aurora, for her part, absorbed the city's sexual mysteries with quiet equanimity. I was frankly surprised that this virgin would show no reaction. I, who had tasted of the fruits of the flesh several dozen times by then, found myself more than a little aroused. So it was that evening, when Aurora and I retired to our private bedchamber, that I could no longer feign total indifference to her.

The daughter of Marcellus was, as I have written, rather plain of face. She was also short and somewhat thick of her middle. Of negative features, I found no more. Her skin was without blemish and exceedingly soft, as were her lips. Her bosom was more than ample and her hips wide. She had a natural smell about her that was altogether pleasing. Her hands were clever. And when she was engaged, the face that seemed so plain in repose took on an aura of intelligence, a vivaciousness that made one forget her shortcomings.

Being a Roman woman, there was no question in my mind of her virtue. I had my proof that night. Her pain, however, was not so great that she did not soon afterward enlist in the joys of Eros and Aphrodite with enthusiasm. Those skills I had attained I passed on to her, showing her what pleased me and how she might be pleasured. In all, she proved an apt pupil. When I finally turned my back on her, she insinuated herself into my curves, laid her arm over my middle, and rested her chin on the back of my neck.

Only afterward, when I listened in the darkness to the slow rhythm of her breath in sleep as I lay awake, did the image of Thalia return to me.

CHAPTER XII

Timon's contingent and the bewildering cargo of six donkeys sailed on our ship from Pompeii for two days without incident. When we tacked past the city of Messana, which lay under Roman control, I breathed more freely. I told myself that if an enemy ship or fleet was spotted, we could at least hurry to the first beach and run for safety.

This is precisely what happened.

We had sailed perhaps three hours south of Messana, well past the toe of the Italian peninsula, where nothing but water stretched to the horizon on our port side. On the starboard lay a mountainous patch of the island that divided the Roman territory from that acknowledged to be Greek. In short, neither side was supposed to settle the region, and only one poorly-traveled road linked the various cities up and down the coast.

Because the wind had been stolen by the mountain range looming to the west, our sailors set out their oars and began to row. The broad-beamed ship relied heavily on wind; manpower could not keep it moving

155

at an optimum rate. We had only six and thirty sailors to tend the oars. Just as the stroke began to get us into a rhythm, one of the men on the deck called out that two galleys sat beached in a hidden cove behind the promontory we had just passed.

I hurried to the stern of our ship for a better look. I saw no scorpion's tail at their sterns, no painted eyes or boar's heads at their bows, which was customary of Greek galleys of this size. The long curve of a Carthaginian and its thatched shelter in the stern was not the shape of either. Nor did I see the distinctive backward curve on the bow of Roman galleys. These were light raiders, built to scout at the advance perimeters of war fleets and to prey upon slow cargo ships. For all I knew they had been built in the Black Sea or beyond the Pillars of Heracles.

Only minutes after spotting us, the two galleys put out from the cove. As their bows came up, I could see the foam thrown by their ramming beaks. I alone had eyes sharp enough to discern that they used two banks of rowers, just as we did. Although they seemed small from the width of their beam, they might have held as many as eighty rowers in each. They were more than ten minutes behind us by the time they got into deep water, but they would not be for long.

"Pirates," I said, as the chief minister came to my side.

"Someone would want us to think as much," Timon said. "They may just as well be from one of the Greek colonies on Italia or a detail dropped here from the Carthaginian fleet. I fear that they may know precisely who we are." He faced to the ship's master and shouted, "Shall we bring it about to the open sea and get back into the wind?"

"And if they carry masts and sails?" I asked, silently cursing the minister for putting us in such a desperate situation. "Your master of ship will tell you that they will catch us within an hour in that case, empty as we are. They are built for speed; we are not."

"I have planned for flight by land as well," Timon revealed. "This is the reason for the donkeys. However, I had not expected enemy ships to approach us from shore, but from sea, where we would have had more time to beach and escape."

I turned and studied the shoreline ahead of us. "If you are correct that they seek you and we land our party on the next beach, then send the ship back out to deep water. If they both follow after the ship, they seek booty. If at least one of them follows our party, then you will have some assurance that they have been placed here to kill you."

Timon nodded sharply at me. "Fetch Archimedes and your wife." Without waiting for reply, he walked toward the ship's master and changed his order.

I quickly summarized our plight for my great-uncle and Aurora. Neither was the sort to panic. I fetched nothing but my armor and weapons as I felt the ship heave toward land. I helped the master break out a rope ladder, which we tossed over the ship's rail.

Even before the vessel's bottom touched sand, I was over the side and down the ladder to the crests of the gently lapping waves. I called for the master to throw down my belongings the instant the ship lightly ground to a stop. As I carried them to shore, Archimedes gamely clambered down the ladder and went up to his chin in the water. While we struggled, members of the crew heaved the braying donkeys overboard from the bow end. Each found his footing and direction in short order and paddled to land. I guided Archimedes toward the beach, but he stopped when his waist was exposed. I caught his bundle and flung it to him. Then came Timon, with a thick pair of satchels over his shoulder and a sword clanging from his belt. Aurora appeared above the ladder.

"Do not let this touch the water!" she shouted to me.

I caught her bundle and then immediately realized what it was.

"Are you insane?" I shouted. "These are your scrolls. I will toss them back up or drop them in the sea. Choose now!"

"I will carry nothing else!" she called down.

"You will carry your dowry. Where is it?"

"I will throw it only if you promise I may carry my scrolls."

"I hid all our drawings among her scrolls," Archimedes called out. "We must take them. Throw them to me!"

I swore as only a soldier can and tossed the bag of scrolls to the old man. He held them over his head and trudged to the beach.

Aurora tossed over the rail the bag that held the dowry and then hastened down the ladder.

Timon's guards wasted no time in climbing. They followed after the donkeys, bearing only their weapons. Amazingly, less than five minutes elapsed between when the ship stopped and when we men pushing in the water and the crew with their oars were able to get it back out to sea. In that short time, the pursuing galleys had cut the distance so that not more than six stadia lay between us.

The cargo ship, now considerably unburdened, moved off with good speed. As it cleared the breaking waves into deeper water, its sail went up and it heaved directly into the path of the wind.

We six on the shore wasted no time as well in rounding up the donkeys, in throwing our sacks over them, and in leading them from the beach toward the clear break in the tree line that indicated a road. When we had reached the rutted and weed-choked via, we mounted our beasts and set off south at less than breakneck speed.

Within five minutes we had traveled to a rise in the road from whence we could look out on the ocean. We saw that our ship headed south by southeast. We also saw that one of the galleys pursued it and the other bobbed near the beach we had just left.

"Push on, push on!" Timon urged.

"You push on," I said, swinging off my donkey and handing its reins over to Aurora. "I need to hang back here and see what they will do."

"They will follow us!" Timon shouted.

"Go!" I commanded, buckling on my sword and grabbing my hatchet and spear. I did not bother taking armor.

My five companions hastened onward. I saw that some of the men in the galley who came to the beach studied us and pointed. I turned and followed after the last donkey until the group rounded a turn in the road. Then I flattened myself against a rock ledge and watched.

The galley had stopped in virtually the identical place that the cargo ship had. Over its starboard side poured six men. They moved to the beach carrying their weapons and armor above their heads while members of the crew jumped overboard and guided the galley backward, to beach it stern first.

I watched the first six men struggle into their armor. Even when they hurried upward toward the road, I lingered. My tarrying rewarded me with a view of six more soldiers descending the galley via two rope ladders. This, I assumed, was the full boarding party of the warship. I waited another minute to be certain that this was all the fighting force they carried. It was.

As I have mentioned, I can run farther without tiring than any other man I have ever met. I ran after my desperate group and caught up with them in short order. I shared with them my plan for keeping Timon, Archimedes, and Aurora safe. Timon approved it and a moment later was kicking his donkey brutally to encourage it to move up the road with unnatural haste.

At last, since they were to be comrades in arms, I asked Timon's guards their names. They were Ioannis and Diocles. I had seen them both in Hieron's palace and knew them to be part of his elite guard. Neither was my size, but both were obviously strong and quick. They strapped on their armor as they listened to my plan.

"We also can play the game of ambush," I said. "Are you skilled in stealth and taking men from behind?"

"We are," Ioannis confirmed.

I pictured them slipping over the walls of Marcellus's home and slitting Aurora's throat in the night.

I said, "The enemy has no doubt placed its six fastest warriors on the road to catch us. The next group follows to finish what the first may not. Let us take them one group at a time."

The two men, both older than I by at least five years, accepted me as the one in charge.

Δ

We chose a place on the road where large rocks closed in on both sides and where a few men could not circle behind us in a fight and take us from the rear. Since the road was poorly traveled, tall weeds and rough bushes crowded in on it from all sides. The opportunities for concealment were abundant. I hid myself on the seaward verge; Ioannis and Diocles crouched behind rocks on the landward side.

The first six enemy soldiers came jogging up the road with good speed. I could hear their labored breathing as the first pair of them passed, and I was glad of it. They were not of equal stamina, so that two came first, then one, then another one, followed by two stragglers.

As the last pair came even with us, I tossed a small stone ahead of me into the bushes. The pair slowed and eventually stopped. They raised their spears and searched the terrain. From behind them with uncanny silence came Timon's guards. Only when Ioannis and Diocles crept three steps from their quarry did the enemy soldiers whirl to face them. By then it was too late. Both had their throats severed, one so deeply that his head tilted to the side as he fell. Even as they died, I dashed from my hiding place and went after the fourth soldier in the group. I had removed my sandals and strapped them to my belt, so that my feet made no slapping noises. I took as much care as possible to tread upon grassy or mossy clumps in the road, all the more to deaden the sounds of my pursuit.

When I was perhaps five strides from the man's back, he turned and swung up his shield in defense. I dropped to one knee and thrust my light spear under his guard and into his groin. He collapsed backward with a scream.

The remaining three men turned from up the road and regarded me. It took them but a moment to realize that their number had been cut in half. They knew that I could not have accomplished such carnage by myself, so they set off at redoubled speed in pursuit of Timon, Archimedes, Aurora, who could just be seen disappearing over a ridge about two stadia ahead.

I ran after the three men, drawing my hatchet from my belt as I did. This apparently foolhardy act no doubt confused the soldiers. I certainly was no match for their combined strength. If they had only turned to face me as one with their light shields and spears, I would have had no choice but to dive for the undergrowth and dodge and jink to safety. Instead, the first two redoubled their pursuit of our lead group, leaving the third to contend with me.

He cocked his throwing arm and harassed me with feints, moving closer each time. His undoubted plan was to draw so near that he could not possibly miss me. I let him come three steps closer. Then, uttering my most terrible war whoop, I rushed at him. This he clearly did not expect. The audacity of my attack froze him in place for a moment, and this was all the time I needed. The instant I knew I was in the range that the Silent Storm had practiced week after week, I threw my hatchet. Before he could bring his shield fully across his chest, the hatchet buried itself in his right shoulder.

The spear flew sideways from his grasp. The force of my strike was so great that the man spun partway around. When he again faced me, he struggled to draw the hatchet from his shoulder with his shield hand. I had my sword in his stomach an instant later.

Ioannis and Diocles dashed past me in pursuit of the remaining two. I was confident that they would not let the enemy near to their chief minister. I, meantime, drew in several fortifying breaths and unstrapped my sandals from my belt. I knew that the second pack of soldiers would be upon me within seconds.

I picked up two dropped javelins on the way back down the road. I saw that Ioannis and Diocles had dragged their victims into the underbrush, but blood stained the dirt in several places. I did what I could to cover it and then hid myself just as I caught sight of the vanguard of the next group.

As with the first of our enemy, the second team advanced according to their lung power and stamina. This group, in fact, was more spread out than the first. A lone soldier came at a full run. Because of his extra effort, he seemed completely drained. He slowed to a halt, bent, and placed his hands on his knees just as I sprang from between a brace of bushes and smashed in his face with a large rock. When I drew my hand away, he collapsed backward like a felled tree. The nose piece of his helmet had been driven deeply into the gore that had been his face. I grabbed him by his ankles and dragged him into the bushes.

Half a minute later, two more of the pursuers came loping up the incline. I hit one of them squarely in the chest with my first javelin. By the time the second spun to find me, I was at his side. My last javelin found the chink in his armor just underneath his upraised throwing arm.

Despite the fact that his chest had been pierced, this man managed to bellow like a speared boar before he died. There was no chance of surprising the last three. I knew that Ares had blessed me far more than I deserved that day. I took to my toes and sprinted up the road away from what I assumed would be a trio lusting for my blood.

I had not gotten more than one stadion when I found Ioannis and Diocles walking wearily down the road toward me.

"I believe they were Greek," Diocles reported. "At least they had the features of Greek men."

"Greek men from where?" I asked.

"We could not tell."

"Do you think they were hired by Timon's enemies in Siracusa?"

"Perhaps. They said nothing. We may never know. They died rather than tell us."

"There are three more below," I said. "Shall we learn from them?"

Both of Timon's guards nodded without enthusiasm. We started down the road, but I will freely admit that none of us moved with haste. The running and the killing we had done had us all exhausted. We were good enough soldiers to know that fighting from such a disadvantage invited defeat. Moreover, if we could ambush them, they could ambush us.

Of necessity, we worked our way down with caution. By the time we reached that place in the road from which I had observed the landing of the galley, the last three soldiers had retreated to the beach. I watched them gesticulating wildly in our direction. I imagined them telling their superior that a great host of warriors had fallen on them from ambush and that further pursuit was tantamount to suicide.

"They are done with following us," Diocles judged.

"They may beach farther south and try again," I said, nodding toward the galley. "I am sure this road hugs the shoreline."

A man standing beside a fire on the beach that had been belching white smoke threw fresh-cut vegetation onto the blaze. Within moments, the smoke changed to black. Out on the ocean the galley that had drawn near to our cargo ship changed direction, describing a circle that would bring it back to its sister ship.

"We will not continue south," I decided. "We will turn around and go north, to Messana. Whether Timon wishes it or not, he needs the protection of our Roman allies to see him safely home."

"I agree," Ioannis said. He looked at Diocles, who nodded his assent. "We have served Timon long enough to make him see this wisdom."

CHAPTER XIII

Timon and the rest of our party reached Siracusa fully eight days after the attack by the unknown galleys, but at least we were all safe. We never learned the identities of the raiders. When we compared notes, we realized that their swords were Spanish, their javelins, helmets, and features were Greek, and their greaves most likely Roman. These clues suggested pirates, but their behavior had not. Some mysteries are never to be solved.

As soon as we returned Archimedes to his home and saw to his comforts, I took Aurora to the house of my father. He and my mother, of course, had been well prepared to receive a Roman woman, since Apollos had set his sign to the scroll that bound me. They welcomed her with characteristic Greek hospitality. Any misgiving they might have had evaporated when they learned of Aurora's noble family and of her ex-consul father who now led the Roman peninsular army. I could tell that they were immensely relieved that Aurora spoke fluent Greek. For her part, Aurora was the soul of grace. My father took me aside after we dined together and expressed his delight in my bride's obvious intellect and breadth of knowledge. He did not offer any sympathy for my profound disappointment over losing Thalia, and I chose to believe that he had not been told of our secret relationship.

Because I was a full-time soldier, my bed lay in the fortress of Euryalus. I beseeched my father to find a small dwelling not far from where they lived for Aurora to set up housekeeping. I also turned over to his safekeeping Aurora's not inconsequential dowry. Apollos' eyes started from his head when he looked on the many coins and their value.

"You have done exceedingly well, my son!" he praised. "To think that this is due to my choice of profession for you! Now let me hear you complain that a soldier cannot get far in life! This is more than enough to purchase a good house and several slaves."

"There will be no slaves in our household," I told him. I explained Aurora's point of view. He accepted it without emotion.

"If she thinks she can change the world by her example, may the gods bless her. So long as she doesn't criticize me for using them."

I told him that she had accepted my words of how Apollos allowed his slaves to purchase their freedom after seven or eight years. He shrugged.

"She is in Siracusa now, and nobody will care much that she is the daughter of a former Roman consul. If she doesn't want to make herself and you miserable, she will temper her tongue and her opinions. There are many these days who feel particularly antagonistic to her race."

Δ

I had barely returned to the fortress and settled in when I received word to report to Hieron's palace. I cleaned myself up, walked down the hill to Ortygia, and worked my way through guards and ministers to the increasingly-familiar audience chamber. This time, I found the king sitting on the throne with his minister of foreign affairs and his minister of finance at either flank. Timon paced the marble floor like a caged African lion.

Although I had been gone less than two months, Hieron seemed to have aged ten years. Two camp chairs had been placed close by the foot of the throne. Hieron gestured for me to sit.

"I deplore the death of your excellent son, my King," I began.

"I thank you. It is a tragedy far worse than my personal loss, as we shall discuss here today." He held up a scroll which looked like one of those Timon had written while we waited for transport out of Messana. "I have read of your remarkable exploits. You now have the friendship of my friend Marcellus. Moreover, you are recognized by a tribune as his father for saving his life. You and Archimedes have acquired all there is to know about the craft of Roman siege. And, as if all this were not enough, you saved my chief minister, the daughter of Marcellus, Archimedes, and even my cargo ship from an unknown foe. Five men killed by your hand within a space of minutes! Four more at Cannae! You will soon become legend."

"I merely serve," I said, even as my being throbbed with pride at my king's praise.

"Because you serve so well, Leonides, I desire even more of you," Hieron said.

I detected a persistent quaver in his voice that had not been there before I left Siracusa.

The king said, "We have not spoken of one other service, which I am sure was the most demanding: I speak of marrying the daughter of Marcellus rather than the woman you love and who professes to love you."

A sharp stitch cut through my chest. "It is so, my King."

Hieron sighed. "There are many forms of love. With this variety the gods should never have cursed us. Ironically, only the lowest of men and women can afford to pursue its unparalleled joy. For those of us with power and duties, it is too great a luxury. But take consolation in this: I am told that it is a creature whose lifespan is measured in weeks or months. Not long after a man possesses a woman and she loses her mystery, he looks to renew the fading joy in someone else. I, like you, was compelled to marry for the good of the state. Philistis was the daughter of Leptines. He was in his day the most powerful merchant in this city. He watched after my interests and those of his daughter while I led the army outside our walls. Likewise my son married Nereis, daughter of King

165

Pyrrhus, to cement our relationship with that great realm of Greece."

"But I am a common man," I protested weakly.

"Not any longer. You rise rapidly out of a moderately wealthy family by your own efforts. Such is the way of special men. You are now the husband of the daughter of the Sword of Roma, for that is what Marcellus is being called. His star is again on the ascendant. Fortunately for us, we were able to curry his favor six years ago when he was a consul. If he were not a Roman, he would be a Greek."

I nodded my agreement of that statement.

"Timon has told you of the swelling sentiment against Roma," Hieron said. "It is so popular that we cannot crush it without destroying the city from within. But we can protect our relationship with Roma if we are clever. I am no longer a man of vigor, as you can see. This must not go from this chamber, but my physicians give me less than a year to live. I concur. This means that my grandson, Hieronymos, will inherit my throne. He turns fifteen soon. That is far too young to rule such a great city on his own. I therefore propose to establish a body of fifteen men to serve as counselors and guardians. Unfortunately, for political reasons I cannot choose only men who are loyal to our compact with Roma. However, ten of the fifteen hold my opinion. Two of these men are to be yourself and your great-uncle, Archimedes."

My brain boggled with this weighty pronouncement of confidence.

"Thank you for this honor. I will, of course, serve as you direct, Sire," I responded. "However, you may wish to change your mind. I tell you with all candor that I am not sure the Romans will prevail in this struggle with Carthage."

Hieron nodded ponderously. "You have proven yourself a reasonable man. Let me then reason with you. Neither of us has visited Carthage. However, I and my ministers have interviewed many Siracusans who have. Their capital is in a weak geographic position compared with that of Roma. More importantly, it lies within a region not one fifth as fertile as that of Italia. You have now traveled through that peninsula. Did it not strike you as exceedingly fertile?"

"It did," I admitted.

"Moreover, Roma has established forty colonies in Italia alone! They have dozens around the Mediterranean, including regions of Sicilia, Corsica, and Sardinia which Carthage once held. Carthage struggles to hold onto Hispania and little more. In total, the Republic of Roma and her confederacy comprise 5,000 towns, cities, and villages."

"But hundreds of these places are in danger of defecting to Hannibal," I argued.

"Not enough. Remember the lesson of King Pyrrhus. Hannibal cannot win over time. Nor can the Carthaginian navy," Hieron proclaimed with confidence. "It is a simple matter of men and materials. Ask our cousin Archimedes to work out the mathematics of this equation for you. If Carthage should miraculously force Roma to its knees, within ten years it would rise to crush him. If you learned nothing else while in that city, you should know now the Roman mind. It is bellicose and determined to dominate. Before Cannae, the Romans marched into battle. Now they march to total war."

"But Hannibal brings no system of enslavement or tribute, as do the Romans," I argued. "Between his military genius and his desire that these other races live freely, can this not succeed?"

"No," said Hieron flatly. "His dream is many independent races. Roma works to unite all under its rule. Its combined weight crushes everything in its path. The leviathan eats the minnow, no matter how clever or brave the minnow may be. Even a school of minnows can never eat the leviathan. Might succeeds in this world. You should not condemn the fact outright, Leonides. It is also why you rise in our army. You are our champion Olympian and our champion warrior. I am prepared to give you whatever you demand for your Silent Storm. If you wish this force to increase to a hundred men, say the word."

"I am satisfied with my cohort as it has been originally designed," I said, fearful of advancing too quickly and creating many enemies within the army.

"Keep your options open," Hieron counseled. "Now, can you assure me that you will hold steady to the course of maintaining alliance with Roma?"

"You have been most persuasive," I said, wondering if he would push me for a more definitive answer. Hieron's silent smile encouraged a bit of boldness. "Although I ask for no more men under me," I negotiated, "I would request one boon."

"I will grant it if I can."

"I desire to learn how you came to know of my love for the daughter of Eustace."

Hieron glanced at Timon, who shook his head ever so slightly. "That, unfortunately, I cannot tell you. You should have asked for forty acres of land outside the city and slaves to tend it. I could have supplied that."

Δ

On my way out of the palace grounds, I was overtaken by a man I had not noted before. I was sure that he had left the palace behind me, however.

"Leonides!" he called out.

I turned.

The man offered a smile too broad to be genuine. His eyes were dark and shone like obsidian. His overall look reminded me of that of a ferret. In his hand, he swung a purse. It jingled with the metallic sound of coin.

"Who calls my name?" I demanded.

"I am not important. I represent certain persons yet unknown to you who would care greatly to make you their friend."

"Who might these persons be?"

"Persons of import. Persons who know which way the wind blows today and how it will blow tomorrow."

"I suppose I should meet such people, since no one I know can predict the future," I said, not without sarcasm. "And what do they wish of me?"

"Merely that you repeat to me, as if to an old friend, the words that passed in the audience chamber minutes ago."

My first instinct was to grab the man and march him back to Hieron. He seemed to know this and stood well enough away from me to avoid capture. Moreover, he was thin, lank, and lightly clothed, and I wore my dress uniform and polished armor. I had no hope of outracing him if he fled. And then I wondered if the man had been sent out by Timon, to test my trustworthiness.

"You tell your masters that I am not a man who can be bought," I replied. "Look elsewhere for your information."

The man smiled again, this time convincingly. He bowed slightly, backed several more steps from me, and sprinted into a dark nearby alley.

Δ

On the same evening as my audience with the king, I took myself to the house of my elder brother, Dion. While Dion held no office, he had an uncanny aptitude for learning the inner secrets of the politics of our city. I believe this was because his business brought him people from all parts of the city and because he listened far more than he spoke. He also never betrayed a confidence.

To Dion I related my conversation with the king. He said not one word until he was sure that I had finished. Then he took a moment to gather his thoughts and clear his throat.

Dion said, "What Hieron did not tell you was that in one way he was glad of the death of his son. In the past few months, Gelon began to side with those who favor Carthage in this struggle. Hannibal's unstopped march through Italia began his shift in thinking. The news of a new Carthaginian fleet tilted it."

"Hieron told Archimedes and me that Carthaginian agents operated within the city," I said. "Do you suppose they were able to get to Gelon?"

"I have heard rumors that they approached Adranodoros and Zoippos," my brother replied. These two were the husbands of Gelon's sisters. "They convinced Gelon."

"And Hieron is celebrated for never eliminating those who oppose him only with words," I remembered aloud.

"Could you imprison or kill your own son and the husbands of your daughters?" Dion asked. "What is more, I have heard second-hand reports that many of the most influential citizens of the city feel the same as Gelon did." He threw up his hands. "Who is to say which side is right? If our city guesses wrong, it could be destroyed. For more than a year, Carthage has had the upper hand."

"But you have heard through me Hieron's reasoning," I said. "Does it not make sense?"

"What? That even if Roma is defeated, it will eventually win?" Dion repeated. "And what good will that do us if by that time Carthage has leveled Siracusa for siding with its enemy?"

"I will not allow that to happen," I affirmed. "And if that is too hard to believe, then know that Archimedes will not allow it."

Dion offered no reply, and I did not solicit one.

Δ

The first dwelling that my father located for Aurora was not adequate. She and I looked at it together, and to her credit she made no complaint. I offered dissatisfaction on her behalf. It had barely enough open area in the back to prepare meals and hang laundry, much less for plantings. Apollos muttered a few words about living beyond our means and how a dowry did not last forever, but then lapsed into a silence. Later, when we were alone, I told him of my higher rank and the salary attached it, and his outlook brightened considerably.

The next day, my father produced a vacant dwelling more to our mutual satisfaction. Its one drawback was that its front door opened onto a narrow alley rather than a main street, but this was compensated for by its quiet and serenity. A spacious back end occupied much of the interior of a block of homes. A plane tree grew in one corner. Four water catch basins overflowed into a small ornamental pool. Beside it was a stone bench perfect for reading. Bushes and vines in need of pruning promised color and verdure in the following spring. It had three bedrooms. As Aurora wandered among the rooms, she figured out loud where her belongings would go. I knew then that she would be content if not happy.

That same day I visited the home of my close friend Apollonius, who was by now a well-married man. He had earned two days' leave from the fortress. Evidently, he had used his previous leaves well, because Amara was expecting a child in the late spring.

Apollonius looked confused and even a bit upset by my unannounced appearance at his door.

"I have survived Roma!" I exclaimed. "I am not a ghost!"

"Thank the gods!" Apollo replied. He gathered me into his wrestler's arms and gave me a fierce hug. "It is wonderful to have you home!"

At that point, he told me the joyous news. I went inside to greet Amara. I did not congratulate her, so not to offend a birth goddess and cause her to lose the child. Congratulations came only after fingers and toes were counted and the baby was deemed fit to live.

When Amara left the courtyard to fetch wine, I said to Apollo, "Have you learned of the engagement of my Thalia to Cleomenes?"

At my question, the huge man blushed. "Yes, I am sorry. Perhaps if you had not been sent to Italia..."

"What?" I jumped in, to rescue him from embarrassment. "Do you believe you have failed me because I appointed you and Amara my go-betweens? What could you have done?"

Apollo hung his head. "Nothing."

"Exactly! Did she send me any messages while I was away?"

My friend nodded. "One arrived about ten days ago." Amara arrived with two bowls of wine. Apollonius asked her to fetch Thalia's sealed missive. When she returned, I asked her to break the seal and read it aloud. Among the three of us, Amara was the only competent reader.

"She writes: 'My dearest love—charged with every fiber of my being against union with Cleomenes, I was nonetheless ordered by my father to accept him as husband. However, do not believe this is the end for us.'" Amara looked up at me and shook her head with grave misgiving.

"Go on!" I urged.

"'While I was forbidden to delay this engagement, yet I could dictate the day of my wedding. Neither my father nor Cleomenes realize that I have chosen the longest night of the year. Such is how I feel about this tragedy. In my heart I am still yours. As proof, I will wear my earrings on the occasion. Send them to me by courier as soon as you receive this. Your Thalia.'"

"What earrings?" Apollonius asked.

"I hold a pair of earrings that belong to her," I said. This was not precisely fact, but in truth I wanted no one else to own them.

"When will you bring your own bride to meet us?" Amara asked in a matter-of-fact tone.

"This news has also come to you?" I asked.

"Through Myreon," said Apollonius. "He told us of Hieron's petition to your father. Myreon began his training under my command when you were away."

"How does he fare?"

"He is no soldier. He waves his sword as if it were a paintbrush. But your brother does not complain. He would not disgrace you."

"She is the daughter of a Roman consul," I said.

"Who?"

"Aurora. My wife."

Apollonius brayed. "Oh, surely! Of course she is."

"I do not make sport," I told him.

The laughter died in his throat. "How could that be?"

I gestured for Amara to sit beside me. I told them in detail of Aurora, her love of things Greek, how she had alienated herself from her own people.

"She reads and speaks Greek!" Amara enthused. "Then she and I can talk. What else can she do?"

"She cooks wonderfully," I admitted. "And she paints murals better than Myreon."

"Truly? And did she come with a dowry?" asked my comrade soldier.

"A large dowry."

Apollo looked at his wife, and she returned his stare. I believed that they were silently asking each other why I still craved Thalia.

"You will find her very opinionated," I said. "She does not sew or weave. She is also nothing special to look upon. Like Thalia, I was ordered to marry."

Amara sipped her wine but said nothing. "I will fetch nuts and raisins," she said, rising.

After a moment Apollo said, "I am not as good a thinker as you, Leonides, but I would forget Thalia. You are climbing high in this city. I would not put the horns on Cleomenes. He could bring you down."

"I would not take the wife of another man!" I exclaimed.

"Then what else can you do, unless he chooses to divorce her?"

I held up Thalia's letter. "It seems I need do little or nothing. She is the one who has promised that we are not over."

Δ

As soon as I could, I gathered together the men of the Silent Storm and assured myself that Xenophanes had kept them in top condition. Menander, ironically, had arrived home from Roma before I did. He was among the ten young men of quality families who had been married off to Roman women. He had been drawn into Timon's scheme with misapprehensions, but when I saw him back in Siracusa among the other members of our elite cohort he bubbled over with enthusiasm.

"She was given a dowry!" was the first bit of information Menander shared with me. "Enough to allow me to purchase the upstairs floor of a dwelling in Tyche! And she is very pretty! Still young. Younger than me by five years. She has one son. He is only two, so he will always think of me as his father. A fine boy."

"What is her name?" I asked my comrade in arms.

"Oh! Drusilla. Her name is Drusilla. Perhaps one day the boy will become a soldier like me. He is Metellus. I wonder if I should insist that he have a Greek name."

The other men had already heard Menander's adventure, so they shouted him down and coaxed from me tales of my various adventures. I began by telling of the Roman defeat at Cannae. I later augmented Menander's verbal tour of Roma, concentrating on its defenses and on their siege tactics. The tale I especially dwelt on was of the two galleys that had pursued us. I related in a general way how I and Timon's two agents were able to defeat a much larger group of men by means of surprise and techniques that we were putting into place with our special cohort.

This I did with the thirteen men who were available on that day for training, as we alternated walking and jogging around the perimeter of Siracusa. I allowed them to rest only when we found a bit of terrain that might work to our advantage during a siege. We analyzed each rill, each tree and bush in detail, worked out how to use features to our advantage, then took turns acting as enemy guards and trying to detect the approach of each man. When we rested to take a bit of food, I told of the Roman army's vexation and humiliation over Hannibal's many surprise tactics. I watched their confidence grow in our potential as I spoke. Before I had left for Italia, our group had begun to develop precisely such unorthodox tactics.

By Archidamus' decree, I was able to muster the full enrollment of the Silent Storm some five days after my return to Siracusa. At this time, word came to one member of my unit concerning the specifics of my accomplishments in the town of Cannae and on the Sicilian coast road, and he had been broadcasting what he had heard. The moment I appeared before my assembled cohort, I was accosted.

"It was not right to keep from us the number of enemy you slew," Xenophanes protested. "Your modesty is as great a fault as being a braggart. How could you not tell your closest comrades these specifics?"

"You tell me what you heard, and I will correct the hyperboles."

Protesilous, it happened, was the man who had heard the stories. In both combats, the number of men I killed and the weapons I used were correctly given. However, Protesilous had heard nothing of specific thrusts, cuts, and parries, which were what my soldiers most longed to learn about.

"Which is it, Ioannis or Diocles, who you know?" I asked the teller.

"I know neither," Protesilous replied. "I heard the stories from my cousin. He got them from his father, who sometimes bathes beside Archimedes."

This knowledge shocked me to my toes. After each of these pitched skirmishes, the old genius had merely patted me on my back. Not a word of praise passed his lips on either occasion. I had not expected more. Yet Archimedes had made known to me several times his opposition to warfare and his loathing of the taking of life. Nevertheless, he had clearly interviewed those who stood beside me in the fights. Later, to others he had heaped praise upon me for exactly the same actions he professed to deplore. This I found as curious as any aspect of my great-uncle's personality. Thinking upon it for several days, I determined that his pride over me as a friend and relative temporarily clouded his sense of moral values. Much as this incident intrigued me, I could never bring myself to broach it with him.

Fortunately for Siracusa, Archimedes' love of his home was as great as it was for me. The same moral equivocation he demonstrated in praising my exploits he applied to his defense of our city. I learned that he wasted no time in making use of all we had learned in Roma. Hieron had given him free rein to employ as many men and as much materiel as he required to make Siracusa impregnable.

He began with the fortress of Euryalus, at the top point of the city, that site which commanded the roads from our tributary towns and which overlooked so much of the terrain on the west side of Siracusa. This solid bastion stood well up on the highest rock prominence. The walls were thick. Often, they simply provided a smooth face to the rock cliff, so that no amount of bombardment, ramming, or tunneling would have helped an enemy. The shape of the walls conformed to the meandering terrain, creating sharp angles. Atop five of these Archimedes directed that towers be added. Beyond presenting his drawings, he revealed nothing of their purpose.

Two weeks after construction began on the towers, Archimedes gave to the engineers more drawings. These specified three sets of trenches radiating in long arcs from the Epipolai gate. The farthest trenches lay at precisely eight-tenths of a stadion. Because I had been with my great-uncle in Roma I knew the reason for this, but I shared it with no one. The second and third trenches lay closer to the gate and fort, and both were backed by embankments from which our forces might engage an enemy as it struggled to surmount the trench in front. An underground passage was dug from inside the fort, leading to the first and second trenches to enable our men to retreat without opening the main gate. This passage was constructed so that it could be collapsed on short notice, denying the enemy its use.

The Epipolai gate itself was modified to conform to precisely the plan Archimedes had laid out months earlier. Behind it lay two more walls in a labyrinthine pattern. Hundreds if not thousands of men would die storming Siracusa from this direction. Every soldier took a portion of his time each day to watch the progress. I could see in their eyes their growing confidence now that the great mathematician was behind our defense.

Also at Euryalus the existing walls were modified, so that slits appeared at about twice the height of a man above the ground outside. Each slit was shaped in a horizontal V, with the larger side facing out. Missiles could be aimed out and slightly down with ease; to put a similar missile into the fort through the same slit under the stress of battle would be a feat.

Not content with fortification, Archimedes started on the engines of warfare. This project moved more slowly. Not until well into the winter was a large building near the Great Harbor emptied and modified to his purpose. The main reason the work could not move with speed was that no more than four and twenty men served as the master's assistants. These men were picked only after the most intense scrutiny. In order that no enemy, be he Roman, Carthaginian, or other, should know in advance what Archimedes had created, no information left the building. So stringent were the measures that these men slept and ate inside the factory. On those few occasions when they were allowed to enter the city, each man was escorted by two soldiers. It is my understanding that most of these were slaves who were promised to be made free men after a period of three years' service. All were young and without wives.

Δ

While I busied myself in my military service, I was also occupied on the domestic front. I was able to return to my new house approximately every ten days. As I expected of a woman of her fortitude, Aurora adjusted well. She got along with my parents and brothers. She so delighted in the culture of the city that my parents or Myreon were pleased to take her whenever they went to the theater or to a poetry reading or song festival. She also made herself welcome among the women of the neighborhood. I noted with admiration her chameleon-like ability to adjust her intellect and subject interests to put those around her at ease. She spoke less than she listened, which convinced those around her that she was a wonderful conversationalist. Whenever I was able to give her warning of my return, she had a feast prepared. She invited me to bring home my companions. It was in this way that she came to know Apollonius and Amara.

Only days after meeting Amara, Aurora began to weave. Amara excelled in the making of tapestries. While the fashioning of clothing did not interest Aurora, the use of threads to create images did. I gave her permission to secure dowry money from my father to purchase a loom and other materials, and she set it up beside that of Amara.

Aurora selected which room was to be our bedroom. She went alone into the marketplace and purchased a carpet on a whim. She also arranged the furniture without consulting me. All of these thing I should have considered impertinences, but I did not truly care since I did not consider it my home.

Only a week after the purification ceremony of the dwelling, Aurora began creating murals. Naturally, she obtained these materials from my father—and, of course, Apollos inquired who would do the painting. I had told him nothing of Aurora's artistic skills. Aurora was not shy in replying. This raised eyebrows in the family and finally set them wondering what manner of woman I had wed. As if to prove to me that she had indeed created the beautiful artwork in her father's domus, she duplicated the four scenes in our dining room. I am sure this also helped her to accommodate to strange living quarters. When she was finished, I hosted a dinner for the men of the family. Everyone was extravagant in their praise of my wife, both for her artistry and her cooking. Only Myreon used faint praise, sulking through the evening as his envious eyes stole again and again to the four murals.

Aurora's ardor toward me, if anything, increased. Her lovemaking became more expert and daring. She did not ask to spend from her dowry every few weeks, as I had feared an indulged consul's child would. There were no requests to purchase scrolls. She was, in short, a model wife. I found these things upsetting rather than reposing me.

Just as Siracusa held the unenviable position of standing physically between Carthage and Roma, so did I stand between Thalia and Aurora. As Siracusa prepared its populace and its wall for the worst, so did I guard my heart. Against the one who legally held claim to it I held back, should the other somehow be able to make good her promise that our love was not ended. I erected mental and emotional defenses on both flanks. Being ever distant from me, Thalia could not perceive this. As one preoccupied in a new land and truly never having had a chance to know me, Aurora did not guess my silent agony. Or if she did, I told myself, she had to be a better actress than a cook or painter.

Soon after reading Thalia's letter concerning the earrings, I had them delivered to her at the house of Cleomenes by my comrade Melampus. I made certain that this was done when he served a day of military duty. Although Melampus assured me that Thalia herself accepted the package from his hand, a part of me doubted. She wrote me no letter of acknowledgment.

Five days before the longest night of the year, I took myself to the house of Apollonius and asked for the scroll I knew must be there. Amara produced it. It simply read, "On that darkest of nights wait in the street outside my prison. See that I am still yours."

After Amara read the words, she sighed and shook her head.

"You do Aurora no favor if you speak of this to her," I counseled. "I believe nothing will come of it at any rate."

"Then don't go."

"I must," I told her. "You loved Apollo when you were engaged to him. I was made a slave for the good of the city."

Amara touched my wrist gently. "But Aurora is a good woman."

"Does that make Thalia a bad woman?" I countered. "And is that enough? Thalia loves me. Has Aurora ever said as much to you?"

"No."

"Ask her if she does," I said.

"You ask her!" Amara shot back. Immediately, she regretted her tone. "I know that she holds affection toward you. She is thankful that you were willing to take her away from Roma. She also told me how you married her to save her life. If I were in her place, I would love you." When I said nothing, she added, "She sings when she weaves with me. A woman only sings if she is happy."

"That is good," I said. I did not want Aurora unhappy; I only wished for myself the kind of happiness that would cause me to sing.

"She should have a servant," Apollos' wife judged. "We cannot afford one, but you certainly can."

"I would let her have a servant," I responded. "But she will have none of it. She must have spoken to you of her opinion regarding slaves."

"She has. But I was thinking of an older woman, for a companion. Why not a freewoman? The neighbors only accept her so much. She would not impose on your mother for more time. I will soon be more than preoccupied with a newborn. She needs companionship."

"Does she say this?" I probed.

"No. But she would not. These Romans are more Stoic than we Siracusans!"

"When she herself tells me, we will seek such help," I said, annoyed at how outspoken Amara had grown since marrying.

"She teaches me Latin, although I am a poor learner," Amara shared brightly.

"Why would you want to learn Latin?"

"So that she has something to give me." One eyebrow cocked. "And one day, as she and I both fear, her people may take this city."

"Say that not in front of me again," I said sternly. "Nor in front of your husband."

Amara blushed and excused herself from my presence.

Δ

Being Greek, the populace of our city looked for things to celebrate, be it the start of planting, the end of harvest, the traditional birthday of a god, or a significant date in our history. Never more than a few weeks passed without some sort of holiday. Thus, the night before the shortest day of the year, I found Apollonius inside the fortress and invited him to drink to the journey of his namesake to the land of the Hyperboreans and thence to return as Apollo Phoebus, carrying the sun in his chariot. I brought with me a portable amphora of potent wine. True to his nature, once Apollo had downed his third libation, he was powerless to stop. I waited until we had drained the vessel, he having drunk two-thirds of the contents, to spring my trap.

"You know that to Homer Apollo was the deadliest of gods?" I asked Apollonius.

"I had heard that," he said, with a thick tongue.

"And that no god except Zeus himself should be more feared?" I continued. "Because Apollo is the bringer of death from a distance, and he is the god of divine justice."

"Good for him!" said my companion, searching the bottom of his cup in vain.

"He is also the god who renders men aware of their own guilt," I told him. "Has he made you painfully aware of your guilt?"

"What are you talking about?" the drunken taxiarch replied.

"The reason why you greeted me with such a sorrowful face when I returned from Italia."

"I was worried about you. What guilt lies in that?"

"Because you also thought about Thalia."

"Well, naturally. I thought that I might have to break the horrible news to you."

"As you broke the news to another."

"Who?" Apollonius asked.

"You tell me. It was probably on a night like this, when you had been drinking too much, as you so often do. Someone mentioned my mission in Italia and the danger, and you began to lament about my impossible love for Thalia."

"Me?"

"Yes, you. Was it to Archidamus himself or to another of the high officers?"

At last the full implication of my accusation settled through the fog of Apollonius' brain. He sat up straight. His eyes filled with indignation. "I would never do such a thing!"

"Who else could have told about our secret?" I demanded.

Apollonius searched his thoughts. "The old woman who brought us Thalia's letters."

I snorted at the idea. "Azar? For what reason? I was paying her good coin. Who would she tell but Thalia's father? I presented no imminent danger. She would have realized that such a confession might move the father to select a more eligible suitor. That would end Azar's need in their house."

The words spilled out my mouth because I had already considered the woman and rejected her. As far as I was concerned, only she, Apollonius, and Amara knew of our love. Amara was, like so many wives, a virtual prisoner of her home. Moreover, she and the other women of her circle had no access to either Eustace or people at the palace.

"Why would I have needed to tell anyone for Thalia to become engaged to someone else?" Apollo asked.

"Timon knew."

"Timon?"

"Hieron's chief minister. He used me as leverage to force Thalia's father to give her away. She was a bribe, to maintain Cleomenes' loyalty to the king."

Apollonius labored to assimilate this news. "Well, search elsewhere," he said with hurt in his voice. "Because I have not betrayed you. I may get stupid when I drink, but not that stupid."

I apologized, compelled by his face to believe him.

"There must have been someone else you confided in," he said, closing his eyes. "Think!"

I thought for days after that and got nowhere.

CHAPTER XIV

Although Thalia's wedding lasted through an entire day, I waited until night's cloak could conceal me before taking myself to the house of Eustace. From the courtyard issued the sounds of several aulos and lute players, competing with the noise of raucous voices. The entire neighborhood was redolent with animal sacrifice. I could tell from the smell that it had been a cow, so that plenty of meat would be left to satisfy the guests after the offering to the gods. I found a niche in one of the walls on the west side of the street and pressed myself into it. As if to mimic my heart, the night was cold.

Eventually, the rented chariot arrived. It was pulled by a pair of magnificent white horses. The chariot itself glittered with gilt ornamentation. It was truly the conveyance of a prince.

The gate opened, and the guests began to spill out. They hooted and called for the bride and groom. At last Cleomenes appeared, wearing a white chiton with a long blue stripe, as would be worn by a professional charioteer. His feet and ankles were covered by calfskin boots with fringe and golden droplets. Around his head sat the unearned olive wreath of the champion. He walked backward, and as soon as he passed out of the gate I realized that he tugged on Thalia to draw her into the street.

As I believe I have written earlier in my tale, the occasion of the wedding feast is one of very few where men and women mix. Also, in the evening women are allowed to enter the street without veils or hoods. Thalia emerged into the street wearing a golden crown. There was no smile upon her exquisite face. I could not tell from where I stood whether or not she wore my earrings.

I started from my hiding place and moved toward the chariot. Thalia had been watching the street carefully. Her eyes caught my approach at almost the moment I emerged from shadow. Her free hand went up to her neck, drawing back her hair. I saw then one of my earrings. I saw also the smile that had won me.

Cleomenes was preoccupied with receiving the reins and mounting a chariot that heaved back and forth from the impatience of high-strung horses. He did not see me behind him.

I lifted my hand. Thalia dared to reach out. Then her focus went past me, and a startled expression transformed her face. An instant later I was hauled backward by two pairs of strong arms. I swung my head left and right in surprise. Diocles and Ioannis had locked me in their skillful grasps. Swiftly, they turned me about and dragged me away from the bridal party.

"Are you insane?" Diocles asked.

"Of course he is," said the other of Timon's agents. "He is insane from love."

"Let me go!" I protested.

"To do what?" Diocles countered. "What will it gain you to antagonize Cleomenes? Do you fancy yourself Paris and her Helen, that you would steal her away?"

"She asked me to come!" I said, thrashing in vain against their strong arms.

"Then she is as insane as you. Do not risk your rising position in the army," Ioannis advised.

"What is that to you?" I railed.

Having reached the end of the block, the two men stopped. "It means much to us," Ioannis said. "Rather than wasting your time here, let us take you to a thermopolium."

Δ

Timon's men took me from Ortygia and into Achradina to a drinking establishment that they clearly favored, as several men greeted them warmly the moment they appeared. The place had a private chamber off the street, and we were allowed to occupy it.

After he had poured out wine for the three of us, Ioannis said, "Let us further your education. You know that Hieron had three children who lived into adulthood."

"Yes, Gelon and two daughters," I said.

"Heraclia and Damarata. Heraclia is married to Zoippos, and they have two daughters. Damarata is married to Adranodoros. None of their children survived."

"But since Hieronymos and his sister survive their father Gelon, Heraclia and Damarata are only aunts and not in direct line for the throne," I said, not wanting to lose the skein.

"True. But others more distant than they have wrested thrones in the past," said Diocles. "Damarata is a constant schemer. Moreover, she is vicious and ruthless. And then there is Harmonia. I would not put past her the murder of her brother so that her husband Themistos could take the throne."

"I am glad not to serve among the palace guard," I admitted.

"You do not know the half of it," Ioannis replied. "Among these wretched excuses for humans, Adranodoros and Themistos are most opposed to our allegiance with Roma. Brother-in-law and son-in-law both worked on Gelon while he lived, to reason him away from Hieron's thinking. We believe they are in the pay of Carthage. Zoippos claims to support Roma, but this may only be to continue the currying of the king's favors."

"Hieron, Nereis, Heraclia, Damarata, Hieronymos, and Harmonia each have their own dedicated guard," Diocles shared. "Naturally, to maintain their positions all of these men claim the same feelings toward Roma and Carthage as their benefactors. Some may be genuine; we feel most would shift opinions like a flag shifts in the wind. But such private thoughts are difficult to plumb."

"And then there are Diocles and myself," said Ioannis. "We serve the king indirectly and Timon directly."

"And you are for Roma," I said.

Ioannis smiled. "Absolutely."

"How many agents like you are there?" I asked.

"We know of one other pair inside the city. We believe there is another, but that one never comes to the palace. Timon has also established informers in Roma, Carthage, Messana, Neapoli, Sardinia, Tarentum, and Korinthos."

I whistled softly at this.

"The price of knowledge is not cheap," Ioannis said.

"Do you bring me here to share it or to glean it?" I returned.

"We speak with you now for two reasons. Both have to do with the aging of the king. Several physicians all agree that he cannot last beyond next summer. Therefore, Hieron does everything he can to insure that Siracusa and Roma remain friends beyond his passing. He works every day on Hieronymos. He brings these Roman women into our city, to show our people that they are just as human as you and I. He feeds the Roman army and allows their war galleys temporary berths in our harbor. He bribes nobles such as Cleomenes for their loyalty."

"Cleomenes will turn the moment Hieron dies," I said, picturing the vainglorious bridegroom in his fancy chariot.

"Then he will look foolish to the populace, for he has been compelled to praise Roma in public," said Diocles.

"Hieron is aggrieved for having robbed you of your love," Ioannis said. "But that does not prevent him from wanting to use you even more. Next to your great-uncle, you have become the grand hero of the city." He glanced at his partner, who grinned conspiratorially. "We have tutored more than a dozen men in your exploits and sent them into establishments such as this to spread the word of your deeds. Word came back to Diocles' ear just this afternoon. Hieron has also paid to have a statue of you erected in front of the Euryalus baths, honoring your triumph as pentathlon champion. You will pose for the head after the body is chiseled. This spring, he wishes you to enter into a special competition designed to determine our greatest warrior. You will win."

"You cannot say that with assurance now," I told him.

Diocles winked at me. "I think we can."

Ioannis said, "After that triumph, you will be asked to address the people of Siracusa from the largest agora. We will provide your speech. Rest assured that you, with your noble Roman wife by your side, will exhort the populace to maintain friendly ties with Roma."

I nodded my head slowly, realizing the price that accompanied fame.

"We will help you as much as we can," said Ioannis. "Naturally, we must stay in the shadows."

His words prompted me to recall the man outside the palace who had attempted to bribe me. I spoke then of him and described his face and form. Ioannis looked at Diocles. They nodded at one another.

"He is in the pay of Adranodoros," Ioannis said. "Perhaps he works for others as well. Thank you for this information. You again prove your loyalty." He leaned closer. "You have earned our respect, Leonides, and that is not a light deed. We have lived for years in a world where no one is to be trusted. You have won us over not merely for your prowess as a soldier but also for your honesty, integrity, and loyalty. There is a personal reason why we have told you all this: We wish you to advance your life in light rather than stumbling around in darkness. In spite of our best efforts and those of Hieron and Timon, if Hannibal continues to win on the Italian peninsula we will not be able to keep this city loyal to Roma. Even if that does not occur, when Hieron dies Timon loses most of his power. He has proven too faithful to his king for the other members of the family to trust him. We are his left and right hands. We will fall with him. When Hieron dies, Timon has already given us permission to seem to distance ourselves from him. We can do this best by joining your special band."

"The Silent Storm?"

"Precisely. All of its members do not serve on a full-time basis. This would be perfect for us. I am certain that neither Diocles nor I would embarrass you if we were members."

"On the contrary," I said. "You are both excellent fighters. My group would have much to learn from you."

Ioannis stretched out his hand. "Then let us agree to this. We will protect your reputation inside the palace as long as we can, and you will protect us when the time comes."

At last I had a bargaining position with two keepers of secrets within the palace walls. I determined to use it. "I will accept you both if you can discover one fact: I must know how Timon came to learn about the love between Thalia and me."

"We know that already," said Ioannis. "In fact, I am glad that you have asked us. It reminds me to impress upon you that you are to speak with no one about the matters we have discussed this evening or may discuss in the future."

"Naturally not."

"Nor may you set them to paper."

"I do not write," I admitted.

Ioannis leaned back against the wall and folded his arms. "We know. Because of this failing, you are reduced to bringing your thoughts to a scribe. Even your most intimate thoughts and secrets."

The realization struck me like a spear in the chest. "The scribe!"

"Nearly all the scribes in the city report to us," Diocles said. "It is our most effective means of amassing information. You wrote of your love for a woman named Thalia. Timon had no interest in this until he was given the task of winning Cleomenes back to our side. It was then that he learned of that man's desire for the woman who loved you."

"Thalia was his as soon as Eustace agreed to give her up for the good of the city," said Ioannis.

"And for a monopoly on the palace's imported wine purchases," added Diocles wryly.

Ioannis threw up his hands in an expression of sympathy. "You had no chance, whether or not you dictated letters to the scribe. However, you could have saved yourself from being assigned a Roman bride. Timon needed you tied up as tightly as possible."

My face must have betrayed my pent-up anger, for Ioannis hastened to add, "You understand, he did not do it out of malice. He merely did his job as well as he could. Diocles and I know these things to be true. We had no part in them." He again held out his hand. "Are we still welcome to your fold?"

I then clasped his arm as well as that of Diocles.

Diocles said, "Another bit of advice: When Hieron makes a suggestion, as he did in giving you free rein to recruit more men to your cohort, he means it as a polite command. Ioannis and I smiled that you did not leap to take advantage of this opportunity. Such is not your nature. Other men would have tried to take 200 under their command when Hieron suggested a hundred. They understand power lies behind many swords."

"I do not wish power for my own end," I replied.

"And this is why you are such a noble spirit."

"I believe the word is naïve," I answered. Both men shook their heads in disagreement. Diocles poured a little more wine in my bowl.

"If you were naïve at one time, it is not so any longer. No, you are noble, Leonides. It is why Ioannis and I want to cast our lot with you. Take Hieron's suggestion and our advice: Double the size of your band. This is twice the power, but it is still not so many that it will arouse suspicion or envy among your fellow officers."

"Very well," I acceded.

"There is one more thing," Ioannis said. "In order that you remain the paragon of Siracusa, you must stay away from the wife of Cleomenes. She is bad business."

"It is Cleomenes who is bad business!" I parried.

Ioannis shook his head. "I do not mean her character. I am sure she is a wonderful woman. I mean that as his wife she must not be touched. Pale as she is, one embrace from her can cover you with mud. If you are unhappy with your own wife, say the word. We can arrange to put you into the arms of half a dozen exquisite young women. Some are married, if that improves the thrill."

I told them that I had no such interest.

"We did not think so," Diocles said. "But please stay away from the quarry owner's wife."

CHAPTER XV

About three weeks after Thalia's wedding, I found myself walking near the home of Archimedes. On a whim, I decided to stop in and see if he might be in his house rather than inside the secret warehouse near the harbor. I found him in his garden, holding his customary long wand and drawing in the wet sand. To my surprise, he already had an audience. Aurora sat on a bench near the sand pit, with a blanket drawn over her shoulders against the cool wind that swooped down into the courtyard for a peek at the genius' work before it blew seaward.

"What brings you here?" I asked my wife.

"I imagine the same thing that brings you," she said. "I am visiting the most interesting man in Siracusa."

"You believe this is a first visit?" Archimedes asked me, a twinkle in his eye. "If you do, you had better come home more often. Aurora visits me at least once a week."

"I pass by three or four times per week, in the hopes of finding him," she freely admitted. "He is rarely home."

"I am about the king's work, as you well know. Your wife is one of the only reasons I come home. If I were forty years younger...no, even twenty years younger, I would steal her from you."

A swift image of Thalia stepping into the wedding chariot came to my mind.

"And what do you two do?" I asked.

"What does any man do with a highly attractive woman?" my great-uncle riposted. "We talk. I flatter her. She accepts it, which appeals to my vanity."

"Do you gossip?" I asked.

Archimedes looked at me askance. "We have no time for that. We debate. Common minds talk gossip; noble minds talk ideas."

"Your uncle allows me to borrow some of his scrolls," Aurora revealed.

"And I borrow hers." Archimedes looked at Aurora. The two burst into laughter.

"What is the joke?" I asked.

"Our drawings of the Roman war machines were not inside Aurora's scrolls," Archimedes admitted. "I lied to you when we were in the water, to force you to save them."

"You two are alike," I decided, shaking my head. "If given a choice of scrolls or a meal to keep you from starving, you would choose the scrolls."

"Absolutely!" both said at once.

"Although now you have set my mind thinking about food," said Archimedes. "I remember that I have not eaten today."

"I shall go and find Irene," Aurora volunteered, rising from the bench. She patted it for me to take her place and moved into the house.

Archimedes watched her disappear. He turned slowly toward me and pointed his wand at my middle. "You must have been kissed by the gods when you were born. To be smart and strong and so successful in your profession as such an early age. All that and to be given Aurora as well."

"She is no trouble," I admitted.

"No trouble?" Archimedes struck me a stinging blow with his stick. "She cooks, she weaves, and she knows how to shop. All these one might expect from a woman. But she also paints, she is well-read and educated, and she knows how to listen! You should have paid Marcellus a dowry for her instead of the other way around."

Everyone who knew Aurora liked her. I was surprised that she had yet to show her fractious side. I wondered how long she would be able to keep up the pleasant persona before lapsing into her tirades on the evils of keeping slaves, the brutality of men in limiting women's rights, the stupidity of worshipping multiple gods.

Her doting, old champion said, "She loves Siracusa. She is very grateful for you taking her from Roma. 'Rescuing' is the exact word she used. She tells me she felt she never belonged there. She believes that naiads spirited her from Greece when she was born." He waited for me to reply. When I remained silent, he added, "She wants to give you something back. Why don't you allow her to teach you to read?"

"She has told you I can't read?" I said in a strident voice, feeling anger well up.

"Calm yourself. I knew it before I met her."

In a way, I was relieved to have the old man admit he knew I could barely read. It had been a terrible burden on me and a constant struggle to pretend when around him. Outside of the homes of the very rich, the scholarly academies, or the few libraries of the world there are precious few scrolls and therefore few opportunities to embarrass myself. However, Archimedes seemed to attract reading materials like dead horses attract flies. People fairly pushed them under his nose for his reaction. I was ever in danger of being found out if he handed me a scroll and asked me to save his old eyes. What affected me most by his revelation was the fact that this man who showed such unremitting disdain for the uneducated man had been so solicitous of my feelings.

"How long have you known?" I asked.

"I overheard your father's remark, about how money spent on teaching you to read could be much better spent teaching you to kill. I suppose you were thirteen then. I did not like his attitude, but he is your father."

"But has Aurora spoken to you about this?"

"No. I have no idea if she knows. Why should you keep it from her? Do you think you were supposed to spring from your mother's womb reading Plato?"

I winced. "It is one thing for her to know, I suppose. But you suggest I should learn to read from her?"

"And why not?" This time Archimedes poked me with the wand. "Because she is a woman? Did you not learn to walk and talk from a woman? Did a woman not teach you your first sense of morals? I say you would give her a present by allowing her to give something of value that she owns to you."

"I will think on it," I said.

"You have untapped capacities, Leonides," my great-uncle lectured. "Do not be embarrassed because you do not yet read. This is a consequence of ignorance and not stupidity. The first can be remedied; the second cannot. You already speak with a remarkably rich vocabulary. I would not be surprised if there is a writer, even a poet buried inside you."

Aurora returned out of the house, as if on cue through a stage entrance. I thought of Thalia and the theater performance. Aurora set down a plate of cheese, bread, and dried fruits on the bench.

"A poet buried inside my husband?" she echoed.

"No, inside the back wall of our courtyard," I responded. "He recited an ode about the nobility of being a slave, and I had to kill him. For you, of course."

This time, Aurora struck me, pounding her small fist against my upper arm.

"Take your wife home!" Archimedes commanded. "I am not so old that I have forgotten that playfulness and punching soon lead to sex."

"When may I visit the warehouse and see your inventions?" I asked.

"When we go to war," he replied, pushing his stick into the sand pit.

"That is not fair," I protested. "I brought you to Roma to view the weapons that have formed your inspiration."

"And if Carthage should declare war on us tomorrow while you are on patrol, and their soldiers capture and torture you for information? No, the fewer men who see what I am devising the better. This includes you."

"I'll wager they are mere copies of the Roman weapons," I said, trying to bait my great-uncle into showing me.

"As like to them as wine is to water," he said. "Now go! Leave me!"

Aurora took my hand and drew me from the garden.

Not five minutes later, as Aurora and I walked side-by-side down one of Achradina's main thoroughfares, I heard my name. I turned and looked into a shadowy alley. Sitting with her back against a wall and surrounded by filthy rags was Azar, Thalia's old nurse. As I paused in astonishment, she struggled arthritically to her feet and hastened toward us.

"The gods bless you!" she greeted. Her manner and tone of voice were so pleasant and unlike her that my shock redoubled. Her clothing was sound enough, but it was dirty. "I wonder if you can help me."

"Why do you need my help?" I asked, stepping between her and Aurora.

"I have been dismissed from the house of Eustace," she said, her lower lip trembling at the admission and all its dire implications.

"Because Thalia is now married?" I said.

Azar's old eyes fixed on Aurora. "That's right. They tried to sell me for a time, but no one would have me. It is their own fault, complaining to everyone they know about me for years. So they turned me out."

I felt Aurora's hand steal to my wrist and encircle it. "And why did Thalia not take you?" I said.

"She blamed me for having to marry Cleomenes. She said I had worked with him against her and you."

Aurora's grip tightened suddenly, but she said nothing.

"This is my wife," I said to Azar.

This news sealed her tongue to the floor of her mouth. She studied Aurora with wise eyes, then murmured a hello and offered a small bow.

"Why are you out on the street?" I asked. "You had a good deal of money only a few months ago."

"Eustace took it all from me. He said it was the price of my freedom. But I didn't want my freedom."

"This is terrible!" Aurora said, coming around from behind me. "You have asked me if I needed a helper."

"I meant someone who could work hard," I said, not liking the set of Aurora's jaw, a look I had not seen since Roma.

"I can work hard, sir," Azar affirmed, her voice trying to sound resolute even as she pleaded. "I just need a day or two to recover myself."

"Of course you do," soothed Aurora.

"Look at her!" I said. "I, too, feel pity for her plight, but she will not be able to do enough to earn her food."

"I will!" Azar insisted.

"We have the extra room," Aurora argued.

"But no bed in it," I rejoined.

"I can sleep on the ground. And I don't need any pay. I'll consider myself your slave," Azar bargained.

"You will do nothing of the kind!" Aurora snapped. She whirled to face me and drew herself up to the limit of her short stature. "I have asked you for little since I came here, Leonides. I now ask to have this woman in our house."

I forced my mouth open and drew in a long breath. "Her presence will be painful to me. I did not want to say this out of respect for you, Aurora, but she was the nurse of the woman I loved."

"A woman who is now married to another," she said evenly.

"That's correct."

"And to spare you some discomfort, we will allow this woman to starve or die from the cold?" Aurora asked. Before I could reply, she said, "I will need a nurse within a few more months. I am going to bear your child."

Δ

Aurora got her way. I who already felt ill at ease in my new home felt even more alienated. For the sake of Aurora, I visited at least every other week. She knew that I was expected to live in the fortress as a professional soldier. She did not know, however, how often I came near our house on patrols or for services to the palace and did not stop.

Azar tried to stay out of my way. She was a simple woman but not without sensibilities. Once in late winter, when Aurora was out in the street occupied in talking with neighbor women, I cornered the old nurse.

"What have you told my wife about Thalia and me?" I demanded.

"I have volunteered nothing," she said, flinching.

194

"Why do you shrink from me? Do you think I will hit you?"

"Perhaps."

"Were you hit in Eustace's house?"

"Many times."

"Did you deserve it?"

"If one drops a pot one has handled for ten years, does one deserve to be hit?" she replied.

"No."

"For such things I was beaten."

"And your sharp tongue? Tell me that was not the cause of several beatings."

Azar lowered her eyes. "I cannot."

"I will not hit you in any case," I promised. "But you have not answered me straight. If you have volunteered nothing about Thalia and me, Aurora still may have asked you questions."

Azar straightened up as much as her old body would allow her to do so. "She never has."

"I find that strange," I freely remarked.

"As do I. But it is also wise on her part. What answer can I provide that will satisfy her? If I say that you were lovers and torn apart, she will despair. If I say you were merely affectionate with each other and dreamed that perhaps one day you might wed, she will believe that I mix in milk to make salt meat sweet."

"She is biding her time," I decided aloud, "winning you over completely, so that she can get the whole truth."

"I do not believe that," Azar said. "Since you say you will not hit me, let me speak plainly: Your wife is a better woman than Thalia. She is selfless and kind."

"Thalia is not?"

"No, neither." She shrugged. "She once was, but not of late."

"Of course not of late!" I fumed. Azar was ready to say more, but I thrust my open hand up close to her face. "You malign her because she did not trust you and would not take you in."

Azar studied me for a few moments. Then she made a small bow. "As you wish." Without another word, she took herself into the street after her mistress.

When I left the house that day, I made up my mind that the company of men was far simpler than with any woman. I resigned myself to the pleasures of honing our warrior skills, of athletic competitions, of drinking, singing, and storytelling. Euryalus became to me two kinds of fortress.

At last, I was completely glad to be a soldier.

CHAPTER XVI

As Hieron had suggested and Ioannis and Diocles reinforced, I increased the number of men in the Silent Storm in the winter and early spring. By ones and twos it increased to four dozen. The silence from Strategos Archidamus or any of the other high-ranking officers was conspicuous, but I now understood a tiny bit of the politics of such maneuvers and did not lose sleep over the lack of reaction. We kept a low profile, carrying out our exercises beyond the city walls, in order not to arouse questions among those not party to palace intrigues. I was assigned a private room, and my cohort was given its own general room on the top floor of the fortress's southeast corner.

We drilled as much as was practicable. My main concern was keeping my men fit and in fighting readiness in spite of uninterrupted peace and prosperity. I was not shy in transmitting to my force my conviction that Siracusa would be fighting for its life within a matter of years if not months. Carthage and Roma hung over our heads like twin swords of Damocles.

Those citizens who took news on its face value were happy to hear that no major battles had been waged on the Italian peninsula since Cannae. They believed that this meant the Roman and Carthaginian forces were roughly equal and that this parity would prevent either from attacking us. My opinion was that sooner or later one would seek our wealth, our harbors, and our supply of men to gain the advantage.

Aurora's father once again proved that he was the best among the Roman Republic's fighting men. Hannibal's agents worked tirelessly to convince the town of Nola to defect from the Roma confederacy. This threatened the transportation and communications routes from Roma into the heart of the Campania. Rather than face the proximate Carthaginian force, Marcellus marched in a long, circuitous route and dug in his army on a ridge that overlooked the town of Suessula, which lay only fifty-five stadia from Nola. The camp, which was named Castra Claudiana in his honor, prevented Hannibal from ranging through Campania. It also made it highly difficult for the Carthaginian general to move his troops north. In my opinion this pinching maneuver, coupled with a refusal to come to battle, worked in the Romans' favor. Brilliantly, by this ostensibly defensive move Marcellus for the first time had put the Romans on the offensive.

With Marcellus entrenched so near, the populace of Nola was convinced not to defect. Hannibal abandoned this goal and moved on to Neapoli. There, Marcellus had providentially already arranged to move in a garrison by sea. As I had learned by personal experience, there existed virtually no ports on the Adriatic side of the peninsula. Those ports on the Tyrrhenian Sea side across the Campania were all controlled by the Romans. The Carthaginian army could not be supplied from distant ports.

We learned that Hannibal had therefore turned south to sack and burn Nuceria, hoping to draw Marcellus out. When he circled back to Nola, he found Marcellus's main legions encamped within its walls. He then attacked, sacked, and burned Acerrae, which lay about forty-eight stadia from Nola. His harsh tactics, we understood, were losing him allies. Marcellus, however, offered no greater mercy. Once he had moved his legions into Nola, he hunted down those who had promoted defection and had them crucified.

The only other major news that came to us, as the days of a new year gradually lengthened, focused on Casilinum. This town controlled the only crossing of the Volturno River, which constituted a major barrier to movement north. The Romans had garrisoned it well enough that Hannibal could not take the town by direct assault. Since the time of darkness and hard earth had arrived, he set siege lines around the walls and went into winter quarters in Capua, not far south.

The town held out all through the winter. However, by the early spring their provisions were exhausted. Marcellus petitioned to relieve the town with a surprise attack against the besiegers before Hannibal could deploy the main force of his still-somnolent army. However, a new consul had been elected to replace the dictator. This man, Tiberius Sempronius Gracchus by name, refused to allow Marcellus to engage the Carthaginians. The resourceful Marcellus had jars half filled with grain floated down the river at night so that the town defenders could scoop them out. Soon enough, the enemy spotted them and took them for their own nourishment. Then nuts were floated downstream to the starving. The Carthaginians devised hurdles made from wattling to strain them out. The garrison negotiated safe passage out of the town, and Hannibal moved his own garrison in.

As of the early summer of that year, this was all we heard of the protracted war between Roma and Carthage. On the seas, the two great war fleets had not found each other.

Δ

In the meantime I stayed busy, not only drilling my group, but also in preparing for the army games that were to mark the festival of Ares. All who aspired to be crowned champion needed to compete in every one of six categories. These were wrestling, discus throwing, javelin throwing, distance running, lifting of weights calculated against each athlete's size, and hatchet throwing. Even though I had won the previous pentathlon, I had fared poorly in the broad jump category, so this was eliminated by Hieron's judging committee as having no possible bearing on martial skills. Naturally, I had given more than ample evidence of my abilities in weightlifting and hatchet throwing. As far as I ever determined, no man between the ages of eighteen and thirty-two was forbidden to enter the contest. Nor was anyone to my knowledge bribed to decline to compete. In this way, one might say that the competition was not fixed. In truth, it had been well designed for me to win.

I carried first or second places in all but wrestling and discus throwing, in which I still finished in the top five. At the end of the three-day event, I added to my previous accolades the title of Defender of Siracusa. Ironically, I was given the reins of the same chariot Cleomenes had rented in order to parade around a great circuit of the city's streets. Behind me marched the men of the Silent Storm. Riding at my side was Archidamus, the city's general. No Siracusan hero had ever been so well manufactured.

The parade ended at the city's largest agora, where the desiccated, walking corpse that was our king greeted me. He personally set the olive branch crown upon my head. I was led to the speaker's platform by a platoon of children. One presented me a bouquet of spring flowers, for which I rewarded her with a pristine kiss. From the platform, I delivered by memory a speech not of my fashioning, but one which I was not loath to recite. It reminded the populace that Siracusa was an independent city, despite its friendship with Roma. As such, it had a strong obligation to protect itself and those surrounding towns who depended on it as much as we depended on them. Toward such an end, I exhorted every male to exercise daily and to hone his skills as a warrior. Only by demonstrating to other races that we were powerful could we dissuade them from attacking us. I called upon not merely Ares, but all the gods to look upon us with benevolence, and prayed that Siracusa would remain free for all time. The words were well received by the throng of thousands. I felt at the same moment incredibly invulnerable and vulnerable.

When I stepped from the marble podium, Aurora awaited me. We were conducted to our home by my cohort, with several of their number volunteering to stand guard lest I be bothered by those who sought borrowed glory by occupying the attention of the blessed.

"You spoke the words perfectly," Aurora praised, as Azar helped her out of her himation.

"I owe that to you," I freely admitted.

The speech had been delivered to me more than two months earlier. It had come from the palace on a scroll. This scroll Aurora had used as the method for teaching me to read. She read passages again and again to me until I had them memorized. Once this was accomplished, the task of matching words to the groups of letters on the scroll became immensely easier. As the speech was meant for the common man, an abundance of simple words had been used. By the day of the parade, I could recognize more than 100 words. You who read this understand well when I say that the accomplishment delighted me as much as all the contests I had ever won. The minds of the great were now open to me first-hand by simply unrolling a scroll.

"I am pleased to serve my husband," Aurora said. I noted that the swell in her belly had just begun to show through her chiton. I realized that I had not thought of Thalia for an entire week. I was simultaneously aggrieved and relieved by this realization.

"As the daughter of a great general, I should be resigned to the ways of war," Aurora continued. "You know this is not so, Leonides. And yet I am proud of you, both as an athlete and as the symbol of our readiness to do battle to protect this paragon of cities."

I assured her that I was equally proud of her and content with my life. I did not think I was lying.

Δ

The morning after my crowning as the city's champion, I returned to the fortress of Euryalus. I found waiting there a servant who held a scroll with a wax seal. The seal was that of the family of Cleomenes.

I took the scroll into the privacy of my quarters and broke the seal. Thanks to Aurora, I could read it. It was from Thalia. She told me that, in spite of her husband's order not to attend the crowning in the agora she had stolen from her household and witnessed it from the rooftop of a merchant she patronized. She professed to be immensely proud of me. She further stated that the flame of her love had not dwindled in the slightest. If anything, it burned hotter. She ached to see me and declared that she would die of a broken heart if I did not bring an offering to the same temple where she and I had passed so many joyous minutes in happier times. She named the day and time and begged me not to disappoint her.

I burned the scroll, not to be done with it but so that no one might find it and know where I would be two days hence.

Δ

Thalia's old nurse had been replaced by a pair of eunuchs. They were so much brawn and so little brain that Thalia was certain neither would suspect an assignation behind her visit to the Temple of Apollo in Neapolis. A bakery stood near the temple, and it was there that she sent them each with a coin, to treat themselves however they wished. Thus, she was quite alone when I entered the hall of offerings.

We both knew the hidden corner from our past trysts. Thalia rushed up to me the moment I appeared and dragged me around the corner and into the shadows of a thick pillar. She pulled away her veil with a sharp tug. I beheld her spellbinding beauty. From her ears dangled the earrings I had given her.

"Kiss me!" she commanded.

I obeyed. A choked sob emerged from her throat, even as she returned my ardor.

"I have dreamed of that kiss a thousand times," she told me, as she pressed her delicate self against my length. I felt my blood pounding and my flesh rise. "Tell me that you love me still."

"You know I do," I answered.

"You are married."

"I had no choice," I apologized.

Thalia pivoted and pounded her fists against the pillar, showing a rage I had never seen in her before. For good measure, she kicked the insensate mass of stone. "Neither of us had a choice. We are both slaves to Hieron's infernal politics."

Voices approached. Thalia pressed herself against the column, and I covered her body with my own. Her flesh was desire itself. I grew light-headed with the scent of her perfume. Presently, the voices faded.

"There is nothing we can do," I despaired.

"You are mistaken, my love," Thalia said. "We can use the very politics that separated us to bring us together. I was given to Cleomenes because he began to campaign with other powerful men for a change of allegiance to Carthage."

"I know this well," I said.

"He now has more than 300 men working for him. Almost 100 of these are citizens. He owns their voices and their votes. Hieron cannot allow him to reverse his opinion again. And yet I know that Cleomenes never changed to Hieron's side. He has been working secretly to insure a shift toward Carthage the moment the king dies. Furthermore, he has had agents of Carthage in our home. I know the specifics of their next visit. If you as the city's champion expose him and allow the palace guard to catch the agents in our home, Hieron will have no choice but to eliminate Cleomenes."

"Do you think that the king would have him killed?"

"Should he not execute a traitor?"

Thalia's rapid and vehement reply rattled me. "You would see the man murdered?"

"He knew I loved you. He did not care. For this alone I want him dead." Thalia must have seen the shock in my eyes, for she immediately added, "But his greater sin is betraying a sworn oath to his king. Hieron will kill him; we will have no part in it."

"Hieron is a benevolent dictator," I reminded her. "He has never once in his long reign had anyone murdered or even exiled for opposing him."

"That was when he cared about his reputation," Thalia countered. "He is now a dying man, desperate to control the fate of the city as he wishes it to be after he is gone. I think he will get rid of Cleomenes if given sufficient cause. If entertaining Carthaginian agents is not enough, then tell me what is, and I will arrange it." Thalia's eyes were fierce. "He has had his way with me for long enough. I do not wish to open my legs to him even one more night."

"When will these agents visit your house again?" I asked.

"Do not call it my house! Say instead my prison. Three days after today, when the sun has set. Swear to me that you will pass this on to Hieron!"

"I will indeed," I said.

Thalia peeked around the pillar. When she had assured herself that we were indeed alone and undiscovered, she smiled and ran her hand up the inside of my thigh.

"Some good things came from my marriage," she said. "The first was getting me out of my bastard father's grasp. The second was proving to me how wonderful the joys of the flesh may be. If I was moved by the attentions of that slug Cleomenes, I can hardly imagine how I will be transported when I lie beneath you."

Her words set the blood pounding in my ears. And yet they could not drown out the thoughts that filled my mind.

"More than one bad thing came from your marriage," I could not help observing. "Azar was tossed out of your father's house."

"That was not bad at all," Thalia declared. "She was eternally a schemer. She gave Cleomenes every bit of information he needed to tear us apart and to win me."

"How do you know that to be true?"

"Because I periodically counted the money she had hidden away. Cleomenes bribed her with twice what you gave her."

"Does that necessarily prove she betrayed us?" I asked.

"She became desperate in her old age. She knew I would escape my father's house soon enough, and she schemed to make the most of it." Thalia's eyebrows furrowed. "How do you know she was dismissed?"

"I saw her on the street."

"How long ago?"

"In early winter," I answered. To test her feelings, I added, "Perhaps she is dead by now."

Thalia shook her beautiful head. "No. She is much too clever for that. She has wheedled her way into some unsuspecting household. Trust me." Her eyes narrowed slightly. "Since we speak of households, tell me of yours. The woman under your roof is a Roman."

"She is."

"Of noble birth, I hear."

"That is also true," I confirmed.

"Do you love her?" she challenged.

"I respect her highly," I said.

Thalia smiled. "That is all I need to hear. She is the daughter of a great and wealthy man. No doubt she brought a good-sized dowry with her. Have you spent any of it?"

"Some," I admitted. "I purchased a house."

"It will all have to be returned when you repudiate her," Thalia said. "But no matter. Cleomenes has no brothers to pass along his businesses and house. I have flattered and delighted him into leaving me all of his estate in his will. His uncles and cousins will not be able to break it. I will have more than enough to replace whatever has been spent of this Latini's dowry. It is time you took your Greek prize, my champion." As punctuation, Thalia kissed me again.

"We must part," I worried.

"Unfortunately," she agreed. "But we part so that we may be to-gether forever. Remember well the day and get it to Hieron's ears." Thalia lifted my hand to her breast and encouraged me to fondle it. As I did, she hunched up her shoulders and gave out a languorous sigh. The next moment, she fled from behind the pillar with such speed that I was left with my empty hand in the air.

I lingered behind the pillar for several minutes, digesting all that had transpired in but a few minutes. More than a little of it disturbed me. I knew, however, that I would do precisely what Thalia wanted me to do.

CHAPTER XVII

As you understand by this point in my tale, the Fates, who I too often accuse of treating me poorly, nearly always smile upon me. Virtually every citizen of Siracusa would have said the same of our king. But both our fortunes were nothing compared with the luck of Cleomenes. I never got the chance to report Thalia's words to the king, Timon, or even Ioannis or Diocles. On the very day that Thalia and I met in the temple, Hieron the Second died.

If anyone in Siracusa did not expect Hieron's death, he had to be blind and deaf. The man had attained ninety years, a feat of which not one in a thousand can boast. Moreover, the state of his declining health could be visibly traced in his stance, his movement, his reedy and wavering voice, his dwindling weight over the final year of his life. Thus, when he passed on, the city was prepared. The body lay in state for two days. It was dressed in a robe so white that its folds were difficult to distinguish. His beard was carefully trimmed. Around his head had been positioned a crown of golden leaves. By his side, as befit a warrior of days gone by, lay his sword and buckler.

I was given the great honor of offering my respects soon after the body was laid upon the catafalque. Everyone in the incense-laden chamber wept, including Timon, his faithful chief minister. His family stood upon the raised steps around the throne, which no one yet presumed to occupy. The various units of the family stood in their own discreet groupings, with Gelon's wife Neries flanked by her son Hieronymos and daughter Harmonia. Harmonia's husband, Themistos, stood behind them. This group huddled closest to the catafalque. Hieron's daughter Damarata and her husband Adranodoros held closest to the throne. The other daughter, Heraclia, clasped her two small daughters to her sides while her husband Zoippos spoke in low tones with Timon. The king's body was hardly cold, and the political alignments were apparently already taking place

I could not get near Timon that day or the next, and his agents Ioannis and Diocles were nowhere to be found. I told myself that, in light of Hieron's death, the visit of the Carthaginian agents had no doubt either been cancelled or rescheduled. Cleomenes had surely eluded some sort of punishment or loss.

The city expected to mourn. They were not denied their grief. The funeral procession began with ninety women wailing and ritualistically tearing at their hair. After this came no fewer than fifty priests, soothsayers, and astrologers of the court and the temples. Hieron took his final ride on a glimmering gilt wagon festooned with flowers and eggshells, the symbol of new life.

The body lay exposed for all to see. It and all the mourners wore white, our traditional shade of grief. Although the full 100 members of the palace guard marched beside and behind the cortege, no onlookers were restrained from tossing their sacks of fruits or nuts onto the wagon. Nor were mourners prevented from smashing tiny vases made for the occasion against the wagon or onto the street.

A second wagon followed after the first, heaped with full-sized vases and amphorae, robes, polished bronze mirrors and other grooming devises, spears, helmet and shield, and a hundred other items Hieron might need in the afterlife. I waited until this wagon approached to move into the center of the street. I was by this time so well known that the pressing throng parted for me, as did members of the guard. Onto the pile of treasures I placed the bronze strigil my father had given for me to scrape the oil from my body on the first day I was sent to exercise at the gymnasium. It was my way of hoping that he would reclaim the body of his youth in the next world. In spite of the fact that I knew the king would die soon, I found myself grieving his passing more than I would have expected. The man had believed in and nurtured me as might a second father. I was relieved that I had not been called upon to deliver a funeral oration.

When I looked up, I realized that Hieronymos, Hieron's only grandson and his intended heir, had come near to me. He led the well-guarded contingent of the royal family from horseback. Although he was now fifteen and considered a man, he had yet to shed the frailty of youth. He held his head high, as he had no doubt been instructed to do, to assure the populace that he could indeed take his grandfather's place. I, however, stood close enough to read the uncertainty in his eyes. A bolt of terror shot through me.

I returned to the edge of the street, where Aurora stood watching by Archimedes' side. To disguise my extreme upset, I offered them a broad smile. Neither returned the expression.

"Peace has just begun for him," my great-uncle commented, nodding at the disappearing wagon. "It has just ended for us."

Δ

The shock of Hieron's death was precisely what Amara needed to jolt her body into giving birth. She had carried the child ten days beyond the expected due date. Aurora said that she had never seen a woman so great with child. In spite of my protestations, Aurora insisted on telling me in detail of the birth. She had attended with Azar, as much to prepare herself for her own event as to assist Amara.

The labor went on for fourteen hours. Typically, babies are born with their skull bones soft and malleable until after birth, the better to ease the passage down the birth canal. The son of Apollonius and Amara later proved that his head was stuffed with brains, and consequently it hardly deformed. This caused great pain and bleeding for Amara and required that she eventually be cut. Aurora said that she did not know so much blood existed inside one human being. Afterward, Amara was too weak to care for her son, so Aurora and Azar moved into her home and attended to her and the baby night and day.

Apollo wished to name his son Leonides after me, but Amara would have none of it.

"He will not be a soldier. He will not have a soldier's name," she insisted. "He came into this world bloodied, but I will not have him go out the same way."

And so he was called Phocylides, after her father. He was healthy and did seem to me and everyone else quite alert and bright from the beginning. Apollonius was immensely proud. He wished me such a son. I wondered if our two children were entering the world at the wrong time.

Δ

One week after Hieron's funeral, Ioannis and Diocles found me at Euryalus. I brought them into my room and closed the door.

"We are now ready to join with you," Diocles said. "We desire a full-time appointment. We know that Archidamus will approve this."

"It must be done now, before Archidamus loses power," said Ioannis.

This statement disturbed me. I had never considered that the death of Hieron would cause our strategos to lose his command over the Siracusan army. If he had wanted to take the empty throne, he had enough loyalty among the professional troops to do so. Moreover, he knew how to accomplish it; he had been at Hieron's side when the man declared himself king. I had thought that a man as covered with glory and so long in his position as Archidamus would have had both the Roman and the Carthaginian sides of the city vying for his favor. I said as much to Ioannis and Diocles.

"You may be right," Diocles granted. "Gelon felt that Archidamus has grown old and too weary to thirst for such power. We cannot tell. Whatever fate may befall him, ours does not lie within the palace."

I asked them about Timon's fate.

Diocles shook his head gravely. "He and Adranodoros head the council to which you and Archimedes belong, but Hieronymos has not asked him to stay on as chief minister. He has appointed Philemon to that position."

"The ship builder?" I asked.

"The same." Diocles shrugged. "A strange profession for a minister of state. I do not believe the man has ever left Sicilia."

"And has he spoken out against Roma?"

"He is a careful man," Diocles responded. "He seems on the surface to be neutral, but we believe he is in the Carthaginian camp."

I told them I had not yet been called to serve as one of the fifteen guardians whom Hieron had put into place.

"And you may never be, if Adranodoros and Themistos have their way," said Ioannis, speaking of the husbands of Hieron's daughter and granddaughter, respectively.

"Should you not stand beside Timon, for his safety?" I asked the pair.

Diocles seemed bothered by my question. He ran his hand back nervously through his hair. "We have never stood by his side. Only in his shadow. He has his guards."

"But attack often comes from out of the shadows," I said, "and you fight so well."

"If certain people want him dead, two more men at his side will not be enough. He has ordered us to come to you. He believes we can now do more good here."

Their unexpected appearance had caught me so off guard that I temporarily forgot how badly I wanted to see them the previous week. I told Timon's former agents about my meeting with Thalia in the temple and made it seem to be over Cleomenes' dealings with Carthaginians.

"Perhaps I should ask you both if you still believe that our city should side with Roma?" I concluded.

"We do," said Ioannis.

"As do I," I agreed. "So, failing to catch Cleomenes in the act of conferring with the enemies of our ally, should we not make him useful in some other way?"

Diocles glanced at his partner. Ioannis nodded.

Brent Monahan

Δ

Two nights after my meeting with Diocles and Ioannis, I stood at midnight outside the house of Cleomenes. By my side were Diocles, Ioannis, and Silent Storm warriors Melampus and Menander. You will recall Melampus as the one who grew up on the docks and who developed the skills to get into any locked and guarded place. Menander is he who avenged his father by climbing over roofs and killing a man in his own bedroom. I was convinced that Ioannis and Diocles also had great skills regarding stealth. I never confronted them directly, but I was certain that they were the men Timon would have used to silence Aurora in Roma if I had not chosen her for a wife.

Diocles seemed eager to take charge of the task, and I allowed it. He had won me over by explaining the difference between murdering a man in his own house and merely interrogating him. The first was best done by only one, especially should the intruder be captured. To interrogate a man, however, took time and of necessity allowed his mouth to be uncovered. This required specific skills I did not own. Further, Diocles stated with conviction that he could learn the exact layout of Cleomenes house, even though neither he nor Ioannis had been inside it.

I shared with the group the fact of the two large eunuch guards. I also knew from watching the house that it had no fewer than five other servants. All of these and Thalia had to be accounted for if we were to enter and depart without exposure. Unfortunately, I had no way of getting a message to Thalia. I assured the men, however, that she was clever and would understand in quick order who was behind the midnight visit.

Ioannis was put in charge of watching the front gate and courtyard from the street. Melampus entered the home over the rooftops. This is not an easy task, owing to the noise created by moving upon tiles. Thick blankets must be laid down before moving and then picked up to repeat the process. Once he had lowered himself by rope to the inner courtyard, Melampus went to the front gate and picked open the lock to allow the rest of us inside. Then moving from door to door, he worked his usual skills in reverse to render the doors impossible to pass through. Sometimes he did this by placing a new lock through old fastening holes,

211

sometimes with a series of wedges, sometimes by means of tying a rope to the door handle and belaying it off somewhere else. When he was finished, he took a guard position at the backdoor.

According to the plans that Diocles had drawn for us, the house had three bedrooms and a storage room on the second level. We expected Cleomenes to sleep in the largest chamber, with Thalia in the room connected directly to it. The third bedroom we expected to find unoccupied, since Cleomenes had no immediate family and no relatives living with him.

As we had anticipated, the third room and the storage space were devoid of habitants. The fourth room did not open directly upon the upper cloister but could only be reached through the main bedroom. Our plan was to enter the main chamber and not awaken Cleomenes until I had reached Thalia's bed. We agreed that I was not to reveal myself to her.

The hinges of the main bedroom door faced the outside. In case this proved to be so, we had brought with us goose fat, which we worked into the cracks of the metal. Diocles was the first into the inky-dark room. He slid along the wall, deftly feeling his way as he went. I moved directly behind him. Several steps in, I needed to advance by myself to where I expected to find Thalia's door. I discovered a rug on the floor by nearly slipping on it. When I finally reached the door and pushed it in, it creaked with a frightening amount of noise.

"Who's there?" Cleomenes called out.

Menander had been waiting at the end of the upper cloister with a lit torch in his hand. At the sound of Cleomenes' voice, he rushed into the room and closed the door behind him.

"What is it?" Thalia asked in a sleepy voice.

I turned with surprise. She had not been in the adjacent room at all but slept beside her husband.

Both Diocles and Menander stood with short swords drawn. Each of us wore a hood of lightly-woven black material over our heads. I carried a dagger.

"Shut up, woman, if you wish to live!" Diocles commanded.

Cleomenes sat up. He had awakened enough already to begin shaking. "What do you wish?"

"Information," said Diocles, who we determined would be the only voice anyone in Cleomenes' household heard that evening. "You have betrayed your king and your own vows, and now you must pay."

"I have done nothing wrong!" Cleomenes called out with an overloud voice.

"Your guards will not save you," Diocles told him. "If you shout again, you will lose the fingers of your right hand. If you lie to me, you will lose your manhood."

At this, Cleomenes drew in a sharp breath.

"We know that you sympathize with the Carthaginians," Diocles said.

"And why shouldn't I?" Cleomenes shot back. "The Romans have stolen all but this corner of Sicilia. Only a few months ago, they began a colony a hundred stadia south into the open territory between us and them. Who are you who would attempt to appease them until they march right in and murder us all?"

Diocles lifted his sword. "Who we are is of no matter to you. What is important is that we are not in the open territory but right here."

"Remember Agricento!" Cleomenes said, alluding to the Roman massacre of the Greek town to our south.

"At least you are not denying your allegiance," said Diocles. "We have watched your house for some time. We have seen Hannibal's agents visit." This he said at my request, to prevent Cleomenes from suspecting Thalia. For her part, she lay on the bed with the top sheet drawn over her and contented herself with listening. "We have also noted you speaking with several citizens who ordinarily do not pass through your gate. I will name thirty. We already know for certain several on this list who sympathize as you do, so do not think to lie half the time."

"And will you kill us all?" Cleomenes asked.

"Worry about yourself. We have chosen you to interrogate because you have publicly supported Roma in exchange for the woman beside you. Therefore, you can only do so much damage. We will do nothing to you if you cooperate. If you lie to us, you will lose all chance of passing on your name."

Cleomenes answered this with a string of oaths and curses. I have no use for men who employ insincere oaths of revenge and curses the gods would never deign to fulfill. I suppose the real reason I rushed to his side and punched him in the mouth was from having to gaze for so long at Thalia lying next to him. However, I justified my action at the time because of his foul tongue.

Diocles grabbed my arm before I could hit him again and pulled me back.

"You have played the brave man enough for your wife's sake," he counseled the quarry owner. "Now I will give you names. You tell me who has spoken to you about creating a government that favors Carthage." Diocles recited his list. Cleomenes nodded or shook his head after each. Diocles seemed satisfied and turned to fetch ropes and gags from a sack he had carried.

A fury overcame me. I had for more than a day held onto the fantasy that Cleomenes would prove himself a real man and refuse to betray his comrades. Then I would have held him with great satisfaction while Diocles and Menander emasculated him. When he disappointed me, I became possessed of a rage. I could not allow him to maintain his manhood, so that he could again and again ravage my beloved against her will.

Growling like a beast, I launched myself at Cleomenes and ripped his nightgown up his body, exposing his legs and genitals. My dagger went up. He thrust out his hands to ward off the blow he expected.

Screaming with her own bestial tones, Thalia threw herself across Cleomenes' body. "No! He has kept his part of the bargain. Do not rob me of a husband!"

I shoved her backward and dragged Cleomenes out of the bed.

"He could bleed to death!" Diocles shouted at me.

"I say no!" Thalia screamed. She threw herself upon me like a lioness. For a moment we tussled, I merely trying to hold her off, lest she do me harm.

Suddenly, Thalia's entire body tensed. She stopped her struggles and lay quietly panting in my arms. I rolled her off me and came up onto my legs.

Diocles threw a length of rope at me and motioned for me to truss the couple up. "We linger here too long. Gag them as well, and let us be gone."

Within another four minutes, we were out the backdoor of the grand house and into the night.

Δ

Two days later, a scroll arrived at the fortress of Euryalus. It bore the seal of Cleomenes, but I knew it came from Thalia. I burned it without opening it.

Δ

All of Hieronymos' guardians were invited to the palace one month after his grandfather's funeral. The occasion was the young king's coronation. It was an impressive affair, with ambassadors from Messana, Neapoli, and several of the Greek colonies on the southern tip of the Italian peninsula in attendance. More ambassadors would arrive in the following weeks, once the word had spread around the Mediterranean that the great and benevolent Hieron had died and been replaced.

The new king was not dressed in the simple robes of his grandfather, who rarely put on grand airs. Hieronymos wore the purple reserved only for the king. He also wore his grandfather's crown upon his head. To these accoutrements of power he had added a newly-fashioned golden scepter, which he waved in an affected manner when he spoke. I had heard that one of his first orders upon taking power was to have called to the palace private chambers the beautiful daughters of two common men. This, his mannerisms, and his imperious attitude did not sit well with me. I ached to take him out into the countryside for two weeks with my cohort and teach him what I knew about being a man.

According to Ioannis and Diocles, in the final years of his life Hieron had been toying with the idea of returning the city to a republic and taking control out of the hands of his family, who he knew to be almost solidly aligned with Carthage. But, as I have been told, and myself observed, the old are especially concerned with maintaining the affection of their children and grandchildren. Thus by kisses, gentle touches, and fond words did Harmonia, Heraclia, Hieronymos and Damarata turn him from his better judgment. Now, the entire city harvested the ill fruit of his poor choice.

Hieronymos had been well instructed to speak nothing of Roma or Carthage from the throne. He talked of Siracusa acting as a great neutral city where all nations might come to trade and make peace. He assured those ambassadors who stood before him that all trade agreements would continue. For the representatives from the seven towns surrounding Siracusa, he envisioned a greater concordance and unity of purpose. I heard this as something which I would fear if I were they.

Those invited, despite being diplomats, could not conceal their lack of confidence in the new tyrant. While the scores of guests dined, I conversed with Timon, Archimedes, and the other seven men favoring Roma whom Hieron had picked to advise Hieronymos.

"Roma seems to do everything it can to confound our cause," Timon lamented. "They purposely kept from me the fact that they moved two more legions into the area around Messana months ago. These were the ones that deserted at Cannae."

I courteously corrected Timon, letting all around me know that these soldiers had been members of eight legions until enough of them collected in Canusium to reform into two. "They fled the field before being surrounded rather than die," I went on.

"And well they should have," said one of Hieronymos' would-be advisors. "Rather than die uselessly, they live to fight another day."

"Except that the Roman Senate does not think that way," I replied. "These men are considered cowards to their Republic. I would guess that they have been moved to Sicilia not for any particular reason of aggression, but because the Roman Senate cannot abide them on Italian soil."

"It certainly seems so," agreed Timon. "They were transported to our island in early winter and ordered to erect an encampment. That encampment was more than ten stadia from the nearest town. This isolation is clearly punishment. What is more, the former consul who survived Cannae and who has been blamed for the defeat has been assigned to command these legions."

"Varro," I remembered.

"The same. He stands in obvious disgrace."

"And yet they are two legions," said Archimedes. "In fact, if they are told to march against an enemy, they will do it with relish and blood thirst, in order to reclaim their honor. This is not good."

"Not good at all," amplified Timon.

Δ

As soon as the bulk of the guests retired, Hieronymos' advisory council was called back into the king's audience chamber. The boy king sat stiffly on the throne. His uncle, Adranodoros, stood beside him. His sister's husband and his other uncle stood to the side, but above us on the same dais that held the throne.

"I have thought hard about my grandfather's wish to have me advised," Hieronymos began. "You are all men of experience and wisdom, and your opinions are well formed. However, you present too many opinions for us to absorb and deal with."

I kept my eyes on the young man, because I knew my expressive face would reveal my upset if I looked at either Timon or Archimedes.

"How can you know that without testing us, your Highness?" Timon asked. "This is, after all, the very first time we have met as a body."

"On the issue of our alliance with Roma, for example," Hieronymos replied quickly, showing that he had been well tutored. "I have already heard too many opinions."

"This is a complex issue," Timon said. "If only one point of view is expressed in your court, we may very well travel down a path toward our destruction."

"You favor continuing the alliance with Roma," said the king. "Others in this chamber favor breaking that alliance and forging one with Carthage. Still others wish us to break with Roma and forge no new alliance. Some believe that we should emulate both Carthage and Roma and begin to gather our neighboring towns into a more subservient confederacy. Others believe that we should be establishing one or two colonies in the territory between us and the Roman colony on Sicilia's eastern shore, to prevent their further expansion. We cannot do all of these."

"Then let us at least debate for a set time in front of you. Allow each man to have his say on an issue, no man speaking more than five minutes," Timon suggested. "In the end we may vote as a body, and then you act as you will."

"I will act as I will anytime I please," Hieronymos said pointedly. He ruined his moment, however, by then glancing to Adranodoros for approval. "I have decided to keep only members of my family as my advisors. We have all learned politics and diplomacy at the knee of my grandfather, and we know intimately the workings of Siracusa and its needs."

"I am a member of your family, Hieronymos," Archimedes said. I am certain he used the boy's name rather than a title of respect to attempt to humble him. His right hand swung out gracefully. "The city's great hero, Leonides, is your cousin as well."

Adranodoros smiled broadly at he stepped nearer to his nephew. "That is hardly an argument, Great One. This city is more than 500 years old. Those of the better families are all related by now. The king means his immediate family. You are dismissed."

Δ

Timon left the chamber with the rest of the ten who were disposed toward maintaining friendship with Roma. We walked as a body in silence down into the main courtyard.

"It is clear that Adranodoros is ruling from behind the throne," said one of the businessmen, whose name was Diophantus.

"And that our days of peace with Roma near an end," Timon decided.

"Unless we rise up and revolt and depose that welp," said a merchant named Micon.

"That would require the assent and help of the army," Timon said, looking at me. "Thus far, Archidamus has refused to discuss politics with anyone. Someone will need to tell him what has transpired today. He must know that peace cannot be maintained much longer."

"I will speak with him," I replied reluctantly.

Archimedes volunteered, "I would head a delegation from the city to argue peace with both the Romans and the Carthaginians once those in the palace are deposed. Perhaps I can convince them that it is expeditious to accept us as a neutral republic."

"And if not, are your preparations for defense ready?" Timon asked.

"The walls and fortresses are as secure and daunting as I can make them," Archimedes replied. "I have also constructed more than a dozen machines that should confound our enemies. Another year is required to complete all the machines necessary to truly keep us safe."

"The greedy creatures!" Micon exclaimed suddenly.

I asked him what he meant.

"Do you believe Hieron's family would offend Roma out of love of Carthage? Not at all. Carthage promises them all the Roman territory to the north, as well as lucrative trading rights. This much I know to be a fact. What else they think they can gain I do not know."

"You have the names of the citizens of the inner circle who would supplant Roma with Carthage," Timon said to me.

"I have memorized them," I confirmed.

"Archidamus does not trust anyone outside of the army," said the former chief minister. "But that does not mean you should trust him completely. Tell him what just happened inside the palace. Then give him the number of prominent citizens behind Adranodoros and the others, but do not list their names. See if the old general has the will to reform this city as Hieron wished it to be."

I vowed that I would do precisely what he outlined.

"Mind your backs, gentlemen," Timon then warned. "These may be the children of Hieron, but they do not have the greatness to win over their opponents as their father did. I fear they will settle their arguments by poison and dagger."

Δ

Archidamus received me with no hesitation. Nor did he act in any way surprised by the nature of my visit. He listened with arms folded across his chest. I could barely detect the rise and fall of his breathing. When I concluded, he cleared his throat.

"In spite of all the training we have been doing these many months," the general said, "we still have only a thousand fulltime soldiers. Hieron had limited the palace guard to 100 men. Those who served men like Timon, known to favor continued alliance with Roma, have all been dismissed. Others have been brought in overnight. Some of them are mercenaries, and I believe several are actually Carthaginian. Did Timon not tell you this?"

I confessed that he had not, and yet in the same moment wondered if Archidamus' words were true.

"In fact," the strategos continued, "I fear that we have trained many of his new guards. My intelligence says that the number is almost 150 today. Did you not see the extra men placed around the two gates?"

This I had observed. Clearly, Archidamus was not as disinterested in the goings-on inside the palace as I had thought.

"I believe I have the loyalty of my men," the old general said.

"You do," I affirmed. "Moreover, of the men I command, some two dozen, are not fulltime soldiers. They will do as I ask."

"Still not enough to storm the palace," Archidamus decided. "And this is not a matter where we can open the armory and recruit fighters from off the street. We might arm the wrong men. Feelings are running high against the Romans, and with just cause. They bully us. They treat us as inferiors. Word is being spread throughout the city of two new legions from Roma encamped south of Messana. A new colony is being built on disputed land. Another already exists there. Hannibal wins. Cities and towns in southern Italia revolt."

"What if we say nothing of Roma and attack the palace in the cause of creating a new republic?" I suggested. "I understand this was an idea Hieron was considering."

"Then why did he not share it openly with the populace before he died?" Archidamus shot back. "Whoever tries to use this story will be considered an opportunist and therefore highly suspect. I do not see me, you, or Timon being able to take the palace from Hieron's family."

"Then they will ally with Carthage, and Roma will attack," I stated.

Archidamus scratched the back of his neck. "But I will not be here. I have made up my mind this very day that I must resign my command."

My heart sank at his words. "You will further unhinge Siracusa."

"I helped Hieron defend Siracusa for fifty years. It is time someone else took my place. You are honored but too young. I will leave the decision to those in charge."

"What have they offered you?" I asked, making an angry guess.

Archidamus looked at first surprised by my words. Then he allowed himself a crafty smile. "You are not so young after all. My ancestors did not come from Korinthos, as did most of those in the city. I will return to the land of King Pyrrhus, where I hope to live out my days in peace."

"But you will hear of Siracusa's changing fortunes no matter how far away you run," I said as I stood. I could no longer listen to his words.

"No city, no empire lasts forever unchanged," the old general said. "Perhaps it is time for this one to fade, or to rise to greater glory. I leave that in your capable hands."

Δ

I had agreed to meet with Timon on the evening of that same day, in the same drinking establishment that Ioannis and Diocles had taken me to after dragging me from Thalia's wedding. I was shown into the private back chamber, where I sat quite alone. Many minutes passed beyond the time we had agreed upon. I was considering leaving when a figure appeared in the doorway. It was the ferret-like man who had accosted me in the palace courtyard and attempted to bribe me. My hand stole slowly to my short sword. I slid it out of its frog and laid it across my lap as he entered.

"Timon won't be coming," the man said. "May I sit?"

"How do you know Timon won't be coming?" I asked.

"Because he's dead. He met an unfortunate accident."

I gestured for the man to sit across from me. "Keep your hands on the table," I cautioned. "What kind of accident?"

"A scaffolding collapsed just as he was passing under an archway."

"And this produced stab marks in his back?"

221

The man shrugged, and his bushy eyebrows crawled up his cunning face. "I wasn't there. I was passed the story."

"And now you pass it to me."

"Just so. I have been asked to pass on two more stories. These are to assure you that you and Archimedes will not meet similar accidents."

My hand tightened around the hilt of my sword. "Why should I believe that?"

"For many reasons. First, because you were pulled into this unfortunate wrangling over Roma and Carthage. You urge no one among your friends and acquaintances to favor Roma. Secondly, you are the city's hero. The people would not stand for something untoward happening to you.

"My second story is similar. Nothing will happen to Archimedes. He is also the property of the city. Likewise, he is no vocal proponent for continued Roman alliance. You are the last one who needs to be told about his disinterest in anything political. He hates war and intrigues. Only through the machinations of you and our old king was he drawn into using his arts to defend our city. This is a good thing, whether we ally with Carthage, continue our alliance with Roma, or go our own way.

"In short, neither of you is considered a threat to certain people." The slender man held up his hand. "However, should you decide to become a threat, you do have a wife. A Roman wife. A Roman wife who is pregnant with your child. She might…"

The man let his final words hang in the air. My face yet again betrayed my rage. He now held up two hands, in a defensive pose. "Do not grow angry with me. These are not words of my fashioning; I am only the messenger."

"And what if I sent 'certain people' a clear message of my anger by carving you up and hanging the pieces outside this place of business?" I asked him, even as I pushed the point of my blade into his stomach.

"That would be foolish, not to mention an unnecessary mess for the proprietor to clean up. I am sure you would not be welcome here again."

I had to grant the man my respect for the degree of calmness and wit he showed with sharpened iron pressing into his flesh. I gestured for him to stand, even as I got up. Before he could flee, I grabbed him by his chlamys and spun him around.

"Let's see how safe from accident I truly am," I said, guiding him toward the shop's back door.

"I tell you, you will find nothing but a sleeping drunk out there," the man assured me.

He was correct. Since he had entered from the front of the shop, I knew that he was a careful man and had taken the time to reconnoiter before approaching me. I wished that I had his loyal services for the Silent Storm.

"Go to your 'certain people' and tell them I do not like them. But I still love Siracusa and serve her. Of that they may be assured."

The man bowed and disappeared into the darkness.

CHAPTER XVIII

Toward the end of the summer, Aurora gave birth to a girl. She insisted that we give her a Greek name. After several days of pondering and trying out sounds that seemed to go with the child, Azar suggested Athena.

"Because she's obviously highly intelligent," Azar explained. "Apollonius and Amara think their baby is smart? He's a donkey compared with this one," she exclaimed with pride.

I had almost come to like Azar. The furtive habits she had developed just to survive across decades of abuse gradually melted away. Even her harsh manner of speaking had softened, although the tone itself was like a sheet of iron being dragged over road stones.

I will not state that I was elated in learning that my first child was a female. However, the moment I laid eyes upon her I was in love. I told Aurora as much.

"That is good," she said. "A daughter needs her father's love. I certainly did with my father. It made those times bearable when he and I

224

disagreed and we did not like each other. Loving is so much easier than liking."

I thought of the difficult life Aurora had led, first not fitting well in Roma because she had a Greek attitude toward life, and then not fitting completely in Siracusa because she was Roman. I thought of her loneliness in the house of her father because he was ever away doing the Republic's bidding, and then hardly seeing me because I was billeted at the Euryalus fortress.

"Is love so important, then?" I asked her.

"I believe so. First, one needs to feel that one is loved merely for being, for belonging to a mother and father. I speak of a love that is selfless and unconditional. If one has that, no matter how badly the Fates behave she still feels secure. Later, one needs to find things to give love and attention to. Only in giving love can a person feel her own value. The more you give, the stronger you feel. Do you not agree?"

Instead of answering her, I said, "You have never asked me if I love you."

"I have received so much else from you that asking such would be greedy," Aurora replied. "You give me a home. You give me most of your salary. You give me your name and your considerable reputation, so that I am a respected woman in the community. You allow me to buy what I want, to cook what I want. You let me decorate our home as I please. You allowed Azar to enter this house when your heart was not in it. Now you give me a fine, healthy baby to spoil."

"Do you love me?" I dared.

"If you need to ask, then I will tell you plainly enough—I do love you."

I sat beside her on the bed and took her hand. Together, we watched our daughter sleep. I felt for a time almost content.

Δ

With Archidamus gone, the whelp king Hieronymos declared that he was the new strategos. He rarely appeared among the soldiers, however. When he did, he arrived in a quadriga chariot built more for show than warfare, drawn by pure white horses. His skinny chest sank from the weight of his useless ornamental breastplate, and he looked quite ill at ease wearing the helmet of a high-ranking officer. Only a fool could have missed noting that the four powerful horses were handled not by him but by a professional charioteer.

The veteran syntagmatarchs jostled with each other for primacy, mostly by bribing the affections of their men and the trainees with extra rations of wine and meat. These were Hippokrates, Epikydes, Paulus, and Archelous. Epikydes, like his brother Hippokrates, made no pretense of liking Roma and proclaimed that Siracusa should be currying the favors of Carthage. Archelous leaned toward Roma. Paulus, who had a Latin father, clearly favored a continued alliance with Roma. The master of horse, Urian, had chosen to retire with Archidamus. The remaining cavalry officer, Lysander, could not be drawn into declaring his preference.

Although I commanded only fifty including myself, Ioannis, and Diocles, I had been granted by Hieron the title of syntagmatarch. No one dared to challenge it. By this time, my champion's statue greeted me in front of the gymnasium. I could now read several hundred words. I had spent several evenings beside Archimedes and Aurora, listening to their debates and musings over points philosophical, and I unabashedly parroted their thoughts in front of my fellow soldiers. In short, I was in many ways a respected man. Consequently, my opinions on the new ruling regime and on the merits of allying with one alien race or the other were constantly solicited. I took Lysander's cue and refused to enter into such discussions. Whenever I was asked, my stock reply was "I am on the side of Siracusa, first, last, and ever." After a time, I was good-naturedly mocked for it, but I was glad that so many knew my public attitude.

The five highest-ranking officers were kept busy all through that summer and into the following year, radically increasing the potential size of the army. Following the Roman example, Hieronymos declared that for the foreseeable future all citizens and freeman living in Siracusa between the ages of eighteen and forty-four would be liable for levy, and that all must be trained and then drilled a minimum of two days per month. The normal operations of the city were constantly interrupted due to lack of manpower. Streets grew dirty and rough. Sewers overflowed. Ships were loaded and unloaded too slowly. Taxes increased. The populace grew restive.

At the same time, also following the example of the Romans that the king professed to hate so intensely, Hieronymous put recruitment pressure on the towns under Siracusa's direct influence. On each occasion, he traveled with two syntagmatarchs, two ministers, and a syntagma of soldiers wearing full battle regalia. The initial speeches delivered by the ministers concerned mutual protection and improved trade and commerce, but the final message was a pointed recommendation that Hieronymos dared any of our satellites to ignore. Each town was asked to "volunteer" at least twenty percent of its male citizenry for training by our army. Further, these towns were to pay for the outfitting and boarding of these men. Their uniforms, footwear, helmets, greaves, spears, swords, and shields were supplied by Siracusa. Thus, although those enlisted hailed from many locations, they all took on the look of Siracusan soldiers and obeyed Siracusan officers.

Within twelve months after Hieron's death, our army was theoretically able to put into the field 15,000 men. This great effort did not escape the notice of Roman or Carthaginian businessmen, sea captains, or spies. With each passing month, entreaties from both sides became more and more urgent. The men who advised the young king had succeeded in making Siracusa a city that neither the Carthaginians nor the Romans could ignore.

Δ

We in Siracusa learned little of events in Carthage, as our Roman allies forbade us to trade with her. Of Roma and her doings we were constantly receiving information, via Roman warships and cargo ships and from common trading partners. At the turn of the year in which Hieron died, the consuls elected were Tiberius Sempronius Gracchus and Lucius Posthumius Albinus. Albinus had been a praetor the previous year and still served with legions in the valley of the Po River. We heard not from Roman lips but from Greek traders that yet another calamity had taken place early in that year. Albinus had been elected consul in absentia, and a week later the two legions he commanded were annihilated by a huge Celtic force. Albinus, in expected Roman fashion, perished with his men.

Albinus was replaced by Fabius, and Aurora's father was made a proconsul. Marcellus spent a good part of the year with his troops at Castra Claudiana. Only after Hieronymos had frightened our tributary towns with news of more Roman legions in Sicilia did word come into Siracusa that the entrenched legions had not been augmented by, but were rather replaced by, the disgraced two legions reformed from the Cannae debacle. Marcellus took the former Sicilian legions, which were the 7th and 8th. This revised information was conveniently never forwarded to the towns surrounding our city.

Nothing of consequence happened that year between Hannibal's army and the three groups of legions that blocked his way north out of the Campania. The truth was that neither Siracusa's Roman faction nor our Carthaginian faction had any news from the Italian peninsula to prove to the populace that one was decisively winning. One bit of information coming from Macedon, however, proved highly beneficial to those in our city who sought to shift it to the Carthaginian side. Philip V of Macedon had concluded a treaty with Hannibal. When this was spread through the city, I could feel a palpable swing in popular opinion away from the Roman cause. Macedon was the birthplace of Alexander, who had conquered so much of the world. This quasi-Greek country was famous for producing fighting men.

At the turn of the next year, when Hieronymos had sat on his grandfather's throne for some nine months, Marcellus was elected a consul for the third time. Tiring of the fact that Hannibal ranged at will across the southern half of their peninsula, the Romans did what they alone in all the civilized world could do and raised six more legions. Like Jason sowing the dragon's teeth, soldiers seemed to pop out of the ground for the Roman side. They fielded a staggering twenty legions at one time. Moreover, to counter Philip's treaty, Roma determined to close down the Adriatic to all but their own trade and war fleets. Within a space of three months, they built 100 new warships. Those still siding with the Romans in Siracusa wisely trumpeted this amazing ability to produce men and weapons that no other power in the world possessed. With such an advantage of soldiers and warships, the Romans were containing Hannibal and slowly choking him. I could see this. Archimedes understood this. Yet many ostensibly smart men in our city refused to understand the inevitable outcome. The common man, however, apparently understood, and the pendulum of popular opinion swung yet again back toward the Roman side.

Δ

At intervals of approximately three months, letters to Aurora would arrive from Marcellus. Sometimes, two or three arrived together, due to the vagaries of fleet sailings. He showed himself to be a loving and faithful father, despite the hardness he had shown to her in my presence. He spoke of weather and crops, of meeting certain notable personages, of books he had read and philosophical debates he had entered into. Never did he speak directly of his military exploits. If I had handed the letters to a stranger, he would have been hard pressed to believe that they had been written by one of the great warriors of the age.

Marcellus expressed in his letters immense joy at becoming a grandfather and looked forward to the day when he could visit Siracusa. He related that Aurora's brother Marcus fared well and was now a tribune. He professed to rejoice that Aurora felt so at home in Siracusa. After being allowed to read these letters I did not know how I could ever oppose a Roman legion. And yet I felt I would be compelled to this very fate, unless Hieronymos was deposed and his family banished.

Δ

Although little news escaped the palace's thick walls, the fact of Zoippos' departure on a mission to Egypt precisely one year after Hieron died became common knowledge throughout Siracusa. Some said that he had voluntarily exiled himself, anticipating deadly times. The same persons, who were in a position to know such things, also claimed that he had begged his wife Heraclia and his two daughters to leave with him. His wife, however, feared losing all power at home. The great author Hesiod wrote "oft hath even a whole city reaped the evil fruit of a bad man." The same is true of an inept boy trying to act the part of a man.

I privately believed that Adranodoros and Themistos were the ones convincing Hieronymos to march into the town of Leontini, and this plan chilled Zoippos' blood. As well it should have; because this action, which occurred one month after Zoippos sailed, was the spark that ignited the conflagration.

Leontini lies about 100 stadia north of Siracusa, near to the coast. This most tenuous of our confederates was the closest major Greek town to that part of Sicilia controlled by the Romans. Because of this, if the Romans did attack Siracusa from land, they would descend on Leontini first. Consequently, its citizens were most wary of arousing Roman ire. Despite the visit of Siracusa's two ministers and its armed syntagma late the previous year, the rulers of Leontini had not voluntarily created a levy to send their twenty per cent of young men to our fortress for training. Therefore, Hieronymos supposedly had made up his mind to enter Leontini himself. The plan was to drag young men out of their houses and off the streets until at least the requisite 192 needed to form one syntagma had been rounded up. These youths would be marched south to Siracusa, escorted by a syntagma of veteran Siracusan soldiers. Eight syntagma marched with Hieronymos. Four other syntagma remained within the city for defensive purposes, with six uncalled to duty.

To show the leaders of Leontini that he was building his army for a purpose, and that Leontini could not avoid being caught in the middle of a conflict, Hieronymos had sent Hippokrates and Epikydes out to provoke the Romans. Each commanded ten syntagma of men. They had been given orders to raze to the ground the two Roman colony villages that had been erected within the disputed territory between the spheres of influence of Messana and Siracusa. These towns lay a bit more than 300 stadia from Siracusa. So that citizens of Leontini might not attempt to ingratiate the Romans by warning them, these two forces set out by sea one day ahead of the army that Hieronymos commanded.

The Silent Storm was assigned the task of sweeping the landward side of Leontini, in anticipation of many young men fleeing in that direction. Because I had been one of Hieron's and Timon's trusted minions, I was given no advance warning of these rash actions. Until we came within twenty stadia of Leontini, our group marched with the main force. For comfort, Hieronymos had brought along with him the cavalry, commanded by Lysander. I walked by Lysander's horse during the journey and attempted to glean from him what he had known in advance and what his opinion was.

As an appointee of Hieron and Archidamus, Lysander also served under suspicion. He professed to have known nothing of the plans until the morning previous to our march, when citizens were rounded up from their work, ordered to don their uniforms and grab their weapons, and loaded immediately onto every available ship in our Great Harbor. He was distressed, but not surprised, by the precipitous actions.

"I suppose they felt they were compelled to do this," the master of cavalry said, speaking of Hieronymos, his uncles and brother-in-law, the brother syntagmatarchs, and every other high-ranking citizen who favored realigning our city with Carthage. "Did you not hear the news trickling through the city yesterday afternoon?"

I was certain he spoke of something momentous. I and my cohort camped in the field that morning and were directed to fall in with the army without even reentering the city. I explained this to my companion.

"You of course know that King Philip of Macedon has pledged to assist Hannibal in his war against Roma. The Romans have already established some colonies across the Adriatic, and Philip believes that they will grow strong enough one day to march on him."

Such an enterprise was daunting in its enormity, but I also could imagine the Romans attempting to conquer Macedonia and Greece once they had finished with Carthage. Their way of life demanded constant expansion.

"Philip brought 120 light galleys from his homeland around to the Illyrian coast," Lysander went on. "His fleet harbored in the Bay of Aulon. He seized the Roman colony of Oricum. He then moved on to lay siege to Apollonia. A praetor named Marcus Valerius Laevinus crossed

the Adraitic with a legion and beleaguered the besiegers. He also blockaded the Macedonian galleys with such a large navy that Philip was
compelled to burn his ships and retreat overland. This has been a long
time coming to us, but a galley arrived from Tarentum two days ago with
the news."

"This is a great victory for the Romans," I said. "Hannibal is once
again without outside supply."

"Indeed. It is enough to swing the opinion of our populace back solidly toward the Roman side. Syracusa's Carthaginian camp could not
allow this. I am sure those who control Hieronymos moved within hours
to create a situation to break the treaty with Roma."

This made perfect sense to me. "If this was not conceived in haste," I
said, "they would no doubt have called in our ally troops rather than using only Siracusan forces. If I wanted to embarrass the leaders of
Leontini into sending us men, I would parade soldiers from the other six
towns in front of them."

"Exactly," Lysander said.

I pondered for a time in silence as we continued toward Leontini under a cool breeze and a bright sun. I worked on how to bring Siracusa
back from the edge of the abyss.

"You and I could relieve Hieronymos of his command and turn the
troops around right now," I suggested. "The news of Valerius' triumph
must be sweeping through the city. Even citizens favoring an alliance
with Carthage will be outraged when we spread the word of this unpro-
voked attack on the Roman villages. Furthermore, I believe that we can
turn Archelous and Paulus to our side, if they are not already there themselves. Then it will be the four of us against Hippokrates and Epikydes."

Lysander contented himself by listening, so I forged on.

"We will command 3,500 men to their 4,000. They have hand-picked
those men in favor of war with Roma. This leaves us those opposed. If
we close the gates on them, they will not have enough advantage to
breach the walls. They have no siege machines. And I can have my great-
uncle place his machines on the walls within a matter of hours."

"We can do what you suggest just as well after we march into Leontini," Lysander responded, after several moments of thought. "What is

232

more, we can take several hundred of their young men with us. We know that these men are not disposed to fight the Romans. They should be happy to restore Siracusa to its old position and to contribute Leontini's name to the process."

"Actually, Hippokrates and Epikydes have given us a wonderful opportunity to unseat them and the ruling family," I decided. "Their desperation has put them two days from Siracusa. This will work."

"Will it?" Lysander asked. "How well will the Romans be disposed toward our new republic when two of Siracusa's generals have just destroyed two of their colonies?"

"We cannot stop that," I answered. "We can only do what we can do. I think that we must certainly be forced to fight Roma if we do not unseat Hieronymos."

"Let us follow our callow general and see how badly he conducts this operation," said Lysander. "There is plenty of time to act before the sun descends."

Δ

Shortly after our conversation, I separated with my men from the main army and moved off the road into the countryside. Thus, I did not witness the startling turn of events that neither I nor Lysander could have predicted.

No army moves as swiftly as single men do. Consequently, those living and working in Leontini received from others using the road sufficient warning to vacate before Hieronymos' army descended upon them. Unlike my fledgling king, I knew how to encircle with stealth. My men had captured no fewer than sixty eligible men by the time one of Lysander's horsemen found us and relayed the fact of Hieronymos' assassination.

A party of ten men who had volunteered to act as scouts and who had entered the town first turned out to be in league against the king. They all hated the ruling family and secretly favored continued alliance with Roma.

Much later, when we were well into war, I learned that Timon had been even shrewder than I had suspected. Fully five years before Hieron died, he had secreted a pair of men into the trust of Adranodoros and Zoippos. These were the men Ioannis and Diocles knew of but had never met. The two had pretended to favor Carthage over Roma and had served as bodyguards to Hieronymos' uncles. One of these was named Dinomenes. He had been specifically assigned to protect Hieronymos during his venture to Leontini. Instead, he had set a trap with the others.

Those who had served as scouts had made sure to show themselves early to the people of Leontini, to guarantee that the town would be virtually deserted when Hieronymos arrived with the main force. Someone among the group knew well the layout of the town. It had been agreed among the conspirators that a certain narrow street that ran from south to north would be used as the path of entry for the army. Several of the scouts hid in an empty house on this street, but not until they had tied a piece of white cloth to its door latch. This was the signal for Dinomenes.

By means of crass flatteries and copious assurances of safety, Dinomenes convinced Hieronymos that he must be the first man to enter the town's agora. In this way, the young king was tricked into leading some 800 men down this narrow street. Dinomenes walked directly behind him. When he spotted the white cloth he paused, ostensibly to loosen a knot because his sandal was tied too tightly. To accomplish this, he set his foot up against the wall of the house, thus blocking the way for the men behind him.

Moments later, four of the scouts burst from the door of the house and attacked the isolated Hieronymos, piercing the chinks in his armor with daggers. He cried out and was unable to defend himself.

Dinomenes took the opportunity of shock to race after the attackers into the house and thence out its back door. He cried out in feigned rage, in an effort to convince the other onlookers that he indeed still served as a bodyguard. His stratagem to separate Hieronymos from his army, however, proved too conspicuous. Several spears were thrown at him by the young king's sympathizers. Blood in the house proved that at least one of the spears had found its mark, although Dinomenes was not wounded badly enough to be captured.

Pandemonium reigned in the narrow street. The lines of men, who had been reduced to moving three abreast, stretched back for several blocks. Many seconds elapsed while the news was transferred to those in the rear. Instead of turning around, those in the back pressed forward to learn what had happened. In the confusion, the conspirators escaped.

By the time I located Lysander, half an hour had elapsed. We saw no advantage in lingering in the town. Moreover, we did not want to arrive back in Siracusa long behind the conspirators. As we began the return march home, carrying the body of the king few respected, I reflected on Archimedes and his projects to make Siracusa impregnable. Many invisible ropes had been pulled in the past two days, launching the ship of war. I wondered if the genius who had once bragged he could move the entire world could prevent his own immediate world from being destroyed.

CHAPTER XIX

Those in Siracusa who wielded power and who favored continued alliance with Roma had been very busy while we had marched to Leontini. Every effort was made to spread the word of Philip of Macedon's resounding defeat and to arouse both the like-minded and the undecided. With half our army sailing and marching north, the speculations of the royal family inciting war with Roma flew about. Within hours of our disappearance from view of the city, throngs totaling more than a thousand men of arms-bearing age had gathered. Many of these I had helped to train in the past months. Those who had supplied their own weapons had them to use. Others brought knives and axes as they left their homes. The moment the conspirators returned with word of the assassination, the mobs advanced on Ortygia and the palace.

A goodly portion of the palace guard had marched out with Hieronymos. Only fifty or so remained. They were powerless to prevent the mass of angry men from storming the walls and then opening the gates. Most, it was reported, instantly realized the impossibility of their situation and fled or hid.

Shouting that the tyrant was dead, the mass rushed through the palace like a spring torrent. While a single common man lacks power, he never lacks an opinion on what is wrong with those who control him. The mob believed that not only the uncles and brother-in-law of Hieronymos were to blame for his callous ways and intemperate actions, but also that the women of the family were equally culpable. According to one member of the palace guard who became loquacious after the family was eliminated, Damarata was the most ambitious. She had pushed her husband Adranodoros to replace Hieronymos. She was overheard to say that her nephew deserved to be removed from the palace "feet first."

So swiftly did the mob act that it is impossible to tell who died first. What is true is that only Zoippos survived, by having exiled himself to Alexandria. Adranodoros and Themistos died with swords in their hands. Harmonia was caught trying to leave through a tunnel in the dungeon and was stabbed more than seventy times.

Heraclia had the most poignant end. One witness who believed himself a bard immortalized her last moments with an overlong ode that he repeated ad nauseum in the city agoras until he died at the hands of either a proponent of the Carthaginian camp or else a sincere critic. Much of this poetaster's details, however, have been confirmed by others on the scene.

When Heraclia learned that the mob had entered the palace and all the exits had been blocked, she gathered together her daughters and fled into a private chapel. So suddenly was the surprise of the attack that their hair was not done up nor their dress complete. As the crowd pressed close to them with weapons drawn, Heraclia raised her hand and invoked the memory of her revered father and brother. She was, she averred, in sympathy with their attitudes toward the preservation of Siracusa. She swore that she had never sided with her sister or Hieronymos.

"What have I gained from this reign?" she asked the crowd, "but my husband's exile? When the boy tyrant was alive I never enjoyed the same high place as my sister, and now you tell me that he is dead. Why should you link me with her merely because we share the blood of our father? Adranodoros schemed to be himself king. If he had succeeded, I would have been reduced to my sister's slave. Send word to my husband Zoippos and tell him that Siracusa is once again free. He will return at once and convince you of my loyalty to your cause. Alas! Here his innocent wife and children beg for their lives!"

At this point, several among the crowd called her a liar and suggested that those nearest her silence her with their swords. Heraclia raised both arms in imperious fashion.

"Can you hate us merely because the Fates caused us to be born to your royal family? If so, then send us away from Siracusa and Sicilia. Exile us to Alexandria, where I may join my husband and my children their father. What harm can we be there?"

"You are of Sicilia," someone in the crowd called out. "What family of this island does not seek revenge above all else?" Many voices murmured agreement. The hearts of the long-suffering and frightened people were hardened, and they wanted blood.

"At least spare my daughters," Heraclia cried out, showing some of her nobility. "They are too young to have even formed a thought against any of you."

With this, a bestial growl of impatience erupted from someone, and several of the mob fell upon her and slit her throat. In the confusion, the daughters ran from the chapel with members of the crowd in pursuit. It was reported that in their desire to survive they took on almost supernatural power, pulling away again and again from grasping hands. In the end, however, enough stabs and blows landed upon them that they, too, collapsed and died. It was a bloody and shameful day in Siracusa's long history, and I am glad that I was not there.

Δ

Now, Appius Claudius Pulcher was the praetor in Sicilia at this time. He was the supreme leader for the Romans on the island. However, Hippokrates and Epikydes paid him no heed, as they had fixated on the stories of the two disgraced legions and their equally disgraced commander, Varro. In their minds, the Romans had sincerely underestimated Siracusa and never expected our peaceable city to rise. Therefore, once these brother generals had leveled the two Roman villages that had been placed on the neutral land between our regions, they elected to set up defensive camps and see if they could draw out these legions of imagined cowards and do to them what the great Hannibal had done some eighteen months earlier. Not once had they bothered to come to me, who had watched these men fight at Cannae and then had stayed with them for days at Canusium. If they had, I would have told them that the Romans' defeat had nothing to do with cowardice, that they had wisely preserved their lives against the only other choice of annihilation. I would have argued that these men above all others would fight valiantly the next time they were put to the test, so as to prove to Roma their mettle, with the hope of being reinstated as citizens.

I had expected that these generals who welcomed an alliance with Carthage would return to their beached galleys the moment they learned of the palace coup, but they lingered in the north pondering a strategy. Within three days of their destruction of the villages the Roman legions did move close to them, but they likewise erected forts and took up defensive positions.

A scout was captured from one of the legions. He would not speak about the nature of the army he served. However, he revealed with satisfaction that Pulcher had already sent out dispatches with a fleet outbound from Messana for Roma, requesting that two more legions be transferred to Sicilia. This news was far more than Hippokrates and Epikydes had bargained for. It did, however, tend to support their contention that the Romans planned an eventual march on Siracusa.

This Roman scout was brought back to Siracusa by the generals to give testimony to Roma's intentions. While the bulk of the fleet carrying their twenty snytagmas floated just beyond the harbor, they petitioned for a conference with those in control of the city and received it. The scout's report provided their means of return. Even those who violently disliked the warrior brothers understood that we could not afford to divide our army in the face of the Roman threat.

I was a member of the group who conferred with our two rogue generals. They argued convincingly that the die had been cast for better or worse, and that all citizens and both halves of the army must work together to protect the city else it fall. They swore on their swords and on the shades of their ancestors that they would attempt no reprisals for the murder of the royal family. In truth, I believe that they were greatly relieved at this occurrence, for they knew the city's history and saw themselves as eventually becoming like Hieron when he was its savior.

But not all were willing to accept Hippokrates and Epikydes back with open arms. Dinomenes, the man who had arranged for the murder of Hieronymos, had returned to the city. He had assigned himself the task of eliminating every high-ranking person who favored Carthage over Roma. His motives were never explained to my satisfaction, but of his zeal there was no doubt.

Soon after the ruling council accepted the two generals back into Siracusa, Hippokrates went to the Ortygian agora to address the people and to justify his actions so that they would love him and allow him to lead them if war came. In this effort he was most effective. He possessed a noble visage and physique, and had a powerful speaking voice and used riveting gestures. Moreover, he paraded out convincing arguments of Roma as aggressor. However, about ten minutes into his harangue, Dinomenes rushed up to him out of the crowd with a dagger in hand.

Now Hippokrates was himself not armed or armored, but knowing the mood of the city he had providentially backed himself up with half a dozen men who carried weapons under their cloaks. Hippokrates, being a strong man, grabbed Dinomenes' right arm before the dagger could fall and wrestled him to a standstill. Within moments, Hippokrates' followers were upon the would-be assassin, and revenged the sad young king.

Δ

It was decided within the post-assassination conclave that Siracusa would be run as a republic, with all male citizens allowed to vote. It was also agreed that an envoy would be sent to Carthage informing them of our break with Roma, but not wishing help until the seriousness of the situation could be assessed. I was the one who declared that we could easily fall prey to Carthage in our eagerness to use them for our own protection, like the farmer in Aesop's fable who hired the fox to guard his henhouse. My words found general agreement.

A final proposal was approved for an ambassador to be dispatched to Messana with a scroll stating our grievances with Roma. These were mainly over the aggressive expansion of two villages into the territory between our two parts of the island. We stated that we hoped for reconciliation, but that this understanding needed to respect us as an equal republic. This meant that our new government would no longer supply tribute to them. We took pains to reassure them that we had not forged an alliance with Carthage and that we merely wanted to remain a free city with free tributary towns and that we would not "have parcels of our land nibbled away as if they were grain cribs and the Roman people so many rats." This last wording was suggested by an owner of vast olive groves to the north of the city. I and several others rather fancied the turn of phrase, but reason prevailed among the body and tamer language was substituted.

Δ

All these things came to pass. To our amazement, no swift retribution descended on Siracusa from the north or across the sea. Neither did Carthage do more than acknowledge with pleasure our rift with their enemy and pledge their friendship. The summer passed in peace and prosperity, even if none of us felt at ease.

And then, in the autumn of that year, Marcus Claudius Marcellus arrived to take charge of the "Siracusan problem."

Δ

Considering that I was the son-in-law of the man who opposed us, I was proposed with high hopes to take the role of chief negotiator. I accepted. Precisely because I was the son-in-law of Marcellus and knew how tough he could be, I insisted to the Roman diplomat that our negotiations take place in Leontini. Marcellus, whose reply was neither warm nor cold, countered that this was unacceptable and suggested Naxos, a former Greek settlement that was now Roman and lay about as far south from Messana as Leontini lay north of Siracusa. We went back and forth in this manner until I realized that his purpose was to have us negotiate on the neutral ground between their lands and ours. This put us in proximity to the two villages our armies had destroyed, the ruins of which mutely attested to our side as aggressor.

We began to negotiate on the anniversary of Thalia's marriage, fittingly at the most dark time of the year. Marcellus focused unwaveringly on the matter at hand and never spoke of his daughter or grandchild during negotiations or even during the breaks. He did, however, have letters passed to me for Aurora via an aide. These were most convivial. They obliquely wished me well and inquired after my happiness as if I did not appear before him every day.

I was amazed at how much time could be wasted in minutia and especially in the laying out of rules and protocols. Our side sinned in this as much as theirs, while we both readied our armies in the background. Men talked merely to be able to say they had participated in such a momentous negotiation and to hear the stentorian sounds of their own voices.

As the days wore on, several others in my negotiating group reported to the council of rulers that I was providing no leverage to soften my father-in-law's demands. I countered that neither had I committed any solecism that allowed the Romans an advantage. I was determined to stay on and do my part to secure the best terms our city could argue. I resisted the temptation to write to Aurora and entreat her to reveal weaknesses in her father's character. I suspected that he had few at any rate.

Our side freely admitted that we had burned and razed the villages, but our contention was that they had been placed there as the first aggressive act. Members of Marcellus' group produced the old treaty between Siracusa and Carthage and showed that no specifics had been made on this point. We argued spirit rather than letter of the agreement. Marcellus demanded that we pay for the restoration of the villages and recompense to the surviving villagers. He also demanded a fine that amounted to five years of our normal tribute. This was considered unacceptable by our group. Any less, Marcellus' legal advisors claimed, would give other peoples in treaty with Roma a tacit nod to injure them in like manner. We declared that we would take the Roman demands to the representatives of the people of Siracusa for their vote. Conciliations were small on both sides and slow to evolve.

Spring came to the island, and the armies left their winter encampments. While we negotiated, our engineers and workmen toiled day and night to fortify Leontini, as a first line of defense against an attack from the north. Owing to winter's impediments and the need not to appear to be preparing for war even as we negotiated for peace, this work went slowly. As the Romans owned the sea, we could not transport lumber and stone in ships, but were reduced to carrying them over land. The defenses were only half improved when two Roman legions attacked.

CHAPTER XX

In order to rebuild his reputation with the populace of Siracusa, general Hippokrates had volunteered to head the effort to defend Leontini. The city rulers had agreed. However, they were only willing to put under his command that quarter of our army that already served under him, totaling a little less than 2,000 men. His objective was to use Leontini as a first line of defense, to test the fighting resolve of the legions, and to inflict as much damage as he could upon them before they continued south to our walls. The entire force under his command in truth totaled almost 4,000, because virtually every male between the ages of thirteen and fifty of the town and the surrounding farms and estates was impressed into the defensive effort. As well, Lysander had been dispatched to employ the city's cavalry before they were hemmed in by our walls and rendered useless.

The perimeter of Leontini was one-sixth that of Siracusa, but the town had never had a proper wall built around it. Peace had blessed it for hundreds of years, and its people had foolishly hoped that this would continue forever. During a five month period, a slow and furtive effort was made to reverse this lamentable state.

As I have already written, winter and an inability to bring wood and stone from any distance limited the operation. Moreover, because our rulers were unwilling to allow Archimedes beyond our own walls or to lose the surprise of his secret weapons of war defending a confederate, the walls were thrown up in a conventional manner. Nevertheless, by early spring the northern and western walls of Leontini, those most likely to take the first blows of a Roman attack, had become formidable. On the eastern side, where the town crowded the sea, they were little higher than a soldier wearing a horsehair helmet. To the south, only ramparts of dirt had been created. Yet even here, Hippokrates had done his best to confound attackers. One of the southern entrances to the town had been walled up. In front of the other, except where road led up to it, he had placed deep trenches filled with sharpened stakes and had them covered over with webbing and dried grasses. Between the southernmost houses of the town and the trenches he had left enough space to fill with a thousand archers and pikemen.

The armory of Siracusa had worked night and day to supply the men of Leontini with bows and arrows, swords, and the type of long lances used in phalanx fighting. Still, by spring many of the town defenders were equipped only with their own axes, knives, and scythes.

Hippokrates may have been mistaken in wanting Siracusa to bet on the Carthaginians rather than the Romans in the titanic conflict that had stretched across decades, but he was not a stupid man. Unwilling to have the army he commanded trapped inside Leontini, should an all-out attack or a siege occur, he had placed only three of his syntagma inside the town, one camped around each of the remaining gates. These men were present both to encourage and train the men of Leontini, and also to prevent cowards from slipping away. In all, this number totaled 576 Siracusan soldiers. The rest of his army, which totaled about 1,400, along with Lysander's cavalry of 120, encamped in a fort hidden beyond a high hill some dozen stadia to the southwest of the town. His numbers were strong because he had lost only three men in the surprise attack on one of the Roman villages in his provocative move against the Roman Republic.

It became clear from the battle that ensued that Marcellus was no Varro. He had managed to get scouts and spies through the surrounding countryside and evidently up to the very walls of the city. Thus, he knew its weak points and even of the covered pits on the south side. Perhaps if we had had the courage to march our entire army to the region, along with the 6,000 allied troops we had built up from the other six towns, he would have continued to negotiate. Or he merely might have sent for another of the legions that were dispersed around Messana and the rest of northern Sicilia. Since we had not presented an all-out army, however, he decided to bring two legions up to the walls and administer one great, crushing blow as an example of the fate that awaited Siracusa if we did not agree to his terms.

Δ

The attack came at mid-morning, after the Romans completed a march of about thirty stadia. The first legion concentrated on the wall and tower in the town's northeastern corner. The attack was preceded by twenty or so flights of arrows which had been dipped in pitch and lighted, to see what mischief could be created by starting multiple fires. This was largely ineffective due to rain the previous night. Because the walls were tall nowhere, the Roman scouts had merely calculated their height. Wide ladders were built twenty percent longer than the wall at the point of attack. In this manner, they could be angled up to form the hypotenuse of a triangle with the ground and the wall and yet not allow any part of the ladders to overshoot the parapets. Thus, the defenders were unable to push them back with forked poles. This attack came in steady waves, using the full force of more than 4,000 men. However, again and again, the Romans would pull back and regroup. Those defenders on the north walls and roofs were nevertheless too preoccupied with these tactics to worry if this was a diversion.

At the same time, half the second legion made a mad dash around the western verge of the town, carrying a dozen wide ladders over their heads. They did not stop until they had reached the concealed pits on the south side. Although they skirted the western wall and moved with speed, it was reported that the Romans lost perhaps fifty men to arrows. Those who carried the ladders could not also defend their left sides with their shields.

The difference between 2,300 and 4,600 men moving at a rush and spread across broken terrain is not immediately discernable. Watching from the protection of the hill to the southwest and from beneath its partial concealment of trees and bushes, Hippokrates and his under officers assumed that this headlong dash was the full impact of the second legion. The ladders were large enough to spot from a distance, so that Hippokrates correctly assumed they would first be laid across the pits to reach the dirt ramparts without much loss of life.

The general reported to us later that he had determined to wait until the Roman numbers had been well diminished by arrows, darts, and long spears from those inside the trenches before falling upon their rear. However, soon after the attacking force had gathered at the south of the city, and he saw their numbers, he called the charge. His hope was to crush the first half of the legion with numerical superiority before the second half arrived in support. As it was, he waited too long. No more than ten minutes after trapping the first Roman force between the town and his men, the sounding of trumpets other than his signaled that more Romans moved in his direction.

Lysander's full regiment of cavalrymen had been held in reserve for such a trick. They charged down the hill onto the western fields, making as much noise as they could. However, they met not only another 2,300 soldiers but 200 horsemen as well. Their charge did nothing more than momentarily stun this wave and hold it back for a few minutes, with the resulting loss of two-thirds of his force. This valiant sacrifice in the face of such overwhelming odds allowed Hippokrates and his army to retreat back up the hill, taking with him also part of one syntagma that had been billeted at the south gate of the town and which had broken through the right flank of the Roman line.

Of the original 576 Siracusan soldiers stationed in Leontini, only 57 returned with Hippokrates. In all, he and Lysander had lost about 1,200 men. He estimated that the Romans had lost a like number, although he could not be sure. Once the town defense was breached from the south, its defenders were left in a hopeless state.

Marcellus did not pursue our army but rather lingered in and around Leontini two days. Miraculously, half a dozen of Hippokrates soldiers had escaped the taken town in the hours after the battle, when the army was preoccupied pillaging, drinking, and raping. The men had hidden in a shop near the town agora and fell upon three Romans sent into it. No one among the legionaries' comrades noted their disappearance. As night fell, three of their number resourcefully donned the uniforms of the killed Romans and led their three comrades boldly out of the southern gate, tied up as if prisoners.

These men reported first to Hippokrates and then to the city counsel that the soldiers under the command of Marcus Claudius had brought no fewer than a thousand men into the agora, fifty at a time, and had beaten and then beheaded them. This would have been virtually every man left alive inside the town after the surrender. The word of this barbarity spread like wildfire throughout Siracusa. In some cases it hardened the resolve "to resist the butchers." In most cases it brought about a panic. The city gates had to be closed to prevent a mass exodus.

Even as hundreds attempted to flee, as many from the six remaining tributary towns wanted to hide behind the protection of Siracusa's walls. We determined that three of the towns were near enough to the north that these should be evacuated of women and children. These were Henna, Megara, and Acilae. Most of their people, however, were to be sent to the other three towns, which lay to the south and southwest. One of these was Agricento, which had suffered so terribly from Roman cruelty not so many decades earlier. These three evacuated towns were emptied of valuables and especially foodstuffs, wine, and olive oil to deprive the enemy. About half these things were sent to the southern towns and half brought into our city, to add to the surplus we had been building up for the past two years. It was estimated that we could last for two years without any outside help. I, however, was determined that replenishing provisions would flow into Siracusa in the coming months, since this was one of the main charges for the Silent Storm. I personally met with representatives from the southern towns and reviewed with them the timetable we had pre-established for running through a Roman siege.

More and more, I felt in charge of the survival of my city, and I also felt capable.

Marcellus seemed to wish us time to prepare, because his army took two days to arrive at our walls. He further gave us three days to consider his ultimatum: We would either immediately throw our gates open to him, or else he would overcome us by direct attack or siege. If the first happened, we could expect that only the leaders of the insurrection would be executed and that we would lose half our existing supply of food, most of our weapons, most of our fleet, and a number of our art treasures. If we kept our doors closed, we could also expect many of our men to be killed and the rest sold into slavery. Siracusa would henceforth be occupied as a Roman province, with not even the boons granted to their colonies.

Δ

I took myself home after receiving this news. Aurora naturally desired to hear all that had transpired. I told her straight out, without softening any of it.

"I cannot believe that my father would kill every man in Leontini," she said. "For one thing, those men have value as slaves. More importantly, he wants us to open our gates."

Her inclusion of herself in our plight was not lost on me.

She added, "He would also know that news of cold massacre would harden hearts and guarantee that the gates remain closed."

"It does seem unlike him," I agreed.

"He has never acted in such a bloodthirsty manner before," Aurora noted. "Why would he begin in Sicilia?"

I merely shook my head in bewilderment. I wondered to my wife if he possibly had direct orders from Roma. We talked in our dining chamber following our meal. Aurora's beautiful landscape murals made warfare seem far away. Over the past few months she had shared with Myreon some of her secrets of depicting how light touches objects. I heard from my father that his work had improved. Immediately, the demand for his murals had increased. Aurora became his favorite woman in the world.

Aurora said, "I will tell you that my father always says what he means and means what he says. If you get the chance to ask him direct questions, he will never lie to you. He will, however, do his utmost not to tell you what he does not wish to reveal. His sense of honor is your greatest ally."

"I do not want to put you between me and him," I said.

"Do not fear," Aurora replied. "My allegiance lies with my husband and Siracusa. This is where I have been loved and made welcome, and this is where my daughter was born. I may not be Greek, but I am now a Siracusan."

For this, I kissed her.

Aurora smiled and lightly massaged my scalp through my hair with one hand even as she nursed Athena. "He knows that you fooled him with Archimedes. That is what he meant when he wrote 'Your husband is more clever even than I had supposed.' This will daunt him and make him wary of direct attacks."

Aurora had already told me about his words, but she was now tutoring me on opposing the power of Roma, as personified by Marcus Claudius Marcellus, the Sword of Roma. A foolish man would have dismissed her thoughts as "those of a mere woman," but I had learned to respect her more than that.

"Thanks to the hospitality of your enemy, you have learned the mechanics of siege well," Aurora continued. "But I must tell you about the psychology of siege from the Roman point of view. Once they begin a siege, they will never end it. Greek states abandoned sieges; Romans never have. They rely on their word and reputation to rob their enemies' hearts of all hope. They have won every siege they ever began. Some have lasted up to five years. No man on earth is as stubborn as a Roman."

"There is always a first time for failure," I countered, "and we are well disposed to cause this. We have large stores laid aside. We have the equivalent of more than two legions behind our walls. We have Archimedes as the creator of our engines of defense. And we have me," I added, wondering if Aurora would laugh.

She smiled. "I rely most upon the last two."

I reasoned aloud, "Roma is distracted on many fronts. They must now defend their colonies on the other side of the Adriatic. They have Sicilia, Sardinia, and Corsica to defend, as well as a few remaining outposts on the edge of Hispania. They have not defeated the new Carthaginian navy. They have yet to defeat Hannibal and his allies. In short, we are but one more distraction to them. They will only be able to concentrate so much power upon us. This we must wear away over time, until their siege becomes too costly."

"I applaud your thinking," Aurora said. "But Marcellus stands behind this army. And he also does not lose. He has never lost."

"Neither have I, and my advantage is that I fight for my home," I said, thinking that this time she must laugh and shrink the comparison of my victories to those of Marcus Claudius Marcellus to true proportions. My wife merely nodded.

"I believe it was Alcaeus who wrote, 'Not houses finely roofed nor the stones of walls well-built, nay nor canals and dockyards make a city, but rather men able to use their opportunity.' So may the protection of Siracusa be its men more than its walls. This struggle may be retold for a thousand years."

A clearing of an old throat drew our attention to Azar, who stood at the entrance to the room.

"May I enter?" she asked.

I gave her leave, asking, "What have you there?"

I caught Aurora's broad smile out of the corner of my eye.

"This is a padded skull cap for you to wear under your helmet," she said, proudly producing the item. "The material cost you nothing," she was quick to add. "It has many stitches, which makes it most durable. It should soften blows."

"No blows ever reach my head!" I proclaimed loudly.

Azar flinched.

I laughed. "I am only teasing you, Azar," I said, accepting the gift. "This should prove very valuable. I thank you." She had no way of knowing that I did not wear my helmet when I served as a soldier with the Silent Storm. I was not about to crush her by informing her of this.

Azar beamed and bowed as deeply as she could. In her joy, she turned to Athena and kissed her on the crown of her head. Then she scurried from the room.

"It has been very important for her to win you over," Aurora said.

I admitted, "I now trust her. I am not sure that she was the good woman you supposed her to be when we took her in. However, because you expected only good of her, she came to behave that way."

"You may be right," Aurora granted. "Azar would never say this to you for fear you would believe her cadging for sympathy, but she has led an abominable life. From her youngest days she has been beaten and abused. Why should she be expected to return good for this? She has told me that she does here exactly the same tasks as she did throughout her life, but suddenly they are easier and almost a joy to perform. It all has to do with attitude. She now wants to be helpful. Before this, if she showed any sign of resentment or disapproval, she was beaten or sold. Not all people are wise enough to respond to kindness with good behavior. The baser ones try to take advantage. But I always give others the benefit of the doubt at first."

I remember this incident so well because of Aurora's last words. When she spoke them, I found myself thinking that I had received a gem of great price for virtually no cost. She was certainly a better person than I was. I also wondered if there was a secret man who had never left her mind, as Thalia had even yet not left mine.

Δ

On the third day of Marcellus' encampment beyond the walls of Siracusa, I went out to him as the main delegate of the city. The stumps of an olive tree grove poked up as high as my knees, to confound the enemy. Because life is so dear and nature will find a way, tender shoots were springing from the barren stems. As I walked over terrain that Archimedes and I had tromped months earlier, I thought about challenging Marcellus to man-to-man combat to settle the war. He had accepted such a challenge once. I knew that I had strength and speed on my side and that he had experience and cunning. Three thoughts prevented me from

252

broaching the idea. The first was that, as the one accepting the challenge, he would have the choice of weapons. He would choose battle on horseback, which was not my forte. This was the man who had controlled a panicked warhorse in the face of his enemies. He had wheeled it completely around to face the sun so that he could salute Apollo and reassure his men that the horse's actions were completely his doing and not an evil omen. The second was that such combat would deprive Aurora of a father, a husband, or both. Even if I won the fight, I would have to face my wife as her father's murderer for the remainder of my life. The third reason was that I sincerely doubted Marcellus would have such latitude in this conflict; Siracusa was too precious a prize.

I made sure that I was the last man to enter the consul's tent. He offered wine, which I refused politely. Around us sat perhaps twenty other men representing both sides. One of these was the praetor Pulcher. Another was the tribune Sixtus Severinus, who had hosted me and Archimedes in Roma. He looked quite ill at ease at having to face me. An inspiration came upon me to show the gathering the irony of this situation. Severinus had stood when I entered the tent. I had raised my hand and offered him my ring to kiss, as the father he had claimed me to be for saving his life. He had looked to Marcellus for direction, and my stern father-in-law shook his head.

"I trust that Cornelia, your son and daughters are well," I said, to show the gathering that I knew his family intimately.

Severinus merely nodded. Men who had become fast friends only a few years earlier were now obliged to kill each other for their countries. Naturally, this would happen only if pointedly polite and formal negotiations broke down. I marveled at how the Fates twist our lives for their own mirth.

I was allowed to begin this round of the discussions.

"At our previous protracted negotiations, you deplored our treachery in attacking your outpost towns. Yet you attacked Leontini without warning even as you supposedly awaited our reply to your terms."

"You told me that they would not be accepted," Marcellus answered with great equanimity.

"Is the score not even now that you hold Leontini?" I asked.

"It is not."

"And why is that?"

"Because it is Siracusa who held the treaty with us, because the army of Siracusa attacked our people first, and because that army compelled the peaceful Leontini to fight."

I was not in a mood to rehash the argument of their illegal settlement of the land. "And now you think that your demonstration at Leontini will frighten us into capitulating."

"It would frighten me if I were you," he replied.

"Say, rather, that it revolts us," I told him. "Do you believe that executing all the men who surrendered helps your cause?"

"What makes you believe I have done this?"

I explained to him the sworn testimony of the six soldiers who eluded capture and fled Leontini in the night.

"They do not speak the truth," Marcellus stated flatly.

"Did you not beat and execute men in the agora?"

"We did. However, they only totaled fifty-two men in all. We executed them by rod and axe in three groups. The first were those who had killed Romans living in their town."

I had heard this sad tale. Despite the intolerance of various races around the Mediterranean for each other, there were always brave souls who moved into alien towns and cities and established themselves. Often, this was to trade goods particular to their homelands. The Leontini had twelve Roman families in their town. When Hippokrates and Epikydes had destroyed the Roman settlements to their north, a number of citizens who resented their Roman neighbors and who coveted their houses and goods murdered them.

"This is fair," I granted. "Who were in the other two groups?"

"The second were the fathers of the town who agreed to build up its defenses and to fight us."

I did not speak my attitude toward this. "And the third?"

"Those were zealots and who pretended to give up but held short swords and daggers concealed. When our men approached them, they attacked as a body and slew half a dozen before being forced to surrender."

"And all of these totaled only fifty-two?" I asked with skepticism.

"I have said so."

"And the rest? Surely you hold soldiers of Siracusa."

"We do not. Your men are enviable in their faithfulness to command. They all died obeying their orders."

"Not even one among 500 survived?"

"Not one," he declared.

"I find this difficult to imagine," I said.

"Then find a better imagination," he countered. "Or else credit more to the abilities of your other top officers to mold and motivate your men."

I sighed with dramatic effect. "But surely not all the men of Leontini died as well. Surely you can bring me twenty who will testify that you did not kill everyone."

"I could produce a hundred," said Marcellus, "but I will produce not one. You have my word that no such massacre occurred, not matter what your soldiers say. I believe they witnessed the three executions and extrapolated. They assumed that we continued after they had fled."

This sounded plausible, but I could not admit it.

"Absent twenty witnesses, the people of Siracusa will believe their soldiers," I said. "You will not have our gates opened, and this will be because of your own vanity. Tell me that you are not a vain and overly proud man," I goaded, knowing that there was more than a kernel of truth in this.

He would not be drawn out. "Let me tell you what you may expect if your gates are not opened at dawn tomorrow," said the Sword of Roma. "I have already had it set down in Greek for you to carry back."

Before the twenty or so witnesses, he repeated the harsh terms he had given me in his tent near the ruined villages: We could expect to be murdered or sold into slavery, and our city would be sacked and reduced to the level of a Roman province. We would have no say in the running of our own city. Tributes would be trebled.

"Now let me tell you what you may expect," I said, as I stood. "You will die outside our gates, Marcus Claudius. You have faced the Celts, the Samnians, the Gauls, the Carthaginians. But you have never faced the grandsons of Korinthos or those of the blood of Alexander the Great. I took no joy in watching Roman men slaughtered on the plain of Cannae, but I will rejoice when those with you meet their end on the plains outside Siracusa. We have already killed more than a thousand, even though you attacked with no warning and with a great superiority of numbers."

I waited for the commander's reply. He refused to confirm or deny my guess as to the number killed or which legions he had used, but I thought I saw in his eyes respect for what he assumed was knowledge.

"Siracusans do not fight like Leontini, as you now know," I said. "We will take two Romans for each Siracusan who falls. You yourself have just told me that we mold our fighting men well and that they are enviable in their faithfulness to command. Within a few months, you will petition Roma to give you an excuse to retreat from here. That is, if Hannibal has not slaughtered another six of your legions, and you are suddenly required to defend Roma's walls."

I had rehearsed the speech several times in my room at the Euryalus fortress. Two years before, I would have been too young, too inexperienced, and too cowed facing such a great warrior. Now, however, I was also a proven warrior and a proven athletic champion twice over. I was also filled with righteous wrath.

Marcellus stood and thumped his fist against his chest in the Roman manner of salute.

"So be it," he said. He gestured to the open tent flaps.

Δ

When war is inevitable, there is no point in delay. That same night, the entire cohort of the Silent Storm exited Euryalus by means of the tunnel that Archimedes had ordered dug. We were dressed in our black, with our weapons cloaked against shining. We had even smudged charcoal upon our faces, arms, and legs, to make ourselves invisible under the moonless sky. Immediately, we split up. The first group, under Xenophanes, stole toward the Roman encampment which was still in the process of being fortified. I had given my men a full report of everything I had gained from my journey to Italia. They knew where guards would be posted; they knew how best to create a great deal of confusion and uproar.

I had borrowed a page from Hannibal's book of tricks and commanded each of these twenty-five men to secure five torches. After they dispatched the Roman scouts who were attempting to crawl up close to the city walls and study them, they spread out across a distance of two stadia. At the traditional time of the changing of the third watch, they each stuck three torches into the ground and lit them. Next, they lit the last two torches and carried them forward, so that seventy-five torches held their place in the darkness and fifty more advanced on the west side of the camp. When they had come within one stadium of the trenches, they planted these torches as well and hastened in retreat.

As I had anticipated, Marcellus sent half a legion of his men marching out of the eastern gate in tight formation, expecting some sort of attack to that side. The remainder of the camp men took to the ramparts, as I had when Hannibal's troops paraded out the day before the battle of Cannae. I imagined these Roman veterans straining their eyes to peer into the concealing darkness, perhaps wondering how many thousands of Siracusans were surrounding them.

I had planned no attack on any side of the fort. The torches had been planted in the west precisely because I desired that the Romans stay near their encampment. I and the other twenty-five of my number had long before stolen beyond their walls another eight stadia to the northwest, where the Romans' secondary camp lay. This was an estate they had occupied, in which they had deposited excess supplies and many of their wagons lest they need to evacuate their main camp on short notice.

In this estate they had stationed forty men. With bow and hatchet we rendered a third of them lifeless by the time the general alarm was raised. Our skills were so honed that we only lost five men in all before silencing the last Roman. At that point, we hitched donkeys to fifteen wagons and loaded them with supplies. It was a paltry amount that would not feed one district of Siracusa for one meal. Symbolically, however, it was an enormous take. These fifteen wagons were driven away by the majority of my remaining cohort while the last six of us took up positions to the southern perimeter of the estate and satisfied ourselves that no reinforcements approached. After half an hour, when we were certain that the captured wagons had been driven well to the west, we set fire to the estate and destroyed the remainder of the wagons and supplies.

I had struck the first blow in the war for Siracusa.

Δ

As you must surely expect, when news of the deaths of the 513 Siracusan men who had died defending Leontini reached our city the outcry was enormous. Unlike Roma after Cannae, our women were not prevented from lamenting in the streets. The screams and weeping were especially strong since these were men of Hippokrates' division, and this general had collected around him those who already had hated Roma.

Throngs gathered in the temples to offer sacrifices for the souls of the valiant departed. Bonfires were built in the agoras. Hair was shorn and clothing torn among nobles, the wealthy, and the poor. Many still distrusted the Carthaginians, and not a few lamented the end of their prosperous dealings with the Romans, but for the time the city united in its hatred of the would-be masters of all Sicilia.

I felt the need to offer prayers as well. However, negotiations with Marcellus and preparations for our successful raid against the Roman supplies took precedence. Once I had completed this task, I hurried to the Temple of Apollo, the god of vengeful death, in Neapolis. I was on my knees in fervent prayer when I felt a light touch upon my shoulders. I turned.

Thalia stood behind me. She wore no jewels or adornment. Her dress was the pure white of a woman in mourning. I drew in my breath in reaction.

"Yes," she said. "Cleomenes is dead. Had you not heard?"

"No," I told her. "I have been occupied without cease since Leontini fell."

"He died defending the town," she told me, through a drawn face.

"Then he died valiantly," I offered.

"I am glad of that for my sake," she said.

I asked her why she came to pray at the Temple of Apollo, so far from their home. "Why not offer prayers at the Temple of Artemis?"

She went down on her knees beside me. "I have prayed there. I have been to every temple, praying on his behalf and on behalf of our city."

"Then it is only a small coincidence that we meet here," I said.

She shook her head. "No. The gods have ordained it. We are not finished."

I remembered with bitterness the night we invaded Cleomenes' bedroom, found Thalia in his bed, and watched her defend him.

"I believe we are," I said. "I am a married man."

"You have in your house a Roman woman, so this cannot be a true marriage. With her kin just outside our walls, send her to them! Repudiate her! Don't you understand, my love? I am a free woman! Or at least I will be after the required year of mourning. This could not have worked out better. Cleomenes freed me from my father. You could not have. Moreover, I now own his home and his businesses. I am one of the wealthiest women in Siracusa."

"You claim to be here on behalf of your husband's shade," I said, "and yet you can dishonor him so with these words?"

"I did not love him," she said, simply.

Her response angered me on several levels. I stood, pulling her up rather roughly. I marched her behind the column that had several times served as our private trysting place. "You say you did not love him? You gave us a most affecting portrayal of devotion in your bedroom the night he was attacked."

Thalia's little chin elevated a bit. "I knew it was you under the mask."

"You only knew after I grabbed you," I said.

"Not so," she countered coolly. "But even if it were, you do not understand what was going through my mind."

"Enlighten me," I invited.

"First, I was soundly asleep when you invaded. I had barely enough time to awaken."

"I watched you," I riposted. "You were completely awake by the time Cleomenes had confirmed and denied the list of names."

259

"You wish to know why I threw myself over him?"

"Exactly. You had heard that he was to be castrated if he did not supply the names. I meant to do it anyway, to prevent him from getting you with child or ever being able to have you again."

Thalia looked to the ceiling as if appealing to the gods to reason with me. "I know that! But were you ready to kill him? Would you have killed him?"

"You heard one of the men say that castrating him would probably kill him!" I hissed at her.

"Probably? Probably?" she repeated. "And what if he hadn't died? You would have saddled me with a husband for all my life who could not satisfy the fires he had ignited. You would never be mine, but neither would he. Do you think I should play the role of Vestal virgin at my age without their benefits?"

The force of her words and her smooth responses mollified me and left me momentarily without words.

"I was furious at you for not having the will to kill him, even behind the anonymity of a mask. I told him that you and I had pledged our love, but he laughed at you and your family. Do you no longer want me?" she challenged.

"I don't know," I said, thinking of Aurora and Athena.

At my reply, Thalia went up on her toes and kissed me with an ardor I had never before experienced. I tried with all my will to resist but found myself responding. Then she pulled back.

"You lie to yourself. If you refuse my love, you condemn me to a living death," Thalia declared. "I have thought of nothing but the clear way to you since hearing of Cleomenes' end. He was after all a decent man. I did not love him, but he was good to me. I have hated myself for not mourning him in the manner he deserves. I have told myself that I am a low and callous woman. But all I could think of was you. This is your doing! You came to my wedding. You gave me hope. And now you tell me that those feelings we proclaimed again and again were just words?"

"I have a wife," I protested.

"I bared myself as a virgin to you. I did this in a common alley, and this is how you repay me?"

"I have a child," I muttered.

"I will give you ten children! When you say you have a wife, you speak of the daughter of our most hated enemy. Are you insane, Leonides? She will either betray us all for her father's sake, or else she will be murdered for being a Roman. Were the Romans in Leontini not murdered?"

I had thought of this several times with dread. I mutely nodded my head.

"Then if you have feeling for her and your child, you will deliver her into the hands of her father. Repudiate her as the daughter of your enemy, and let us get on with our lives. Trust me; they will not starve!"

I still could find no words.

"You had no choice in marrying her, as I had no choice with Cleomenes," Thalia argued. "You are a young man. You cannot waste your life and mine with some misguided loyalty. Speak to me!" she hissed.

"We cannot do anything about our love for one year at any rate," I argued, temporizing through an agony of ambivalence.

"Not officially at least," Thalia quickly replied. "That does not mean we cannot establish a nest for our love. I will buy a place in Epipolai, far from both your home and mine. Near to your fortress. I will make myself your courtesan, your plaything. You may do with me all those things you have dreamed in your fantasies. I am an experienced woman now, but you will teach me more. We will invent together such joys as neither of us alone could devise."

"I cannot think on this now," I said, my head about to burst. "I have suffered the loss of too many comrades."

Thalia nodded. "We are both in a troubled state. This is an inappropriate time to talk of love and futures. But I could not find you here and steal silently away. I tell you that the gods wish this for us. I will purchase the house and let you know where it is. We can speak of using it at a later time."

I merely nodded.

Thalia kissed me again, and this time she ground her midsection against my thigh. Her kisses ran from my lips and trailed across my chin and down to my neck. I steadied myself with one hand against the temple column. She dropped to her knees and pressed her face into my groin. I pulled her immediately to her feet and kissed her quickly, then fled the temple.

CHAPTER XXI

Because Archimedes bestrode the beginning of my tale like the colossal Helios of Rhodes, my reader no doubt wonders why he figured so little in the middle. This was because he had his duties and I mine. Although they were both directed toward the same end, we perpetually moved on different paths. In the six months before the Romans attacked Leontini, I recollect that I saw him only four times. Once was at the baths, once in the agora, and twice on visits to his house with my wife.

Archimedes had not changed perceptibly since my teenage years. Aurora agreed that he had lost neither physical strength nor mental acuity since she first met him in Roma. He was, in brief, a marvel for his age. The only change in his house was the death of Crito, due to infections from the loss and the breaking of teeth. Irene reported that my great-uncle was home so little, however, that she was able to carry on without her beloved husband.

Now had come the time when Archimedes and I were destined to unite again. Soldiers of the Silent Storm left Siracusa by tunnel, skiff, or rope twelve at a time, in six pairs. Three pairs scouted south and three north. When they went out, they carried food and drink to sustain them for five days. Their purpose was to watch trails, roads, and the ocean, so that no Roman stratagem might catch our city unawares.

This left thirty-three of my well-trained men inside the city with nothing to do. The four generals, Hippokrates, Epikydes, Archelous, and Paulus, drilled their men in the open places of Euryalus and Epipolai and assigned them to guard the walls. Owing to their competitiveness, none wished to contribute soldiers when Archimedes issued a call. They believed these men would lapse to the old genius' charge. This was true to a certain extent, but once the fighting began the direction of Archimedes' engines would by necessity fall to individual soldiers who directed a large force of non-citizen laborers. I and Lysander, whose cavalry had been reduced by two-thirds and was useless inside the city, volunteered our men to work with Archimedes.

At last the doors of the secret warehouse were opened to us. Inside, we found fifty weapons of five separate designs. These I shall describe as they came into use. Suffice to say at this point that Archimedes had devised machines that gave every man who looked upon them hope that Siracusa would not be taken.

These engines were not easy to move. All but a prototype of each had been disassembled to cart them to their optimal locations. Given enough laborers, every one could be broken down in half an hour or less and rebuilt within another hour, so that they could serve in several quadrants of the city during the course of a single day. In consultation with Archimedes, Lysander and I agreed that ten machines of various types should be placed at the Great Harbor, five at the Little Harbor, five at the fortress of Euryalus, twenty along the walls that faced to the north, and ten along the western-facing walls.

Where the cliffs doubled the height of the walls, no machine was deemed needed. Likewise, where the walls skirted swamp and marsh none was positioned. After a short time, all the machines were removed from the towers of the Euryalus fortress, because no spies probed the area for weakness after the first week. Clearly, its towers, the slits in its walls, the three lines of trenches, and the changed gateway more than discouraged Marcellus and his commanders. I will tell you now that not once was the fortress attacked during the long siege.

"I have one more invention that may be of use on our ocean side," Archimedes told me, several weeks into the siege. "It has been the most difficult to devise, and it will only work on days of bright sun, but it may be worth the trouble." This machine was kept in a separate room of the warehouse, and no amount of cajoling could convince my great-uncle to show it until he had it perfected.

"We must practice once your machines are in place," Lysander said.

Archimedes shook his head. "You only need to tell my workers where and when to use them. They have practiced already."

"Where?" I asked, for I had heard nothing of this.

"Inside this building."

"But it is so small compared with the throw of the machines," I said. "How was practice possible?"

"We rehearsed the actions without the destructive elements," Archimedes answered with impatience.

"Then how do you know that they will do what you say they will do?" Lysander asked.

"It is called physics, young man," my great-uncle replied. Even though Lysander was in his late thirties, anyone under the age of sixty Archimedes considered a young man. "The laws of physics never vary. Therefore these machines will behave one way and one way only...provided you do your jobs correctly. You report that you have reliable men posted outside the city to watch for the approach of a fleet?"

I affirmed that we did.

He said to me, "I think that perhaps the reason your father-in-law has not begun an assault is that he awaits ships."

"If that is so," I responded, "my men do not even need to get back into the city to warn us. We have established a system of smoke signals."

Archimedes picked up a metal ratchet with a critical eye and examined it. "That is good. The engines removed from Euryalus are being repositioned in the Great Harbor. The minute we learn of a fleet heading toward Siracusa, we must anchor 100 inflated animal skins in its waters."

To Move the World

The old genius at least shared the reason behind these strange words. When we heard it, Lysander and I almost became eager for the battle to begin. We supervised the redistribution of the various machines according to the capabilities that Archimedes dictated. We ached to test them, but despite the siege, the inventor feared spies. He was adamant that the element of surprise in battle would prove half their value.

Δ

Once the business of placing the war engines was finished, I was able to return to my room at the fortress, where I found a communication from Thalia. She had not wasted any time finding a place where we might meet in secret. It lay at the western edge of Epipolai, near the inner wall of Euryalus. Many who lived in this area assumed that this would be the place where the Romans would attack and the first of the city districts to fall. Therefore, they were selling or renting out their homes at low price. Both Menander and Apollonius moved swiftly to secure beautiful homes with large courtyards for their families. They were able to rent them and still live within their salaries. They each in turn pressured me to do the same, but I was content to leave Aurora and Athena where they were. I also did not want to be too far from my great-uncle.

Thalia sent to me explicit directions to the street and thence the little house that she had secured. I wrote my reply, sealed it with my signet, and gave it to a trusted courier. My message was that I could not violate the sanctity of her year of mourning. There was more behind my reluctance, but I could not write this. I was ashamed to admit to myself that I was still in her thrall. I wrote that if I was to come to her, it must be a year hence. As I set the words to papyrus, I thought that the odds were good of my not being alive to have to make the choice at all. I received a reply from her the following day, begging me to reconsider. Her reasoning was that Cleomenes had robbed me already of months of her love; his shade should not prevent me from claiming her as soon as possible. This letter I did not answer. I received no more messages.

Δ

Aurora and I had had a standing invitation to my father's home for weeks, but my hundred-odd preparations to defend Siracusa made acceptance impossible. Once the machines were put in place I set a date. We had spoken about my family several times since the outbreak of hostilities. During a war, there are few professions as unnecessary as that of house painter. Although I had often harangued my brothers and father about the need to be prudent due to the war between Carthage and Roma, and Siracusa's dangerous position between them, not one had economized as he should have. Aurora and I, therefore, decided to help support them. Since my father held the dowries, we said that he could merely use them as he and my brothers needed them. We knew this would not be abused. We spoke of the money as loans. I assured them that we had enough with my salary, my winnings as a city champion, and my reward for bringing Archimedes safely home from Roma. We implored them to use the money to lay up stores of food, wine, and oil before prices rose beyond reason. This struck a resonant chord with them.

While we dined on those sorts of food that would not keep for any time, Myreon said to me, "Your offer of this loan is greatly appreciated. However, what I truly need is to be transferred to your command."

Myreon had the misfortune of being assigned to one of the syntagmas that Hippokrates commanded. He had served at Leontini and only by good fortune had found himself in the syntagma farthest back in the charge. He had witnessed warfare first-hand but had not struck one blow.

"This man seeks to win glory on our backs," Myreon said. "He thinks to become another Hieron by soldierly exploits. He talks of sallying from the gates when the Roman forces begin an assault. He believes our courage will come as a great shock."

"Marcellus will be ready," I assured him.

"Of course he will. Hippokrates will either die at the front of the ranks or else win glory. I want no glory."

I explained to Myreon that I was powerless over Hippokrates. I also assured him that my men put themselves in harm's way every few days and that he had better prospect of surviving if he stayed where he was.

Dion chimed in, "Do you wish to live forever, Myreon?" This was a common saying of bravado among the young men, all of whom I am sure wished precisely that.

"That's easy for you to say," my younger brother shot back. "You serve with Paulus and supervise slaves who cook. You will be the last one sent out the gates."

"I will ask Paulus if he wants a mural painted in his quarters," Dion said through a wicked grin. "Perhaps he will trade you for one of his men."

"Perhaps I will see that he tastes your cooking," Myreon replied. "Then you and I will exchange places."

The night wore on more or less in this nervous and carping manner. I felt like Siracusa itself, for I was besieged by my family for hours with questions on every aspect of the conflict. I was happy to escape the house with Aurora.

Δ

Over the course of two weeks, the Romans tested the security of our city walls in several places and at varying hours, but always they did this with fewer than 500 men, who retreated as soon as their officers could judge how quickly and in what numbers we responded. Maintaining our composure, the engines of Archimedes remained silent.

During the same period, the Siracusans were not passive. Six days into the siege, shortly after the middle of the night, the full contingent of the Silent Storm so efficiently cleared the plain of enemy between our walls and the Roman camp that a hundred archers were able to follow after us and crawl unobserved to the very defensive ditches surrounding the encampment. While they fired some two-dozen volleys of flaming arrows soaked in pitch over the ramparts, I and my men created a wall of large shields and methodically pulled the stakes from an area twice the width of a man and about a third of the way up. Within minutes, the rain of answering stones and arrows grew so thick that we were forced to retreat.

Glancing over our shoulders, however, we watched with great satisfaction the pulsing glow from half a dozen burning tents and huts. I had devised the plan, to rob the Romans of good sleep and to make them understand that we were not afraid to go on the offensive. For the next full week, observation of their camp showed that at least two centuries of men had been assigned night patrol in case we returned.

On the twelfth day of the siege, just as we had planned, 120 donkeys weighted down with sacks of food trotted through the Euryalus gate. This relief came from Henna. Hippokrates got his wish to march out beyond the walls. This he did as the sun reached its zenith, only a few minutes before the donkey caravan arrived. His well-disciplined troops jogged out four abreast, and within minutes no fewer than 1,500 men formed a battle line curving from west to north.

Unfortunately for the ambitious strategos, the Romans were caught totally by surprise by this caravan. As I had hoped, they believed that such action would only commence once the town had begun to exhaust its resources. Consequently, they were improving some aspects of their camp and not thinking of war that day. I laughed heartily as the donkeys and their drivers not only had time to reach the city gate, but also to unload and escape. I laughed both at us making fools of our Roman foes and at Hippokrates, who stood at the right front corner of his mass of men with his armor shining and his spear held aloft, perspiration trickling down his cheeks as he waited in vain for someone to fight.

I did not laugh later when I realized that this last thumbing of the nose in front of Marcellus would cause him to react far more than I would have in his place. Owing to the three lines of trenches and the threatening towers on the fortress, he dared not build closer than two stadia from the walls. Yet at a little more than this distance, where the road from Euryalus cut through a ravine, he built a wall. Our main artery to inland Sicilia was effectively made useless for commerce.

Three days later, Hippokrates and Epikydes together marched out the Euryalus gate, this time with 2,000 men. In less than an hour, they had knocked down most of the wall. As they retreated, the fearsome Roman cavalry galloped into view.

The next day, behind a human wall of Roman foot soldiers, their wall was rebuilt higher and thicker. This time, a small fort was erected adjacent to it. Atop the fort, catapults aimed with menace at the deserted and rough fields between their wall and the Euryalus gate. There would be no more sallying with impunity out of the Euryalus gate.

This was the extent of hostilities in the first four weeks. No flags were waved for further negotiations. The harbors were not blockaded. Several small convoys of trading ships ran brazenly in and out. The people of the city grew foolishly bolder and encouraged each other to make bragging statements. Triumphs of ancient Greek city states over foreign enemies such as the battle of Marathon were recalled. No one dared to recall the disasters. The forehandedness of Hieron was blessed, and everyone wondered what their great Archimedes had prepared for the proud and aggressive Romans.

They did not have much longer to wonder.

Δ

The first true attack began at night. We were prepared. The scouts of the Silent Storm had spotted the arrival of the fleet that no doubt had been sent for before Marcellus and Appius Pulcher marched up to our walls. It totaled sixty quinqueremes, the pride of the Roman navy. Eight of these ships were refitted for a unique attack upon the Ortygian side of the Great Harbor. They were lashed two together with the inside oars shipped, so that they formed four double-wide galleys. Upon these on the prow ends were placed planks to even the decks. Two towers of a height equaling approximately four men standing on each others' shoulders were set up near the bows on their outer beams. Between these towers, lying flat on the deck, was a ladder much like the ones carried to the south of Leontini. It was wide enough for two men to climb together and high enough to reach to the top of our sea wall when it was hoisted up on pulleys attached to the ship's mast. Because it looks like a musical lyre when erected, the Romans called it a sambuca.

The strategy was straightforward: The oarsmen would row directly for the sea wall in four places. When the wall was brushed by the ship noses, anchors would be dropped to keep the ships close. Approximately eight men on two levels of each tower would use pikes, darts, and arrows to clear the wall of defenders. The ladders would be raised by pulleys, and two men at a time would scurry up them to take the wall.

Meantime, archers and engines that hurled stones and spears would be employed from as many of the other galleys as could be maneuvered into the harbor, sweeping more of the wall and creating havoc and diversions.

To further aid this plan, Marcellus launched his first major attack late at night. This evening was clear under a full moon, which lit the waters enough to expose the galleys when they were yet at Naso Point.

At the same late hour, the bulk of the Roman army assaulted part of the Achradina wall, with catapults, belly bows, regular bows, and flights of men climbing ladders. This part of the wall they had never openly tested. It is my belief that this was purposely done to encourage our forces to concentrate elsewhere.

I shall deal with the latter assault first. Archimedes' many walks around the city's outer walls had given him an excellent idea of where an enemy would most likely focus an attack. Thus, when some 3,000 Romans impinged upon the Achradina wall, the old man was ready. He had had placed in the rough field beyond this wall several low and unobtrusive stone pyramids, often concealed from Roman view by brush. The sides of the stones drawn from the earth and dark were turned to the Roman side. Their white top sides faced the city. These piles were set at two precise distances. As the Roman army advanced close to the farther line, which lay about eight-tenths of a stadion from the city, three catapults released torrents of fire that exploded upon impact, lighting up the plain. The fires that burned across the layers of straw, threshing, and chaff which had been strewn there weeks before not only lit the area for our archers but also compelled the soldiers to concentrate between them.

Less than a minute later, the same catapults hurled into exactly the spaces between the fires bundles of stones that were each large enough to kill a man. The throwing capacity, accuracy, and reload rate of Archimedes' machines surpassed all descriptions we had received of Roman engines. At least a dozen men fell with each volley. The fusillade repeated at intervals of about three per minute with never a sign of flagging.

When the surviving legionaries crossed this hellish space, they soon reached the second set of marker pyramids. This signaled men on the wall to bring another three engines into action. These hurled five spears each. Again, because the sighting was so accurate, the devastation was appalling to the Romans and extremely heartening to our soldiers and laborers. At least a third of the spears found their marks, so tightly packed were the attackers. In a few cases, the same spear pierced two men at a time. Both these sets of weapons were not operated by twisting animal sinews, as the Romans practiced, but rather by using a group of slaves to draw up great weights via pulleys and then allowing that weight to plummet them down. Further, the engines were set on large pivots with pin spacers, so that they could be precisely repositioned in a matter of moments.

Finally, when the vanguard of the enemy army advanced within twenty lengths of the wall, the slits that had dotted the wall in so many places, not far above the height of a man, released dozens of darts each from little machines that Archimedes had also designed. Likewise, rocks hurtled down upon the men, some so large that the earth shuddered when they landed. Soldiers disappeared under their weight.

From atop the wall two sets of archers also fired upon the Romans. These men did not need to aim their weapons, but merely pulled to their limits and pointed to the tops of sticks that had been set upon the wall. Obeying Archimedes' laws of physics, the arrows landed where the soldiers marched, even though our archers did not expose themselves to aim. Some archers had normal bows; some used composite bows reinforced with horn and sinew. The latter filled the plain just below where the farthest stones fell; the former rained down upon the space just in front of the multiple spears. At no moment were the advancing soldiers free from attack. As they lifted their shields to ward off the stones and spears, the arrows came more or less straight into them. They had more chance of running across an agora in a rainstorm and keeping dry.

Only about half of the Romans who charged reached our wall, and these cried out ceaselessly with moans of despair. Many were wounded. A few threw up their ladders and dared to climb, but soon enough trumpets called them into retreat. It was a most costly lesson in Siracusan defense.

Δ

In the Great Harbor, even greater mischief awaited the 3,000 men who Marcellus commanded. The moon goddess clued our men as to when the lead galleys reached the first line of animal skin floats. In a fashion similar to the treatment afforded the land troops, three catapults hurled immense stones with astonishing accuracy into the galleys. Oars were torn off several at a time. A mast crashed backward upon its deck. In one case, a great stone pierced through the deck and the hull, causing the ship to sink within minutes.

Those ships gliding into the range of the second set of floats were met with meteors of fire that were extremely difficult to quench. Two galleys had the misfortune to choose this distance to turn broadside, so as to use their catapults and spear-throwing weapons. After sustaining more than half a dozen hits each, their captains ordered retreat upon their own recognizance.

At the flanks of the eight rafted galleys rowed another eight ships, loaded with men who were to transfer via great planks called corvuses, or beaks, once the walls were secured. These ships held small throwers on their decks, but these only launched one spear at a time. A number of soldiers, however, served as archers, and they did their best to aim at the tops of the walls that seemed largely devoid of men.

As all these galleys touched against the Ortygian walls, suddenly out of slits sailed more than 200 darts. These were released at the exact level to sweep across the Roman decks. Every thirty seconds, another 200 or so burst from the spaces, with virtually no opportunity for the Romans to retaliate. These engines were improvements upon the Roman "scorpion," so named for inflicting multiple deadly stings.

While the shipmen were engaged erecting shields against the darts, climbing the towers, and raising the ladders, from over the island's ramparts swung half a dozen machines that looked like gallows. Each moved swiftly and silently and stopped directly above a ship as if it were a living thing and had its own eyes. Three of these held stones as large as ten talents' weight. These were released with incredible violence. One stone tore off the rail of a ship. Another crashed through a ladder and tower device, broke all its foundation to pieces, shook out its fastenings, and dislodged it completely from the bridge. A third stone plummeted straight down, landed squarely amidships, and drove through to the harbor bottom, taking the galley down within minutes.

The remaining three devices that swung out over the walls held great grappling hooks. These seemed to operate more blindly, but not one failed to hook into some part of a galley or another. When they had dug in, they began to draw upward. Despite weighing many tons and carrying dozens of oarsmen and soldiers, the ships were borne inexorably out of the water so that their bows came halfway up the height of the wall and their sterns dipped into the harbor. In this manner, two of the rafted ships were swamped and sunk. One support galley was hooked in a rowing port, which allowed the hoist to draw the ship over on its side. A century of men spilled into the waters screaming in terror. Suddenly the ropes that held the hook were released. The ship crashed down upon the breakwater rocks and split open.

Hundreds of archers suddenly appeared on the walls, and these fired down upon those soldiers who had already not drowned from the weight of their armor. Not half an hour had elapsed since the first galley crossed the outer markers, and Marcellus wisely ordered that the trumpets be sounded for a swift retreat. In the confusion, one galley collided with another, snapping off oars with sounds like cracking thunder.

The fortress of the Plemmyrion on the south side of the harbor, which had lain dark and silent until this moment, suddenly came to life. Another of Archimedes' hurling engines began raining buckets of hen-egg-sized stones with uncanny accuracy upon each ship that passed through the harbor mouth. The two ships that ventured too close to this fortress were also punished with volleys of lethal darts. Never had Roman galley slaves bent to their oars with such energy.

When the final missile was thrown, eight Roman quinqueremes lay sunk or listing hopelessly in the harbor. Many more required extensive repairs. The joy of our army was immeasurable.

Δ

Archimedes, who had slept through his triumph, was fetched at first light to view the havoc he had engineered. The dawn fully revealed the sunken ships, the flotsam, and the scores of bobbing corpses in the clear, blue water.

"Am I expected to rejoice at this sight?" he asked his adoring minions. Their expressions fell in disappointment. He turned his back on the harbor. "You did your work well. Congratulations! I have not slept enough. I shall appear later today in our factory, to see if I can make myself into an even deadlier god."

Δ

This last story came back to me a full day after the attack. I sought Archimedes out myself late in the morning to heap congratulations upon him, unaware of his visit to the sea wall and his bitter comments. He stood beside a recently manufactured engine that was leaving his factory, inspecting the various pulley systems, levers, and counterweights.

"There is nothing to congratulate," he said. "There is only for me remorse at having to pervert science by using it to such evil ends."

"But you have saved your city!" I exclaimed.

"And have I lost my soul?" he countered, walking toward the harbor. "Does this undo the good of my water pump and other inventions that benefit my fellow man?"

I reminded him that he had saved the lives of his countrymen, against a bellicose people he did not like. He was, however, obdurate in lamenting what he had wrought.

Then suddenly he waved his hands in front of his face, as if to shoo flies. "Have you ever thought that philosophy is a luxury of those with free time?" he asked me, catching me off guard.

I told him that the notion had never entered my mind.

"Races of still hunters and gatherers do not spawn philosophers. They are too busy moving around and collecting food to stay alive." A landward breeze ruffled the old man's thin hair, as if Nature herself caressed him. "Likewise, pondering the merits of good over evil is a luxury in times of war. One must live, so the time to reflect is again possible."

I thought that we would have much time to reflect, trapped inside our city. But I understood what he meant and gave no reply.

"Although I have always been a bachelor," he told me, "nonetheless have I created children. These are offspring of the mind and therefore can be immortal. My water screw, my leverage systems, my formulae and studies of hydraulics are important. These I wish to live on after me." He turned and looked at the yet-unused engine of death. "But not these perversions of science. When this war is ended, I charge you to destroy my weapons. The last thing I want to do is to contribute to the world's store of destructive knowledge. I shall make this known to the rulers as well, but you must give me your solemn promise that they and my designs for them will be destroyed."

This I did promise.

CHAPTER XXII

I n the short time between the losing of Leontini and when the Romans had drawn a curtain around Siracusa, Hippokrates and Epikydes took pains to hurry to two of our confederate towns to help them defend against Roman attack. These were Megara and Acilae. Seeing that he could neither take our harbors nor seal them up due to Archimedes' machines, Marcellus set about at least denying us succor from such towns and their fields, vineyards, and orchards.

We had anticipated this would happen at least by harvest time. Perhaps the business of running donkeys so boldly in and out of the Euryalus gate early in the siege had been a miscalculation. Likewise, I was too eager to destroy the Roman storage camp. If these had not so provoked and embarrassed the Romans, perhaps they would not have focused so soon on the surrounding towns, allowing the townsmen more time to prepare for defense. Instead, two days after the first major attacks on Siracusa a large part of the Roman army marched on Megara and Acilae. These towns were quite like Leontini in that they had never known warfare and had neither bothered to build up daunting fortifications nor to train their men in the fell business of warfare. They lived as if in a dream, which is enviable except when the wolves circle the house. Like Leontini, they became unfortunate object lessons in the failure to learn the price of freedom.

Thus, Marcellus was able to take both towns with little trouble. It was reported to us by my scouts that Megara's men had fled after only a token resistance. Those living in Acilae, however, had been busy in the making of an encampment some fifteen stadia northeast of their town, where they gathered in all their valuables. This they had done in an effort to spare their homes and shops. The fort was a simple design of earthen ramparts and pits lined with stakes. It was built too small and even so was not completed. Again, only 500 of these men had come to us for training. The remaining 1,000 owned no weapons of fighting quality. Therefore, when 3,000 Romans arrived to give them battle, they did not have the wherewithal to march out of the gates. The methodical Romans were able to use their catapults and spear engines and a seemingly limitless supply of arrows to accost the little fort until a third of the Acilaen men were killed without being able themselves to attack. After the Romans rammed down the two poorly-fashioned gates, their numerical superiority allowed them to kill the remaining thousand with minimal losses to their side. The goods and valuables were collected down to the last coin and vase. Then Acilae itself was entered and scoured. A town that had held nearly 8,000 people only three weeks earlier stood as empty as Cannae had.

Marcellus now had a summer before him and half the region and its planted fields in his possession. No matter how long we resisted the siege, his army was certain to have enough food.

Δ

One might wonder if, considering 1,800 of the Romans' approximately 9,200 man army had been killed at Leontini and in the combined assault on Siracusa, and if 3,000 of the remaining soldiers were led into the countryside by Marcellus to reduce our tributary towns, why our 8,000 citizens and resident allies did not rush from our gates and attack those Romans left besieging our city. One might opine that a numerical superiority of almost two to one would be enough to overcome the Roman camp.

Two notable things prevented this.

The first was that I had lost two pairs of my scouts in the preceding days. The rest of my cohort had returned to the city, rendering us blind beyond the horizon seen from our walls. Thus, we had no idea until the men of the Silent Storm roved once more on patrol that so many of the Romans had vanished. Consequently, we did not know when they had departed, if they had left forever, or if they would return the next hour.

The second reason was that the great majority of the Roman fleet survived. Although they did not attempt to enter either harbor for another two months, they sailed back and forth across the ocean, daring any convoys to come to our aid. We had no idea how many soldiers or marines stood on those decks. Finally, while Hippokrates and Epikydes, ever our hot bloods, wished to attack the Roman camp, Archelous, Lysander, Paulus, and I outvoted them. We were in favor of inviting other attacks which would either wear down the antagonists' numbers by hundreds each time or else thoroughly discourage them and finally cause a Roman army to retreat for the first time from a siege.

Marcellus returned to Siracusa with about 250 fewer men, according to reports that were gathered in the following weeks. He set about increasing the size and strength of the little fort that opposed the Euryalus gate. He sent patrols to the south side of the city to assess the swamps and marshland that rimmed the Great Harbor. While the Romans are known to be excellent engineers and to build within one day a wooden bridge that can cross a sizable river, the unhealthy conditions there and the vast expanses of muck made him wisely abandon any thought of taking the city from that quarter.

Other than these activities, the Roman army settled down to gross inaction. They did not probe our walls; they did not build huge towers to assault us; they heaped up no earthen ramps; nor did they attempt to tunnel beneath the walls. Such was the respect for Archimedes that they evidently decided to starve us out. This seemed illogical, since their armada was ineffectual in preventing individual ships and even small convoys from entering and leaving Siracusa. This was due to the fact that our harbor opened directly into wide ocean. Moreover, those galleys seeking to enter our harbors might beach to the south and await a strong northerly wind. In this manner, by means of oars and sails combined, they could move into the protective range of our engines quickly, while the Roman ships were reduced to oar power alone. Generally, these friendly ships sailed away on dark nights with impunity, as there are remarkably few shoals or treacherous stretches of water to fear once our harbors are left behind.

In this manner, more than a thousand of our citizens left Siracusa over the next year and a bit more. Most of these were women, children, and men over fifty with money enough to book passage at high price. No healthy men between the ages of seventeen and fifty were allowed to leave. A great number of those who left were families with relatives in Thessalia or the Peloponnesus. Some braver hearts fled to the Greek colonies at the tip of the Italian peninsula, depending upon Hannibal and his allies to protect them.

The city was not entirely magnanimous in allowing these families to depart. They were required to leave all food supplies behind, and they forfeited their dwelling places. In truth, if the siege went on for years, we would be glad to be rid of those who could not fight but only consume.

Do not believe that the entire city was resentful in seeing others with means of abandoning Siracusa. Many rejoiced at the opportunity to acquire new homes at low cost. A great number expressed high confidence in the abilities of Archimedes' engines, Dionysus' and Hieron's walls, and our army to hold the Roman army at bay indefinitely. We had huge storehouses of grain, dried meats and fruits, nuts, wine, and olive oil. Hannibal still harassed the Romans on their own soil, and threatened to crush more of their legions. Most heartening, word spread around the city that negotiations were in progress with the Carthaginians. I was not part of these, but careful plans were made for our forces to combine on the island and to crush the besieging Roman army. At the same time, a clear understanding needed to be forged as to what the Carthaginians could possess and what remained ours. Patience was not confined to the Roman camp.

Spirits were so high that the few hundred native Romans in our midst seemed quite safe. Many had lived in Siracusa so long that Greek neighbors had forgotten their original heritage. Of the ten Roman widows whom Timon had had married off to Siracusan men, five were repudiated soon after Marcellus came to our walls and were placed on a galley to find their way back to Roma as best they could. However, the other five were evidently beloved by their husbands because they and their children we kept within our walls. Among these were the wife and son of Menander.

Aurora expressed no fear of her heritage, although before falling asleep I often counted with dread those who knew her lineage. Since work was difficult to find within the city, men could be hired cheaply. I asked Aurora if I might place two guards around our house, but she would have none of it. She would not even allow me to purchase a fierce dog for fear of Athena's safety. I taught her how to use a long dagger.

Aside from me, the populace seemed quite positive for the early months of the siege.

Δ

This universally optimistic attitude vanished at the end of the summer, when two more legions arrived to swell the Roman camp. We no longer had spies operating in the Roman Republic to tell us who these men were or their fighting history. Nevertheless, the addition of another 9,200 or so soldiers at our walls not only reminded us of the Romans' resolute nature regarding siege, but it also indicated that the war could not be going so badly on their own soil if they had so many men to spare. Moreover, such superior numbers might even prove too much for Archimedes' engines if they should concentrate on one section of our walls.

Every few days, the legions paraded in front of the walls on the plateau, just beyond the range of Archimedes most powerful stone hurlers. Twice, we opened the gate directly in front of them and even marched out several syntagmas, attempting to coax them closer. Both times, they refused. None of those among the officers could understand why such numbers had been assembled if only to maintain a siege. As the months wore on through fall and into winter, we learned that parts of this army were periodically moved to one region of the island or another, to dissuade insurrection and to capture or recapture towns. Yet always they returned. When they did, they would parade before us as if they might momentarily attack. Yet they kept their distance from Siracusa. Neither was one flag raised to indicate they wished to negotiate.

Δ

Encouraged by the success of Archimedes' engines, the city rulers ordered that a dozen more hurlers be built and placed. Also, another twenty scorpions were created, and thousands of bolts were fashioned by men made idle by the siege. None of this was under Archimedes' direction. Having fulfilled his promise to Hieron, the old mathematician retired from the business of war. Only one other martial project occupied him, and this was more a matter of science than warfare. He had been working on the nature of curves and the ability of certain surfaces to focus light. As he had much spare time, and I found myself at a loss for full-time activity, we came together again, often with Aurora at our side. I at last was able to interest him in the game of Senit, which I had brought back from Egypt. Naturally, he could not merely enjoy the sport of it, but needed to analyze what made it a challenge and how the mathematics of it worked.

Archimedes eventually showed us his closely-guarded discoveries. He lost me when he speculated about the nature of light and its abilities to be bent and reflected, but I saw clearly enough what he could make it do. By means of highly polished bronze bowls he was able on a bright afternoon to concentrate the sun's rays and set a piece of papyrus aflame.

"There is no end to our ability to harness Nature," Archimedes said. "We need only coax secrets from her with diligence."

Toward the end of the first summer of siege, my great-uncle was able to test his latest invention. It seemed that Marcellus was game enough to try another attack on the Great Harbor. This push came at mid-morning, concentrating on the Plemmyrion fortress on the south side. This time, our lookouts at both forts saw that large war engines had been bolted to the decks of many ships. As the galleys neared, the arms of their engines were drawn back in preparation for assault.

Before our foe could launch an offensive, the two great mirrors that Archimedes had commissioned swung into action on the fortress walls. They were mounted on pivots and turned from horizontal to angles that split the difference between the sun's height and the level of the galleys. Within seconds, they reflected Apollo's force onto the two lead ships. According to Archimedes, who stood beside me on the Ortygian walls, their focus was not sharp enough owing to imperfections in the mirrors. He had envisioned concentrated points of light no bigger than a man's fist setting the ships' sails on fire. Instead, the beams were almost as wide as the ships themselves. Yet were their intensities frightful.

The ships seemed to lighten several degrees in color. Soldiers on the decks shrank back and then turned away as if struck by objects of weight. Those carrying shields dropped them. Some even fell prostrate onto the decks. Moments later, both ships veered away, followed by the rest of the fleet. Without causing any real damage, the threat alone of Archimedes' latest wonders had convinced the Romans to run. Until that moment, I had considered the fighting man and the iron in his hand the true power in the world. Now I realized that knowledge and its application were greater. Later, in speaking with Marcellus, my thinking would be borne out. On the night of his two-pronged invasion and again when the mirrors were used, many of the Roman soldiers believed that the gods themselves fought on our side.

When I brought this tale back to Archimedes, he said, "The gods never fight for or against men. They simply offer us the gifts of intelligence and diligence, so that we may be like gods ourselves. Woe to us, Leonides, if we use these gifts but do not temper our base passions."

Δ

At the end of the summer, an extraordinary event occurred. It was first brought into Siracusa by foreign Greeks. The next year, I heard another version from Marcellus himself. Both, however, were identical in their essential elements.

On the island of Sicilia there exists a town of no great size or import called Engyum. It is nonetheless ancient. Furthermore, many in the region believe that it is the home of a goddess called the Mothers. The goddess preceded the Greek settlement. A temple already had been built to her. Some said the builders were Cretans.

Now, this town stands physically closer to Carthage than to Siracusa. For this reason and reason of constant trade, its inhabitants were favorably disposed to treaty with the Carthaginians and resistance to the Romans. One among the noblemen of the town, however, believed, as Hieron did, that destiny favored the Romans. Consequently, he pleaded with his equals to alter their thinking. This man's name is Nicias. Not only to closed meetings of the rulers, but also in the town's agora had he delivered impassioned pleas for the citizens to change their minds.

So powerful were the arguments of Nicias that many people's opinions were converted. This sorely angered the other nobles. They resolved to deliver him into the hands of the Carthaginians. Seeing that he was secretly watched, and receiving a warning from a sympathetic party, Nicias contrived to feign insanity. He visited the temple of the Mothers and spoke numerous blasphemies in loud tones. His enemies decided they could use this to bring him to trial and then turn him over.

When he was brought before the assembly, Nicias was asked to justify his behavior in the temple. At this, the man began to roll upon the floor. This struck the witnesses dumb. Before they could respond, Nicias came up on his knees and turned his head backward as far as it would go. Looking over his shoulder he began to wail, first using the lowest tones of his voice and gradually modulating up to the highest pitches. This being done at the full power of his lungs, many in the hall clapped their hands over their ears. Not content with these two displays, Nicias cast off his mantle and rent his tunic so that he was naked but for a loincloth. After throwing the clothing at the ceiling of the chamber he ran toward the entrance, screaming that he was being pursued by the invisible spirit of the Mothers.

So superstitious of the fury of the Mothers was the assembly, no man dared reach out and detain Nicias. All rather shrank from him as he passed. Continuing with the same mad ranting, the clever fellow ran down the street and out the town's main gate.

Nicias is married and has children. His wife, having been made aware of her husband's plan, had stood outside the assembly hall. As the astonished judges entered into the daylight, she declared that she would pursue him and bring him back. Thus, were she and her children also able to escape from Engyum. Only a little way down the road the family united. Without pause, they hastened to the Roman encampment at Siracusa and told their story to Marcellus.

Possessing a sense of humor, albeit of the grim side, Marcellus was greatly amused by the tale. Having nothing better to do since he would not attack us, he decided to travel with a legion to Engyum and lay hands upon the rulers of the town. This place also had failed to learn the lessons of Leontini, Megara, or Acilae.

With hardly any trouble, Marcellus marched into the town and captured everyone before they could rise from their beds. Nicias had traveled with the Roman general at his command, so that he could point out the leaders. Upon learning that the intent of Marcus Claudius was to beat and then behead the men, Nicias employed the same oratory skills by which he had swayed so many of his fellow citizens. With tears in his eyes, he implored mercy for those in chains and blamed the blandishments of the Carthaginians for so deceiving them that their eyes had been blinded to the glory of Roma.

According to Marcellus, he had never heard such a flurry of convincing words, had never seen such gesticulations, nor experienced such swaying tones from any speaker, be he Roman, Carthaginian, Celt, or otherwise. This reason as much as the logic of Nicias' argument decided him toward clemency. When he shared this with Nicias, the man proclaimed with pride that Marcellus had clearly never heard the speech of the average Greek. This Marcellus commented upon, revealing that his son-in-law was Greek, and that I had stemmed from less than noble stock. I as well had impressed him with my logic and power over words. Therefore, he granted that Nicias might well be correct in his statement. For his oratory powers and his sense of justice and mercy, the general rewarded Nicias with much land around Engyum and with rich presents.

When I first heard this tale inside Siracusa, and then again from Marcellus' lips, I realized that this son of Roma was taken by things Greek more than even I or Aurora suspected. Archimedes had his engines; I held a vital key to Marcellus' character.

Δ

I had not yet spoken again with Marcellus when autumn of the first year of the siege arrived; no overture was made from the Roman side to settle the matter with words. While he had conquered more than half the region around Siracusa, I would not allow him to benefit without some cost from its harvest. My reasoning was applauded by all the generals, although Hippokrates and his brother elected to hold the city while a syntagma from each of the other divisions and half my cohort ventured out. I understood that Hippokrates' highest wish was to be considered the savior of Siracusa. I believed that he was short-sighted in his decision of not allowing some of his men to pillage and burn with us, since depriving the Romans of food would go a long way toward prying them from our walls. I held my tongue, realizing that he was as implacable as Marcellus in his way.

To be certain that we would not be betrayed, before we stole out of the city Paulus, Archelous, and I gave Hippokrates and Epikydes a false itinerary. To their credit, the Romans did not appear where we pretended we would be. The brothers were, essentially, loyal Siracusans.

We departed by three means, all on the same night. The first syntagma, under Paulus, left by galleys through the harbor mouth. The second with Archelous rowed in skiffs through the hummocks of the marshes. My group of but twenty-four men rappelled down the wall on the southern side of Euryalus. All three groups set out in southward directions for several hours, then camped without fires among dense vegetation. The next day, we lost sight of each other, setting off for the fertile fields around three of the captured towns. Our plan was to follow the spines of hills and mountains, making pursuit or engagement difficult. We would live off the land and endure whatever Nature and the

Romans threw at us until we had created havoc.

The fields were but days from maturity. Captured Sicilians would be certain to do most of the harvesting before they were shipped off in late autumn to be sold by Greek slave traders. The timid resistance put up by all but Leontini's and Megara's residents coupled with Marcellus' softer nature toward people of Greek extraction, however, had limited this number of captives. We knew that hundreds of Roman soldiers would be sent out to round up inhabitants for the gathering in of grains, the grapes, and then the winter olives.

Our forces could not do more than feed ourselves. We needed to move too quickly to carry more than a few pounds of the fruits of the fields and vineyards. Our purpose was to scorch the earth and deny the harvests to our enemy. Unfortunately, the summer season had been a wet one. Fields did not catch fire easily. This proved a great disappointment to us. Another vexation arose from the fact that Marcellus had sent out virtually all his cavalry to oversee the harvesting. I had not counted on having to face men on horses.

I devised another means to harass the Romans.

Near to Acilae lay a hook of hills well known to one of my band. The hook's inner curve faced to the east, and barley was planted in the nestling arms of the hills every few years. Due to the elevation and good drainage from the abundant runoff of the hills, the barley in this place grew quite thickly. It also stood high, above the average man's belt. However, the fact that the sun's last hours every day were denied to the fields by the same hills guaranteed that the crop would come in later than in other parts of Sicilia.

These fields lay at the junction of two roads. The field to the west was so large that its yield could have fed the Romans' horses for a month. Because the field was late in maturing it had been ignored. Therefore, I set out with my men to turn it into a trap.

We had brought with us a considerable amount of rope, for scaling cliffs and other purposes. In the back third of this field I had my men sink dozens of stakes, which protruded from the earth to the height of a man's thigh. Each of these had been notched at the level of the knee to accommodate a rope knot. We wove long rope trips in among the barley, so that they were difficult to spot even close up. Set back from the side edges of the field so that these also could not be spied, we planted a forest of sharpened stakes, to protect our flanks. Then we rested, spending our time fashioning many makeshift spears from saplings.

Two days later, the Romans and their conscripted workers arrived. The laborers were chained together until released to harvest the barley. From a hidden vantage on the hill, I counted about 250. About a quarter of these were women and children. Unfortunately, the cavalry who guarded them numbered 100.

The prisoners were divided into two groups, one to harvest the fields on the opposite sides of the roads, and the rest to work their way toward us. Protesilous commanded our left flank, and I took the right. We went on our hands and knees forward about halfway into the field and waited. This we did so that when the workers found us, they were too far from their captors to alert them with a startled gasp or outcry. From this distance we could hear the scourges of the Romans falling upon the hapless workers' backs, to discourage slowing down as they dumped their filled baskets into the wagons lining the roads.

When the first of the miserable Sicilians came into our range, we caught their attention without much noise. We consulted with them even as they sickled the sheaves of barley from their stalks and assured them that they had an excellent chance of both avenging themselves and escaping. We showed them furrows that we had dug into the soil to lead them to two gaps between the rope traps. Then we retreated.

Those captives we had informed of the plan returned to dump their baskets. As they passed the others, they whispered the word. To their credit, the prisoners did not run in desperation toward us, but rather took their time working toward the hilly side of the field, careful to get to every member of their group.

Finally, when the entire hundred and more workers were in the back half of the western field, they dropped their baskets and hastened along the furrows we had made. The cavalrymen noticed this mass movement almost instantly, but they lost several moments debating what to do. We could hear their frantic shouting to their companions who watched the other fields. I crawled up the tree-covered hill until my eyes cleared the tops of the barley stalks. I saw that the master of the corps gave orders for ten horsemen to ride to the left flank of the field and ten to the right. He himself charged through the stubble of the harvested barley with about thirty others. I was certain that even though they sat astride steeds, their range of vision over the plants did not extend down to where my men were hidden.

I edged down through the hill's masking vegetation to my men, who were passing spears to the laborers as quickly as they came through the barley. I instructed them as to the Romans' strategy. I directed four of my men and about a dozen of the armed workers to crawl to the left of the field and an equal number to the right. Protesilous and I and the rest held the two open spaces in the center of the field. We formed into rough approximations of syntagma lines, on one knee as we had been trained.

The charge of cavalry is a fearsome sight even from a distance. It is terrorizing to face in the open. Even from the opposite side of ropes and stakes, however, they were a force that only the brave of heart could oppose. I did not blame the half dozen or so prisoners around me who dropped their spears and ran up the hill as earth and barley shook with the pounding of hundreds of hooves. To their credit, three times as many held their ground.

"You will not have to deal with them all," I called out. "We have seen to that. Mind only those in front of you. Do not hesitate to spear the horse! Plant your spear in the ground and aim it with both hands!"

As I directed the workers, my men clapped them on the shoulders and reassured them that professional soldiers stood on their flanks. Our formations knelt not far behind the line of the second ropes. The open alleys that we defended were three men wide.

Owing to a shorter distance to cover, the thirty horsemen who galloped straight across the field arrived first. The trip ropes worked to perfection. Horse after horse tumbled forward, pitching their riders headfirst to the ground. Men I had stationed just beyond this rushed forward to finish the work with spears.

Five horsemen spotted us from their high vantage and charged at us. I watched them rein in momentarily when they realized that among the workers knelt warriors. Before they could react and coordinate their retreat in the narrow space, I and my soldiers leapt up and charged. We speared and hacked them to pieces. A similar situation occurred in the alley Protesilous commanded. I recall that three of the cavalry on the left flank and two on the right charged into the sharpened stakes. Another two were killed by hurled spears. Less than half the mounted troop retreated from our position. A great cheer went up from both my men and the triumphant prisoners as the Romans galloped away. This cheering soon died in our throats.

While we were collecting the horses that had not been badly wounded by the ropes or stakes, a shout went up from the cavalry commander.

"You rebels! You think you have won here? Unless you surrender, we will kill every last one of the prisoners we still hold. Like this!"

We heard the shriek of a woman.

Protesilous swung up onto one of the captured horses.

"Son of perdition!" he cried. "He was not pretending! We must save them!" He dug his heels into the horse's flank and encouraged it forward.

"Stop!" I shouted. "There are more than seventy of them, on horses!"

Protesilous, who was an excellent horseman, wheeled his mount around to face me. "Then give me five more who ride. We will pass them with a spear attack and flee down the road. When they follow, you can rush out and gather up the rest of the prisoners."

"They will not all be drawn away," I exclaimed.

The Roman commander shouted, "I shall kill another in a minute, unless I see you coming forward."

"Better to die heroes than allow this!" Protesilous proclaimed.

I pointed my bloodied sword at him. "If they kill those people, the disgrace is on them. It does not make us cowards to preserve our lives. You will climb off that mount and follow me."

I watched the muscles in the powerful man's neck knot. With a scream of rage, he thrust his spear into the ground.

"What is your name, Commander?" I asked, standing as tall as I could among the barley and facing the Roman.

"Tell me your name first," the Roman commander countered.

I told him who I was.

"I am Cassius Piso."

"Cassius Piso cannot be your real name," I shouted back. "That is a Roman name. You must be an ally of Roma. No Roman soldier would so dishonor himself by killing prisoners to make his enemy surrender. Come forward and give us battle!"

"You have too great an advantage where you stand," he answered. "We will dismount and give you battle on foot." There was a pause. "We have seventy and one men. You have more than that among you, I believe. If you are not a coward, you will come forward into the barley and fight there man to man."

Protesilous looked at me with begging eyes.

"I do not like this," I told him. "Have we lost anyone among the Silent Storm?"

"Heracleides was pierced in the side, but he may live."

I said, "That leaves twenty-three, including you." I looked around at the prisoner men, all of whom held spears and sickles and some of whom had taken swords from the cavalrymen's corpses. Their number was about sixty. "Do you expect us to win against seventy-one trained Roman soldiers with only this few?"

"We fight for our friends, our women, our children," one of the men who had been a captive said. "We will fight with heart."

His comrades nodded sharply.

I glanced at the rest of my men. They awaited my word. I knew that whatever command I gave, they would follow. I quickly communicated a plan, sending seven men out on each flank, to duplicate Hannibal's tactics at Cannae.

"Very well!" I cried out to the Roman commander. "We will meet you in the middle of the field."

"We dismount and advance!" Cassius Piso called out.

I cried back that we advanced as well.

I made sure that we walked slowly, not trusting the Romans in the slightest. While we moved, I labored to count their number, but they had massed in a line as tightly as an ancient phalanx. Behind them, the horses whinnied and wheeled on the road, kicking up dust. I wondered how such restless creatures stayed together in a pack. I signaled for my troops to stop moving.

"It is a trap!" a male voice called out from the road where the wagons stood. "They will ride!" he added, as he attempted to flee into the barley.

A spear hurtled from the road and caught the man in the back. He disappeared with a scream.

"Fall back!" I commanded my men.

An instant later, I watched half a dozen cavalrymen swing up onto their mounts, holding many reins in their hands. Their plan had been to bring the horses to the bulk of their men once they had drawn us toward the middle of the great field.

As a body, my force turned and ran. The valiant Sicilian's sacrifice on the road had given those of us in the center the time to retreat to the safety of the open alleys. This was not so with the fourteen men I had sent out on the flanks.

"Protesilous, Melampus," I shouted, pausing while men bounded through the stalks around me. "Run for the ropes!"

I made sure that I was the last member of our retreat. The ground behind had already begun to shake as virtually all the Romans had swung onto their mounts. I used the strength and length of my legs to propel me toward the open alley and my turning men. The horses and their riders advanced at full charge.

"Hold!" I commanded.

The cavalry seemed to know where the ropes and the alleys were this time. They came at us in twos. As each neared our line, one turned right and one left. They hurled their spears and bolted away parallel to our ropes. Then they engaged our disarrayed flankers with swords and hooves.

I could do no more than see that my line held. I heard desperate duels to my right and left. Then Cassius Piso shouted out a retreat, and the horses thundered back to the road.

I gestured for our men to drop to one knee, concealing themselves in the barley. I ran up the hill to survey the strange battlefield. We had lost another seven men in our center from the Roman spears, since none of the prisoners held shields. The Romans had lost but two more. Their nearly seventy circled and wheeled in the harvested section of the field. I saw that fewer than fourteen men on the flanks had reached the safe ground beyond the ropes.

"I will make good my promise and kill the rest of the prisoners!" Piso cried out to me.

"Then you are a disgrace to your uniform," I called back. "But first you will have to catch them!" I saw that the road and the opposite fields were devoid of prisoners. Our stand had at least bought them the time to flee into the hills and rills. "If you fail, you will have to harvest the barley yourself. Think well what you do, Cassius Piso," I continued. "I say my name again: I am Leonides. I am the notorious son-in-law of Marcus Claudius Marcellus. When I return to Siracusa, I will confer with him. Then I will tell him just what manner of treacherous coward he has serving under his command. Do you understand?"

No reply echoed back from the road. This heartened me. I watched two dozen of the horsemen ride into the far fields of barley to pursue their prisoners.

When I returned to the line behind the ropes, I was confronted by Melampus. His face was contorted with grief.

"Nine of us returned from the flanks," he reported. "Protesilous is dead." He reeled off the names of the other five members of the Silent Storm who had been killed by the cavalry charge. Heracleides bled to death, dying in my arms. Thus, the courageous fifty and one of the Silent Storm were now but thirty and four.

Δ

We made much noise in passing through the brush and scraggily trees, up and over the hill that backed that bloodied field. Cassius Piso was not only a coward, but also as cock-sure of Roman superiority as his brother officers had been at Cannae. I lingered in concealment behind our retreat, using my keen eyes to count the number of prisoners recaptured, beaten, and then returned to striping the fields. In late afternoon, they moved with the wagons a distance of about thirty stadia toward Siracusa. They camped in a defile bounded on three sides by steep cliffs, compelling the exhausted prisoners to construct a small rampart and trench between them and the road. I am certain that Cassius Piso felt he could not be overcome from such a place by fewer than 300.

I accomplished the task with seventeen and another ten prisoner volunteers. The ropes we had used to trip their horses we had salvaged before retreating. These we used to guide ourselves silently down the rock cliffs in the middle of the night.

I myself killed five Romans within the space of two minutes. It did not bother me to kill the first two in their sleep. No one touched the commander. He my comrades left until last, so that I could face him myself.

I brought his head home to Siracusa—a gift for the Sword of Roma.

CHAPTER XXIII

The winter passed slowly inside Siracusa. Privation was not common, but deprivation was. The populace missed being the royal city of Sicilia. They missed the flow of people from other parts of the world and the commerce and enlightenment that visitors brought. They remembered with longing the simple ability to walk out of open gates and wander through the countryside. Quarrels erupted over trifles. The coin necklaces that many women wore "for bad times" lost row after row. Those who were plump were beaten without warning for being gluttons or for suspicion of hoarding. The temples were more frequented than ever before in my memory. More people seemed to be sick, and more of the elderly died. A number of persons committed suicide. How many I do not know, since this news was suppressed.

Fortunately, we also received happy news that winter. Hannibal had at last gained entrance to Tarentum. This had been made possible by yet more Roman cruelty. It seemed that notable diplomats from several of the Greek towns of the southern tip of the peninsula had been held invidious hostage in Roma to prevent their cities from opening the gates to the Carthaginian army. By valiant means, hostages from both Tarentum and Thurii managed to escape from the underground hell that the Romans called a prison. These men who never should have been seized were recaptured, scourged, and then pushed to their deaths from the Tarpeian rock on the Capitol. When this news reached their native cities, both were opened up to Carthaginian troops.

At Tarentum, the Romans who had entered the city for "protective reasons" managed to block the harbor from a citadel they held onto at the harbor mouth. Hannibal could not dislodge them. Moreover, they could be resupplied from the sea. The resolute Tarentines confounded the Roman garrison nonetheless, dragging their blocked ships across a peninsula to take them to the sea.

This news of more brutality from the Romans hardened the resolve of our people. At the same time, the reports of the turning of two Greek cities to the Carthaginian cause made us feel that we did not struggle alone. I wondered if any Roman consul or general would one day show the courage to offer an open hand rather than one with a bundle of sticks or an axe to those who lost after resisting their encroachment. Aurora had found a home among Greeks, but I know I never would have acculturated myself to Roman life.

At the turn of the year, Pulcher was elected consul and relieved from Siracusa. I understood that he served no purpose in the camp, as a man with Marcellus' credentials and experience would have none other giving him military orders. No praetor replaced Pulcher to stand by the side of the Sword of Roma. When the four legions continued to hold back from attacking our walls, I knew for certain this time that the waiting tactic was the doing of Marcus Claudius Marcellus.

Δ

I have already written that I found myself with too much free time, and that I visited my home often. The inevitable result was that Aurora was again with child. Fearing to worry me, she refrained from making her announcement until she was in her fourth month of pregnancy. This was as spring burst upon Sicilia, wafting even into our closed city.

I had been wondering if she might be with child, but in truth I merely believed that she was growing heavy because of the change in our diets. Aurora had always favored fresh vegetables and fruits, and these became more and more difficult to find. I believe that both this and her condition contributed to the extra weight she added. A taller woman, even a woman of Thalia's height might be able to carry the pounds without notice, but Aurora was small. As if she did not have enough problems, and perhaps because of these other problems, she also developed a constant redness about her face like that of a heat rash. I could tell that she was miserable, but in her unchangeable fashion she refused to complain.

Azar prescribed a grain paste as an old wives' cure. It provided no improvement. I did my best to act as if I had noticed nothing, but this angered Aurora. She stated on my behalf that her weight and her rugose face upset me. The more I denied this, the angrier she became. She called me a liar. I quit the house for my fortress quarters, believing unwisely that this was a prudent course of action. I returned only after ten days. Aurora informed me in a bitter tone that I had recently been coming home at least once a week. This set off another argument. This time I stormed out, breaking her bust of Homer that perched on a pedestal as I slammed the door.

I made sure that I created enough excuses to stay away for two weeks. When I returned, Aurora had taken to her bed with prolonged bouts of the sickness that usually affects woman only in the morning. I had spent a sinful part of my salary getting her imported dates as a peace offering. She could not eat them.

I found myself thinking more and more of Thalia and the house she had secured in Euryalus. Once I even took myself past it out of curiosity. However, I never knocked on the door nor sent a message to her home in Ortygia. I told myself that that dream had vanished and could not be reclaimed. Nevertheless, I kept track of the days until Thalia would fulfill her year of mourning.

I was in a miserable state.

Δ

As if the sickness in my own house was not enough, Archimedes came down with an illness of the lungs that would not clear. He was laid low for two weeks with a fever. During that time, he dropped weight that the old fellow could not afford to lose. When at last he believed he had regained enough strength to attend the baths, I took him there. He was near to exhaustion merely reaching the place. We rested on couches for an hour, talking of many things.

I remember well that occasion.

He began by saying, "Thank you for bringing me here, friend."

"Have you stopped calling me 'Cousin', then?" I asked. I had been more than happy when he had stopped calling me "Strategos". Now, ironically, I was one in a sense.

Archimedes coughed and cleared his throat. "To call you 'friend' is a greater honor. One cannot choose one's relatives, but one decides who merits the title of friend."

I said, "But I have been told by many that friends come and go, and relatives are more important because they can be counted on."

"Truly? Ask all the wives, husbands, sons, and daughters of royal families who have been murdered because they were not trusted. We want to believe that relatives must be faithful to us, but it is no more true than with friends. Relatives do not come and go because they do not have that option. How do you define a friend, Leonides?"

I thought for a moment before answering, as Archimedes had taught me to do by his own example. "It is someone who defends you in your absence. Someone willing to tell you when you are wrong, although he does not do this in front of others. It is one who will sacrifice for you rather than giving mere lip service. Do you agree?"

Archimedes smiled and closed his eyes. "According to Zeno, 'A friend is another I...' I have heard it said that 'a faithful friend is the medicine of life.' It is certainly another in whom you see your beliefs and values mirrored. Pythagoras believed that 'friendship is equality.'"

"You believe all these," I said.

"I do."

"But do you have your own thoughts as well?"

"I believe a friend is one who wants for you the good he wants for himself. You are my friend because you wish me well in all things."

I assured him that I did.

"Although I hate war," he said, "I do not denigrate your work as a soldier. I have come to understand that you defend against the makers of war, and that to do so means fighting fire with fire. In this, I wish you the best."

I felt as if a great weight had been lifted off my chest as the man I most revered said these words.

"You have a love of learning and an inquisitive mind," he judged. "We share this to our mutual satisfaction and gain."

"Gain?" I exclaimed. "I possess none of your genius.

Archimedes held up his hand. "But you have wit and your own unique way of looking at life. It is a more generous attitude than I have. You know, I have met several men who might be counted geniuses. You would think that like minds would naturally compel friendship. But this is not necessarily so. These men pretended to be my friend to pick my brain. I could tell that they were jealous and sought my friendship to be able to use my name to impress others. No, I have had not had many true friends in my life, and yet I have been fortunate in this regard. My father said that if at the end of one's life one could count all true friends on the fingers of one hand, then that person was blessed. As I approach the end of my life, I number my friends at eight."

"Who are they?"

"Two were husband and wife. They lived in Agricento. They had remarkable minds and extraordinary kindness. Intellect and loving kindness rarely run together. I am a particular offender. They were murdered by the Romans. I also knew a woman in Siracusa."

At this moment Archimedes' eyes drifted away, and I knew that he was seeing with his mind's eye. An expression of pure joy and peace came onto his wrinkled face.

"She was older than me and married, but we had a confluence of thinking. She was the only woman I have ever met who could grasp abstract mathematical concepts." He sighed.

"Who else?" I prompted.

Archimedes smiled slyly. "Myself, of course Aristotle said 'A man is his own best friend.'"

"That is only four."

"Crito and Irene. Finding them was like you finding Aurora. I did not deserve to, but I had great luck. And then there are you and Aurora. She is a friend to us both, far better than a mere lover and helpmate, Leonides. She embodies my fondest quotation regarding this subject. It was also made by the sublime Aristotle: 'What is a friend? A single soul dwelling in two bodies.' How fortunate you are to have found your soul match out of this whole wide world." He raised his eyebrows at me. "And how unfortunate that you do not yet fully know it."

I felt at that moment ashamed. I did know it, and yet I had thrown up a wall time and again against this obvious truth. I had pitted her against not the woman Thalia but the perfect creation of my mind that Thalia portrayed, like an actor in the amphitheater. Azar was correct that I did not really know the maiden she had served. All I knew were moments made passionate by forbidden love. I knew Thalia only when she had chosen the time and looked and acted her best. I had not seen her in times of ill health or ill temper. I had looked upon her physical perfections and extrapolated them into mental and spiritual perfections, as if one could possibly predict the other. I resolved to discard my dream once and for all and return to Aurora the love and friendship she threw at me in great bouquets.

When we were done with the baths, Archimedes was so enervated that he could not walk even the few blocks back to his house. Small and light as he was, I would not risk finding that he was too heavy to carry halfway to his house. Thus, the greatest man in Siracusa was reduced to riding in a vegetable cart that I pushed. Rather than expressing embarrassment, he declared to me that he loved the conveyance and should pay the vendor for the cart so that he might ride in it everywhere.

In this I recognized beyond words his love and friendship.

Δ

I hurried home, burst through the door, and gathered up my wife before she could utter a word. In the middle of the day, I carried her to our bed and made slow and very passionate love to her. She cried when we lay side by side. Her tears told me that she understood a change had occurred in me. I did not defile the moment with unnecessary words.

I found Azar in our courtyard playing with Athena, who was as precocious a child as ever I have seen. I turned her over to her mother and told Azar that I needed her to come with me to the shops. The old woman shot me a suspicious look but asked no questions.

When we were but a few paces from the threshold of our home, I said, "I would know the real Thalia. Tell me not of her beauty, but of her blemishes."

Again, Azar regarded me with a clouded look of mistrust. "Did she not allow you to look upon her body in the alley near the Arethusa fountain?" she asked.

"I mean the blemishes of her character, her spirit," I said.

Azar framed her words for long moments as she hobbled along. "You know the expression that the tree is shaped as the wind blows it."

"Certainly."

"She is an unfortunate product of her parents. I blame them for her imperfections. She was a perfect child. Not merely in features, but in attitude and instinctive charity. But her father is calculating and cold. He rules his household and his shops by fear rather than kindness. He begins an acquaintance with every man suspecting him of the worst and only softening as the man presents his good side again and again. He takes especial joy in reciting the faults of others and speaks of their misfortunes as if he applauds them.

"The mother is vain of her looks and believes that these are the only thing a woman must perfect to be a success in life. Oh, she also puts high value in girls who can play musical instruments. She played the lute when she was young, but once she caught her husband's attention she put the instrument away herself. She fears aging as you and I fear the Romans. Any woman who is younger or prettier than she is regarded as an enemy outright. She believes that great beauty is like royal birth, in that it allows and perhaps even obliges one to lord over others less blessed. The crueler and more imperious her behavior, the greater she supposes her beauty must be for people to bear her. She loves possessions. Her jewelry is a better friend to her than any other woman.

"Both parents scheme. They say out loud that they would rather cheat and best others before they allow others to do the same to them. Are these harsh enough winds to bend even the most perfect tree?"

"Poor Thalia," I said aloud.

Azar stopped short in the street. "Do not say that, Master! I once feared to tell you these things because I knew you would refuse to believe them from me. Now I feared to tell you precisely because I knew you might respond with great pity. When Thalia was little, I did my best to explain the error of these behaviors in ways that would not have her carry them back to her parents. Too often this happened nonetheless, and I was severely beaten. When little, she was not responsible for adapting her parents' ways, for a child is most successfully taught by example rather than words. However, I warned her of these faults over and over. Now she is an adult. She has her own mind, and she could cast these imperfections off if she wished. But I fear she does not."

"You have not known her since she escaped her parents," I argued. "Perhaps her better self, her original self has come to the fore."

"Perhaps," Azar granted reluctantly. "But this is not for you to determine. You have your own wife to look after. She is worth ten Thalias. Trust this old woman who has known them both."

The former slave stood looking at me, waiting.

"I do trust you," I said. "I will stop thinking about Thalia."

At that, Azar broke into a great gap-toothed smile. "It is rare that a woman of my age is given a precious gift. This is one I have longed to receive for many months." She grabbed my hand and kissed it.

I had no business in truth among the shops, but we continued on. Azar, relieved to be done with the subject I had broached, shifted into praise of Athena. She speculated on our second child and confided in me several superstitious rites she had performed to guarantee that it would be a boy. I pictured our daughter growing up very straight, blessed only by gentles breezes. We walked and talked, and I knew that I had three prize women under my roof.

Δ

On the first anniversary of the death of Cleomenes, another scroll awaited my return to the fortress. I knew what it was. I should have sent it back by courier. I did not. I should not have read it before I burned it. I did. I do not know why some men who stand on firmest ground yet desire to walk to the edge of the abyss and peer down.

CHAPTER XXIV

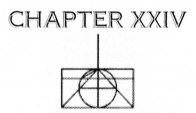

As the spring turned to summer and the promised help from Carthage did not arrive, more and more Siracusans clamored for the reopening of negotiations with Marcellus. Those who ruled the city estimated that about one third of the populace favored this, and the percentage climbed each month. They, I, and the other generals agreed that there was no point in this. Marcellus would only repeat his demands. He clearly was biding his time until we weakened, even as he used the area north of Siracusa as a staging point to keep the majority of Sicilia under control. From time to time, he or another of his generals surreptitiously marched a legion off to punish some part of the island. Their navy seemed to shrink and grow as if on a whim. Sometimes, they would sail or row back and forth in squadrons in front of our harbors for days on end, denying us replenishment from the sea. On other occasions they disappeared. We supposed that they sometimes ferried a legion to another part of the island, to speed up their ability to respond.

One particularly favorite exercise of Marcellus seemed to be extending the fort that lay directly west of Euryalus, sitting across the road. He had by this time learned that I sent my scouts out not more than six at a time, so he posted squads of twelve in pockets around the fort to deny us a good look at the handiwork of his engineers.

Because Lysander, Paulus, Archelous, and I were purely soldiers and not politicians, Hippokrates and Epikydes stole the march on us at the palace, wheedling and scheming with the ruling body of citizens to increase their power. The rest of us awoke one day to find them in supreme command with the blessing of the ruling body. Further, the losses their divisions had sustained were now fully supplied out of those of Archelous and Paulus. Because of the majority sentiment of the populace, our camp was powerless to oppose them.

The brother-generals gained even more control when the Carthaginian army landed on the southeastern corner of Sicilia. This came as a surprise to the city. I was one of the first to learn of it, as Menander and another member of the Silent Storm had been scouting in that direction. Their report was that this force included 25,000 infantry, 3,000 cavalry, and twelve elephants. Foolishly, I and the rest of the city expected that they would march directly to us with their full army. A week later they still had not arrived. We learned that some 15,000 men had been sent inland to recapture those towns I earlier recorded were taken by the Romans. The rest lingered south of us, investing the few towns that had not been taken, while brassily asking for our blessing in these enterprises.

The Carthaginian general we secreted into our city was named Heppos. He entered with my scouts and six of his own soldiers. We reported to him that our forces inside the city, along with isolated troops from our tributary towns, comprised almost 10,000 infantry and 500 cavalry.

We knew that Marcellus could not marshal more than 17,000 men against us. Therefore, we decided to close a ring around him and besiege the besiegers. In order to accomplish this we needed to wait almost six weeks, until the Carthaginians had not only recaptured the towns from the Romans, but also erected strong walls in these several places.

Precisely what we had not wanted had come to pass. Within seven weeks of the Carthaginians landing, they controlled every part of southeastern Sicilia except for Siracusa. I could not imagine us later pushing them out with ease. So intent were they on keeping our confederate towns and the yield of the earth that was so near harvest that they left 5,000 of their men inside them. We argued that there would be no need for this if both our armies combined to crush the four Roman legions. Clearly, the Carthaginians were so delighted at taking all this land that they could not be swayed. We had indeed invited the fox into our hen-house. All the fears of Hieron had come to pass, but he was safely in his grave, spared from witnessing the horror of it.

At last, 23,000 Carthaginians and another 2,500 of our allies con-verged upon Siracusa, from the south, the southwest, and the west. The Romans by this time knew full well of their presence. They pulled into their two fortresses.

With great joy, the more than 7,000 soldiers we marshaled poured out of the Epipolai and Euryalus gates and formed into crisply-drawn syntagmas. Even Lysander's forty horsemen trotted out to join those on horseback from around the region. Behind them, bold crowds streamed onto the barren plain and the city walls with food and drink in hand to witness what they expected would be the long-awaited slaughter of the hated Romans.

This was not to be.

When we approached the Roman fort to the west, we found our-selves dodging a hail of stones and other missiles. Our quick survey assured us that that the fortress was no longer small nor made only of earth. They had extended the walls to encircle an artesian well, guaran-teeing a constant supply of water. Everywhere, the walls were high. The Romans had been busy creating a truly daunting edifice. We estimated that it held as many as 1,000 of their men, and that to take it by assault we would probably lose 3,500 warriors. Therefore, we decided to encircle it and starve them out. If they were well provisioned, this might take as long as a year. The anticipation of this protracted time, however, was far more bearable than the same time trapped inside the city.

Marcellus' main camp was all but impregnable. He had stolen a page from Archimedes' engineering notes and erected hurling towers. He had also created three rings of trenches. Taking the camp by brute force would surely kill at least 10,000 men. Neither we nor the Carthaginians favored such a plan.

At last, a flag of truce went up upon the Roman wall. We carried an officer's tent up just beyond their outermost trench and erected it. Junior Roman officers emerged from the camp to be sure that we would honor safe conduct and to state the terms of the discussion. I volunteered to walk back with them to bring their leaders to the tent, but they smiled and told me that they had been ordered by Marcellus to allow no one near their camp.

Marcellus appeared in the most splendid uniform I had ever laid eyes upon. It was gold, black, and red except for the leather, which had been oiled. His armor glinted in the sun. The bristles atop his helmet were black as midnight and incredibly long. He was, in a word, splendid.

The consul was flanked by only two under officers, a scribe, and a translator. We faced him with seven top officers, five under officers, two scribes, two town fathers, and a translator. Marcellus did not seem daunted by the discrepancy in numbers.

Paulus had been chosen to present our terms, since he spoke Latin fluently. He read them from a scroll. They demanded the immediate cessation of hostilities and the withdrawal of the Roman troops to behind the old neutral ground. Further, they were to cede Lilybaeum on the far west coast of Sicilia back to the Carthaginians. We asked no recompense for the destruction and murders done in Leontini or the other towns. This was to counterbalance our destruction of their two provocative villages. Further, the treaty committing Siracusa to send grain and monetary tribute to Roma had gone on long enough and must be considered at an end.

Marcus Claudius Marcellus listened politely. When he was certain that Paulus had finished, he replied in passable Greek.

"I regret the time you have taken to forge your document. As a soldier at the command of the Senate and the people of Roma, I am not at liberty to respond myself to your terms. Moreover, since you have us surrounded, I have no means of sending a message to Roma at any rate. You are free to send your ambassadors directly to Roma, but I am certain that they will not welcome them."

"Will they throw them as well from the Tarpeian Rock?" Archelous asked.

"That was a regrettable act," Marcellus allowed.

"So then," I broke in, "why did you signal for a talk? Do you wish to set the terms for battle?"

"Not at all. We are content where we are. I thought it was high time to trade prisoners."

This somewhat rattled me. I had for months assumed that the Romans had been taking our scouts and executing them, even though we had found no bodies. Only in the past four months had I given the order to capture enemy soldiers whenever possible.

"We hold seven of your men," I said.

Marcellus looked surprised at this. "But we have lost more than fifty scouts and lookouts," he said. "We assumed that you had brought them back into your city."

"Most are buried in our trenches," Paulus revealed.

Marcellus shook his head gravely. "Most unfortunate. We hold as well some sixty of your citizens, captured from two galleys attempting to escape Siracusa. Do you wish them back or not?"

"Of course we do," Hippokrates proclaimed. "We will exchange one of your soldiers for two of our people. Do you not tell the world that each Roman is worth two Greeks?"

"I do not tell the world such a thing, Strategos," Marcellus replied. "I hold your people in high esteem. Most of your people."

Paulus and Archelous readied their hands to hold the powerful Hippokrates back, but the man was on good behavior. His white teeth, however, appeared through his handsome black beard.

"Will you offer gold?" Marcellus asked.

"Have we assembled all these men for such a trifling matter?" Hippokrates broke in.

"I did not ask you to bring so many," Marcellus replied through a smile.

"I can work this exchange out with the consul," I said to my side of the tent.

Hippokrates stood and swept the papers off the writing table. "Yes, do that. You have a Roman woman you can trade him." Having delivered his strike, he moved with haste from the tent. Several others followed. I invited Marcellus outside. We were allowed to walk away together across the trampled and barren plain.

"First of all, thank you for slaying Cassius Piso," my father-in-law said. "He was a poor soldier and a poorer Roman, but his family is powerful. I sent his head back to Roma in a handsome box."

"Give me a list of the rest you want killed and let me know where I may find them," I replied.

Marcellus laughed. "You are in charge of the night fighters."

I shared with him our name.

"Yes, they deserve such a title. And you have acquitted yourself well. But you have lost at least a score of these men if I am not mistaken. It is dangerous work. Would you make your wife a widow?"

"You mean my wife and child," I told him. I then added the news about the child Aurora expected. I also spoke well of Aurora.

"Perhaps I might see them," he said. "When we finally work out the exchange, I might come into your city gate. Can your citizens be trusted not to tear me apart?"

"I would see to it," I said.

Marcellus nodded at this and kicked a stone that had once been a missile. "And how is your servant? What was his name: Alonzo?"

"You know that he was Archimedes," I said.

"But I knew this too late. And I am glad of it. It would have crushed my heart to have given the word to imprison such a great man."

I noted this further sign of Greek worship and tucked it into my mind. "Even though he was the author of your resounding defeat at our walls?"

Marcellus smiled lightly. "Even so. I must say that I was greatly diverted by his display. Rarely has the Roman army been defeated, but this was for practical purpose done by one man! I constantly chide my engineers for their inability to create such marvelous engines. As we fled from your harbor I said, 'Must we give up fighting with this geometrical Braireus? Must we flee from the multitude of darts which he showers upon us at a single moment? Does he not use our ships like wine vessels, dipping them into the sea so that he may drink? Is he not more powerful than the hundred-handed giants of mythology?'"

"A speech worthy of a Greek," I praised. Then I added, "I would not have been amused in your place."

"The better man had his day. But your city will not win. We will win."

"How is that possible?" I asked. "Fortune has turned on you. You waited to starve us out, and now you face our army and one of Carthage. We outnumber you better than two to one."

"Then attack me," he invited.

"Why do that when we can starve you out?" I asked.

"Does Aurora wish to leave Siracusa?" he asked, shifting the subject.

"No. Do you think we hold her hostage?"

"I do not. Has she then become a Greek?"

"She was halfway there in Roma," I replied.

"So she was. Does she ask to speak with me on your city's behalf?"

"No. She knows better. But she does wish that you go away with your army in peace and one day return alone in peace."

"She wishes too much. One Roman prisoner for each Greek one. For the rest of the Greeks we hold, 1,000 denarii each." He paused and looked squarely at me. "We are not an unfair people."

"Are you not?" I replied. "And what of Agricento? Even though its Greek citizens did not invite the Carthaginians in, when your army took over the town they killed the citizens."

"That was many years ago."

I feigned confusion. "Oh? Have Roman methods changed?"

"It was an object lesson to other Greek towns. If they were too complaisant to resist the Carthaginians, then they learned from Agricento that they would have to answer to us eventually. Better to build up their defenses as they should and keep everyone out."

"As we have tried," I said.

Marcellus looked momentarily at the ground and made a few noises in his throat. "This is different. I would not have murdered the citizens of Agricento. I do not want to murder your citizens either."

"Then find a way to leave us in peace," I implored. "You are wise. You have much power in Roma. How many other men have been elected consul three times? There must be a middle way short of your having to enter our city."

310

"I wish there was. If we leave, you will not be free at any rate. You will have the Carthaginians snoring in your beds beside you."

"That is another matter. Make a separate peace with us, and we will leave you alone to fight the Carthaginians on this very plain. We will watch from our parapets."

Marcellus snorted with derision. "Did they not pledge to come to your aid months ago? After they arrived did they march straight here, or did they spend the summer investing and capturing every Greek settlement in your part of the island? At least we hold to our word, harsh as it may be," he defended.

"But are you fair, in your word or your behavior?" I asked him. "What about the Greek ambassadors hurled from the Tarpeian rock?"

"You must understand how threatened our people are," he said. "They truly believed Hannibal was marching on Roma after Cannae. They still fear this."

"They must bear such stress with Roman courage," I counseled. "Is this not a consequence of your expansion into regions the Carthaginians once held?"

Marcellus walked beside me for a while in silence. "You expect a great deal of this soldier," he said at last.

I held up my hand. "No closer to the walls, if you please. I cannot guarantee your safety unless I warn them first. Your pretty uniform makes you a wonderful target, and I should be quite vexed if a stone meant for you landed on me."

My father-in-law laughed.

When we had turned back toward the tent, I said, "You are more than a soldier, just as I now am. A change must be made in the way the Romans make war. If you cannot affect this, who can?"

Marcus Claudius Marcellus, the Sword of Roma, nodded. "I will think on this. Meantime, let us take the first step with an exchange of prisoners."

As I went back into Siracusa through the Epipolai gate, I heard the sound of a shepherd boy playing his pipes. I found him with his sheep on a sad patch of open ground that was all but grazed out. That the sheep were thin could be perceived even through their fleecy coats. His tune was nevertheless merry, as if he had no idea what forces raged around him. I envied him.

Farther down the road, three men were straining goat's milk through cloths to form cheese. They seemed contented in their work. Although I had been amply honored in the profession my father had chosen for me, I did not view it to be honorable. A phrase that had been used to describe me, "good at killing," seemed to me a supreme irony. How could killing many men constitute a life well spent? As the months had worn on, I had become better and better at killing and at the strategies that allowed my comrades to kill effectively. This disturbed me more and more, in spite of Archimedes excusing of the soldier who defends rather than conquers. I pondered this in my heart and shared it with no one.

Δ

Because it was so ancient and so prosperous, Siracusa had expanded into all the flat and solid ground around its harbors. Consequently, the Romans had needed to squeeze their two forts into the little flatland that had formerly held olive groves and straddling our main road west. Other than this and the deadly plains within eight-tenths of a stadion from our walls, there simply was no space on the seaward side of the hills.

The Carthaginians debated for a day as to where they would place their fort. At last, they decided upon the expanse of land just beyond our marshes and swamps. They did not consult with us in this. Only after they had begun, I went out with a small delegation. We told them of the Athenian army so many years earlier that had pitched their tents in the same place and who had been more than decimated by fevers. Heppos and his superior marked the Athenian troubles down to weak lungs and poor attention to their gods. When I pointed out how bothersome the mosquitoes were, he informed me that the species in Carthage were twice as large. I perceived the same type of self-satisfaction and undeserved pride in this man that I had experienced in the Romans before Cannae. I decided that in this case that I would need to do something about it.

Δ

Two days after I walked with Marcellus, the city rulers approved the exchange of all prisoners. On the third day, Marcus Claudius set foot inside our city walls and met his granddaughter. I stood by my wife and child for a time, but soon enough I stepped away so that Aurora might have a private conversation with her father.

I could not help but watch their faces and movements out of the corner of my eye. For some time, the conversation was pleasant. Then I watched Aurora's eyes narrow and her jaw thrust forward as she spoke her mind with vehemence. Marcus maintained his demeanor. For a time, he answered her. Then suddenly, he turned from her and walked away. He came straight toward me.

"Have you beaten her?" he asked, his expression tense.

"Of course not."

"I thought as much. She is worse than ever. Now she calls me 'the butcher for voracious meat eaters.' I warn you: I will not take her back."

"I do not want you to," I assured him.

"I have given you a dowry. You keep it and her."

"What of the child?" I asked. "Does she please you?"

"She seems smart enough. Does her mother teach her Latin?"

"Not yet."

Marcellus nodded several times with great energy. "She will learn it soon enough." He started away from me. "I am glad that they are well. Tell her that." His hand thrust out in a dismissing gesture as he headed toward his waiting officers.

I approached Aurora and asked her what she had said to him. She confirmed that she had labeled him a butcher for the Roman Republic.

"If they are truly a republic, then they are all madmen," she fumed. "Otherwise, why would they desire to expand without end? All this pride over a constitution and the willingness of every citizen to serve it for the greater good of the state. If they allowed women in the Senate, they would not have this mess! They are merely little boys grown up, waving swords because it is not proper to wave their penises!"

"If you had held your tongue, he might have come to our house and taken supper with us," I suggested.

Aurora picked up Athena, who was patting the ground and making

313

herself filthy. "I do not want the man in my house."

"Our house," I corrected. "We could have invited Archimedes as well. Your father has a sense of humor about being tricked by us. Even about the machines Archimedes set upon his army. We could have flattered and impressed him, perhaps allowed him to convince himself he cannot take us by attack or siege. We could have shown him the peace and contentment of our home and made him ashamed to threaten it."

Aurora glared at me, but I could see that I made sense.

"I rely on your wisdom," I told her. "You showed none today."

"I am sorry, husband," she said, bowing as best she could with her burden. "I will labor to improve myself."

"If I get another opportunity, do not waste it," I warned her.

Without reply, Aurora turned and headed back toward Achradina with Athena in tow. I found myself standing alone in the plaza.

Δ

I visited Archimedes and presented him with my problem concerning the Carthaginians.

"If they stay in that area, a number of them will surely sicken," I concluded.

The old man had not ceased drawing figures in the dense sand of his courtyard pit all the while I explained the situation. "And what is the problem with that?" he asked. "If we allow two- or three-thousand of them to die, will that not be fewer we must chase out of Sicilia? The cool weather will be here soon enough. The fevers always pass at that time. They won't all die."

"You are playing with me, Uncle," I realized.

"You and Hieron give me tasks that only a god should be given, so why should I not play god? You say they do not want to move anywhere else?"

"They would relocate to the summit outside the Euryalus gate, if they could overcome the Romans' smaller fort. That is why I am here. We lack the time to starve the Romans out. I wonder if you can devise other engines to defeat them."

Archimedes handed me his stick. "Draw me in as much detail as you can what you know about this fort."

I first sketched the terrain, paying particular attention to the two small plateaus on either side of where the road had been. As I have written before, the fort had been built squarely across the road, to prevent the smuggling in of provisions. These plateaus rose the height of two men above the rest of the place. Storming the fort from either of these would necessitate much lower ladders or platforms. Then I drew what we knew of the fort and, from personal observations of the stones and other missiles flying out from within, I advanced my guesses of the types of machines they employed and where they were positioned.

"Obviously, you assault where the walls are lowest," Archimedes decided.

"But that is where they have placed their engines."

"And why should we worry about that?" he asked me, with a sly twinkle in his eye. He did not allow me to sputter for too long. Rather, he bade me wait in the courtyard while he went to his bedroom. He returned a minute later holding a folded blanket under his arm.

"If I invite you to strike me in the stomach with your hardest punch, do you think you can hurt me?" he asked.

"Of course."

"I think the same. Do not attempt it. However..." At this point, he opened the blanket with both hands and held two ends up just below the level of his eyes. He stretched his arms out toward me. "Now, standing where you are, strike me as hard as you can in the stomach."

I punched directly into the blanket, but with only half my force. It billowed back. I had not even reached Archimedes' torso.

"Come on, use your full strength, Oh Great Olympic Champion!" he chided. "I guarantee you will not hurt me."

I tried again, this time with great effort. This time, my hand reached the old man, but by the time it did the blanket had absorbed most of the strike's energy.

Archimedes lowered the blanket. "You say that the Romans are isolated inside this fort."

"Precisely."

"So that they cannot obtain more materials to build other machines."

"I would expect."

"Perhaps they can move their machines. Perhaps they cannot. But the point is that they cannot make more powerful ones. The ones you describe have the power to hurl a rock one-quarter your weight about four-tenths of a stadion."

I verified what I had previously told him. Archimedes nodded. He handed me the blanket.

"Fold this for me. Then accompany me to my factory. I will have what you need within the week."

Δ

Archimedes was true to his word. His workers, long idled because of the Roman refusal to attack our walls or harbors, plunged into the project with zeal. Within five days they had manufactured two towers. These were not the cloud-scraping towers used in past foreign wars, such as the iron-clad monster named Helepolis that Demetrius Poliocetes used in his unsuccessful attempt to take Rhodes. They stood only as tall as five men on each other's shoulders. But they were precisely what I required.

They were fashioned mostly of wood, with each corner leaning slightly inward for reasons of stability. Their bottoms were actually low wagons with wheels that could be pivoted slightly to turn them. They had three levels, with enough space on the second for six men to stand and for three on the top. The uppermost level contained one of Archimedes' hurling engines. Through the very center of the machine were square holes so that weights could move up and down. Naturally, many pulleys and ropes were used. By these means, heavy stones or pitch balls for fire-starting or even buckets of rocks could be sent up and loaded into the hurling cup. While the three on top loaded, the five below hoisted the counterweight for hurling.

Except for replacing sinews with counterweights, none of this creation is extraordinary. What proved the genius of Archimedes were the two thick arms that extended from each platform, as Archimedes' arms had extended toward me. Attached to these arms were nets of nautical

316

rope, stuffed with damp seaweed. Whether stones, spears, or arrows were directed at the tower, the netting absorbed the initial blow and sprang back, distributing the force along its entire length. Stones would tumble down to the ground in front of the tower; spears would pierce halfway through and then hang down; arrows did the same; fireballs bounced back without setting the wet netting aflame.

I will grant that about fifty of the Carthaginians were killed moving the towers into place on either side of the fort. However, once they were positioned and set to work with steady bombardment the tactic worked flawlessly. Archimedes had designed the hurling machines so that they could be swung back and forth in an arc of thirty degrees, to focus on various portions of the fort. Moreover, since the counterweights could be lifted to any height desired before dropping, the range of our missiles were precisely controlled. Because the towers sat on the plateaus, they looked slightly down over the fort walls. According to the men who worked the machines, their devastation was enormous. In the course of the first day, only seven operators had been killed by enemy fire, but they were quickly replaced. In this same time, more than 300 volleys were let fly from the towers. There was no question in my mind that men were dying inside the fortress by the dozens.

At the end of the first day, the towers were drawn back out of enemy range. In consulting with Heppos, we agreed that a storming should be attempted after five days of bombardment. At the same time, the Carthaginian army would take up positions surrounding the fort so that a sudden counterattack could not be launched against the towers. The Siracusan army, meantime, would parade back and forth across the plain to the north of the Epipolai district, holding the Romans in their main fort and denying any rescue attempt. I was more than content with our plan. I lay my head down that evening with a full expectation of success.

Once again, the Fates laughed at me.

CHAPTER XXV

At the end of the second day of attacking the smaller Roman fort, our men in the towers and those supporting them reported strange occurrences among the Carthaginian army. A number of the African men shivered in their lines. Also, many of the men seemed bothered by the sun and perpetually shielded their eyes. A third observation was that perhaps one man in every fifty passed out. I have known men who stand too long at attention and pass out from lack of use of muscles, but these afflicted soldiers had been moving back and forth upon the plain and over the hills and the plateaus.

On the morning of the third day of bombardment Heppos came to Hippokrates and said that he wished to assail the fortress immediately rather than wait any longer. Hippokrates, thinking that there was no harm in having the Carthaginians do our work at any time, agreed. He and his brother moved immediately with the bulk of our army to the plain outside Epipolai. Archelous was with them as well. This left Paulus, me and our men to guard the city. I commanded the fortress of

Euryalus that day. I was standing on the battlements with the morning sun to my back when the Carthaginians arrived. Although they were a formidable mass, my eye could tell that their numbers were not what they had been the previous day. Nevertheless, at least 15,000 men converged upon the little Roman fort. With such odds, we expected the fight to take less than an hour.

I could only see that prong of the attack that concentrated on the wall that faced Siracusa, nestled within the pass between the plateaus. Even this was distant enough for me not to be able to view individual soldiers but rather waves of them. The 3,000 or so that I observed carried with them only perhaps fifty ladders. Many of these had been begged from our city, as the area all around us had been denuded, first by Siracusans for defense purposes and then by the long-encamped Roman army.

Considering that they had withstood two days of stones and burning pitch, the Romans fought with vigor. The ladders were too long, made for taller walls. Almost as soon as they touched the walls they were pushed back by pikes. Great masses of Carthaginian soldiers were needed to secure their bases so that their men might climb. When they assembled, cauldrons of burning liquid were poured down upon them. They died by the score. I saw then why most generals preferred starving a city out or taking it by guile rather than by frontal assaults. The carnage was gruesome even from my vantage point.

Eventually, however, the fortress walls were breached. Men poured over the ramparts like ants atop a dead animal. I later learned that Marcellus had placed 1,200 in the smaller fort. How many had died from the bombardments we never learned, for the Romans were slaughtered to the last man. As we had expected, they took with them to the Underworld almost 3,000 Carthaginians.

About an hour after the battle had ended, I could no longer keep myself inside the city. I put Xenophanes in charge of the fortress walls and ventured out through the tunnel. I took with me one of our soldiers who spoke Carthaginian. We eventually found Heppos standing among his lieutenants. Several of them were bloodied, but he looked fresh and resplendent in his armor. They stood just outside the fort's gate and watched their men with wary eyes. Their backs were to us, and none had yet noticed our approach.

Before I could address Heppos, he cried out to a group of guards standing beside the gate. They lowered their spears and blocked the way to two of their comrades.

I asked my companion what was happening.

"The general said, 'Those two there! Stop them!'" he translated

One of the lieutenants then called out.

"He says, 'That one there as well. It is upon him as well.'"

I studied the three men who had been singled out. All of them walked with their knees too bent. I hastened toward the solitary man and studied him. His forehead was dotted with perspiration, and his eyes were red and swollen.

Heppos called out to me.

My companion translated, "'Do not touch him! He is sick!'"

We backed away and went to the cluster of officers. I charged Heppos to explain to me what was happening.

Through the translator, I learned that sickness had broken out in the Carthaginian camp three days earlier. At first it was thought to be the fevers that arise in the hot weather and particularly near to wet lowlands. But many men began to complain of violent headaches. These same men were also vomiting. Two days earlier, thirty men had died. The day after, 300 were dead. These mostly had shown signs of a dread illness that made the skin around their necks, in the area of their groins, and under their arms swell up into discolored bulbs. Their tongues had swelled as well, grown fur, and had turned brown.

The priests who had come with the Carthaginians' army declared that the gods were angry with the campaign. The time had not been propitious. Heppo's superior had resisted their dire predictions and decided the sickness had something to do with the place where they had camped, since we had informed them of a similar thing happening to the Athenians 200 years earlier. His plan was to take the smaller Roman camp with all haste, regardless of losses, and to move those men who were still healthy up to the heights.

This made perfect sense to me. I knew, however, that the flatland, including the plain just beyond our lines of trenches, could only support about 10,000 men. With a grave look, Heppos informed me that perhaps not many more than this number would be allowed to leave the first camp.

Δ

The migration of the Carthaginian army went on through the day. On the following morning, however, the decision was made to withdraw from the region. More than 2,000 men had already died, and another 3,000 were confined to the old camp, in various stages of dying.

The priests had had their way with their countrymen. According to the signs they had read, their army should only have been sent to relieve Siracusa. Instead, the greedy officers had wasted time investing and conquering other towns, and had taken plunder from those who should have been allies. For their impiety, the gods were sorely displeased and the army had been cursed with a plague. If they did not retreat immediately, the priests predicted, all would die.

I have never seen such a huge contingent of men vanish so quickly. They were so intent on saving themselves, much of their equipment and provisions were left behind. I was the unfortunate one who was nominated to lead two syntagmas down to the mouth of their original camp to prevent the dying from escaping and bringing the contagion to us.

I had already faced many men in mortal combat and stared at Death disguised behind their fierce faces. At those times I was frightened, but never was I so terrified as I was looking into this encampment.

My heart went out to the dying, who begged for physicians and priests. They were covered with grotesque swellings. The legs of several were sullied with excrement, as they could no longer contain their bowels. Some collapsed before us, with their lungs heaving. Almost all staggered as if they were drunk. Half a dozen stumbled resolutely toward us, until we were compelled to kill them with arrows.

The air wafting from the camp was already tinged with a disagreeable odor. In the days to follow, as the corpses lay unburied, the stench became horrible. We began a campaign to burn the entire place inward to the very water's edge, but the fires attracted Roman spies, and we feared that Marcellus would catch several hundred of our men out in the open. He no doubt already knew that the Carthaginians had withdrawn. He did not, however, allow his legions to leave their camp. I put myself into his head, and thought he was made cautious either by fear of contagion or, if his spies were not this knowledgeable, of being ambushed by an enemy army that lay only a few dozen stadia beyond the hills that backed Siracusa.

Only weeks later, when the cold came to Siracusa did we send men through the marshes to clean up the camp. These at first were the denizens of our prison, deemed to be expendable. When they did not die, we sent slaves as well, to bury the bones and to burn the rest.

Δ

In the two days after the little Roman fort fell, a large portion of our army and more than a thousand other men from inside the city were used to break the fort down stone by stone, to at least deny it to our enemy. During that same time several supply caravans arrived overland, but the appetite of the Carthaginian army had been so great that our confederate towns and cities had little left to send us. I directed four teams of my men out scouting, two to shadow the Carthaginians on their southward trek, two to watch for new support for Marcellus and his legions. The autumn and early winter of that year were dreary, both in weather and in the city's mood. In truth, all we gained from the long-awaited Carthaginian rescue was the reduction of a menacing fort, the death of about 1,200 Romans, a few extra months of food stores, and the adding of enough captured and abandoned weapons to our armory to arm even the women of the city.

The siege had not been lifted.

The ground inside and outside Siracusa was rough with thousands of new graves. Each day, I grew to regard war more as the most senseless endeavor of mankind.

Δ

322

In the early autumn, Aurora bore to me a son. He was healthy and unblemished, save for one cherry-colored birthmark on his hip that looked like the sign of a heart.

"He will be a lover of men, not a killer," Azar judged from the birthmark.

"That is well," I said. "One soldier in the family is enough."

"May he live in times such as you were born in," Aurora said, cradling the child.

I could think of no better benediction.

We named him Anaximander, after a very ancient philosopher whose thoughts Aurora had transcribed onto one of her scrolls. This man was evidently the first who had evolved the theory of everything in the cosmos coming from one source. His thinking greatly influenced my wife and later influenced me as well. I liked the sound of the name. Naturally, the boy was rarely addressed using this long name. He was called rather Petrus because he was as thick and strong as a rock.

Δ

As winter heaved its last gasps of cold air and the sun climbed noticeably higher in the sky each day, I received yet another letter from Thalia. I knew I would not go to her, so I dared to open it. In it, she professed her yet-undying love for me. She told me of how she swelled with joy and pride whenever she heard tales of my exploits. She declared that her father had admitted that giving her to Cleomenes had been a mistake and that he wished I would have been his son-in-law. She spoke about others who had fled the city by ship and swore that she could never leave so long as I remained. She confessed that she often stood in front of my statue and offered prayers, since I was her living god. She dared to create salacious images of us in a bed of sexual delights. She assured me that she still kept the house in Epipolai, should I desire to make it our love nest. She described the street and the house in detail. She reminded me that her period of mourning was well past. I do not know how long she labored on her words, but she could not have thought of better means to tug at my heart.

I knew of more than one man who had a mistress as well as a wife, and I must confess that I desired to be one of them. I loved Aurora now and greatly respected her, but I was also a man trapped inside our city with not enough to do. I needed excitement and release from unrelenting tensions. I was being offered the most beautiful woman in Siracusa with no qualifications. I, as well as my city, was under relentless siege. I thought of what I might lose with my selfishness, however, and I vowed to take no action. I pushed this letter to the bottom of my pack and considered myself quite noble each time I saw it and resisted temptation.

In short, I was not yet fully a man.

Δ

The Roman war fleet continued to sail back and forth in front of our harbors, but they never again attempted to enter. We did not know where they went when they disappeared. My scouts and I observed that often they sailed straight out into the sea. We theorized that they had despaired of catching midnight runs into our harbors from beaches and other harbors to the south, and were trying to intercept ships farther out and during daylight.

This was indeed the case.

One of the ships that sneaked out of our harbor in darkness was overtaken on the way to Greece. Among those passengers seeking to escape Siracusa was an important Lacedaemonian businessman named Damippus. He oversaw much trade between our city and our mother state. We, of course, knew nothing of his capture until an officer was sent by Marcellus to our city walls with a flag signaling a desire to negotiate again.

Once more we opened talks. Once more Marcellus entered the uppermost district of the city—this time with three of his officers. This was via the Hexapylum gate. So that they might not be able to peer too deeply into our defenses, we had set up a table and chairs a little way inside the gate. They also brought a hunting dog, for Marcellus declared that as the spring was almost upon us he wished to hunt directly after concluding the negotiations. I thought this a blatant display to show the commander's contentment with staying in Sicilia, and a blatant way of telling us that his army controlled all the region around Siracusa, but I refused to comment on it.

"Much of your work was undone while the Carthaginians visited," I said to him with equally affected nonchalance. "Many towns and villages once in your thrall are again free and now decidedly your enemies. Be watchful that some neighboring warriors bent on revenge do not cut your hunt short."

"I have been accused of being heedless before," the Sword of Roma replied, "but I do not fear the so-called warriors outside your walls." He grinned. "Did not my second fort work to perfection in anticipation of the Carthaginian arrival?" he asked.

"You lost 1,200 men," I replied.

"Even so. Worth the sacrifice."

I inquired what he meant.

"I compelled them to locate in the same place that the Athenians camped when fevers helped to cause their defeat in the time of Dionysius. I am a poor student of philosophy and mathematics, but I have studied my history well. If their forces and yours had attacked my fortress as you attacked the one on the road, you might have won." He gestured to the chair he sat upon. "Just because I merely sit does not mean I am not scheming."

"Except that you have lost by attrition more than 1,500 men in the past six months," I said, "and Roma will certainly not send you more men than four legions to conquer such a peaceful city. What good will your scheming do in this regard?"

"That is for you to worry about," he answered.

"You have taken in the regiments formed from the remaining survivors of Cannae," I said.

"Your intelligence is correct. They long to reclaim their honor, and they long to sack your city."

"May their ill fortune continue," I told him. Then I said, "In all your scheming, have you thought of a means to settle our differences without warfare? There is still a sizable Carthaginian army roaming somewhere in Sicilia."

"We are winning," Marcellus proclaimed. "We have changed our tactics concerning patrol of the sea, and we are stopping many more vessels that seek to enter or leave your city. You will soon enough begin to starve."

"Then let us be satisfied with the matter at hand," I relented.

At that moment, the hound that had been held by one of the officers broke loose and bolted down the street that ran parallel with the outer wall. The officer cried out and ran after it. Archelous, who was with our group, sent three of his men to assist the Roman. They had some difficulty in finding the dog, and did not return until our negotiations had concluded. Damippus had been rescued, at no small decrease to the palace treasury.

Δ

About a week after this, as spring was almost upon us, one of the Roman brides that Hieron had brought to Siracusa was murdered. It was a foul deed, done as she walked to one of the temples to pray. Most of those who witnessed the incident said that the slayers were two large women carrying knives. A few, however, believed that the pair were small men in disguise. Owing to the veils our women must wear in public, no one was certain.

The citizens of our city knew that the food reserves were dwindling. They were also mightily afraid for their lives, and they sought to direct the energy of their fears and frustrations against some easy target. I judged at this juncture in the siege that our populace hated the Romans and the Carthaginians equally and permanently. Those of us with a degree of foresight saw that the unfolding sequence of events could only spell doom for our city. Even if the Romans retreated immediately from our walls, the city could not stop the transformation. No one in the world beyond our walls seemed to have the will or the power to prevent it from occurring.

Fire from Zeus' thunderbolt falls upon a space of land and lays it barren and scorched. Grasses and flowers grow first. Then bushes spring up and push the flowers aside. Finally, trees grow until their canopy kills everything beneath them by depriving them of light. Thus, I understood the sorrow that Siracusa must eventually fall under the shadow of the empire of the Romans or of the Carthaginians from a similar evolution.

I was most obsessed with immediate dangers, owing to the murder of the Roman woman. I greatly feared for the safety of my wife and children. Several of my friends counseled that I should move them into a house close by the fortress of Euryalus. I did not believe that would stop a sudden attack any more than where they resided. Moreover, if I moved them, they would be among strangers. I had seen Aurora interact with some of our neighbors, and they all seemed respectful if not unanimously warm toward her. I did wonder to my wife if she might not do better to move back to her father's house in Roma for a time. I would negotiate with Marcellus, and he would have her, Athena, and Petrus transferred to a ship bound for Italia. This angered her greatly

"I have no place there," she said. "It is as foreign to me as is Babylon now. This is my home. Even if I returned to Roma, do you think a woman who is the wife of the greatest thorn in their side except Hannibal will be welcomed? Do you think Athena or Petrus will be welcomed to play with other children? I understand that no fewer than 200 Romans still live within Siracusa's walls. Until many more are murdered, I shall not be afraid. Perhaps this woman did something to incur the wrath of another woman. We cannot tell. I will not have you overreacting."

I said no more. But I came home almost every other night from the fortress and made my bed beside my wife. On the floor next to me lay both my sword and my hatchet. I installed a second crossbar on our front door. I also instructed both Azar and Thalia in the employment of long daggers that I brought home. This tutelage they were both willing to take. Finally, I forbade Aurora to go into the streets without me. All these precautions lowered my guard somewhat.

In this I was foolish.

Not long after I had fitted the second crossbar, I returned home to stay the night. At the bidding of Azar, who ever longed to stay in my favor, I had brought home much of my soiled winter wear. She labored all that afternoon at the stone rainwater trough that was reserved for washing. I fear that she spent so much time in the cold water slaving on my behalf that she caught a chill. She took herself straight to her bed directly after the supper was prepared.

I played with my children and listened to Athena recite until it was time for their bed and cradle as well. Aurora and I sat in the courtyard watching the sky turn from purple to indigo to black, talking of times long past and great kings and happy things. At last, we went to our own bed and made love.

In the hour just before dawn, I was awakened by Azar's voice.

"What is it?" she asked, not too loudly. Then she exclaimed with surprise. "You shall not!" Before I had halfway opened my eyes, my hand was on my sword.

A dark figure rushed toward me from the bedroom door. I saw in the gloom that it was a man holding a sword. His thrusting hand was extended.

I shoved Aurora away as hard as I could and tumbled off the bed in the opposite direction. The intruder's sword sliced into the mattress.

I came to one knee and raised my sword. The dark figure drew back his weapon and swung it at me. I blocked his attack. From another room, Azar's outcries continued.

My opponent was a highly skilled warrior. I found the barest opportunities to block his thrusts and strikes much less to rise to my feet. I despaired of being able to overcome him.

Suddenly, an object sped across the room and struck the figure in the neck. It did not harm him, but it struck so unexpectedly that he made an involuntary turn. In that moment, I launched myself forward and drove my sword at his stomach. He wore chain mail, which absorbed the blow. I had anticipated that such a competent adversary would be well protected, so I did not satisfy myself merely with my thrust but threw my body against him, driving him hard into the wall. He grunted heavily as the air was driven from his lungs. The sword fell from his hand and clattered against the tile floor.

Powerful and determined, the intruder reached with his right hand between us and struggled to wrest from my grasp my sword. In the next moment, our free hands clawed toward each other's throats. I felt that he was a mighty man and nearly my equal, but I fought for my family. My hand tightened inexorably around his windpipe. He coughed and then he gurgled, but never once did he speak. After several moments, his hand relaxed slightly around the sword. I angled it up under his armor and drove it into his gut. Then I twisted it and pushed until I felt the tip of the iron meet the wall. I yanked it out and let the man collapse onto the floor.

I knew from Azar's screams that another man was inside my house. I glanced around the bedroom and saw no one. I ran into the courtyard.

A man knelt over Azar's unmoving figure, gasping for breath. He struggled to rise. I spotted in the gloom the dagger in his hand. I kicked it from his grasp, and then delivered a second kick to his head. He flew backward into the ornamental pool. His face barely cleared the top of the water.

Aurora emerged from Athena's room clutching our screaming children. She set Athena down and commanded her with a firm voice to stand with her face to the wall.

"Where is your dagger?" I asked.

"I threw it at the man who was attacking you," she replied, as she moved with haste toward the hearth where the banked flames waited awakening for the morning meal. While I dragged the second man out of the pool, she carried fire to the three lamps that hung on posts around the courtyard.

"Look to Azar!" Aurora directed, jostling Petrus up and down to lessen his wailing.

"This man is yet alive!" I replied. "Return Athena to her bed. Azar needs you."

I dragged the sopping-wet, unconscious man into the light of one of the lamps. I saw with surprise that it was the thin, ferret-eyed messenger who had tried to bribe me in the palace when Hieron lived and then later came to me in the wine shop to tell me of Timon's death. He wore a black chlamys. I saw that his costume was ripped on the side, and that this area was soaked with blood. I pulled the rent aside and found a small but deep wound. I slapped his face lightly to bring him awake.

Aurora gasped. "Azar is dead!"

She reached to the old nurse's right hand and took from it the dagger I had given her. She held it up to show me. The bottom half of the blade was coated with blood.

The man's eyelids fluttered and rolled back. "They say third meetings are auspicious," I said to him with an even tone. "Who sent you?"

"Certain persons," he answered. His teeth were clenched in pain, but he managed to affect an evil grin nonetheless.

"It is always 'certain persons' with you," I replied. "You are dying, man. If you would be revenged on them for putting you to this, tell me who they are."

He winced in pain. "If I do that, then you will be safe. How then shall I be revenged on you for my death?"

"I did not kill you. An old woman did."

"An old woman. What shall I tell Charon when I see him?" he jested, even as blood welled over his lips.

"You will not have to. She will meet the ferryman before you. She will say that she loved her family more than you hated us."

"I merely serve," he said.

I pushed my finger into his wound, causing him to yelp. "Someone will identify your body soon enough, and then I will know who sent you for me."

"You think so?" He laughed softly. "Who says that we were sent for you? Is your wife not the daughter of Marcus Claudius Marcellus? How many in this city hate him? What way is easier to punish him than by killing his daughter and grandchildren?" Before he could say more, he was seized by a paroxysm of pain so great that he fell unconscious. I could not awaken him again, despite much effort. Within a few more minutes, his breathing ceased.

Able to do nothing for poor Azar, Aurora first calmed Petrus and then went in to our daughter and got her back to sleep. I, in this time, sought out the would-be assassins' means of entry. In my language thieves are often called "wall-diggers." This is because most city houses are not built of stone, but only of hardened clay mixed with straw, which is often stuffed in molds around the house's wooden framework. It is not a matter of great effort to dig through such walls. What is more, it can be done without much noise. Such was the case with this entry. A small side alley between two other houses ends at the back of our courtyard. The two men somehow knew of this and excavated a hole big enough to slip through.

The place of stealthy entry lay just next to the room in which Azar slept. Possibly because she had gone to sleep so early in the evening she might have awakened to find the pair. Or else they made not enough noise to be heard in our bedroom but enough to reach hers. In any case, they had obviously both made their way inside by the time Azar discovered them. The brute killer had reached our door, and the smaller man stood guard in the courtyard when Azar accosted him. An ordinary servant might have felt that full duty was done by merely shouting out an alarm. To Azar, her house and family were threatened. As I lifted her from the cold stone, I wept thinking of her ultimate sacrifice of love.

Δ

In the hours and days that followed, I did everything I could to determine the identities of the would-be assassins. The big man served among the troops of Hippokrates, but he was not one of the general's regular soldiers. When he did not serve in the army, he was a stevedore on the city docks. He was a man known to keep his own counsel and not to make friends easily. None of his acquaintances in the harbor or in the army could or would shed light on who had sent him.

As to the other man, although I had his body hanged in the agora in Achradina and later in Epipolai with a sign offering a large reward for information about his identity, no one came forward. This astonished me.

I have said that before I won the olive wreath as pentathlon champion, I did not know more than 200 persons in my city by name and perhaps another 200 by face. I will say with all humility that, by the time the Carthaginian army fled our region, I was recognized by perhaps one in every five citizens, servants, and slaves. I am sure that some of this was due to my prominent statue, the features being remarkably well duplicated by the sculptor. Yet to think that this man who had bedeviled me for months was known to virtually no one was beyond my imagining. I came to understand that there are creatures of human shape who are more like vermin in their thinking and behavior. They like to keep to the shadows and skulk through life, stealing crumbs rather than earning loaves. This was clearly one of those wretched few, and I was glad that Azar had killed him.

Since I could not determine the guilty party behind the raid upon my house, I refused to listen to Aurora's dismissals any longer and posted two guards to patrol the area night and day. Since Aurora was the daughter of the man who led the army that was camped at our doorsteps, the city counsel was content to pay for this service. Nevertheless, I continued to come home every night that I was not on duty.

Spring arrived with warm breezes and the smells of new life, but a cold deeper than that of winter enveloped my soul.

CHAPTER XXVI

As I have written earlier, the people of Siracusa are ever eager to celebrate. This is one of the traits Aurora most admires in us. Never had we been more intent on enjoying our lives than in the spring that came three years after Hieron's death. No one knew if he or she would live to see the next year. This ensured that the spring festival of Artemis was observed to the limits of decorum and sometimes beyond.

In the morning, the temple of Artemis was filled out to the courtyard with the pious and with those wanting that reputation. In anticipation of the crowds, some of the less formal sacrificing took place in the plaza fronting the building. Directly afterward, syntagmas of men in their best military outfits drilled in the four agoras. The marketplaces around these agoras, though only lightly stocked with wares, were crowded. A poetry contest was held in Ortygia. To Aurora's great disappointment, women were not allowed to observe it, much less to participate. Nor were the women allowed to view the athletic contests, in which I for the first time in years did not participate. We had a morning singing contest which Aurora attended with much delight. In Roma, public music is confined to Saturae medleys, and these she declared sounded like funeral lamentations. In the afternoon we hosted not the usual troupe of foreign actors, but rather a group of home-grown Thespians who had resurrected a classic comedy, and the amphitheater was filled an hour before the play began.

With the royal family all dead, the front row with its high-backed marble seats was reserved for the top officers of our army and for their wives. Athena and Petrus had been delivered over to my mother's keeping for the day. Ironically, I sat almost precisely where I had sat several years ago, when I first laid eyes upon Thalia. More ironically, she sat in the same place on the left side, close by the orchestra.

This was the accustomed place for the family of Eustace. I do not know why I had not expected to see her there. I had feared running into her, since the theater accommodated about one-sixth of the entire population, but I never expected her to sit in the same seat. Aurora had so looked forward to the play that I had no way of excusing us from it.

Once again, Thalia sat in the open with her face uncovered. She was now fully a woman. Impossible as it seemed to me, she was even more beautiful. I tried with all my will not to look at her, but when an actor's movement brought him near her, my eyes could not resist. She, for her part, looked boldly at me.

"Is that she?" Aurora asked me in a whisper, as the audience offered generous laughter.

"She? Who do you speak of?" I dissimulated.

"Don't make yourself more absurd," she said. "The woman you have been stealing peeks at. Is this not the infamous Thalia?"

"Yes. She sits with her family," I told her.

The comedy continued. To me it was as funny as the tragedy of Oedipus Rex. At length, the first act concluded. The actors retired; the audience stood to stretch its muscles; vendors slipped through the crowd hawking refreshments.

"The widow of Cleomenes is extraordinarily beautiful," Aurora decided, in a sad tone, picking up the thread of our exchange as if we had not had a hundred actors' speeches in between. "It is little wonder that she is your mistress."

I have received several wounds in my day. None has been more than temporarily harmful, but the evidence of some still remained upon my flesh. In light of my months of agonized mental struggles to avoid Thalia, this wound hurt worse than any I had received from iron.

"Where did you hear this?" I asked.

"You sound surprised that I know," was her reply.

"I am surprised because it is not true."

"And what if I said that I did not care?" she asked.

I looked into her expressive face, which labored mightily to affect an air of non-concern. "Then I would call you a liar."

I noted that our words had attracted the attention of several around us. I took Aurora's arm and drew her to the side of the amphitheater, where several plane trees provided a shade that would be welcome in warmer days.

"I will freely admit that she has offered herself to me. I will also freely admit that her offers have tempted me. But I have been true to you, and this I will swear at any altar."

"Why should you spurn her?" Aurora demanded.

"Because I love you," I said at last. "You have won me from her, and I am glad. You are the better woman, Aurora."

A sudden welling of tears streamed down my wife's face. Her throat worked up and down, and her mouth opened, but could find no words. Instead, she hugged me and pressed her face against the material of my uniform.

"You have made me very happy," Aurora said softly. "I would die for you, you know."

I stroked her hair. "I would rather you lived for me. I am very glad for your tender feelings, but we are in a public place, and I would have you act as the wife of a leader."

This gentle rebuke caused her to gain control of herself in quick order. She dabbed at her eyes. "I will raise my veil so that I do not attract more attention," she said. "This is the first time I am glad of your custom."

While she was hiding her face, I asked, "Was it Azar who put these thoughts into your head?"

Aurora shook her head. "I am ashamed to tell you this, but this past winter I finally could stand it no more. I took advantage of her tender feelings toward me and coaxed from Azar a great deal of information about Thalia, her family, and her relationship to you. However, she said nothing of Thalia as your mistress. Rather, she believed that you were faithful."

"She was right," I said. "Then what made you suspect me?"

"First, fear. And then this woman's beauty. It is storied around the city. I know men. They are petrified that their wives will cuckold them precisely because they think so much of philandering. Can you deny that this is the way of men?" she challenged.

"It is our nature," I answered. "But some of us resist it for greater reward."

"You were always clever with words," my wife judged.

"And this is all?" I continued to probe.

"No. Not all." She lowered her eyes. "There were words of caution from Amara."

I knew that Aurora and the wife of my boon friend Apollonius had grown extremely close over the months. Aurora had taught Amara much about the subtleties of design, so that Amara's already-masterly weaving became the envy of her neighborhood. They shared the experiences of motherhood as well. I also knew how protective Amara had grown of Aurora, calling her "a poor Roman dove among Greek cats." This made perfect sense to me. My eyes swept through the crowd to pick out this couple, but I knew that such heady entertainment was not to the liking of my wrestler friend. Consequently, his wife would not be in attendance either.

"I will not be angry at Amara," I promised. "What did she tell you?"

For a moment, Aurora said nothing. Then she drew in a fortifying breath. "As you know, Apollonius has moved his family up to Epipolai because of the large houses that may be gotten for little money."

I saw the story beginning to form before the words were spoken. Amara lived but two long blocks from where Thalia's second house lay.

"When Amara was at the public well drawing water," Aurora went on, "she happened to overhear two other women talking. One spoke of hearing about the wealthy woman from Ortygia who had taken a house on their block. This woman knew of the fact but also had never herself seen the wealthy woman visiting the house. It seemed, however, that her next-door neighbor had spied from her window a military man entering the place alone. He had looked around furtively, as if to assure himself that no one he knew recognized him. The woman had said that the man was handsome and, from his uniform, she knew that he was among the highest ranking in the city."

"It was not me," I vowed. I exclaimed with exasperation. "And from this scrap of a city wife's tale, you have concluded that I have taken Thalia as mistress? A tale told to you third-hand?"

"I am ashamed, husband," Aurora said, although she did not sound ashamed to me.

"Did Amara confront either of these women?"

"She did not know them to speak with them."

"Then she could not ask anything. Did the woman who spoke say that she saw Thalia there at the time she saw the man?"

"No."

"In its meandering travel from ear to ear, might someone have missed that the man entered another house, or that he carried a scroll on business?"

"I do not know. I merely heard three facts that seemed to link you to Thalia."

"A wealthy woman, a handsome military man, and a high-ranking uniform."

"That is the sum of it," Aurora confirmed.

An actor with a horn signaled the end of the intermission from the second story of the playing area.

I took Aurora's arm and steered her back down the rows toward our seats. "I think there will be another pause before this comedy is finished. When that happens, I suggest we cross the orchestra to Thalia. I will introduce you to her, and you may tell her of your suspicion. Do not neglect to tell as well that you have given me permission to take her as mistress."

"Now you sound like my father," Aurora complained.

"You mean the man who has several times counseled me to beat you? I am decidedly not Marcellus."

"If you were, I would not be here," my wife said. When she had taken her seat, she made a point of staring at Thalia. When their eyes met, she offered her rival a generous smile, even as she wrapped her arm around mine.

As we left the amphitheater, I dared to ask Aurora, "Were you seriously resigned to accepting Thalia as my mistress?"

"For a time. For only a short time."

"That does not seem like you," I said frankly.

"It is not my nature. But I thought it better to take the risk of letting you experience her and to learn her bad sides than to have you idealize her all your life and ruin our marriage. But I also understand that Azar explained her faults to you. So, you are no longer permitted to have her, husband," she told me, through a hard and haunted smile.

I determined to visit Archimedes when next I took my leave. I knew that he would be immensely entertained by all of this folly.

Δ

After the theater, the majority of the populace retired either to their homes or to professional houses of entertainment, to share feasts and wine that everyone knew would not be available soon afterward. At our house we had taken in two young women who had lost husbands in our conflict with Roma, one of whom also had a young daughter. This daughter was especially well liked by my children. For their sakes we celebrated the festival with food and drink, but a pall hung over the house. We toasted to the shade of the departed Azar, and I did not attempt to conceal a tear that came to my eye.

I could not tarry long beyond dark, however, because I had duty in the fortress. I stayed as long as I dared, but about halfway through the first watch I began the slow climb out of Achradina toward Epipolai.

I decided at the last moment not to walk by the streets but rather to move along the walls, acting as an impromptu master of the watch. While I discovered no one missing from his post, I found to my dismay that several men were far too drunk to keep a watchful eye. I redoubled my march up to the fortress, to find competent men to relieve these dere- lict soldiers. As I was about halfway along the north wall, I came upon a man asleep at his post.

Boiling with rage, I kicked the heap of shadow as hard as I could in his thigh.

"Get up, you poor excuse for a soldier."

The man grunted and rolled over. I saw with shock and despair that it was Apollonius. I hauled him to his feet and slapped him across the face. His eyes snapped open.

"Leonides!" he said. He was too drunk to feel embarrassment.

"Do you not understand that the enemy waits beyond our gates for just such carelessness as this?"

"I am drunk," he said.

"You are no soldier!" I barked at him. This caught his attention through the fog. "Turn around, and look out at the plain, Apollo! Look for your enemy! Do not dare to fall asleep again, or I may kill you with my own sword, friends though we may be."

He heard these words, and his breath came in sharply. He struggled to hold his eyes fully open. "I will try."

"No, you will obey and succeed!" I countered. "The safety of your city and your family depend on it." I picked up his spear and placed it in his hand. "Now walk! Walk back and forth briskly, and do not stop!" I commanded.

I left my friend staggering through his round. I no longer felt I had the luxury of walking the long route, but elected instead to descend the wall and cut across Epipolai directly toward the fortress. Even I, having drunk but two cups of wine more than my usual habit, felt my footsteps heavy as I jogged through the streets.

As I entered the district's agora, I heard the blood-chilling sound of a Roman trumpet. Its metallic blare did not come muffled over the walls from the plain beyond but clearly sounded from on high. I knew that something horrible was happening. I drew my sword from its sheath and redoubled my pace. I overtook two of Hippokrates' under officers who were jogging up the street. They turned with alarm at my noisy approach and recognized me.

"The wall may be breached somewhere," I told them.

"We think the same," one of them said. "We go to fetch Hippokrates."

I said that I would come with them.

"He is in a house just around the corner," said the other.

When we turned into the street, I saw with great surprise that it was the very street in which Thalia had secured the little house to be our love nest. My surprise trebled when the officers moved directly to it and knocked upon the door. I lingered back a few paces. Although night surrounded me, yet did the light of understanding fill my mind.

The first officer banged on the door and identified himself. At first, he received no reply. Then he shouted out that the Romans were attacking. This got the door open within a few more seconds. As I had done on the night of Thalia's wedding, I hung back in the shadows of a nearby doorway. I watched as Hippokrates appeared, half dressed. He blocked the door so that his men could not enter. I heard him issue commands for one soldier to race back to the fortress and gather men while the other was to bring up a second force camped in the Neapolis district.

The two saluted him and retraced their way on the run back to the street, hardly acknowledging me as they passed.

I immediately advanced to the door and banged on it. "Strategos!" I called out, in a voice I purposely disguised by making it low.

Hippokrates threw open the door. He had slipped on his leather gear and belt but had not taken his helmet, breastplate, greaves, or sword. Thalia stood behind him, wrapped in a sheet. She gasped when she saw me.

"He has forced himself upon me, my love!" she cried out.

Hippokrates whipped around. "You fool! Do you think he would ever raise his sword to you? He has come for me. Have you not, Leonides?"

"I am pleased to find you here," I said, truthfully. I had inadvertently stumbled upon the puzzle of the handsome officer who had been seen

340

visiting Thalia's Epipolai house.

Hippokrates shrugged and smiled easily, as if we were all members of the same family and having a little row. He walked over to the bench on which he had laid his breastplate and greaves. He sat and began fastening on the protection for his lower legs.

"Are you indeed pleased?" he said. "I am curious how you could know about me and Thalia. I was ever careful not to visit unless you were with your wife."

I stepped into the house. It was a hovel in comparison with both Eustace's city home and that of Cleomenes, dark and with nothing but a bench and a small table in the front room. It was lit by two oil lamps hanging from wall irons. I shut the door behind me.

"I have my spies as well," I dissembled.

"You aren't thinking of killing me over her?" Hippokrates asked. He glanced up at my sword, which I had not realized I still held high. I noted that while he labored to looked unconcerned, that his hands shook slightly as he fastened on his greaves.

"She is a free woman," I returned. "I have no claim over her."

Thalia had backed away toward the door that I assumed led into the bedroom. As she moved, she tried to arrange the sheet in a decorous manner.

"She is a free woman indeed," said Hippokrates. "I made her so. You should know what manner of woman you have lusted after."

"He is a liar!" Thalia exclaimed, her words issuing like the hissing of a snake.

"How do you know what I will say to call me such?" asked the general. "But, then of course, you know exactly what I am about to say." He returned his words to me. "When her husband was levied into my command, she sent a note to me saying that she wished a conversation in private. I expected this was to bribe me to advance the man or to protect him. Several men have had their wives do the same, sparing themselves the embarrassment of begging on their own behalf. I met with her. She brought a good deal of gold. What she wanted, however, was not the sparing of her husband, but his death."

Thalia retreated one more step into the dark bedroom.

"Stay where you are, Thalia!" I warned.

"I am not decent," she protested.

Hippokrates burst into laughter. "From her own mouth! She knows her city history well. She suggested that when the opportunity arose that I should do to her husband what Hieron did to the mercenaries against the Campanians. She provided me with a handsome down-payment for this service."

"You put him inside Leontini," I said.

"Not merely inside Leontini but with the syntagma that defended the weak south side. Not merely in that division, but in the front line. You may speak with a taxiarch who survived from that syntagma if you wish verification." Hippokrates finished with his greaves and lifted the breast-plate over his head. "They were the most likely to die. I even held back my ambush for a time to be sure. I am too good a soldier to hold back for too long, however. I was afraid he might survive, but he stood his ground and died like a loyal Siracusan. Someone had to stand in that place. Thalia simply made my decision much less difficult."

I glanced at Thalia. Hatred burned from her shadowed eyes.

Hippokrates stood as he slipped the breastplate down past his arms. "Of course, I made the mistake of falling in love with her, just as you have. I thought that she merely did not wish her husband. But she wanted him gone for you. I was quite jealous and unable to get her attention. And then you rejected her."

I understood completely. If I had flown to her, Thalia would never have considered Hippokrates. But he was an excellent consolation. He was handsome, if somewhat too old for her. He was a general during a war. By the time Thalia knew that I would not come to her, he had made himself the controlling general. I am sure that this woman who knew about Hieron's betrayal of his mercenaries also knew the history of the dead man's rise from general to dictator of the city. It was not at all out of the realm of possibilities that if Siracusa survived the turmoil with Roma that Hippokrates would emerge as the city's next dictator. Then she would reign by his side.

"I love you still, Leonides," Thalia said.

"And I hate you for that," Hippokrates admitted to me. He strode to the table, where his helmet and sheathed sword lay. He held out his hands in a friendly gesture. "But neither of us can be concerned with this matter right now. We are soldiers, with a city to defend. Let us do what we do best and worry about her tomorrow, shall we?" He picked up his sword.

"If this were merely about Thalia, I would agree," I said, moving one step closer to him. "But there is also the matter of the attack on my home. You made a mistake sending a man from your regiment to eliminate your rival."

"I don't know what you are talking about," Hippokrates said. His hands, however, continued to shake.

"You also sent the little man who ran between Hieron's children and you while the king still lived. You used him one time too many." I knew from his face that my guess was the truth.

Hippokrates dashed across the room, grabbed Thalia by the hair, and pushed himself behind her.

"I say that we will settle this later," he growled at me. "Otherwise, we both share the guilt of this woman's blood. For I will kill her if you advance. Unfortunately, there is only one door out of this poor excuse for a house."

"You are a coward," I said to him.

"No. I am a patriot who has made some poor choices. I sent those men for more than you. I sent them to rid this city of the issue of the man who besieges us. Your life is as filled with mistakes as mine, Roman lover." He let go of Thalia's hair and reached for her neck.

At that moment, Thalia whirled around and bit Hippokrates hard on the forearm. Before he could react, she had thrown herself to the floor.

I tossed the table aside and lunged for Hippokrates. He parried my first thrust and backed into the darkness of the bedroom, making himself invisible.

Thalia scrambled forward like a cockroach on her hands and knees.

"Flee, Thalia!" I said. "The Romans are pouring over the walls of Epipolai right now. Get down to Ortygia as fast as you can."

The woman was nothing if not obsessed with her own welfare. She grabbed a himation from a peg that hung near the door and disappeared

343

from the house.

"And will you allow Siracusa to fall to the Romans while you wait for me to emerge?" Hippokrates asked from the cloak of darkness.

"Not at all," I replied. I lowered my sword for several moments, both to give my arm a rest and to see if he might thunder out of the room on the attack. He was content to wait. "Do you think you can win her back if you slay me?" I asked the darkness.

"Do you believe I want her back?"

"Yes."

"You are right."

"Then why did you use her as a shield? How does that show your love?"

"She is like me, a very pragmatic woman. She will come to understand that I did it to make her a queen. Why do you not do your duty, Leonides, and save Siracusa?"

"Very well. If you will not face me now, I go," I answered.

The passage between the main room and the bedroom had its own door. This door opened so that if Hippokrates hid on the side of the room away from the street his view of the front door was blocked. If he hid on the opposite side, he could only see the inside of the main room. I sidled toward the front door, opened and closed it with noise. Immediately after this, I stepped into a corner of the room where one lamp hung. I quietly lifted the curving bronze instrument out of its cradle and lengthened the wick. Then, holding it behind the left side of my body, I moved swiftly to the bedroom doorway, scudding my feet lightly as I went.

Hippokrates guessed wrong. He had supposed that I would charge into the room with sword raised. When he heard me move, he stepped into the open space thrusting out his sword. Instead, he was met by flying oil which struck him squarely in the face. Even as he gasped in surprise and pain, his sword arm swung blindly back and forth, seeking me out. I dashed the lamp onto the tile floor at his feet. The rapidly-spreading film of oil burst into flame.

The general retreated. I first threw the bench through the door to make sure the space beyond was cleared and then wedged the overturned table into the door's opening.

"Consider the room Leontini, and pretend that you are Cleomenes," I called out, as smoke began to fill the little house.

Hippokrates replied with a fit of coughing. I moved back cautiously and grabbed the second lamp.

A moment later, Thalia's large mattress pushed roughly into the table and halfway through the door. Its bottom had already caught flame. I tossed my second bomb over the top of the mattress, directly at the sounds of coughing. The second lamp's liquid also caught fire.

Hippokrates bellowed out his rage, pushed again at the mattress, slipped and fell feet first on the floor. The mattress crumpled and landed on top of him. He was covered in oil and flame. The table toppled over, so that two of its legs held the mattress down. The general's arms and legs flailed wildly. Through the choking smoke, he did his best to scream

I rushed to the front door, swung through it and out into the night, and then held tightly to its handle, denying Hippokrates escape. I held fast for more than two minutes, until I could feel the heat of the room escaping under the door. When I at last dared to kick it open and look inside, the general had not moved from the floor in front of the bedroom doorway. Thalia's love nest had become his crematorium.

Δ

Since one of Hippokrates' officers had run to raise the alarm at the fortress, I elected to return to Epipolai's agora. This was the place where we had instructed and drilled the citizens to assemble in case of attack to the district. As I ran, I was heartened to see scores of men hurrying to the point carrying their weapons. I was at the same time disheartened. We had not planned on the panic among the citizens who were not expected to fight.

Roman horns sounded from several parts of the district, as if they had already conquered it. This threw the people into frenzied flight. Carrying all they could from their homes, with some even wheeling carts and barrows, a screaming mass rushed toward the gate that divided Epipolai from Neapolis. I knew that this area would soon be a confusion of desperate people, with street after street blocked. Even the Romans would not be able to move forward there. In a way this was good, as it thwarted the enemy from advancing into yet another of the city's districts.

"Leonides! It is Leonides!" one of the men cried out.

The soldiers gathered at the sound of my name and looked to me for direction.

"Where are your helmets, your shields?" I asked them, looking at the rag-tag group with dismay. Many of their faces were puffy with drink and sleep. They registered my concern; their eyes begged for hope.

"No matter," I said with bluff confidence. "We fight for our homes!" I raised my sword. The group shouted and shook the weapons they had brought.

"Leonides! I am here!" Menander came running into the agora, fully outfitted. I remembered that he had moved his Roman wife and son into this district.

"Good! Here is a fighting leader, men!" I cried out, even as I glanced around the agora. I saw the fifty or so tents that had been erected to sell wares. Each of them had a pair of poles extended in front to hold up awnings. Although they were all fashioned of wood, some had points on their tops. "Grab those poles for phalanx spears!" I commanded. The throng, which grew by the second, rushed to grab them.

"The Romans seem to be everywhere," Menander worried. "How can that be?"

"I don't know," I told him. "I am surprised they could find even one way inside. But they will surely send their first men to the Hexapylum gate to open it for the bulk of their army. We must go directly there."

Menander and I quickly arranged the men in ranks and files, with those who held spears and shields to the front. The moment we had most of the tent poles in hand, I led my makeshift force off at a trot.

The agora lay about five streets from the Hexaplyum gate. We were prevented fully two streets away from reaching it, as the gate had clearly been opened. A disciplined century of Romans moved down the street toward us. They marched six abreast, which was the full width of the street. Their large, squared shields were held high in their left hands; their right hands pointed long spears directly at us.

I glanced left and right. Menander came up to my flank.

"You command those with spears and shields. We must hold this group until reinforcements arrive."

"But we will surely be flanked by others coming down the side streets," he worried.

I said, "We cannot worry about that."

"Where will you be?"

"I will put the others into these alleys on our left. If you can, instruct some of the men with only swords to fall on the ground and to attack once the first line passes above them."

"I shall."

"I shall also."

I turned at the new but familiar voice. I saw my brother Myreon. He trembled with fear, but he smiled at me and clapped my shoulder. I squeezed his hand. There was no time for more.

Menander shouted for the men to move forward. I watched the terror in their eyes. The Romans were less than half a block away.

I turned to the twenty or so men who carried not more than swords.

"This is a formidable foe. We cannot face them for long. But we can outflank them in these narrow confines. They cannot transfer their shields to their right side, so we will attack them from these alleys on their right as soon as the front two lines pass. Do you understand?"

The men indicated that they did and disappeared into several spaces between buildings. I held one of the wooden tent spears. I raced to an alley ahead of the others. Here, by myself, I slipped into the night shadows.

For an agonizing time, all I could do was listen for the inevitable meeting of warriors. I knew that our men would fight with the desperation of those defending their homes but that they faced a larger and better armed force.

It happened that the initial clash occurred directly at the mouth of the alley in which I hid. For a time, our poles held the Romans back well. Then the enemy realized that they were only tipped with wood, and those just behind the first rank of men began hacking at the spear points with their swords. This was not easily done in the tight confines. The press of men surged back and forth. I was heartened to see our side hold

347

for so long.

Then, one by one, our spears were broken or pushed aside. The Romans plowed forward, each man shoving on the back or shoulder of the man in front of him. The shouting was terrible to hear.

I waited until the fourth rank came even with my black alley. Then, making no sound, I ran with all my speed at it and drove the spear through the first man and into the second. I had moved with such velocity that I came very near the first man I speared. He glanced at me just as the spear went through him. I recognized him as one of the Romans who had befriended me on the rampart at Cannae. We faced an element of a highly-motivated Cannae legion.

The entire mass of Romans faltered at the surprise of being attacked from the flank. For a moment, the far side of their vanguard was driven backward by the Siracusan force. Even the shouting died for that moment. In the relative silence, I heard the sounds of bowstrings twanging and the hissing of arrows in flight. I looked up and realized that Roman soldiers had surmounted houses along the length of the street and were firing down into the Siracusans.

I ran to the back of the alley, jumped upon a dividing wall, and climbed onto the nearest roof. A Roman archer stood at the edge with his bow drawn. I ran forward and pushed him off onto the century of Romans down on the street.

A moment later, an arrow whizzed past my ear. I saw then six other archers. Two of them aimed at me. The night was not entirely dark, and my silhouette could be seen as easily as I saw theirs. I ran for the place where the wall was. As I prepared to drop down an arrow caught me in my left shoulder, piercing the muscle and running through, so that I could see the point sticking out of the side of my chest. The pain felt extremely hot. I dropped to the wall and thence to the side away from the Romans. Here I found the rear of another alley.

I leaned my back against the alley wall, driving the arrow far enough forward so that I could snap off the point. Then I reached with my right hand over my shoulder to draw the rest out. I could not reach it.

I ran toward the fortress of Euryalus. Twice it was necessary for me to reverse my path, to avoid tides of Romans who poured down the side streets. By the time I reached the fortress, Roman soldiers were already marshalling around its inner wall, examining it to see if it could be breached. Our men on the battlements were pelting them with spears, arrows, and stones. I knew that I could not get inside. I also knew that I would never reach the gate into Neapolis before it was sealed.

The undefended west wall of Epipolai stood behind me. I found the nearest set of steps and climbed. Walking along it, I looked down to find a place where rocks rose highest toward it on the outside. Such a place was impossible for the Romans to move many men up, but for one man to drop down was merely insane. I studied the dark ground and wondered what disaster the shadows held. Then I climbed onto the parapet. I let my sword drop, to judge the distance. The sword stuck into the ground, indicating that the ground in this place was rather soft. I moved a bit to the side and jumped, bringing my legs up slightly to absorb the shock of my landing.

The instant my feet touched the earth, I collapsed onto my right side. Nothing inside me snapped. The quills of the arrow, however, had met the wall as I fell back, and the remainder of the dart went farther into me, causing me to cry out. I pressed myself flat against the cool earth and listened. Men moved outside the walls in the distance. I was certain that Marcellus had employed the full force of his legions, breaching here, threatening and decoying there. Romans tested the trenches in front of the Euryalus fort. They did not, however, venture farther south than this.

I picked myself up and limped south, down the craggy slopes. I had injured a muscle in my right leg from my fall. The arrow remained inside me. I was not fit to defend myself much less my city. In time I reached a skiff and a paddle that the Silent Storm kept hidden in the marshes. I climbed into it and began the laborious process of attempting to paddle with only one arm. Across the harbor and high on the plateau to the north, flames enveloped sections of Epipolai.

CHAPTER XXVII

The valiant efforts of our army allowed the vast majority of the populace living in Epipolai to escape to the lower districts of the city. When the cost was counted, we realized that nearly 1,500 of our soldiers had been killed. Moreover, another 300 were trapped inside the fortress. I knew that only enough stores had been laid in there for six weeks. All of Epipolai had been taken, which constituted about one-third of the size of Siracusa. Moreover, it sat upon the high district, so that the Romans could direct their missiles down upon the rest of the city from above. This was not with total impunity, as our holding tactics inside Epipolai had allowed the wall that divided it from the rest of the city to be closed off and well fortified. Stones, flaming pitch, and other missiles needed to fly over this wall before raining down upon the city. Nonetheless, they had a devastating effect on several blocks and upon the morale of the entire populace.

The Romans had destroyed about one-third of the buildings in Epipolai on the night of their invasion. In order to make room for their army and machines, they knocked down several more blocks of structures. Many saw this as the prelude to the total destruction of Siracusa. The Romans had been known to pull down an enemy town or city stone by stone and brick by brick and to sow salt in the fields around it, so that it might never rise again.

Among those men who fell defending Epipolai were my brother Myreon and Apollonius. It was carried to me that Apollo had been found among three Roman soldier bodies, still in the place where I had commanded him to do his duty. His family had not escaped into the lower districts, and no one knew if they had been killed or carried off into slavery. I was told by Menander that Myreon accounted bravely for himself at the end, despite his months of fears. He had elected to pretend to fall and then to spring up among the advancing century, stabbing at legs, groins, and bellies. The tactic, performed by half a dozen men, had thrown the Romans into a greater panic even than the men who attacked them from the alleys. Of all the stands made that night, our defense against the main advance was deemed to have been the most successful.

The charred body of Hippokrates had been identified by the Romans only from his armor and helmet. How he had come to die in a fire was a mystery to everyone. His brother had been killed as well in the defense of the district. This left Archelous and Paulus in charge of the remaining troops. That these two generals had favored Roma in the city debates months earlier mattered now not at all. The fate of the city seemed to be in the hands of Marcellus.

My wound had become infected, and I spent one week in my bed, delirious with fever. Consequently, I took no part in the negotiations to exchange prisoners. I could not take advantage of my special relationship with Marcus Claudius Marcellus and learn the fate of those unaccounted for or how the attack had been so successfully staged.

Menander had managed to survive the debacle. When the last remnants of the men he commanded were forced back into the agora, he had elected to save himself, taking virtually the same path I did. He, however, had found a rope and had repelled down the wall to safety. He visited me every day. As soon as I could recognize him and speak, he sat by my side. He told me what he knew of the battle as I related my efforts to him.

In the pause that followed, he said, "My family is among those not accounted for. As I left, I told Drusilla to scrawl in chalk outside our door that Romans lived inside. I hope she and Metellus are safe."

"The Romans take good care of their own," I reassured.

"But she is no longer theirs," he fretted. "They were happy to be rid of her."

"She will be returned to you eventually, if that is her desire," I said. "As soon as I am able, I will meet with Marcellus and speak to him on your behalf."

Menander hugged me lightly.

"Is war not madness?" he asked. "Drusilla and I are Roman and Greek, and yet we get along happily. Why can disputes not be reasoned out?"

"Because war is easier," I said, thinking on what Archimedes had told me.

"It is easy if you give the command from a palace or a senate!" Menander railed, rising from my bed. "It is not easy when you are looking at a line of enemy spears."

"I know," I said.

He realized how much he had tired me and slipped out of the room the moment my eyes closed.

Δ

I was not ready for military work for seven weeks. On the day that I put on my helmet and took up my shield once more, the fortress of Euryalus capitulated. Its 300 men were taken prisoner. They had held out fully one week beyond the last of their provisions, no doubt hoping for some miracle. The Romans had finally realized that none of Archimedes machines had been placed there and that they had been intimidated by empty towers. Once they understood this they moved in around the fortress as close as bowshot range. Even when they had more than 10,000 men surrounding the 300, they did not attempt to storm the place, so respectful were they of the skills of Archimedes and of the engineers from the days of Dionysus.

The first war council that I sat on following my return from injury discussed the possibility of using Siracusan criminals and slaves to help fight the Romans. The incentive was to be freedom. I related what Marcellus and other Romans had told me of this debate concerning the defense of Roma against Hannibal. We decided that not all men would be enrolled, but only those whose crimes were small and those slaves who had proven themselves loyal to their families.

Despite losing its fortress and upper district, Siracusa was yet a formidable city. Many of Archimedes' machines had been moved up to the Neapolis wall and were directed at the Roman emplacements. Half a dozen Roman engines were destroyed before they realized just how accurate Archimedes' wonders were. The entire Roman army retreated to the back half of Epipolai, and no serious assaults were attempted on the Neapolis wall after this.

We also had thousands of hale men still prepared to defend the city. Since the legions had first arrived, we and the Carthaginians had been causing steady attrition among their ranks. Even in the dismal, uncoordinated defense of Epipolai, we estimated that we had killed as many as 500 Romans.

The pressing problem was provision. We now had several thousand refugees from the upper district stuffed into available housing. All the stores of food that they had kept in their homes had been lost. They, along with the rest of the populace, had to be fed. Houses directly below the Neapolis wall were destroyed as well. Spring was upon us, and no one could plant, tend, or shepherd. We had enough to hold out into the middle of the following winter. Then, when need was greatest, we would begin to starve.

Twelve cargo ships from Carthage had managed to slip into the city ten days before the war council. Together, what they brought would not feed us all for even one week. However, they spoke of another Carthaginian effort to relieve us. As many as 130 war galleys and 700 supply ships were promised. We believed that these numbers were highly inflated, and yet they gave us great hope.

I advanced a plan to attack the part of the Roman army patrolling the plains, since so many of their number were now inside the city. We set this aside for a time, until after the Carthaginian fleet had arrived and the people were in a more positive mood. Word had come to us that Hannibal was still marching up and down the southern half of the Italian peninsula, harassing the great Roman Republic. We voted to conclude the meeting and to reconvene after the supply ships docked.

Δ

I do not know how the word of the Carthaginian armada slipped beyond the palace walls. I suppose when a people are greatly in need of hope, such news cannot be denied them. At any rate, left with nothing to do, thousands each day lined up along the shorelines of Achradina and Ortygia, watching. I believe that this alerted the Romans as to a major attempt at relief. What is certain is that when my scouts spotted several hundred Carthaginian ships approaching our coastline from the south, they also spotted about seventy Roman biremes, triremes, and quinqueremes of war sailing toward them. For whatever reason, upon seeing this, the admiral of the Carthaginian expedition lost heart. His galleys changed direction for Tarentum, and his cargo ships returned to Africa.

When my scouts returned to the city and reported this we knew that our situation had grown desperate.

I went to Archimedes and asked him what should be done.

"Bend to the inevitable or break completely," he advised.

"But Marcellus will not bend," I argued. "The Roman way is never to compromise, never to relent from a siege."

"Then this shall be the greatest challenge of your life, will it not?" he replied. "You have told me of several things that might be used as I use pulleys and fulcrums. This is not Roma or even the Roman Senate you negotiate with. It is a man who admires the Greeks and their way of life and who admires you in particular. Get from him what you can. We have now seen that the Carthaginians will not treat us any better than will these Latin dogs."

I must have looked completely forlorn, because Archimedes murmured soothingly and patted me on my good shoulder.

"Do not be so hard on yourself. You are doing all a man can do."

"I am not enough man to oppose Marcellus," I answered bitterly. "That is the truth of it."

Archimedes poked me hard. "First of all, it is not only Marcellus you oppose. You may sway him, but he is ultimately answerable to the might and the will of the accursed Roman Senate. Secondly, you are more of a man than you suppose. I have watched you carefully since you returned from Korinthos. How long ago was that?"

"Six years."

"That long?" He sighed. "You will see when you are my age that the years fly faster as you grow old. But that is not my point. I wish to tell you that I have observed a wondrous man in the making when I have watched you. At first, you were the ideal that many men believe encompasses the real man. You were strong, fast, and greatly skilled with instruments of death. You know now that you were only half a man with these attributes. Since then you have gained compassion. You have learned to resist temptations, how to delay gratification, to accept responsibility, how to take advice, and to form your own opinions. You have even begun to understand your limitations."

"Much I owe to you," I acknowledged.

"True. But even more to Aurora. What is important, however, is that you did the learning. Many have the truth placed directly in their faces time and again, and they never gain from it. No, you are well on the way to becoming a complete man. But, as you will see, this journey never ends. For what is important is never where a man stands but only the direction in which he is moving."

I did not know what to say after such praise from the most admired man in Siracusa. Archimedes saved me from my compulsion to blurt out something.

"Tell your father-in-law that Archimedes expects him to behave with compassion and to treat us with dignity. Otherwise, he will not be invited into this Greek home."

I stood.

"And also tell him that when he has given you terms that we can live with that part of the agreement is no duplication of my machines. We will destroy them before the Romans enter the city. I will supply no plans. Neither will my laborers be tortured to reveal what they know."

"It shall be done," I promised.

As always, I left him drawing in his courtyard pit.

Δ

A most unusual parlay occurred three days after the Carthaginian fleet turned heels. I walked out of the Achradina gate as a general of the Siracusan army, as a spokesman for the city council, and as a private citizen. I walked with not even a scribe at my side. Waiting at a safe distance from the city was Marcus Claudius Marcellus. He, too, came alone. We stood facing each other on the wrecked and nearly barren plain.

My arm was still held in a sling. He pointed to it. "Can you walk?"

"There is nothing wrong with my legs," I answered.

"Good!" Marcellus gestured to the road. We started off at an amble.

I said, "Let us begin with the thousand and more citizens missing from Epipolai. We wish to know the fate of each of them."

Marcellus shook his head. "There are perhaps 200 held by us. Few are soldiers. Several are Roman citizens."

"A woman named Drusilla and her son Metellus?"

"They are among the few," Marcus confirmed. "Unfortunately, many died in the flames."

"Not from rape or slaughter?"

"I am told not. However, I entered in the morning. I cannot personally vouchsafe that this is so."

"It may be what your soldiers know you want to hear," I said with vehemence.

"You sound surprised that so many died," he returned. "Did I not warn you that this would be the consequence of resistance?"

I stated, "Because you allow it. If you tell your men they will be punished for rape and murder, they will think twice."

"Not easily said to men who must sit on their heels for years, with no one to stare at but each other, taunted by enemy walls and machines. I will have lists of those surviving made for you. The women and children you may have back."

We began to climb. I could wait not one more moment to learn the truth of the taking of Epipolai. "How were you able to breach the walls?"

He smiled as if he knew this would be an inevitable question. "You and Hannibal are not the only ones who can be devious. You surely remember when we negotiated for that Greek businessman taken on the ship. The negotiations were inside the Epipolai district. One of my officers brought a dog with him on that day."

"You said that you wished to hunt."

"I was already hunting. What is more, I found what I sought. Or, more properly, my officer did. The dog is a high-strung creature with a habit of running. He was released on purpose, so that the officer could confirm an observation we had made from the outside. Your walls are uneven in height, due to the hilly terrain. There is one place where the rocks rise up, near to one of your towers. He was able to count the number of courses of your wall from the inside and take an accurate measure of the height. After that, it was simple to create two ladders exactly shaped for the sides of that tower. I know you Greeks, how you love to celebrate. I figured correctly that many of your men would be unready for warfare after the festival of Artemis."

"But how could you get so many men over the wall so quickly?"

"We did not. Do you think this because of the noise of our horns?"

"Yes. I had been on the wall not ten minutes earlier. Your horns sounded everywhere."

Marcellus nodded. "That was another trick. Most of the first men who spread along the walls carried horns. We also sent several of the first men down onto Epipolai dressed as civilians. They were able to slip past your soldiers and blow the horns they had concealed far beyond where we had reached. This was to convince your people that we already entered the city in force, to create a panic."

I was satisfied that at least we had been beaten by a worthy adversary. "To accomplish this, you waited months."

"Years. For that and several other reasons. Patience is indeed a virtue." His eyes swept the countryside, where the shoots of grasses and buds on brambles had begun to poke up hopefully through the trampled plain. "It is a fair spring day. A day to plant and to plan for futures."

"What future do you see for us?"

"The time to open your doors has passed. My word was that your city would be destroyed. The leaders of this insurrection against our treaty will be scourged and axed, and your men, slaves, the poor, and citizens alike, will be sold into slavery."

"I thought that was the dictum from the Roman Senate and not your own word," I said.

"That is true."

I turned us west. "Then let us reason, you and I. With those terms we will not sit passively and starve. We will not throw down our weapons to meekly bare our necks. Remember the Spartians who fought at Thermopylae under my namesake. How many surrendered?"

"None," my adversary said. "They died to a man."

I lengthened my stride. "Taking, it is said, thousands of Xerxes' soldiers with them. How many men have you lost already?"

"Enough."

"Yes. Enough is my exact count for our side as well. Most of those who began this trouble from our side are already dead. I, however, live. So do other reasonable and intelligent men inside the free quarters of our city. I can guarantee you that we will take two Roman legions with us before you enter Ortygia. These are Greeks you fight, Marcus Claudius. We believe it is far better to die free men than to live as slaves."

Marcellus gave me an assessing glance. "You have been to Roma. Can you not fathom how little latitude I have?" he asked.

"I understand that you come from a race of implacable men who are making the entire world their enemy. I entered the Temple of Jupiter Feretrius to admire the armor you offered to that god after you defeated the Gallic chieftain. It was only by chance that I heard the prayer of one of your priests. It chilled me to my marrow. Shall I repeat it?"

"Please."

I told him how the priest had not wished merely defeat of the Carthaginians, but plagues upon them and the total destruction of their capital city and their race by fire and earthquake. "If this is the act of rational humans, then I want no more part of the human race," I told him. "This must stop. What better place to modify and mollify than in Siracusa? We are not barbarians who sweep down from the north to attack Roma. We are Greeks, who had drama, medicine, games and philosophy when your people were building mud huts in the middle of marshes. We have been friendly with Roma for six decades."

"That was the doing of Hieron."

"Not alone," I countered. "Hieron was guided ever by the will of the majority. He held feasts every few months to read the minds and moods of our influential men. More wished friendship with Roma than with Carthage, and even more would have been friends except for harsh Roman behavior such as we witnessed in Agricento. But you curried Hieron to be your best ally in Siracusa, Marcellus. You sent him spoils from that same Gallic war. You hold Greeks in high regard. Nothing speaks more plainly of this than that you allowed your beloved daughter to marry a Greek."

My father-in-law nodded more than once.

I exploited his open mind. "The Greek states on the mainland have turned into shadows of the great people they once were precisely because of the same kinds of senseless wars we now fight. Because Hieron was clever enough to save us from decades of conflicts, we have maintained and improved the arts of Greece. We have great artwork, philosophy, poetry, architecture, theater, and medicine here. Would you erase it in blood and fire, or would you bring some of it back to Roma, to make your people more than just common conquerors?"

At these words, Marcellus flinched. I knew that these arguments struck to his very heart and soul.

"But do these pursuits not make a race soft?" he asked. "If a people do not conquer and grow, then they eventually die."

"But how shall you grow?" I returned. "Roma grows not like a child, into something of beauty, strength, and wisdom, but rather like a cancer, a tumor that has for its efforts nothing but size. Moreover, it kills its host and, thereby, itself."

I had hoped this would open the great man up, but he was struck so ambivalent by my arguments set against the decrees of the Roman Senate that he could not frame a reply that would satisfy either himself or me.

To fill the silence, I asked, "Tell me about the Cannae legions here."

He laughed bitterly. "You could not have asked a more pertinent question. You know how I felt when the Roman Senate would not allow the families of those captured at Cannae to ransom them?"

"Yes. You deplored the decision."

"Likewise did I deplore the decision to send these men away from Italia as punishment for not staying on the battlefield and dying uselessly. They were sent here and told that they could not camp near any town. They had no hope of winning their return to Italia unless they won some stunning victory. I am being considered again for consul. Now, this sort of adulation should carry a certain power, should it not?"

"It should give you considerable power," I enthusiastically granted.

"Have I not covered myself in glory serving Roma all my life?"

"You have."

"Do you think they allowed me to lead these two legions willingly? No! The Senate said they were too cowardly to fight with me. How then were they supposed to earn their way home, I asked. 'They are not' came the reply. I petitioned again. They said I might use them if not a single one be honored on any occasion with a crown or any military gift, as a reward for whatever virtue or courage might be shown. They acknowledged that these men would again show courage and virtue, but they could never expunge their so-called sin against the state. Do you know that we honor greatly the first man to gain an enemy's fortified wall?"

I told him this was the first I had heard of it.

"It is true. Such acknowledgment must be given, for surely a hundred die trying before the first succeeds." He shook his head miserably. "As you correctly reckoned, we lost more than a thousand men at Leontini. And yet Leontini was not considered enough of a victory to ransom honor. Now these poor fellows sit outside your city, hoping to crush it completely so that they may go home to their loved ones. Not because they hate you in any way, but because they are lonely and in disgrace."

I said, "This is what I mean about your people's implacable nature."

"It will be our undoing."

I stopped walking abruptly. "Then change it, Marcellus!"

"How?" the champion beseeched me.

"By betraying your country for its greater good. I am here doing the

360

same for my city."

Marcellus looked first up at the fleecy clouds that scudded toward the toe of Italia. Then he turned and looked out at the glimmering sea.

"What will I say when I am brought before the Senate, for I surely will be?" he asked me.

"Tell them this, and say that you heard it from Leonides, who was named after the immortal Spartian general: The Romans are great warriors, but they pale in comparison to the ancient Spartians. Harder warriors the world has never known. And yet, when these same Spartians finally conquered their mortal enemy, Athenai, yet did they relent from their sacred vow to raze the city to the ground so that not one pillar might stand upon another."

Marcellus' jaw worked at my words, and I thought I might see the man's eyes brim with tears, as they had when he gave his daughter to me.

"And do you know why they relented?" I continued.

"Tell me."

"On the evening before the planned destruction, they held a great high festival. One of their number stood to recite a poem. This was by the great Euripides. Do you know his work?"

"I do. He is a favorite of Aurora's."

"He is. That is how I came to know his genius and this tale. This Spartian soldier's stern and hard comrades listened to the embodiment of the human soul as captured in Euripides' words. And they wept. And they forgot vengeance and declared that any city that could birth such a man should never be destroyed." I paused, seeing the tears I sought. "Archimedes sends you his warmest regards and invites you to dine with him. He knows you to be a man of intellect and honor, a man who respects the Greeks. He has confidence I will bring back an understanding that my city can accept. He is so confident, in fact, that he has told me you are not to learn about his weapons when you enter Siracusa."

At this Marcellus laughed. "They are indeed fearsome. And I can well understand why he does not wish the world to possess them."

"Then let us defy those who say all must end in blood and settle on reasonable terms," I said.

Marcellus began to walk again. "Let us."

CHAPTER XXVIII

The terms of surrender were, naturally, not to my liking. Nor were they liked by any man in Siracusa. They were yet so harsh that those of us in charge decided not to inform the public of the worst parts of them, lest many of us kill each other in rancor before the Romans entered and created the final havoc.

Siracusa would become a province of Roma, without any citizenship privileges to be granted to those not Roman. The remaining men who had campaigned openly and schemed to bring Siracusa to the Carthaginian side would be crucified. Citizens were to be disarmed. We were not allowed an army. All our slaves and non-citizens would be taken and sold abroad. The city would be opened to sack for one day. In this time, no one was to resist the Roman soldiers. They, in turn, were not allowed to charge through the town in wild fashion, raping and killing while they plundered. Rather, one-tenth of the army at a time would be allowed inside the city, each assigned to its own district. These soldiers would be supervised by their commanding officers. Our officers would walk beside them to see that these promises were kept. All plunder was to be collected into general piles, with any Roman soldier holding back to be killed. When the take was calculated, half would be given to those in the Roman army not of the two Cannae legions and half sent to Roma. The art of our great buildings would be carried off. Our navy was confiscated. In short, we were to be reduced from one of the gems of the Mediterranean to a sad tributary city in a matter of hours. But Siracusa's citizens would live and the city would stand.

I walked beside Marcus Claudius Marcellus on that dread morning. He was naturally concerned for the welfare of his daughter and grand-children. We, therefore, charged ourselves with the supervision of that half of Achradina in which my family lived.

Our entry point was through the Achradina gate. I listened along with the more than 1,000 soldiers as the rules of their sacking was reviewed. In this I was satisfied. However, when I looked into the eyes of these foreign men who had been forced to live in squalid conditions for so many months, so far away from home because of our city's rebellion, I saw there a thirst for revenge. The same men who had looked almost refined and composed inside the camp at Cannae seemed now completely transformed into things subhuman, and I wondered if it was simply my own fears. I did not think so, however. Many years had passed since Cannae, and these men had been told they were less than men for all that time. I think that they had come to believe it, and I shook at their great number, shifting impatiently and fumbling with their sacks and bags rather than listening to the officer's words.

At last the city gates were thrown open. A hundred wagons went in first, pulled by donkeys being whipped without mercy to speed them along. When the last of these had made its way about one street in, the soldiers were released. With a roar, the mass pressed forward. The people of the city waited beside the buildings, holding nothing in their hands. Despite their labors to look completely inoffensive, many were knocked to the street by the dashing throngs. Some were kicked on purpose and stepped on. All were spat upon.

Marcellus, I, and several officers waited until the dash of men had passed. We followed at a brisk pace. I was focused on reaching my home quickly. Marcellus was concerned with reaching Archimedes and seeing that the old human treasure was kept safe. We both believed that the soldiers would be slowed in the first streets, intent on covering every room in every house and shop and not missing a single coin or thing of bronze, silver, or gold. We could not, however, see where those at the head of the mass had gone.

The Achradina gate lay close to the water. It opened on the same street where the many houses of joy plied their trade. Much noise and numerous exclamations of dismay and indignation issued from inside these places.

"Your whores think that they should be paid for their services, and our men want them for free," Marcellus speculated. "Listen to them debating."

"This may be a problem," I worried. "Many men believe that a prostitute cannot be raped."

"We shall see," he said. "This is but the first trial of the clemency you have cajoled from me."

When we had moved to the last house of prostitution on the street, an anguished cry came out of the upper floor. We stopped and looked up. The bloodied body of a woman sailed over the balcony and landed on its back at our feet. I recognized the woman named Iris who had comforted me so many years before.

"Bring out the man who has done this!" Marcellus commanded. Three officers ran into the establishment. A minute later they wrestled out the door a wild-looking creature half-naked and covered in blood.

"She was only a whore!" he cried out. " A Greek whore!"

"On your knees!" Marcellus ordered the man.

"This is not fair!" the soldier protested.

"Officer, do your duty!" the general commanded.

One officer had taken his sword out of its sheath while his comrades yanked the condemned man's arms up roughly behind him, preventing him from rising. The executioner swung swift and true, decapitating the murderer even as he protested his fate. The head rolled down the street and came to rest against the body of the prostitute. The body crumpled in a heap. The legs twitched for several seconds and then lay still.

Marcellus ordered, "Have his head mounted on a post, with a sign in both Greek and Roman reading 'Roman Murderer/Executed by Roman Justice.'"

"Where shall we erect the post?" one of the officers asked his commander.

"On the inside of the gate we just passed through."

"But that will not prevent anything until they return," I protested.

Marcellus gave me a grave look. "Did you really think this would happen with no bloodshed?"

"Then why did you not allow me to keep a few of my soldiers and post them around the homes of the Roman citizens and Archimedes?"

Marcellus rocked back at my words. "I would have, if you had formally asked this."

I looked at his under officers, who stared anywhere but at us. "I did."

The Sword of Roma snapped his fingers at one of the officers, a centurion. "Accompany him to his house and see that his family is not disturbed!" He asked me for directions to my home and that of Archimedes and then pivoted and addressed the remaining officers. "You and you come with me! I cannot believe that Archimedes is not protected!"

We each ran off at our own pace. I could have easily outdistanced the centurion, but I had no power without him. We passed scenes such as I never want to witness again. There were simply too few officers to control the soldiers. Bodies, especially those of men my age, lay in the streets. Women staggered from houses in a daze, holding babies who had been taken by their heels and smashed against a wall until their crying stopped. Furniture, bedding, pots, toilet articles, in short things that the soldiers had no use for, were thrown wantonly out into the streets. Soldiers cavorted wearing women's cloaks and feathers. A pool of wine and a broken amphora lay in the street where soldiers had fought over it. Romans dashed back and forth, as if afraid that they would miss some bit of mischief if they tarried anywhere too long.

When I came at last to our house, I found the words I had myself chalked in Latin, informing those who might happen up the alley that therein resided people protected by Marcus Claudius Marcellus himself. I found as well my wife standing with my old sword in her hand, ready to protect what she held dear.

"Put that down, Aurora!" I bade, "The centurion will stay here. We go to the house of Archimedes. Your father will meet us there."

"I have no wish to see him."

I was not in the mood to argue with her. I took the sword from her hand, let it drop to the floor, and said, "Archimedes will be mightily upset by today's infamies. He is an old man and unused to such violence. You soothe him."

"Very well," Aurora relented. "For his sake."

The centurion had in his possession the fasces, which was a bronze bundle of rods around an axe, symbolizing the power to scourge and behead. This he handed to me. I held it high as we left our home, and we were not impeded from wending through the frenzied streets to my great-uncle's house. As we entered, we heard Irene wailing. We rushed inside.

Marcellus stood with his officers flanking him. His shoulders were slumped. He stared at something on the ground. He turned and saw us. His lips had reared back from his lips in his distress. He gestured for us to approach.

Archimedes lay in the center of his drawing pit, quite dead. His precious blood still seeped into the sand. In his right hand he clutched one of his drawing sticks.

"I only just arrived," Marcellus told us. "I took a wrong turn, and then I was lost. We finally found someone who…" His voice trailed off.

I looked across the courtyard. A Roman soldier stood there with his sword in his hand. It was stained with blood. In his left hand he held the bronze instrument that Archimedes had bargained for in the Roman market. He could not have looked more guilty.

"Tell me what happened here," Marcellus said to the soldier, in a voice so soft that it might have been mistaken for lack of caring.

The man shrugged. "I came in looking for things of value. I did not find much, so I thought that they had buried the rest. This crazy old man was drawing on the ground. I asked him where his money was. He turned his back on me. I figured he was deaf, so I went to him and spoke loudly. He spun around and started hitting me with that stick. He was shouting something in Greek. I do not speak Greek."

"He said, 'Do not disturb my figures!'" Irene told me softly. I could see in Marcellus' eyes that he understood her.

"He was clearly insane, so I defended myself." The soldier held up the bronze instrument. "Look! He has things of value. He didn't want to give them up."

Marcellus walked slowly around the courtyard, careful not to step upon the complex equations in the drawing pit. He took the bloody sword from the hand of the soldier and immediately thrust it into the man's stomach.

"You have murdered Archimedes!" he screamed. He looked up to the sky with infinite sorrow. "A lump of clay has murdered genius!" he cried to the gods.

As the soldier sank to his knees, clutching his guts, he looked up at his commander as if imploring him for explanation.

"I preserved the city for this man and what he represents, and you have taken it from me!" Marcellus ranted in answer. He threw the sword against the dying soldier's back. "Die slowly for your sin."

Only then did the Sword of Roma come to himself. He looked at me and the other shocked onlookers with his head cocked to the side. "Speak of the foolishness of this soldier if you must, but say nothing of my rage. It will serve no good for Romans or Greeks."

Thus did the Siracusa I knew and the man I most admired die on the same day.

CHAPTER XXIX

Four years and more have passed since Siracusa surrendered to the Romans. Much has transpired. The city is administered as a province by a Roman praetor, with a questor as the financial advisor. Those surrounding towns that had been confederates to Siracusa in the time of Hieron were now truly tributary under Roman rule. The Greek inhabitants are no longer considered citizens but subjects. They have no military, administrative, or judicial power. The western half of Sicilia also fell under this praetor's direction, so that the entire island is under their control.

The structures of the city remained as they were on the day of our capitulation, but its treasures were removed to Roma. This would seem on the surface a calamity of monumental proportion. However, the truth is that they served us and the rest of the world far more in that primitive capital city than they had where they were. Our paintings, architectural models, marble pediments, woodwork, furniture, bronzework, pottery, glassware, statues, and even large portions of tessera murals were put on display in several of Roma's public buildings. This created a sensation such as Roma had never known. Most of its citizens had never beheld such beauty. The displays sparked a reverence for all things Greek, a newfound desire to pursue the artistic side of life, and an earnest desire to emulate our lifestyle. Thus, in a large manner, we had conquered them. Simonides of Cios, who long ago wrote "The city is the teacher of the men," would have smiled at the appropriateness of his words to this supreme irony.

Virtually every statue and bust in the city had been carted off, including the great Zeus wearing the crown with the silver mixed into the gold. Some citizens said that the crown should have been recast, that this impiety had led the outraged Thunderer to desert the city. I by this time agreed with Archimedes and Aurora, that the gods created us and the world but rarely interfered in the affairs of men. We are generally to blame for our own woes, whether we choose to accept this or not.

My statue went as well. Every time I thought of it I laughed, imagining Romans unwittingly admiring the figure of the man who had bedeviled and killed so many of their compatriots.

Moreover, the success of Marcellus' mercy to our citizens was not deplored, but rather applauded when it was revealed how difficult we might have been to conquer and how few Roman soldiers relative to the task had died. Marcellus, in fact, was the Roman who most regretted his decision not to murder or sell off all our men. For his mercy, he was ironically compelled a year after the end of the siege to defend himself in a Roman court. His triumph had caused him to be elected consul a fourth time, but this did not prevent him from needing to appear before the Senate to answer charges of brutality. This stemmed from his inability to prevent some eighty-six murders during the course of the day in which the city was sacked, in compliance with the terms of surrender that he, I, and several others had drawn up.

When these charges were brought forth by certain former citizens of Siracusa, Marcellus was in Roma. The Sword of Roma entered the Senate and first conducted other business with them. However, when this matter was brought forth, he relinquished his seat and stepped down to the place where the accused must stand to offer their defense.

According to some in the petitioning party, when they saw Marcellus in his magisterial robes of state, he was even more awe inspiring than in his warrior's armor. Moreover, he carried himself with complete confidence and calm. Nevertheless, they read out their petition of unwarranted brutality, along with other lesser grievances.

When Marcellus' turn came, he reminded my Greek brothers that their soldiers had committed many hostilities against his army and, with the aid of the great Archimedes, had killed many and compelled four legions to remain around Siracusa for almost two years. In light of this, he had been more clement than any other Roman commander in that state's history. He concluded by telling the body of his son-in-law, who had opposed him in the taking of Siracusa. He read out my exploits and deeds and spoke of my valor and honesty. He asked the Siracusans to confirm this, which, although they sensed a trap, they were obliged to do. Marcus Claudius then read a statement I had sent to him in support of his honest efforts to treat the people of Siracusa with dignity when its gates were opened.

I had written this letter in my own hand and placed my seal upon it, so that it could not be impugned. When this group of Siracusans had decided to come to Roma to embarrass Marcellus I no longer lived in Siracusa. Word of their intent came to me, however, and I was compelled to rise to the consul's defense, if only to prevent the Roman Senate from regretting Marcellus's compassion toward the Siracusans and to turn once more to unbridled brutality. I was damned if a group of petty businessmen who had swiftly forgotten their relief at not being executed or sold into slavery would end the new method of Roman treatment toward enemies before it had truly begun.

When Marcellus had finished defending himself, as was the custom, both he and the Siracusans retired from the chamber. In short order, the Senate found in favor of Marcellus, and the Siracusans publicly apologized for their rashness. Amazingly, when they returned to their city they led a movement that issued a proclamation sent back to Roma: If Marcellus or any of his issue should at any time return to the city, the people of Siracusa should wear garlands in celebration and offer special sacrifices to the gods.

Aurora and Marcellus' grandchildren in fact returned to Siracusa twice a year, but no garlands were worn or animals sacrificed. This is because we traveled there with no fanfare, preferring anonymity. We returned to the city during high festivals when the markets were most active, in order to trade the yield of our estate for those few items we could not produce.

As part of his payment for taking the south of Sicilia, the Roman Senate granted to Marcus Claudius Marcellus estate lands on the island to be chosen by him to the equal of the size of Siracusa. He naturally consulted with me and his daughter in this regard. He already owned two estates on Italia from former triumphs, and he hardly visited them, so busy was he charging from one conflict to the next. I chose a tract of land well off the main roads and over a tortuous range of mountains, so that no future army might travel there easily. This estate was all but self-sufficient, with fields, orchards, vineyards, woods, and plentiful water from mountain streams. It was able to sustain hundreds of souls if it had all been worked, but we left much of it to grow wild. We invited twenty families to work the land, and not one man or woman was a slave. The estate was so bountiful that we were able to entertain at any time and for indefinite stays a dozen learned men and women. This we did, creating a de facto school of art and philosophy in the remote back country of Sicilia.

This school was mightily aided by the library we amassed. It consisted not only of those scrolls Marcellus had given to Aurora as a young woman, but more than fifty removed from the library of the palace that had nothing to do with the affairs of state and so were not desired by the Romans. The third source came from Archimedes, who had bequeathed his scrolls to Aurora in his will. Because the city had been conquered, Marcellus determined that they were not the old man's to give. He confiscated all of Archimedes' original works and returned them to Roma as one of the greatest collective treasures taken from our city. He left with his family, however, all that was not rare or unique. Ten days after Siracusa capitulated, we found ourselves owning one of the greatest private libraries in the Mediterranean.

Owing to the respect in which he was held by both the citizens of Siracusa and Marcellus, Archimedes was buried with highest honors and much mourning. His grave was located on the heights of Siracusa, looking out across the sea on the vastness of the world, where the keenest eye might see the mast of a ship appear before the ship itself.

I gave to Marcellus the slip of paper that Archimedes had entrusted with me. From this, the consul caused to be created a large monument over the grave with a marble sphere beside a cylinder. Beneath it, in Greek, were the formulae for the mathematical discovery of which the genius was most proud, carved just below his name.

True to his word, Marcus Claudius did not work to discover the secrets behind the great engines of war that Archimedes had used, as many were fond of saying, "to single-handedly hold off the entire Roman army." He understood that if such machines went into the field some would ultimately be captured and copied, and then warfare throughout the Mediterranean would be that much more terrible. For my part, I have refrained in this commentary from describing in detail their workings, although I did study these wonders and understood their genius.

Δ

I conclude by relating the fates of the major players in this living drama.

Thalia predictably emerged from the ordeal of Siracusa's siege not tarnished, as they say, but gilded. The Roman who was sent to Siracusa to serve as questor was not only relatively young but a bachelor. Six months after his arrival, he found himself married to the widow. On the balance, she could not have done better for herself.

Hannibal spent most of the year after Siracusa's fall trying to raise the Roman siege around Capua. In a major battle that coordinated the Capuans attacking the inner Roman line whilst the Carthaginians attacked the outer one, Hannibal was nonetheless forced back without ultimate success. In desperation, the great tactician marched toward Roma, trying to draw the Roman legions from Capua. The Senate, however, would not be frightened and did not rise to the bait.

Under Quintus Fabius, who was known as Cunctator, which in Latin means 'The Delayer," a plan was put in place to refuse large battles and to dog Hannibal's rear constantly, seizing his baggage trains and culling his stragglers. This is proving successful.

Hannibal was compelled to abandon Capua.

Twenty-eight of the major conspirators in the city's defection from Roma committed suicide. Of that enormous city, only fifty-three more were scourged and beheaded. Seeing that Roman policy had turned more clement, the other rebelling towns of Calatia and Atella also surrendered. The example of Marcellus' mercy in Siracusa was producing tangible results that the Senate could not ignore. Archimedes had made me believe that I could convince Marcellus. I had made the once implacable general believe that he could sway the Roman senators. Thus, from the efforts of but three men, the world was moved.

Since then, the fortunes of Hannibal have grown increasingly worse. Although the two Roman Scipio brothers were killed in Hispania, Nero shored up the Roman holdings with 6,000 infantry and 300 cavalry. The Roman Laevinus concluded a treaty with the Aetolians, the traditional enemies of the Macedonians, which effectively kept Philip from attacking the Roman colonies along the Greek side of the Adriatic.

So confident are the Romans of eventually defeating Hannibal by attrition and starvation that they decommissioned two legions. Two more of the Sicilian legions have also been unformed.

Marcellus, whom Hannibal had ever feared, was put in charge of recapturing Apulia. The year after a string of triumphs in this effort, he set about recapturing the Adriatic coast and forcing Hannibal even farther south toward the tip of the Italian peninsula. Tarentum was betrayed back into Roman hands, leaving Hannibal with little more land to roam over than that of Lucania and Bruttium. All the while, Marcellus dogged after him, moving his camps as close as he dared to limit the space around which Hannibal's men could forage.

On one such occasion, Marcellus wished to take a wooded hill that lay between the camps. Hannibal knew that this would be his strategy. I have related at least twice the reckless valor of Marcellus, to such a point as to be foolhardy. Thus, he and Titus Quinctius Crispinus, who had been elected consul at the same time Marcellus received the honor for the fourth occasion, rode out with an escort of only sixty cavalry and thirty velites. When they reached the crest of the hill, they were surrounded by some 400 Numidian warriors. Despite a desperate effort to break out, Marcellus was killed and Crispinus badly wounded. I am told that even though the second consul escaped, he later died from his injuries. Even so, Hannibal did not gain ground; Roma has a seemingly inexhaustible line of heroes willing to die for their state.

It is said that upon hearing of the death of his feared foe, Hannibal hurried up that hill. He gazed on the body of Marcus Claudius Marcellus for some time in silence, appearing to murmur a prayer as well. As prize he took only the consul's signet ring. The body he had cremated with high honors and the ashes put into a silver urn with a golden lid, with the intent of being delivered to Aurora's brother. Only a little way toward the Roman lines, however, a troop of Numidians overtook the messenger and stole the urn, dumping out Marcellus' bones.

When he heard about this unfortunate occurrence, Hannibal said, "It is impossible, it seems, to do anything against the will of God!"

Hannibal yet roams across part of the land which the Romans deem to be theirs by destiny. How this most protracted conflict shall end is not yet determined, but I cannot see Roma losing.

Upon hearing of her father's death and the incident with his remains, Aurora, of course, wept. When she had recovered, she said, "The will of God had nothing to do with this. It was my father's will that caused his sad end. Every time he was asked to fight, he accepted. Since the Romans are ever at war, there was hardly a moment when he was not serving. He was the Sword of Roma. He could not have helped but to die on a field of battle."

I have chosen otherwise. When I was relieved of my sword and shield on the day Siracusa opened its gates, I handed them over with no regret. I had held true to my duty as long as I could. I had served to the limits of my abilities in defense of my home. There was nothing more to raise a sword over.

I am, however, not standing still but continuing to move. I content myself with running the estate, which is in truth owned by my son. In my considerable spare time I read, I study, and I write. I spend hours with friends, sharing knowledge, making music, and simply delighting in their company. I play with my children until they tire of me.

Aurora declares that she has found total contentment in her estate and her family. She has no desire to visit Roma even if the world suddenly should lapse into a temporary peace. She knows that she is loved, for who could not love such a gentle, wise, and compassionate creature? Certainly not I.

Athena is her mother's girl. She finds me too rough for her tastes. I am, I must admit, a boy's father. He wants to hear over and over of my exploits as a warrior. He delights in fighting with me with wooden swords and using me as his horse in imagined battles of great pitch. As Plato has written, "Of all the animals, the boy is the most unmanageable." But I do not neglect his instruction in that other side of being a man. I teach him through the scrolls the thoughts of the great minds of ages past. I repeat again and again the many sage words that Archimedes shared with me. I do not neglect to give him my own observations and to share my shortfalls. Perhaps, if I am wise, I will have produced a man who will one day move the world.

NOTES ABOUT THE
NOVEL'S ACCURACY

This novel follows the course and the details of its events as accurately as possible. However, two centuries before the birth of Christ the keeping of historical accounts was in its infancy. Where precise facts and figures were not known, authors from closely-following years, decades, or centuries supplied best guesses. Exaggeration in sizes of armies, armadas, and numbers of soldiers lost in battles is particularly suspect. Moreover, in the extended conflict between Carthage and Roma, since Roma was the winner its writers told their version only. Authors borrowed from earlier authors without giving credit or verifying accuracy. Authors, be they Greek or Roman, sought to please the conquerors and bent history to Roman favor. Historians were also few and far between. With this in mind, I nonetheless sought out roughly contemporary sources whenever possible, i.e. Plutarch, Livy, Pausanias, Polybius, Proclus, Vitruvius, Dio Cassius, etc. and labored to follow "history" as closely as I could.

The idea for this novel came to me more than three decades before I set pen to paper. As an avid boyhood reader of Gibbons, Renault, and many others who dealt with this period, either historically or in historical fiction, I stumbled upon this fascinating footnote in the Punic Wars. I traveled to Syracuse, Sicily in 1973 and personally viewed the landscape, the harbors, and the surviving walls and structures such as the amphitheater and the caves formed from quarrying.

The character Leonides, his family and friends, Thalia and her family, Aurora, Cleomenes, the chief minister Timon and his henchmen, and the tribune Sixtus Severinus are all inventions of convenience. As much as possible, Archimedes, King Hieron and his family, Hannibal, and the consul Marcus Claudius Marcellus, are as described in several histories.

All major events in the novel, to the extent that they are accurate in the depictions of contemporary historians, are presented as realistically as possible. The relationships among Carthage, Syracuse, and Roma are true, and these segments of the Second Punic War happened in the order and time sequence in which they appear in the novel. Fortunately, the story line allowed every basic event to occur without requiring factual manipulation for the sake of more exciting storytelling. Most interesting to me is the fact that the conquered in this tale did to a large extent conquer the conquerors. The sacking of Syracuse and the display of its culture in Roma did effect an enormous influence toward the civilizing of the Roman Republic.

Especial care was given to the depiction of everyday life in *To Move the World*. Some of my favorite resources included:

Everyday Life in Ancient Times. National Geographic Society.

Plutarch's Lives. trans. A. H. Clough, Little , Brown, and Company.

Citizens of Roma. Simon Goodenough, Crown.

Greece and Roma at War. Peter Connolly, Prentice-Hall.

Archimedes. E. J. Dijksterhuis, Princeton University Press.

Brent Monahan

Printed in the United States
38636LVS00004B/409